Colonel Porter led his Confederate mounted cavalry in a column of fours straight as an arrow toward the Union artillery battery like a giant fist ready to strike. The Union artillery had held their fire to the front, afraid they might hit their men concealed in ambush in the ditch. Now, sensing danger, they wheeled their artillery to face Porter's men. As one, the six gun battery roared to life and emptied their big guns into the face of the Rebel cavalry charge. The canister and case shot loaded in the cannons turned them into giant shotguns. The front rank of the Rebel charge melted away into a bloody, convulsing heap. It was a hopeless tangle of dead and dying men and horses.

KANSAS, BLOODY KANSAS

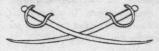

RANDAL L. GREENWOOD

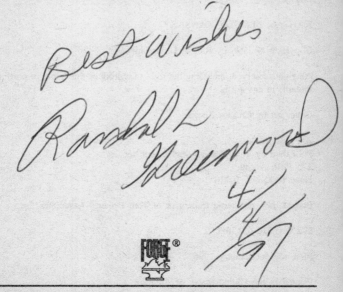

Best Wishes

Randal L Greenwood

4/4/97

A TOM DOHERTY ASSOCIATES BOOK
NEW YORK

This is a work of fiction. All the characters and events portrayed in this book are either products of the author's imagination or are used fictitiously.

A Forge Book
Published by Tom Doherty Associates, Inc.
175 Fifth Avenue
New York, NY 10010

Forge® is a registered trademark of Tom Doherty Associates, Inc.

ISBN: 0-812-53456-5

First edition: January 1996

Printed in the United States of America

0 9 8 7 6 5 4 3 2 1

Lovingly dedicated to my mother, Midge Greenwood. She has blessed her family with love, but most importantly, Mom taught me to believe in myself, reach for the stars, and follow my dreams.

Acknowledgments

I want to thank Robert Gleason formerly of Tor Books for giving me a start in this profession. It was his foresight that made this series possible. I would also like to thank Harriet McDougal, Nadya Birnholz, Lisa Wiseman, and staff for completing the job Bob Gleason began. Pat LoBrutto did a masterful job of line editing my manuscript. A bravo to my agent Nancy Yost of the Lowenstein Agency for smoothing out the bumps along the way. Thanks to Linda Quinton, Larry Yoder, and the sales staff of Tor/Forge Books for getting out there and selling my books. You make it work.

A special thanks to Kenneth and Midge Greenwood for proofreading my manuscript and catching most of my mistakes. Their encouragement kept me motivated. My father has always been my hero and has been with me every step of the way. My mother, Midge, and Aunt Evelyn Prather have been a guiding light and encouraged me to keep my eye on my dream and never lose faith in my ultimate success.

Thanks to my wife, Rebecca, for seeing to it I had the time to write and for helping keep a roof over our heads. To my children, Evan, Amber, and Ciara, who understand when Dad has to write.

I want to acknowledge three of the finest novelists writing western fiction today, Johnny Quarles, James Reasoner, and Elmer Kelton, for taking time out of their busy schedules to read my first novel and encourage a newcomer. I will never forget the help they have given me. Your friendship is deeply appreciated.

I wish to thank Wilson Powell of Batesville, Arkansas, for his historical information and descriptions of the area. Last but not least, I'd like to thank a man I've never met, John Grisham. I read his author's note in his first book, *A Time to Kill,* and found encouragement. At the time, I was attempting to find an agent and publisher for my first novel and his ultimate success after numerous rejections from agents and publishers inspired me to keep trying. Thanks to his story and the encouragement of others I hung in there.

I used these books and sources for authentic information about Jo Shelby's cavalry and the guerilla war in the Trans-Mississippi region: *Shelby and His Men, or The War in the West* by John Newman Edwards, published in 1867; *General Jo Shelby, Undefeated Rebel* by Daniel O'Flaherty, published in 1954; *William Clarke Quantrill, His Life and Times* by Albert Castel, published in 1962; *Gray Ghosts of the Confederacy* by Richard S. Brownlee, published in 1958; and *Quantrill and the Border Wars*, by William Elsey Connelley, published in 1909.

Contents

Foreword

This book is a historical novel. General Jo Shelby and his Iron Brigade were real. All the campaigns and battles in this book actually happened, although the part my characters played was actually done by various real persons. My characters are fiction, and are not made to represent anyone truly living or dead. There wasn't a Third Kansas Cavalry during the war, but their actions portrayed here were common to many Kansas regiments such as Jennison's Jayhawkers.

The conversations between General Shelby and my characters of course are fictional, but remain within the scope and personality of Jo Shelby. Briarwood and all the plantations except the Lightfoot Plantation are works of fiction, but the things that happened there really occurred across Missouri and Arkansas and throughout the South.

It is my hope to give an impression of the war in Missouri and Arkansas. The Trans-Mississippi region, located west of the Mississippi River, has largely been ignored by history books and writers in general. The bloody border war between Missouri and Kansas erupted into a fiery, total war unequaled in the history of the United States.

The Union ordered entire counties emptied of southern people, their homes and property stolen or destroyed. There were roving bands of guerillas, bushwhackers, and freebooters working for both sides, and some that just stole for themselves. Through all this, there were men of honor and courage that fought in regular army units, both Union and Confederate. Both sides fought for what they believed was right. To the South it was a war for independence and the Second American Revolution. We may not agree they were right, but we must honor their bravery.

Quantrill and the other guerillas are largely condemned, but I think it is important to understand their motivations. It is time the Jayhawkers and the Kansas Red Legs are recognized for their evil and share equally the blame for the terrible atrocities and hate formed along the border. If this forgotten history is brought to life in some small measure for my readers then I have accomplished my goal.

Randal L. Greenwood
Hugoton, Kansas

1

Frozen Bivouac

Corporal Calvin Glen Kimbrough turned away from his picketed horse and walked purposefully toward the burning campfire. He glanced around him, watching the gray, shrouding mist of freezing rain fall through the stand of cottonwood trees surrounding him. An icy rivulet of water fell from his wide-brimmed hat and trickled down the back of his neck. An involuntary shudder ran through him and he pulled his rubberized rain poncho more tightly around his neck as his teeth continued to chatter. Even the warmth provided by the captured Union overcoat beneath the poncho was no match for the cold. He wondered if he would ever feel warm again.

He reached the edge of the campfire and, after brushing off the log, sat on a section of a dead tree trunk. The surviving members of Collins' Second Missouri Battery seated around the fire acknowledged his return grudgingly.

Each was content to explore his own thoughts and brood about his own discomfort.

Calvin watched the falling, slanting rain dampen the struggling fire, each raindrop sizzling among the red-hot coals and winking embers of the blaze. Licking at the bottom of the logs, the fire fought to stay alive. He held his gloved hands to the struggling flames and gathered some warmth in his numb hands from the fire.

He studied the miserably wet souls sitting near him. They were a battle-weary, frozen group of soldiers stuck in the icy grip of a northern Arkansas winter. Sometimes he wondered who the lucky ones really were. Those who had survived the frozen hell of the battle of Prairie Grove only to suffer endlessly on this miserable retreat, or those who died swiftly in battle. Sometimes living was a kind of punishment in itself, though he felt he should be glad to be alive.

He stared at the parked artillery pieces lined up behind their caissons. Already the steel barrels were coated with a thick sheen of ice. The hanging icicles clinging to the deadly iron only made him shudder more as yet another chill ran through him.

So much had happened to him and his family since August of 1862. The recollection of that time was forever burned into his memory and he recalled that momentous event that changed his life. He could still picture clearly the day his brother Ross Kimbrough and the remaining members of Captain Jo Shelby's old Lafayette County Cavalry returned home to recruit a new Southern brigade from the very midst of their enemies. He had joined them that day along with his brother Jessie.

Calvin had never wanted to go to war, and like his father he worked to avoid it by taking a neutral stance. In the first two years, he tried to keep to his college studies at the University of Missouri, but the conflict forced him from school. When school closed, he returned home to help his father run the thoroughbred horse breeding operation at Briarwood Plantation.

His father, Glen, was a Union man who worked hard to counsel peace and settle government differences so the Union would be preserved. The coming of the Civil War dashed that hope from him, but still he resisted becoming involved for he believed it was not his fight.

It all changed the day Major Benton Bartok of the Third Kansas Cavalry rode into Briarwood. He informed them of Governor Gamble's new decree requiring all men between the ages of fourteen and forty-five to join the Union militia. Those who didn't were to be considered traitors and treated as such. Glen didn't want to fight against the Union, but he was a Southern man born in Kentucky and he couldn't bring himself to fight against his southern friends and neighbors.

Forced into choosing sides, he urged his sons to join their older brother in service with Captain Jo Shelby's Confederate cavalry. Bartok and his Jayhawkers burned their home to the ground, killed their father, and left the Kimbrough women homeless just weeks after Shelby's brigade marched South.

The last letter they received had brought the sad news of events at Briarwood. The Kimbrough women, now refugees, were on their way south to Arkansas. Worries about their safety crowded Calvin's mind during times like this when he had a chance to think.

His older brother, Lieutenant Ross Kimbrough, was in charge of Jo Shelby's scouts, and his younger brother, Jessie, was a member of Company E, Fifth Missouri Cavalry, of Shelby's brigade. Calvin recalled almost ruefully how he had chosen to join Richard A. Collins' Second Missouri Mounted Artillery, attached to Shelby's brigade. In the last few months he had suffered conditions he had never thought possible in all the sheltered years of his life. He had already participated in three separate battles and engagements at Newtonia, Cane Hill, and Prairie Grove.

The last battle at Prairie Grove, just three weeks ago, had been a hideous, desperate struggle fought in frigid conditions. If there ever was such a thing as hell freezing over it must have been Prairie Grove. During the battle, Ross was wounded seriously in the leg and Jessie was wounded slightly in the chest. A note had arrived a day after the battle telling Calvin of Ross's wound. Jessie was on sick leave and would take Ross to stay with the Covingtons from Batesville, Arkansas.

Ross had met their daughter, Valissa, on his way home to Lafayette County to recruit the new brigade. A couple of days had been long enough to ignite an intense romance. Hopefully, Ross would be allowed to stay with Valissa's family while he recovered from his wounds. There, at least, he should be removed from the fighting. So now Calvin had his brothers to worry about, too. Never had he felt more alone as he shivered near the pitiful fire in this freezing drizzle.

Out of the corner of his eye, Calvin saw movement. He looked up at a new arrival in their camp as an officer swung down from a spirited, black cavalry mount. Calvin recognized him immediately as the soldier tied his horse to a nearby cottonwood and strolled toward the campfire with the rolling gait of a man used to long hours in the saddle.

"Good afternoon, Captain Stryker," Calvin said, rising wearily to his feet.

Captain Evan Stryker of Shelby's headquarters smiled slightly as he waved for the men around the campfire to remain seated. "Take it easy, men. It's too miserable out to stand on ceremony." Stryker found an empty space on a wet, icy log facing Calvin. Some of the soldiers eyed him curiously.

"What brings you out in this weather, Captain?" Calvin asked.

"Things are kind of quiet up at headquarters. I thought since I had a little time I'd ride down here and see if you'd heard anything from Cassandra or your brothers."

"I haven't heard anything new, Captain. We got a mail call, but there wasn't anything there for me." Calvin could read the disappointment etched in Evan's face.

The captain shrugged his shoulders as he nodded in reluctant acceptance of the disappointing news. "I was afraid of that. Since I didn't get a letter, I hoped you might have heard from her." The officer bowed his head as he stared into the struggling flames, alone with his thoughts.

Calvin smiled a little as he began to relax. He was afraid at first Captain Stryker might be bringing orders to resume the march despite the terrible weather and was relieved to see his visit was of a more personal nature. As he studied the officer across from him, Calvin remembered the impression the handsome Texan had made on him the first time they met at Briarwood Plantation.

Evan's dashing good looks and his easy southern charm had not been wasted on Calvin's oldest sister, Cassandra. When the brigade marched south, Cassandra promised to write the young Texan. Ever since then, Evan Stryker had kept in touch with all the Kimbrough brothers. Calvin knew Evan's affection for his sister was more than just a passing fancy. At first the Texas officer had intimidated the Missouri corporal, but now he considered him a good friend.

Evan was compactly built and of average height, and he never failed to draw admiring glances from the ladies. Cassandra was particularly fond of Evan's strong jaw line and dimples in his chin and both cheeks. His brown, thick mustache curled up at the ends; the rest of his face was clean shaven. His eyes were deep brown and his face always seemed on the edge of breaking into a smile.

Calvin recalled that the Texan had been wounded at the battle of Elkhorn Tavern, and it was near the end of his recovery from his shoulder wound that Evan Stryker met Calvin's brother Ross Kimbrough and Colonel Jo Shelby. Shelby and his company were marching toward home to form a new brigade to fight west of the Mississippi River. Captain Evan Stryker's old regiment had been dismounted and moved across the river to fight in Mississippi. Evan had not been anxious to become a foot soldier or to fight so far from home, so he had applied for transfer to Colonel Shelby's personal staff. As far as Calvin knew, he was the only Texan serving in Shelby's Missouri Brigade.

At the moment, ice clung frosty white to his mustache; Evan slapped his hands together and rubbed vigorously as he tried to restore circulation. He held them closer to the fire to gather some warmth. "Don't get too attached to this fire, boys. There's talk up at headquarters we might be marching to Missouri soon."

Calvin shot a look of disbelief at his friend. "That's not even funny, Captain. We're already half frozen."

One look in his eyes and Calvin knew the Texan wasn't kidding. "I wish I was only joking, but I'm afraid General Marmaduke and Colonel Shelby are serious. We've got to do something to make the Yankees pull out of Arkansas or they'll soon take Little Rock. Colonel Shelby wants to make a raid behind General Blunt's army and cut his supply lines. With winter in full force they'll have to abandon their campaign."

Calvin felt his heart sink. The trauma of the last battle was still fresh in his mind and the struggle of the last few days had been almost unbearable. Was there to be no end to this suffering? What sane men would try to fight a war in these awful conditions? Dying in battle was one thing;

it was quite another to freeze to death marching around in the dead of winter. Anyone with any sense would hold up and wait to fight in the spring, but this war was already beyond reason. He realized daring men like Jo Shelby would gamble even their own command if it might lend an advantage over their enemies. He shuddered as he contemplated another campaign. "How soon till we march?"

Evan slid the toes of his high-topped boots near the burning embers before he responded. "I don't know exactly. Shelby wants to wait for a break in the weather before we move out."

At least that was comforting. "I thought you meant right away."

"I don't expect it to be immediately, but if the weather clears we could go soon. I just didn't want you boys wasting your time trying to build a winter camp when we'd just have to leave it behind." Evan noticed that his horse had turned its tail into the driving sleet. The dreary weather held little enticement to get back in the saddle and leave the meager comfort of the struggling fire. "I guess I'd better move on. Colonel Shelby wants me to check in with Major Shanks."

Evan envied the young man's six foot three inch body, built lean and hard as hickory wood. His pale blue eyes offered just a hint of color against his sandy blond hair. A light sprinkling of freckles spilled across his nose and cheeks. In the time he had known him, Evan knew he was intelligent and studious with a love for reading. Unlike Jessie and Ross, this middle Kimbrough brother tended to be more quiet and reticent. At first Evan was put off by the boy's reserved nature, figuring him to be arrogant, but after a while he attributed it more to being shy than to anything else.

Evan put his hands on his knees and pushed himself to his feet. "Try to keep warm, fellas. I'll catch up with you later." He gave a lazy salute and moved toward his waiting horse. He slipped into his saddle and felt the stinging, driving sleet slash at his face and shivered. He made up his mind to deliver his dispatches quickly and get back to headquarters as soon as possible where, maybe he could finally get out of this weather for awhile.

2

The Flaming Fire of War

Near Ozark, Missouri
January 1863

Colonel Jo Shelby held his binoculars to his eyes and scanned the city of Ozark, Missouri, from the hilltop. To the north a cloud of dust marked the probable retreat of the Union garrison. Smoke began to lift in lazy, slow spirals as it swirled on the wind. He swung the field glasses toward the orange flames licking the base of the smoke and focused the knobs with his leather-gauntleted hand. After a moment he lowered the glasses. "Blast! They've set fire to their fortifications and some of their warehouses! Somehow they must have spotted us. It doesn't look like Captain Elliott and the advance will be able to block their escape to Springfield." Colonel Shelby released the field glasses and let them hang by the leather strap around his neck as he slammed his fist into his hand in frustration.

"I'll bet some of those men who escaped this morning from the little fort on Beaver Creek gave them the warning. Colonel McDonald tried to catch them, but they ran too fast," said Evan Stryker.

Colonel Shelby whirled to face him. "Stryker, tell Colonel Gordon to hurry his men forward. He is the advance now that Elliott is circling between the Yankees and Springfield. Perhaps we can salvage some supplies if we hurry." One look into his commander's eyes was all the urging Evan needed as he vaulted into his saddle and spurred his horse forward. He caught up with Colonel Gordon less than a mile away.

Evan Stryker slid his horse to a stop in a little cloud of dust near Colonel Gordon's mount. The colonel, surrounded by his staff, waved his battered campaign hat in a sweeping, forward motion. "Move it, men! By God, we don't have all day!" His cavalry troopers, riding in a long column, moved past his position in a blinding cloud of dust at a gallop.

Captain Stryker saluted briskly. "Colonel Gordon, Colonel Shelby requests you move your men to the advance at the double-quick."

Anger flashed in Colonel Gordon's eyes as he eyed the captain with a stern look. "What does it look like we're doing, Captain, taking time out for tea?"

Captain Stryker felt his face flush with anger. Brashly he responded, "I don't make the orders, Colonel. I just deliver them."

A nervous tick alongside Colonel Gordon's right eye showed his anger. He puffed up like he was ready to spit nails when all of a sudden he eased the air out of his lungs and an amused smile crossed his face. "Right you are, Captain. I'm sure Colonel Shelby had no way of knowing my intentions. Please give him my regards and tell him we are advancing as quickly as possible." Colonel Gordon snapped off a lazy salute as he turned his horse toward his men. "Move up! Double-quick, men!"

Evan wheeled his horse and set the spurs as he rode back toward the commander. Colonel Gordon's response was all too common. Sometimes, he let it get to him when he shouldn't. Often officers didn't appreciate the orders Evan carried or disagreed with them altogether. Many resented seeing him at all—but he had his job to do. Sometimes, it was more than he could handle.

He tried to let the anger flow from him as he rode rather than keep it bottled up inside. He didn't want to be on this winter campaign any more than the rest of them, but something had to be done to force Union General Blunt out of Arkansas. This attempt was their only real option, even though the operation would be risky. After many discussions between General Marmaduke and Colonel Shelby, the decision to march had been made. On the last day of 1862, they had moved north.

The weather had warmed considerably since the bleak days of the retreat from the battle of Prairie Grove and the encampment at Lewisburg. Although the nights were brisk, the days were mild for early January.

They had crossed the White River at Forsythe, in Taney County, Missouri, and moved toward Springfield. Two more days of marching had brought them to the doorstep of Ozark, Missouri. The first surprise of the assault was now shattered. Evan only hoped it wasn't an omen of bad things to come.

Two hours later, Evan Stryker accompanied Colonel Shelby and the rest of his staff into Ozark. A smile creased the colonel's face when he realized the Yankees had failed in their attempt to destroy their supplies. Although they had set fire to their fort and to their supply depot, the flames had failed to destroy all the food and ammunition.

In fact, badly needed supplies surrounded the hungry Rebel troopers.

Evan let his eyes sweep the town. Union tents stood in line where their owners had hastily abandoned them earlier in the day. Many had failed to take little more than the clothes on their backs with them. Smoke still drifted on the wind, but already Confederate soldiers were getting the best of the flames. He watched gleefully as the soldiers began to examine their loot. He didn't mind the enemy leaving without a fight, for tonight he would sleep in a good tent or house and dine on food seldom available to Rebel soldiers, courtesy of General Blunt's Union Army of the Frontier. A nipping frost was already blowing in from the north, making him all the more happy about the situation. Soon, after they had gathered what they could use, he knew Shelby's men would complete the destruction begun by the Federals. When they rode on, there would be nothing left that could be used against a Southern soldier. He swung down and walked toward the supplies, hoping to pick out something choice for his supper.

Calvin Kimbrough pushed hard against the carriage of his cannon as he wheeled it into place at the edge of a strip of timber. Every crew member worked quickly and efficiently to bring the battery into battle. Once the cannon was clear of the caisson other men began detaching the horses and moved them to the rear. Using their long-practiced drill, honed in battle, the four artillery pieces were ready to fire in less than five minutes.

Calvin stepped forward and squinted through the pendulum-Hausse sight at the enemy cavalry. He took a couple of full turns on the elevation screw as he aimed the barrel for the largest concentration of troopers.

"Number three, shift right three inches!" shouted Calvin as the number three crewman used the trail spike to aim the gun to the right. "Hold it there!" Calvin yelled as the sight lined up on the enemy. Taking one last quick glimpse, to make sure it was right, he removed the sight and stepped behind the field piece. "Number one crew ready to fire, sir!" he shouted.

Now, as he waited for orders to fire and the other three crews to complete their tasks, Calvin studied the battle-field. A large gathering of Union cavalry was milling about ahead, busy trying to harass their lines. Colonel Thompson held the Confederate right, Colonel Jean's reg-iment was forming behind the battery, and Gordon held the left. To the far left stood Colonel McDonald's men, while Ben Elliott's men served as cavalry. All the rest of the Confederate cavalry were dismounted to fight as infan-try and their horses led to the rear by horse holders.

The order to fire rang in Calvin's ears. The number four crewman yanked his lanyard as the cannon belched forth flame. The recoil drove the piece up and back as the bit-tersweet smell of black powder smoke drifted back over the crew.

Calvin's eyes involuntarily blinked from the roar of the cannons as he watched the path of the shot. A geyser of dirt erupted in the Union formation as horses and men went down in a bloody sprawl. A ragged gap formed in the Union lines where once there had been living flesh. Two of the four shots hit their mark; one fell short and one went long.

Calvin stepped forward as his men rolled the cannon back in place and the reload drill began. By the time he sighted on the Union cavalry they were already turning tail to run. He elevated the barrel to lengthen the shot, hoping he would catch them as they ran. Again he pulled the sight and stepped to the rear. As soon as number four had the primer ready, Calvin yelled, "Fire!" Again the cannon bucked as the shot arched toward the enemy. The fuse was cut short and the artillery shell exploded in the air over the retreating cavalry, emptying a number of saddles and bringing down many horses. Calvin winced at its effectiveness and was glad he was not out there with the enemy.

Lieutenant Collins shouted, "Cease fire!" Colonel Gilkey led Jean's regiment around to the front of the battery. The Confederate dismounted cavalry dressed their ranks and marched forward under Gilkey's leadership. Behind them hurried orders were given to bring up the caissons and horses. Collins' men would limber their guns and prepare to move forward now that the battle lines had moved past them.

Fifteen minutes later, Calvin slid into his saddle and fell into line behind the caisson pulling his crew's cannon. Already the Union cavalry had left the field and the long Confederate battle lines advanced toward Springfield. Once again the battery unlimbered and took positions with an unencumbered view of the battlefield. As they worked, the Confederate lines advanced and dressed their ranks. A steady barrage of artillery fire began from the Union fortifications. Shells screamed overhead, crashing into the earth. The land seemed to tremble under their feet. After they positioned their artillery piece, Calvin studied the Union lines as he waited for orders to fire.

In the center of the city was a large and formidable earthwork, flanked by rifle pits and long, deep trenches for infantry. A strongly built wooden stockade stood on the southern side of the town enclosing a brick girl's academy, now used as a military prison. The guns of the large redoubt to its rear gave it added protection. Calvin saw fresh Union troops marching forward to man the trenches and rifle pits. The banquettes of the earthwork and the embrasures of the stockade were blue with Union uniforms. Calvin watched the gleaming sunlight dance off thousands of gun barrels and bayonets along the enemy embattlements.

Suddenly, a Union officer accompanied by his staff and

personal escort rode out of the fortifications and traveled along the Confederate lines, studying their dispositions. The Rebels opened fire as they moved past, but the fire sputtered to a halt. Southern soldiers could not ignore the gallant bravery exhibited by the Union general Brown, and a rousing cheer echoed above the roar of guns as a tribute to his reckless bravery.

While others cheered, Captain Ben Elliott and his advance Confederate force watched from the backs of their cavalry mounts. Instead of admiring the bold move of the Union officer to rally his troops, Elliott saw the move as an insult to his men. He would not let this move go unchallenged. He gave the order to advance, and leading the front rank of charging Rebels rode the young Quantrill guerilla Billy Cahill.

Billy leaned low over the neck of his horse, Bess. He drew comfort from the polished walnut grip of his Remington thirty-six caliber revolver pressing firmly into his palm. He wore three more revolvers of different makes in the deep pockets of his guerilla shirt and carried two in a brace of saddle holsters in front of him. He glanced to his left and eyed his old friend Frank James keeping stride; on his right was Riley Crawford. Leading them all, Lieutenant William Gregg's powerful mount began to outdistance the others. The Union escort pulled up to form a line of battle, but they never expected the attack about to sweep down on them.

Many of Elliott's command belonged to William Clarke Quantrill's already famous Missouri Bushwhackers. While Quantrill was away in Richmond, Virginia, applying for a general's commission, his men were temporarily attached to Shelby's brigade. Where the fighting would be the toughest these young, fearless lads would lead the way. Since November they had already participated in the battles of Cane Hill and Prairie Grove, Arkansas. Now in January 1863 they were again in the thick of the fight.

Billy Cahill grinned wickedly as he dashed at the blue coated enemy. He would kill every Yankee he came close to until his pistols were empty or they were out of range of his flashing blade. He felt no fear, only anticipation. Union blood would be shed in retaliation for the torture and murder of his father. Jennison's Jayhawkers took everything of value and burned the Cahill farm to the ground. Only Billy and his mother were left. A few weeks later, the fifteen-year-old lad had joined Quantrill's raiders to seek revenge and the rest was history.

By now the distance between the Yankee escort and the Rebels was a scant twenty yards. The panicked Union troopers fired a ragged volley from their Sharps carbines while sitting on the backs of their pitching horses. Black powder smoke drifted on the breeze temporarily obscuring their targets. The Yankee shots for the most part went high, though one bullet plucked at Billy's sleeve.

He was close enough now to make out the features of the Union troopers. He thumbed back the hammer and fired, following with a second, and a third shot. One Yankee slid from his saddle to fall under his horse's prancing feet, while a second somersaulted over backward from the shot through his chest.

Billy felt a surge of excitement, and all around him Elliott's Rebels began their firing. The whole front rank of the escort fell before the rebel charge. The rest of the Union staff and troopers rode hell-bent-for-leather for the protection of the Union fortifications.

Never before had the Union soldiers faced such concentrated firepower. Quantrill's men and many of Shelby's regular troopers relied on many pistols for close-in fighting. The standard issue for Union cavalry was single-shot carbines. Once fired, they were virtually impossible to reload from the back of a galloping horse. The Rebels could easily fire five to six shots and pull additional revolvers to shoot before the enemy could respond. The result was predictably bloody.

Billy lay low on Bess as he rode alongside a terrified Yank. Billy grinned as he deliberately pointed his revolver at the wide-eyed Union soldier. The trooper was trying desperately to jack another cartridge into his Sharps carbine while precariously perched on the back of his galloping horse. When he was aware of what was coming, the frightened soldier let the carbine slip through his fingers and fall in the trailing dust behind him. Billy thumbed the hammer and squeezed the trigger before the man could offer to surrender. The gun bucked in his hand and through the powder haze from his gun Billy watched the shot take the man high in the forehead. The dead body cartwheeled from the back of the horse to lie crumpled and still in the dirt below. Billy's eyes searched for his next victim as he looked after the remainder of the fleeing Union bluecoats. They were drawing in close now to the fortifications. A cloud of smoke spouted from the fortifications as musketballs plowed into the dirt around him or whined by his ears. He wheeled his horse to race toward his own lines. Elliott's men returned to safety with minimal losses.

Frank James turned and watched Billy pull the cylinder pin on one of his empty revolvers. He loosened the wedge with his pocket knife, slipped the empty cylinder out, and slipped an extra loaded one into the revolver. He put new pistol caps on the loaded chambers.

"I saw that Yankee general reel in the saddle just before they reached the fortifications. I think I winged him pretty good, Billy," said Frank James.

Billy never took his eyes off the gun while he finished the job. "Too bad you didn't kill him. Been one less damn Yankee to deal with." He thrust his freshly loaded revolver into his belt.

A rolling roar of sound like distant thunder reached their position. In an instant they recognized the sound of gunfire. They glanced to the left and saw McDonald's Confederate cavalry regiment advancing to the attack on a Union infantry regiment placed before the Union stockade. In the forefront of the mounted charge, Billy could see the gallant Colonel Jo Shelby leading the troops. He rode several yards in front of his men, his extended sword catching the sunlight. Jo's long, dark hair streamed beneath his black plumed hat, trailing out behind him. Encouraged by the attack, Ben Elliott's men surged forward to join the charge.

By the time Elliott's men caught up with the attack, McDonald's men had annihilated the lead Union regiment and their maniacal rush carried them against the stockade like a tidal wave breaking on a distant shore. The Missouri Rebels burst through the gates left open to allow the retreat of the Union regiment, while others swarmed over the walls. The garrison housed within the stockade succumbed to the Confederate charge.

Still the Rebel enthusiasm was not dimmed as their adrenaline-fueled courage swept them past the stockade and against a line of rifle pits beyond. Here the Union stand was more determined as volleys of musketfire greeted the mounted Rebel cavalry. Saddles emptied quickly up and down the line as horses stumbled and fell.

Musketballs whirred past Billy's ears like maddened swarms of bumblebees. Almost simultaneously riders on both sides went down. The man on the left rolled off lifelessly to the ground, while the rider on the right flipped over the head of his horse as the horse somersaulted dead beneath him. Somehow in the confusion around the stockade Billy had lost contact with his friends, Riley Crawford, Frank James, and Bill Gregg. Now he was glad they weren't among the men who were falling.

He felt Bess gather her haunches under her as he approached the first line of rifle pits. He could see the gleaming guns with their ominous gun barrels aimed in his direction. Then, Bess was in the air and sailing over the ducked heads in the rifle pits. He fired, but missed the nearest Yankee as he fought to keep his seat when Bess touched down roughly on the other side. He wheeled her quickly and turned his revolver on the Yankees nearby. Most were busy trying to reload or aiming at other Rebels still charging toward them.

Billy was forgotten in all the chaos swirling about him as he pulled two fresh revolvers from his saddle holsters and slid from the saddle. Deliberately and coolly he walked toward the Union soldiers in the rifle pits with a revolver in each hand. No one seemed to notice him as he stopped less then six feet from the backs of the enemy soldiers. With practiced skill he thumbed back the hammers and fired his guns as if he was at target practice. When finally the last hammer fell on an empty chamber on his smoking guns, eight Union soldiers lay dead in and around the pits before him. He jumped into the nearest pit and shoved a dead Yankee out of the hole. He then eased himself down against the cool earth and began to methodically reload his weapons. A strange calm had descended over Billy and he worked at the task as if it was no more than a required chore back home on the farm before the war. By the time he finished reloading and his head appeared above the rim of his rifle pit, Bess was nibbling at the yellowed dead grass along the edge of the hole, her reins trailing behind her.

He took hold of her reins as he patted her gently on the head. She pricked her ears up and pulled away from him a little. "Think I'd forgot all about you, Bess?"

Billy studied the terrain near him. A quick glance showed the line of rifle pits were empty and the Yankees who had escaped were fleeing into a graveyard to the rear. Clusters of tombstones of every size and shape jutted out of the ground. In among these macabre symbols flitted soldiers in Union blue. Many were using the stones for cover while others were simply passing through on their way to the rear. Swirling clouds of dark gray powder smoke drifted and swirled across the cemetery giving those among the stones a surreal aspect. The Union soldiers took on a ghastly appearance like blue-uniformed ghosts dancing among the tombstones.

By now, more Confederate troopers had swept past the line of rifle pits and were threatening the denizens of the graveyard. While much success had been gained on the left, those in front and to the right of the large earthwork were taking a fearful beating from the deadly play of shot and shell from the Union army's fortified artillery. Twenty large guns spewed their deadly cargo against the Rebel lines.

Other Rebel soldiers from Jean's regiment, originally in the center of the attack, mixed with men of Mcdonald's, Gordon's, and Elliott's commands. These dismounted men from Gordon's and Jean's regiments joined him in the rifle pits. An all-out attack was begun to pressure the enemy out of the graveyard before them.

Captain Evan Stryker felt his horse stagger as the concussion of an exploding shell thrust a geyser of rock fragments and dirt into the air just a few yards away. He knew his horse had taken a fearful blow and kicked free of his stirrups just moments before the horse collapsed underneath him. He rolled across the ground head over heels and slid to a stop. He lay there for a moment gasping for breath and fighting to drag air back into his lungs. The hard impact had stunned him. He crawled back to his black horse which was struggling to rise to its feet. Dark blotches of blood seeped from the horse's side and jagged blood-stained bone jutted from a broken foreleg. Evan patted his mount on the neck as he pressed the barrel of his revolver inches from the horse's head. A quick pull of the trigger and the horses' suffering was ended. Evan removed his saddle and accouterments and moved toward the nearest rifle pit. He reached it as he heard the piercing scream of two conical shells hurling toward him. He dove into the nearest hole as the shells thudded into the ground several yards away. Flying dirt obscured his vision and when he blinked his eyes he was staring into the gun barrel of a thirty-six caliber Remington revolver.

"Howdy, Captain, welcome to my humble home," said Billy Cahill wryly as he eased the hammer down gently. "What brings you by for a visit?"

"Kind of stormy outside. I thought I'd get in out of the lead hail flyin' around out there for a moment or two, if you don't mind."

Evan's eyes studied the young lad of fifteen sitting before him. The boy had long blond hair pulled back and stuffed under his felt hat. A sprinkling of freckles spilling across his nose added to his youthful appearance. When Evan looked in his dark brown eyes he saw a hardness and experience far beyond the boy's years. He sensed there was danger in those eyes and in that instant he knew, Billy would have killed him without a moment's hesitation had he been a Yankee. It was a relief they were on the same side.

Billy's face broke into a smile. "Seems like a good idea to me." His face became more serious. "Where were you headin'?"

'I've got a message for Colonel Shelby from Colonel Thompson. The artillery is playing hell with our right. Do you know where I can find him?"

"Last time I saw him he was near the stockade. General Marmaduke had joined him there for a conference."

Captain Stryker's disappointment showed clearly on his face. "I've got to find him, but I've lost my horse."

Billy still held Bess's reins in his hand and he glanced over the edge of the rifle pit to see if the chestnut mare was still okay. "If you don't mind riding double I'll try to get you to the colonel."

Without waiting for a reply, Billy climbed out of the pit

and swung into the saddle. Evan followed and swung up behind the young bushwhacker; the two of them rode at an angle away from the cemetery. Shots furrowed into the earth around them while others buzzed by their heads. Both men ducked low in the saddle instinctively as the chestnut covered the ground in long, ground pounding strides. In less than fifteen minutes they pulled to a halt under the protection of the wall of the stockade.

Colonel Shelby was in a heated debate with General Marmaduke. He halted long enough to hear Captain Stryker's report. Just as Evan finished his account sent by Colonel Thompson, splinters of wood flew from the stockade wall as a cannonball ripped through the barrier.

Colonel Shelby's face twisted in anger, "Blast, we've got to do something about that damn artillery piece!" He pointed vigorously at the cloud of powder smoke hanging over a rise just beyond the cemetery. "That one cannon is stopping our progress in this whole area. Stryker, ride to the front and tell Major Bowman I want that cannon captured or silenced and I want it done now!"

"Yes, sir!" replied Captain Stryker, but he didn't move from where he stood at attention.

Colonel Shelby looked perplexed. "What seems to be the problem, Captain?"

"I need a horse, sir. Mine was killed by enemy fire earlier, sir."

A look of understanding passed across Shelby's features. He turned toward one of his orderlies. "Mathews, give Stryker your mount. I'm going to need you here for a while."

The look on Mathews' face left no doubt the young man was not eager to give up his horse, but he complied with Colonel Shelby's direct order.

In moments Captain Stryker and Billy Cahill were once again riding toward the rifle pits. As they neared the hole where they had met earlier, Captain Stryker swung down and jumped into the pit while Billy held his horse. In short order, Evan brought out his equipment and attached it to the saddle of his new mount. He looked ruefully at Billy. "I hate to leave, my saddle behind, but I don't have any way to carry it."

"Whatever you're gonna do, Captain, do it quickly. I don't like being a large bulls-eye in the middle of the battlefield."

Stryker hurried the transfer and climbed into the saddle as both men spurred away. Soon they located Major Bowman and many of his men hiding behind the lee side of a gentle hill near the cemetery. After dismounting and turning the horses over to a horse holder they reported Shelby's wishes.

Major Bowman grimaced when he heard his orders. A calm spread across his face as he accepted the challenge. He turned toward the men around him. Shouting above the roar of battle he said, "Men, Colonel Shelby wants us to capture the cannon on the other side of the cemetery. He's counting on us and by God, we will not let him down." Major Bowman pulled his cavalry saber from its scabbard. "Now who will follow me?" A loud cheer went up from the men crowded behind him. Without further hesitation the major crested the hill and ran toward the graveyard with nearly forty men following him including Billy Cahill and Captain Evan Stryker.

Billy ran a zigzag pattern across the field and past three or four rows of graves before he flung himself behind a large headstone for cover. Above the sounds of battle he heard the thunderous roar of the six-pound artillery piece a short distance away; screams and shrieks of the wounded filled the air. Billy knew it would take them a while to reload and he was up again and running toward the cannon, now less than twenty yards away. His eyes grew wide in terror as he watched the crew serving the piece. He knew in an instant they were nearly ready to fire and the black,

gaping maw of the deadly barrel loomed dark and dangerous. It seemed pointed directly at him and, in that instant,
he felt he was facing instantaneous death head-on. He
yelled "Get down!" as he slid to a stop behind a thick
headstone and fell on his face across the grass-covered
grave. The deep-throated roar of the cannon made his head
ring. Canister balls shattered the headstone as tiny slivers
of rock and granite splayed everywhere. He felt the warm
trickle of blood running down his cheek as he raised himself up to his knees, guns in both hands. He began to fire
at the crewmen through the swirling haze of spent powder
smoke. He watched as his shots struck home and several
of the artillery crew went down.

Other Rebels were rising from the tombstones amid the
pall of smoke like ghostly wraiths seeking revenge. Major
Bowman ran toward the Union lieutenant in charge of the
gun. "Surrender or I'll fire!" he shouted. The Union junior
officer smoothly raised his pistol and shot Major Bowman
in the chest. In nearly the same instant, Bowman fired his
revolver and the Union officer clutched at his chest before
sagging across the gun trail. The last of the Yankee crew
turned to run, but were swiftly cut down by a Confederate
volley. As the soldiers gathered around the captured piece,
a hearty cheer ripped from the throats of the survivors of
the charge.

Twenty eager hands gripped the wheels and trail. In
minutes the dead were cast aside and the beautiful artillery
piece was moved by hand through the cemetery and toward the Rebel lines.

Captain Stryker moved beside the gallant Major Bowman. Blood frothed at his lips, indicating he was shot
through the lungs. His breathing was shallow and rattled
horribly when he gasped. He looked up into Evan's eyes.
"We took it, didn't we?" His voice more a statement of
fact than a question.

Evan swallowed hard, biting back the tears as he replied, "We certainly did, Major. The boys are taking it downhill now to our side."

Major Bowman coughed violently as his face contorted in pain. "Tell . . . Shelby, tell . . ." His words faded from his lips as his eyes rolled up vacantly toward the sky. Hot tracks of tears seared Evan Stryker's cheeks. He blinked them away and lowered the major to the ground. Then, reached up and gently closed Bowman's eyes. Evan thought it was ironic for a man to die in a graveyard. A place of peaceful rest disrupted by the violence of war. He turned in time to see Billy Cahill stumbling toward their lines.

Billy had stuffed one of his empty revolvers in his belt and another still hung limply at his side, firmly gripped in his hand. He was gently probing a wound along the scalp just above his forehead.

Captain Stryker caught up with him easily. "How bad are you hurt, Billy?"

"I don't think I'm too bad. I've got a nasty cut on my scalp, but I don't think it's serious."

Evan glanced down at Billy's arm. A jagged sliver of granite nearly three inches long protruded from his arm. When Evan pointed it out to Billy, Billy stared at it blankly as if realizing he was hurt there for the first time. "I'll be damned! I didn't even know it was there."

Evan Stryker gripped the sliver and with a quick yank pulled it free. Luckily, it hadn't penetrated deeply. A large drop of blood oozed from the wound and spilled down the side of his arm. It didn't look serious and Billy pulled a clean handkerchief from his haversack and bound his wound. Then both found their horses.

Corporal Calvin Kimbrough smiled as men from various companies of Shelby's command rolled a beautiful field piece and caisson they had just captured from the far side of the cemetery into position. In short order they worked in a few volunteers and had the weapon firing alongside the rest of Collins' battery. Now the gun was hurling shells at the bluecoats instead of defending them.

Collins' battery had changed locations several times as the battle lines ebbed and flowed. They were now stationed to the left near the stockade where the brigade had made deep inroads into the Union lines. The soldiers were fighting in the very streets of Springfield and the artillery barrages from both sides fell among the homes.

Retreating Union soldiers set fire to homes and warehouses filled with supplies to keep them from falling into Rebel hands. Other houses started burning from the explosions of artillery shells. The flames quickly spread against the winter skies. A stiff wind fanned the flames, which quickly encircled whole blocks of buildings. Amid the stifling heat and smoke and crashing timbers the soldiers of both sides continued their desperate struggle. Roofs caught blaze, sending showers of burning sparks and hot coals swirling across the city and fortifications. The area around the stockade became a living sea of flame threatening to annihilate the Rebel soldiers. Once again, Missouri was burning. Forced from their cover, a rain of bullets swept their lines from the concealed Union infantry, while the Union artillery, firing from the main earthwork in the center, zeroed in on the Confederate lines. Where Union soldiers had failed to stop them, hell's burning flames were able to turn aside the advancing Rebel lines, leaving them cruelly exposed.

Those who staggered back took shelter in the captured stockade, still free of fire, while others hid in the trenches and rifle pits. General Marmaduke was now convinced they could not take the city. All day they had been unable to penetrate the center or the right flank and now their progress was blocked by fire and stiffening enemy resistance.

After dark the Rebels withdrew from the field in orderly fashion, by regiment. They took with them over two hun-

KANSAS, BLOODY KANSAS 27

dred Union prisoners and the captured cannon, and left behind a portion of Springfield destroyed by fire and many Union dead strung across the battlefield. The battle of Springfield, Missouri, was over.

Cold and blustery winds sent banks of lead gray clouds scudding across a foreboding sky as Shelby's men marched down the road toward Rolla, Missouri, the day after the battle at Springfield. All along the way at every crossroads and little village, a small stockade was erected and maintained by a company or two of Union defenders. Each in turn was abandoned by the fleeing Yankees and destroyed by the advancing Rebel army. Telegraph poles and lines were ripped down and destroyed, crippling the Union communication lines. Badly needed blankets and overcoats, food and provisions swelled the Confederate supply. Still the Yankees failed to pursue.

Shelby and General Marmaduke linked up with Colonel Porter at Sand Springs. With his supply line cut between Springfield and Arkansas and his communications destroyed, General Blunt turned his Union Army of the Frontier away from Fort Smith, Arkansas, and marched back toward Springfield to reestablish his supply lines. When General Blunt was one day away from Springfield, General Marmaduke turned his army and Shelby's brigade south toward Marshfield in Webster County, Missouri. The plan had worked and Blunt was drawn away from his attack on Arkansas.

Farnsworth House

Cassandra Marie Kimbrough studied herself in the mirror in the bedroom at Covington Manor. Today they would move into Farnsworth House and she wanted to look her best. She let her eyes drift over the long, blond hair cascading over her slender shoulders and was pleased with the luxuriant shine. She studied her face and saw a fair complexion with prominent cheekbones and a fine, slender nose. She looked into her eyes, the color of sky blue. She often was complimented on the beauty of her eyes, but as she stood there, she saw a hardness she would never have expected before the war. She knew instinctively the cause of that hardened gaze as her mind wandered back over the last few months.

Everything had changed that awful day in June 1862 when Major Benton Bartok and his Kansas Jayhawkers stopped by Briarwood Plantation. From the beginning, Bartok made it clear he would have her anyway he could and would use his office of district commander to bring pressure on her family if she was unwilling to comply. Brave and proud, she resisted his advances until he tried to rape her during a Fourth of July ball at Riverview Plantation. Only the swift intervention of her brother Jessie had saved her. From that day on, Jessie was a hunted man.

Her new suitor, Evan Stryker, caused problems with a friend, Gilbert Thomas, who wanted more from her than friendship. Gil had asked Cassandra to marry him before he marched away with the brigade. She knew she didn't love Gil, so she turned him down as gently as she could. It sparked bad blood between Gilbert Thomas and the Texan, Evan Stryker, further complicated by both being officers of the same brigade.

After Shelby's brigade rode out in August of 1862, Major Bartok reclaimed his domination of Lafayette County. Angered by Cassandra's rejection, Jesse's escape, and the recruiting of an entire brigade under his very nose, Bartok sought to extract his revenge on Briarwood. In September Bartok struck, and when his Jayhawkers rode out, Briarwood was left in smoldering ashes and Cassandra's father, Glen Kimbrough, lay dead.

Left homeless and with little more than the clothes on their backs, Cassandra, her mother, Ellen, and her younger sister Elizabeth, accompanied by their two loyal servants Jethro and Fanny, turned for help to Gilbert's father, Harlan Thomas, at Riverview Plantation. After a brief confrontation with Captain Bob Anders of Bartok's command, Cassandra and her party continued south accompanied now by Katlin Thomas, the fiancée of her brother Jessie, and Katlin's slave, Becca.

The party was attacked by a band of Union deserters and Cassandra was forced to shoot the leader point-blank. Cassandra was amazed at how easy it was for her to kill. All the pain and anguish visited upon her by the Yankees finally pushed her to the breaking point and she exploded in violent anger. She felt no remorse, but a strange feeling of exhilaration after killing someone who needed it. She was no longer a helpless victim, but would fight back when the situation called for it.

Not long after her mother, Ellen, ill with pneumonia, died in a tragic accident. They continued south and with help of an unexpected source, Major Kenton Doyle of the Union army, secured a pass through enemy lines, finally reaching safety at Covington Manor near Batesville, Arkansas.

Cassandra's older brother, Ross, now convalescing from wounds received at the battle of Prairie Grove, had met Valissa Covington on his way to Lafayette County to help recruit Shelby's brigade. Although their time together had been brief, a romance had begun. Cassandra remembered her brother and the way he talked about Valissa Covington and her family from Batesville, Arkansas. In desperation, with nowhere else to go, Cassandra headed for the Covingtons'. Valissa's family took the Kimbroughs under their wings and found them a place to stay. Cassandra felt exceedingly grateful to have a place to live, called Farnsworth House.

The house belonged to a man named Joseph Farnsworth who had gone to Europe to oversee his blockade-running business. While away from home he had left his plantation in the care of his good friend, Andrew Covington. Andrew thought it would be wise to have people living there to protect the home, and the Kimbroughs gratefully accepted. Today they would see the place for the first time and Cassandra felt an odd mix of excitement and trepidation. One last glance in the mirror and she held her head proudly. She would handle this as she had everything else. She smiled to herself as she walked out of the bedroom and went down the stairs to join the others.

Near Batesville, Arkansas

Cassandra didn't know what to expect as they traveled the short distance between Covington Manor and Farnsworth House. She had been told it was a fine and beautiful home, but little more. Indeed, Andrew Covington had never given the impression the house was at all unusual. As they rounded the final turn leading to the large home near the White River, she wondered why.

She had seen many plantations and fine homes on her journey south to Arkansas. Most had the familiar characteristics of Greek Revival: large columns and facades reminiscent of drawings she had seen of ancient Roman and Greek ruins in southern Europe. She had even seen plantations and fine homes adopting the Italianate towers and round-arched doorways that served to make that style distinctive, but none of the homes she had seen looked anything like Farnsworth House.

Before her stood a turreted and castellated house built of gray, weathered stones. In the front of the house, paralleling the river, was a large round turret constituting about a fourth of the entire structure. From this turret a double door opened onto a circular veranda that wrapped itself around the front of the house. Large white columns supported a gothic-styled roof. The turret attached neatly into a large two-story rectangular-shaped main structure. A smaller round turret extended to a level of three floors. The back of the house consisted of a smaller two-story rectangular shape dominated by round chimneys. Beyond the rear of the house stood a brick-and-wood barn and a carriage house with attached riding stables. She was surprised there were no slave cabins on the property.

Cassandra was awestruck by the unexpected and unusual appearance of the home. "Valissa, why didn't you mention the Farnsworth House looks like a castle?"

Valissa looked a little defensive. She shrugged her

shoulders then answered, "I don't know. I guess since I grew up around here and spent so much time here, I don't think of it as a castle."

"Come on, Val, it looks like a picture right out of some fairy tale. I'd call it a castle if someone asked me to describe it."

"I don't think so. I picture a castle having tall walls surrounded by a moat and a wooden drawbridge. Farnsworth House doesn't have anything like that."

"Yes, it does lack the castle walls, the drawbridge, and the moat, but the embattlements on the top of the towers and along the roofline make it look like a castle to me. Why, I could just picture some fair damsel in distress calling for her rescue from the window of the tall tower."

Valissa laughed. "I don't think your hair is going to be long enough to let some prince climb up there like Rapunzel."

"I can sho' 'nuff tell you one thang, Miss Cassie's too tenderheaded for that kinda nonsense. Why, it's all I can do to get a comb through her hair without her screamin' about how much it hurts! Ain't no way that gal gonna ever let no man go climbin' on her hair no matter how long her hair gets," responded Fanny.

Cassandra laughed. As they neared the place, a tall, dark man came running from the veranda. When the carriage stopped in front, he was there to help the ladies down.

Cassandra noticed him immediately. He had rugged good looks and a frame heavily muscled and lean from working in the fields. Even though he was wearing a coat, she could tell he was no stranger to hard work. His skin was dark, but lighter than the average field hand. He had straight white teeth and a cheerful smile.

"Mornin' to ya, Miss Valissa" he said. "You're lookin' awful pretty today."

"Thank you, Jeremiah. It looks like you've taken good care of the place for Father."

"Yes, ma'am, I reckon I have."

Jethro parked the wagon carrying their few possessions behind the carriage and joined the others. As soon as they were all out of the carriage Valissa began her introductions. "Jeremiah, I want you to meet these fine people. This is Cassandra Kimbrough, her sister Elizabeth, and her brother Jessie. This is Jessie's fiancée, Katlin Thomas. And this is Jethro and his wife, Fanny. They will help with the house care."

Valissa hesitated, looking for Becca, who stood behind the others. They moved, so for the first time Jeremiah could get a good look at Becca, who stood shyly, eyes cast at the ground. "This is Becca. She belongs to Katlin."

Jeremiah couldn't believe his eyes. Before him stood a beautiful girl with skin the color of liberally creamed coffee. He stared at her large dark eyes and flowing black straight hair. Her lips were full and sensuous, and her cheekbones were high and proud. They were set off perfectly by a rather small and narrow nose. He just stood there with his mouth hanging open, staring at her.

Valissa jarred him back to reality. "Jeremiah, aren't you going to say something?"

He quickly found his voice. "Ah, yes, ma'am, I'm sorry. Pleased to meet you. It'll be a real pleasure to work here with you." He held his hat so tightly he was nearly tearing it, he was so distracted by Becca.

"Jeremiah belongs to Father," Valissa explained. "He's been preparing the house since Father invited you to stay here. Before that he has been the caretaker. Father said that he could stay on and help you if you need him."

"Thank you, Valissa. I'm sure we can use his assistance while we unpack from this long journey, and Katlin is going to need some help preparing for the wedding," said Cassandra. "I'm sure we can keep Jeremiah busy, if he doesn't mind staying here with us for a while."

"No, ma'am, I'd be happy to stay." He smiled broadly

as he stole another glance at Becca. She returned his smile then looked back down at her feet shyly.

"Now that everyone has met Jeremiah, let me show you around the house," said Valissa as she led the way to the double doors on veranda.

The first room was a large round room with a spacious ceiling reaching two levels. The room had long windows located high on the wall, letting sunlight filter down on the floor of the room. A group of four windows were located near the double doors, two on each side, that gave a view of the river and the circular veranda.

"This is the ballroom. Joseph Farnsworth loves to dance and we've attended some grand balls here over the years," said Valissa.

"Oh, Jessie, let's have our wedding right here in this room. Isn't it lovely?" Katlin's eyes sparkled with delight as she squeezed Jessie's arm.

Jessie smiled at Katlin. His love for her was easily seen in his eyes. "Any place you want is fine with me, just as long as it's soon," Jessie replied. The two young lovers had been separated when Jessie joined the army. Now Katlin had joined him and the wedding was being planned.

"Before you get too excited, let me show you the rest of the house." Valissa smiled, then turned and walked through the room and down a short flight of steps. At the bottom of the stairs they entered a double hallway. One hall went straight before them, dividing the large rectangular main section of the house. The other hall cut at right angles to the first one.

To their left was a short breezeway leading to a wide, circular staircase, neatly tucked into the smaller of the two turrets on the house. In the opposite direction was a doorway, which opened onto a small porch.

Valissa stood in the center of the two adjoining halls. She pointed at the stairs. "That leads to the second floor, and the observatory at the top of the tower." She turned and pointed to the porch. "That leads to the landing on the river. That's the way most people approach the house when they arrive by riverboat. On some grand occasions Mr. Farnsworth would take everyone onboard one of his riverboats and we would cruise the river, dancing and dining the night away." Valissa smiled, lost in remembrances of those nights that seemed so long ago.

She turned and led them down the larger, central hallway. The party followed, eyes roaming in wonder at the beauty of the mansion. "Lawdy, lawdy," said Jethro in admiration. "This is a might handsome place. It's sho' gonna be a pleasure livin' here."

Fanny hastily added, "Gonna be a pleasure just gettin' away from that witch Etta an' back in a kitchen of my own."

Valissa turned to look at her with stern disapproval. "Where I come from, slaves do not speak until they are spoken to. Besides, you have no right to pass judgement on Etta. She is an integral part of Covington Manor and if you were my slave I'd have you beaten for talking that way."

Fanny put her balled-up hands on her hips and took a belligerent stance. "Well, I hate to tell you, missy, we ain't your slaves. We ain't nobody slaves no mo' an' I says what I think."

A shocked expression quickly passed over Valissa's face and she flushed crimson. Never before had she met a slave allowed to talk to a white person with such impertinence. Her father, had he been here, would have caned Fanny or forced her from the house rather than stand for such behavior.

Cassandra, sensing the danger looming should a serious rift develop between them and the Covingtons, stepped between the two women. She faced Jethro and Fanny. "Jethro, I think it would be best if you'd take Fanny out to the wagon until we finish seeing the house. Fanny, you

are free, but you work for me. We are guests of the
Covingtons and they deserve our respect. Would you
please apologize before you go?"

Jethro stepped forward quickly, an embarrassed expression on his face. He grabbed Fanny by the back of the arm
and tried to pull her away before she caused any more
trouble. Fanny yanked her arm free of his grasp and shot
a look of disdain at her husband. "I don't need help findin'
my way out." She looked back at Valissa. "I'm sorry if I
said anything out of place. It's just Etta and I don't see
eye-to-eye when it comes to cookin'. I ain't sayin' what
she does is right or wrong—she just does it her way. I like
to cook my way." She let her arms relax as she stood there
proudly. "I'm sorry for the way I spoke to you, Miss
Valissa. Ain't no way to talk to folks who've taken us in
like you have." She bowed her head slightly, "I'm sorry."

Fanny turned and led her husband down the hall before
a response could be issued. Valissa shook her head in
amazement as she watched the two walk toward the front
entrance.

Cassandra spoke softly, "I hope you will accept my
apology, Valissa. Fanny has always been headstrong, but
she is loyal and very good help. She's been with us so
long I'm afraid she has become a part of our family."

Surprisingly, the tension drained from Valissa's face, replaced with a strange little smile. "I think I understand
why Etta and Fanny don't get along. They are both stubborn, mule headed, and strong willed. They are so much
alike and so determined to have things their way, they
can't accept the other's ideas. I believe the two of them
were stamped from the same mold." She sighed deeply.
"We love Etta despite her arrogance and I see much of
Etta in Fanny." She paused for a moment as if she was
pondering the truth of what she had just said. "Let me
show you the rest of the house."

Valissa stopped at a set of doors directly across from

one another. "This is the library." They entered an impressive room where against one wall stood a large brick fireplace with a stone hearth. Arranged in a semicircle around it were several overstuffed chairs. The walls were filled with books and bookcases reaching to the ceiling and a sliding ladder was mounted on a track to aid in reaching books on the uppermost shelves. Windows were placed above the bookshelves to allow light in from the river side of the house. "Mr. Farnsworth loves to read. I believe he has the best personal library in this part of the country. He likes to collect books and has brought them in on his riverboats."

"My father always loved books. We had a library at Briarwood, but it was nothing compared to this," Jessie said.

Valissa continued the tour of the ground floor, showing them through the parlor, the dining room, and Joseph Farnsworth's personal office.

She led them back into the hall and continued to the kitchen. "All the cooking for the household is done here. The quarters for the house slaves are located above the kitchen area on the second floor. Joseph doesn't run a plantation and keeps this as his home, so he didn't need slave cabins. You will find the stairs leading to the bedrooms over there. I think you will find the rooms quite comfortable. Jeremiah, if you'd be so kind to show Becca the way, she could select her room. I'll take the others upstairs and show them the guest bedrooms."

Cassandra, Elizabeth, Jessie, and Katlin followed Valissa back down the long hallway, turned to the right, and climbed the beautiful winding staircase in the turret. They made a three hundred and sixty degree turn as they climbed to the second floor of the house.

There they entered a long hall directly above the one on the floor below. "This first room is the master bedroom. There are plenty of other rooms, so I think it would be better if we kept Mr. Farnsworth's personal bedroom unoccupied. I'll show it to you. If you're like me you'll be curious." They entered the room quietly, and with great reverence. The center of the room was dominated by a large canopied bed. Lush ruby-red fabric draped the windows. Above the fireplace hung a gold ornate painting of a beautiful woman.

'Who's that in the painting?" inquired Elizabeth.

Valissa glanced at the portrait before responding, "That's Pamela Farnsworth. She was Mr. Farnsworth's wife."

"Where is she now?"

"Buried behind the house about a quarter of a mile. She died in 1860 from the fever. Her death nearly destroyed Joseph."

"How old was she when she died?"

"Elizabeth! You're being too nosy," said Cassandra.

"Oh, I don't blame her for being curious," responded Valissa. "She was young, maybe twenty-three when she died. They never had any children."

This news surprised Cassandra. "Well, how old is Mr. Farnsworth?"

"I'd say he's in his early thirties."

"That young? I thought by the way everyone talked he would be much older."

"I can see how you might reach that conclusion. I guess since I've known him for years I never thought much about it. Father says he is an accomplished businessman and has built well on what his father left him."

"If this house is any indication, I'd say he has done very well," said Jessie.

"Let me show you the rest of the house. I'll ask you to keep this room and Mr. Farnsworth's office closed."

Cassandra nodded in agreement. "We're just blessed to have an opportunity to enjoy this beautiful home. I think it is the least we can do to respect the privacy of our host.

I'm glad you showed it to us, but we'll leave those two rooms alone."

Valissa took them to the other rooms on the floor and they all selected bedrooms for their use. When they returned to the ground floor, Fanny, Jethro, Becca, and Jeremiah were busy unloading the wagon and carrying their possessions into the house.

Long before sunset Valissa was in her carriage on her way to Covington Manor. Jeremiah was impatient, but he tried not to let it show. All he wanted was to get Valissa home as quickly as possible and return to Farnsworth House. He pictured the beauty of Becca in his mind and her shy smile. The way her dress hugged her curves. He licked his lips in anticipation as he though about her. Yes, sir, things were gonna be a whole lot more interesting around there with Becca at Farnsworth House.

Temptations

Ross Kimbrough stared at a light freezing rain splattering against the window of his bedroom at Covington Manor. The steady rhythm of the rain added to the monotony and gloom he felt inside. Day after day of lying in the bed as his leg healed from its wounds gave him plenty of time to think and brood. His thoughts often turned to his mother and father and growing up at Briarwood Plantation. Those had been happy days filled with adventure, but now they were gone; swept away by time and war.

He felt a fresh surge of anger welling up in him as he thought about his parents. He knew the name of the man responsible for the destruction of Briarwood. Major Benton Bartok of the Third Kansas Cavalry had led his Jayhawkers on to Briarwood Plantation and ordered his men to burn out the Kimbroughs. Ross's father had made a stand and tried to defend his home and his land, but the

Yankees killed him. With callous disregard they stole everything of value, then burned what was left, leaving his sisters and his mother homeless. Left to face the coming winter without shelter, they were forced to trek south toward Arkansas. His mother died of pneumonia along the way. The loss of his home and his parents were all the direct result of Benton Bartok's devilish raid. Ross vowed to make Bartok pay with his life for what he had done.

Ross first received the news of the death of his father and the destruction of Briarwood when he was at the camp called Cross Hollows just before the battle of Cane Hill. The memory was forever burned into his mind. He had fought with his grief and anger as best he could, but as chief of Jo Shelby's scouts he was left with little time to deal with his emotions. The battles of Cane Hill and Prairie Grove followed swiftly on the heels of the distressing news.

Focusing his anger on the Union troops had been therapy for him, of a sort, and he delighted in killing as many enemy soldiers as he could. They were the first payment of many he intended to extract from the Union army. His killing spree ended when he was wounded at Prairie Grove. His brother Jessie brought him to Valissa and Covington Manor to recover.

In the last few days as his head slowly cleared from fever and delirium, he began focusing his anger and his hate on seeking revenge against Benton Bartok. He knew he was still far from being well enough to make the journey to Missouri, but in time he would. He started formulating a plan that included Billy Cahill and his friends from Quantrill's raiders.

William Clarke Quantrill should be returning from his trip to Richmond and arriving in Arkansas sometime this winter or early spring. Once he arrived, Ross thought it would be a matter of days before he would take his men and march again for Missouri. Ross promised himself he would ask Jo Shelby for a few weeks' leave so he could travel north with Quantrill. Once there, he would kill Benton Bartok and avenge the death of his parents.

The decision gave him grim satisfaction. He would see Benton Bartok in his gun sights and watch him die. Only then would he truly be free of guilt and be able to go on with his life.

No matter how hard Ross tried he still blamed himself in part for the death of his father. If he hadn't led Shelby's men north things might have been different. He should have been home to fight beside his father. He should've stayed and protected his family and their home. Even when others told him the outcome would have been the same and he couldn't have done anything to prevent it, in his heart Ross wasn't convinced. Only one thing would ease the pain and the guilt. "An eye for an eye and Major Bartok will die," he said to himself over and over again in a little singsong tune playing in his head.

The door swung open and Valissa Covington walked into the room. He found himself smiling—only moments before he would have thought it impossible. Valissa worked that kind of magic on him. She carried a tray of food and set it down on a nightstand near the bed. "How are you doing this morning?" she asked.

"Better now that you're here."

She smiled as if she didn't believe him and put her hands on her tiny waist. "I'll believe you after I see for myself. I want to change your bandage and see how your leg is doing. When I'm done I expect you to eat every bit of this food Etta prepared. You need to rebuild your strength."

"Yes, ma'am, right away, ma'am," he said with an ornery smile and loose mock salute.

Valissa tried to look stern, but couldn't help a smile. She waved his effort off as she pulled the blankets back to expose his wounded leg. She gently began unwrapping the bandages.

Valissa Covington without a doubt was the most strikingly beautiful woman Ross had ever met. Her deep auburn hair caressed her shoulders in thick, soft waves. Her fair complexion lacked even a hint of freckles or blemishes and set off the prettiest eyes he'd ever seen. She had green eyes the color of new grass in the spring, with just a hint of blue.

Ross loved her eyes, but he knew it was her sensual full lips that enticed him and set his groin to twitching whenever she flirted with him. She could break his will anytime she wanted by turning on her charms and she knew it. In fact she seemed to delight in teasing him to see how he would respond.

Her aristocratic high cheekbones were set off perfectly by deep-dimpled cheeks and as exquisite a face as he could imagine. She stood five feet five inches tall, and the blue day dress she wore hugged her breasts snugly, tapered to a narrow waist, and clung to her hips before flaring to the floor.

Valissa lifted the bandage from the wound on Ross's leg. She thought it looked—and more importantly, smelled— like healthy flesh. It wasn't completely healed, but there was steady, noticeable improvement. She looked up at him, jubilation clearly visible in her expression. "It's healing. Every day it looks better." Her eyes locked on his.

Ross was lost in the joy of the moment. He felt content, like a fat cat being patted and stroked in front of a warm fire in winter. He was sure if a human could purr he would be doing it now. He absolutely basked in the glow of tenderness engulfing him. When their eyes met and she held his gaze, she had him. He knew he was in love with her to the very depths of his soul. He never wanted anything more than he wanted her, and all thoughts of Benton Bartok fled his mind. He was captivated by her beauty.

"Good Lord, but you're beautiful. I have never looked into more beautiful eyes."

She revelled in the compliment. Her soft, husky voice never failed to fire his passion. "If you think you'll get somewhere by flattering me," she paused, "you're probably right." Her eyes danced with impish delight.

He could no longer resist. He pulled her to him, his lips eagerly seeking hers. Suddenly, he felt a searing pain. He jerked back quickly. She shifted her position and the pain eased in his leg. She looked shocked, then concerned.

"Are you okay?" she asked.

"Yes, I'm sorry I jumped. Your elbow was pressing into my wound. It was my fault."

The moment of passion had been broken, but his feelings for her were painfully evident to him. He had to let her know how he felt. "I love you, Val."

"I know you do." She looked away from him and began to rebandage his wound.

He had hoped she would respond with "I love you, too." When she didn't he felt a slight rebuff—perhaps she didn't want to commit herself. "You know Jessie and Katlin are going to be married." He hesitated only slightly. "We could make it a double wedding."

She stopped her work, then looked into his eyes. "I care about you, Ross, and I enjoy being with you." She stopped as she carefully threaded her way through what she must say. "I . . . I don't want to get married right now, Ross."

Ross felt as if someone had thrown a pan of ice water in his face. He had been certain she had felt the same passion, the same desire that he felt. Was he wrong? Had he so badly misjudged her feelings? He felt a strange mixture of hurt, fear, and anger welling up inside him. It was as if someone had run a cavalry saber through his belly and was draining his life's blood away. "I though you loved me, and wanted me as much as I want you."

"Please, Ross, don't misunderstand, or be angry with

me. We really haven't spent much time together. We just had those two days together at the Lightfoot Plantation and these last few weeks together since your brother brought you here. I'm not sure what I feel right now. I do care about you, but I'm not sure what love really is." She got up and began pacing by the bed. "I know I'm strongly attracted to you." Valissa stopped and looked into his face and his deep blue eyes. She loved his thick, blond hair and his darker, trimmed beard. She let her eyes linger on his handsome features and his broad shoulders. "You excite me in ways no other man has before, but I just need some time." She walked to the window and looked out at the freezing rain.

Ross felt frustrated. He knew he didn't want to waste a single minute he could be spending with her. "Don't you see, Val, we don't have much time. My leg is healing now and soon I'll have to rejoin the brigade. I want to spend every moment I can with you before I have to go back to the war."

She turned and faced him. "That's part of my reluctance, Ross, the damned war! Suppose we get married and you go off to battle and never come home again?"

"Then I'd die a happy man knowing that for a while I had your love."

He could see the fire in her eyes. "Oh, that's just fine and dandy! We get married, you go off and die a hero, and I'm left a young widow. It's all very easy for you, but I have to live on alone. Everyday for the rest of my life I would have to face the empty hole you would leave in my life. I'm sorry, but I don't want to take that risk."

"I didn't start the war! I have my duty. You wouldn't respect me if I turned my back on my obligations and hid behind your skirts."

She put her hands in tight fists upon her waist. "I don't expect you to leave the army, Ross Kimbrough, and if you do shirk your duty then you're not the man I think you are."

"Do you think I want to die a hero?" Ross yelled. He reached his hands to her imploringly, "For God's sake, Val, I wouldn't want to die when I have you waiting for me."

She softened her stance, her hands sliding into the pockets of her day dress. "It's not a question of whether you want to live or die. In war it just happens. I wouldn't feel right if I thought you weren't doing your best because of me."

"I can't give you any guarantees, Valissa, if that's what you want. Life just doesn't work that way. Hell, I could just as easily get sick and die as catch another bullet." He shook his head in disgust. "What about me, Val? What do I do if something happens to you? Do you think it would be any easier on me than it would be for you?"

"You're in the war business, Ross. Every day you're in battle you duel with death and only God knows if you will survive."

Ross began to feel his frustrations grow. Somehow he had to convince Valissa to get over her fear of his death or they would never have a life together. "Val, war is a risk, but so is life. I can't promise I won't die, but you have to keep things in perspective." Ross rubbed his hand through his hair. "Sometimes you just have to take some chances and not be afraid to gamble on life. We can never be certain what tomorrow might hold for us, but if you don't dare to believe in the future then you might miss the chance for something really special. Love is a risk and there are no guarantees, but that's what life if all about."

"Just try to understand, Ross, I need some time to think this through. Father and Mother need me. They already have one son dead and another one off to war. Something this important shouldn't be done on a whim or on the spur of the moment." She walked to him and leaned down and kissed him. It was tender, but lacked the fire of the earlier kiss. She turned and walked to the door. "Get some rest, Ross. I'll be back later."

Ross was left confused and his mind swirled with mixed emotions. He felt hurt, rejected, and disappointed, while at the same time he felt love, tenderness, and burning desire for Valissa. Mixing into this wild tableau of emotions were self-doubt and fear that he might not be worthy of her love, though he would never admit it to himself at a conscious level. Overpowering all the rest was his frustration and anger at his failure to get her to agree to marry him. He wanted to marry Valissa now, and if she loved him he really didn't understand why she wouldn't agree. His self-doubt began to build. What if she wasn't in love with him? The thought tightened his stomach with the clutching cold hands of fear that was worse than any battle he had ever faced.

He wanted to chase after her and try to convince her to change her mind, plead with her to tell him how she really felt, but his pride wouldn't let him. "Hell, no!" he thought. "I'm not crawling to her, begging her to marry me." Deep inside he knew that was exactly what he wanted to do. Instead, he sat there brooding over Valissa and his misfortune.

The hours crawled slowly by for the remainder of the day. He pouted and felt sorry for himself, lost in his self-imposed gloom through the fine meal brought in and served by Etta, the housekeeper. He had tried to read awhile after supper, but his heart and mind hadn't been in it. He finally gave up and drifted off into an uneasy sleep. He lost all sense of time as he dozed in and out of his miserable dreams.

Ross rolled onto his side and after several minutes, he felt the bed move. His sleep was sound enough so that at first, he didn't comprehend what it all meant. He felt a soft kiss on his cheek and a warm hand caressing his arm. Startled, Ross rolled onto his back. He felt warm breath upon his face and ardent, passionate lips pressing down on his mouth. The soft aroma of jasmine filled his senses and in that moment he knew it was Valissa. His lips parted and he felt the soft, warm probing of a tongue against his. He reached up, overcome with passion, and pulled her to him. His fingers wrapped around the nape of her neck, caressing her thick auburn hair. He rolled toward her as she rolled onto her back. He let the kiss linger, savoring every sweet moment of it.

Finally, overcome with curiosity, Ross pulled himself free from her kiss long enough to ask, "Val, what are you doing here?"

"Shhhh!" she whispered. "Don't wake my parents!"

He realized then the risk she was taking. He tried to study her eyes in the dim moonlight coming through the window, curious about what she was thinking and feeling. "I thought you didn't want to marry me."

"I said I didn't want to get married right now," she corrected him. "When the war is over then we can see how we feel."

"What if your parents find out you're in here with me?"

"If we keep quiet and don't make too much noise, no one will know I was ever here except you and I." She hesitated for a moment and her voice was low and sultry when she whispered, "Besides, it's more exciting this way, isn't it?"

Her soft voice fired his passion even more, and this clandestine meeting beneath the sheets in her father's house had an intriguing allure. Ross felt the pulsing surge of his lust. The danger of being caught in bed with her raised his excitement to even higher levels. The sweet temptation to take her here and now under her father's roof sent his heart racing. He felt his breaths coming in ragged little gasps as his pulse quickened. "Yes, he said huskily, "I want you, but are you sure this is what you want? I still want to marry you." He could barely make out her face in the dark.

"I told you, Ross, I don't want to get married while the war is going on, but I'm here right now if you want me. Do you want to make love to me or not?" she whispered challengingly.

All hesitation passed as Ross succumbed to his burning lust. Months upon months had passed since he had last felt the warmth and comfort a willing woman can provide. He felt a pulsating throb in his groin as his hands ran over the soft cotton of her nightgown. He felt her stomach rise and fall rhythmically under the palm of his hand. He could feel the warmth of her body through the soft material. His lips eagerly sought hers, as the time for talking slid past, swept away in the heat of his passion.

His hand slid upward to caress her breast and her nipple grew taut, responding to his touch.

She pulled slightly away from him. "Wait a minute," she said as she pulled the gown over her head and tossed it on the floor. He peeled off his nightshirt. He pulled her to him and felt his skin tingle as the warmth of their bodies pressed together, her breasts firm against his chest. She lifted herself and swayed slightly, brushing her nipples lightly across the hairs on his chest, leaving tingling trails of delight. He rolled her on her back, while keeping the weight off his injured leg. His hands slid to cup her breasts and his mouth followed. Valissa arched her back and sighed in ecstasy. He slipped his hands free and slid them down her sides until he grasped her hips firmly with his hands, pulling her tight against him, his member throbbing against the firmness of her belly.

His lips found hers and he found her mouth warm, wet, and willing. Her breath came quick and hot on his cheek as he pulled their lips apart. He began tracing a line of soft kisses down her neck and between her breasts as his hands slid from her hips back to her breasts. His tongue darted teasingly toward her nipples as he held her breasts in his hands and squeezed them together. A soft moan escaped her lips as her body involuntarily shivered in delight.

He continued to kiss and tongue her as he slowly traced his way down her belly. She raised her knees and opened her legs wide to his maddeningly slow advances as he caught the sweet scent of her. His fingers and mouth probed her until she began to shake and quiver with delight. Then, overpowered by his lust, he entered her and felt her warmth wrap around him.

He began to thrust out of his animal need and she answered his every move as she nibbled his earlobe. He felt her tongue dart into and around his sensitive ears, matching his hard thrusts, while her hot breath fell softly on his neck. Her fingers clutched his back, then slid down and squeezed his buttocks as she urged him deeper and harder into her. He felt her begin to tremble and shake underneath him as she whispered his name amid her restrained, soft, passionate moans. She fought to keep her voice low as she was swept over the delicious brink of ecstasy.

Responding to her passion, Ross surrendered to his flaming desire in a fiery eruption. It was all he could do to keep from screaming out in blessed release as the tension of lust subsided. Somehow, he managed to keep quiet as he shook and shuddered with delight and his taut muscles began to unwind. He felt giddy with delight as a soft, tender warmth crept over him. He felt joy and gratitude for the pleasure she had shared with him and loved her even more than he had before.

When it was over they lay exhausted in each other's arms, revelling in the afterglow of love shared. They made love again later, but this time the pace was slower and less urgent. When their lust had been quenched, Valissa slipped quietly away to her room before the first rays of sunlight caressed the cold winter skies. Ross was left tired, drained, and happy.

Their lovemaking had been better than he had ever imagined it could be. He caressed the pillow where her head had been only minutes before and wished she were still with him, warming his bed. Nothing he had ever experienced had touched him this deeply or filled him with such ecstasy. He knew what made the difference; he was in love. Head over heels, king of fools in love, and God have mercy on his soul.

5

Rendezvous with Death at a Disputed Barricade

Near Hartsville, Missouri
January 1863

Captain Gilbert Thomas took two quick swigs of fine Kentucky bourbon from his pocket flask and felt the burn of the fiery liquid as it traced a path down his throat. He slipped the flask quickly into his uniform jacket and handed the reins of his horse to a nearby horse holder. He looked down as he adjusted his tunic and hoped the bourbon would soon soothe his nerves and still the shake in his hands. He pushed his way through the ranks of dismounted soldiers of Company E, Fifth Missouri Cavalry, until he faced them. Nervously, he studied the town of Hartsville standing before them. What he saw was not to his liking.

On a hill across from them stood a splendid six-gun Union battery defending the town. On closer inspection, he saw a ten-rail fence set beside what appeared to be a dry, deep ditch maybe a quarter of a mile in front of the hill. The fence followed the meandering ditch until both ends of it disappeared into groves of trees on each end of the meadow. In these stands of trees Union cavalry lay in wait and were making themselves known. An uneasiness settled on Gilbert's nerves as he licked his lips. Already his throat felt dry. He wanted another drink, but he dare not risk it in front of his men and his commanding officers.

He looked down the ranks of the brigade as they formed to march across the field. Horses were to the rear and the dismounted soldiers lined up as if on parade. Gilbert pulled his cavalry saber from its sheath and held it low. He used his other hand to pull his revolver from its holster and waited for the order that would send them toward those deadly cannons staring across the meadow.

His nerves were taut and his hands continued to shake as his stomach turned in fiery protest. "It's too soon, much too soon," Gil Thomas thought as he felt sweat bead under his hat brim and trickle down into his eyes despite the cool weather. In the last two months they had fought the battles of Cane Hill, Prairie Grove, and Springfield. Springfield. Even the word made his heart race harder. It had been a hopeless task taking on those fortifications around Springfield and, in the end, the attack had failed. In the wake of the battle, many of Missouri's finest were left in the cold embrace of death or left behind wounded. It was only a miracle he had survived this long and the thought occurred to him he was expending his luck at a rapid clip.

Gilbert wanted to turn and run. Just get aboard his horse and ride away, anywhere but here, but he knew he wouldn't. These men had followed him into battle and Jo Shelby had given him his commission and he would not bring shame on them or his name. He looked again at the fence, seeing if he could detect any movement behind those rails. Everything remained calm and he saw nothing moving. It didn't seem right. Had he been on the other side of the field he would have had his men behind that fence, not scattered in the woods. He was only glad the Yankees had not thought of it.

The order finally passed down the ranks and Gilbert stepped forward by the company color-bearer. He listened to the flag gently popping on the breeze as he held his sword high and motioned his men forward. "For . . . ward at a walk, ho!" he shouted. He saw Porter's mounted Confederate brigade on the road advancing at a walk in a column of fours on the enemy's left flank. On the far right he could see Thompson's regiment. Behind his regiment he heard Collins' battery unleash a salvo at the distant Union battery on the hill. Involuntarily, Gilbert flinched from the deep-throated boom of the guns as the shells screamed by, arching overhead on their deadly flight. Great geysers of dirt and debris erupted from the hill, but still the enemy guns remained silent.

In response, Collin's battery fell silent out of fear of hitting their own men marching across the meadow. An eerie silence fell across the field as Gilbert and his men marched forward. The air felt crisp against his face and the cold, brown leaves of winter crunched under his feet, sounding somehow strangely out of place. Great flocks of wild pigeons darted over the field in wildly swooping flights. They looked so graceful and safe up there against the azure blue sky laced with strands of white clouds. He wished he were up there with them.

His every nerve felt strangely alive, every sound vibrant. He could hear the soft, crunching tread of his men's footsteps on the dry leaves, the soft rustle of their woolen and cotton pant legs as they walked. The strange metal tink of canteen and cartridge box as they bumped against the walking soldiers. Every now and then a nervous laugh or a dry cough as a soldier cleared his throat would resound above the other noises.

As they neared the ten-rail fence, Gilbert halted to dress the ranks of his company. Just as his men started to vault over the fence and he slipped his pistol in his belt to free his hand for climbing, all hell broke loose. At nearly point-blank range, three companies of Union soldiers concealed in the deep, dry ditch fired a shattering volley. Shelby's men were caught off guard by this sudden ambush and the line staggered and reeled under the impact of the sudden assault.

The rattle of the volley sounded like a large string of firecrackers all popped off at once. Splinters flew off the rails and cut burning trails of pain across Gilbert's forehead. A rolling cloud of gray burnt powder smoke swirled over him as he ducked behind the cover of the fence. Around him lay the crumpled remains of what had been proud living and breathing Confederate soldiers only moments before. His heart raced away as fear tugged at his insides. Next to him a young boy clutched at his stomach, trying desperately to push his intestines back into his ruptured body. The lad's face was twisted with pain and his eyes large with disbelief. Colonel Shelby's horse went down in the first volley, but miraculously he arose from the mists of gunpowder smoke and urged his men forward on foot.

In that moment, Gilbert knew he must fight or die. If they ran from here across the open meadow the Union soldiers would make easy targets of their exposed backs. No, far better to stand and fight for the ditch than to take several volleys in the back. With a loud Rebel yell he rose to his feet and jumped over the fence. A bayonet tugged at his sleeve as he drove his saber through the first Yankee he reached.

The young boy looked wide-eyed and terrified as blood spilled from his lips. Gilbert roughly shoved the Yankee off his blade as his hand reached for his revolver still stuffed in his belt. The horrifying scream of the Rebel yell echoed in his ears as the Southerners charged the Union soldiers in the ditch. The contest became a desperate struggle of hand-to-hand combat in the narrow confines of the ditch and the fence. Above all the chaos, Gilbert sensed he was firing at blue targets who became a blur in his numbed mind while his blade cut wide, killing swaths before him. Gilbert leaped into the ditch.

Captain Evan Stryker had been beside Colonel Shelby when the first shattering volley hit them. He watched in horror as his commanding officer went down in a sprawl, spilling from his saddle. Without thinking, Evan swung down from his horse and raced to the side of his commander. As he reached him, Colonel Shelby staggered to his feet while his sorrel mount kicked out its last moments of life, blood spilling from an ugly chest wound. The two men stumbled away from the flailing hooves.

"Are you hit, Colonel?" Captain Stryker asked.

A slightly dazed look crossed Shelby's face as he said, "No, I don't think so."

When he snatched his hat off his head, they were both amazed to see that his brass hat badge which pinned one side of the brim to the crown was distorted and holed by a minie ball shot from a Union musket. The metal had deflected the shot. Jo Shelby survived. Around them, the battle raged and without further concern for his safety, Jo Shelby climbed the rail fence before them and urged his men on.

Still surprised by the events around him, Captain Stryker stared after his commander for a moment. He let his eyes take in the swirling milieu. Very few officers around him were still standing. His senses returned as he leapt the fence and followed his commanding officer into the fray. Evan landed on the other side, pulled his revolvers, and began firing at the mass of blue and flashing steel in the ditch.

Captain Gilbert Thomas found a momentary lull in the fighting and realized suddenly his revolver was empty. He returned his bloodied saber to its sheath before he turned and climbed the ditch wall. He knelt near the fence while he fished a loaded extra cylinder for his pistol out of his coat pocket. With practiced ease, he quickly slapped the loaded cylinder into his gun. When he looked up, he spotted Captain Evan Stryker fighting alongside Colonel Jo Shelby.

Involuntarily he felt his jaws tighten as a surge of hate flashed through his veins. There was the damned Texan who had stolen his only love from him, Cassandra Kimbrough. He had known Cassandra nearly all his life, and because of that friendship they had constantly been thrown together at numerous social occasions and visits. From the start Gilbert had been infatuated with the blond, blue-eyed beauty.

Cassandra never seemed to consider him more than a friend, but Gilbert hoped in time he would bring her around to loving him. It had all changed the day Jo Shelby marched into town to recruit a new brigade and brought Evan Stryker with him. In just a matter of a few days the damned Texan had turned on his charm and stolen Cassandra away from him.

When Gilbert had asked Cassandra to marry him, she refused his request. In his heart, Gilbert knew things might have been different if Stryker had not come along and swept her off her feet. From that day on he had hated the Texan and promised to extract revenge. They had fought a duel and Gilbert might have killed the Texan then if Colonel Shelby hadn't come along. Shelby had made them swear an oath to settle their differences after the war.

Promise or not, he was now deep in the midst of a swirling battle and he held a loaded revolver in his hands.

Evan Stryker was making himself an inviting target. Gilbert lifted his loaded revolver and aimed it squarely at the Texan. With his thumb he cocked the revolver and he was ready, but he found himself hesitating. A part of him didn't want to pull the trigger while another part of his brain screamed to kill him now while he had the chance. The Texan turned to face Captain Thomas and his eyes widened in horror as he saw the cocked and aimed gun pointed directly at him.

Both men froze for a moment, Evan Stryker afraid to move and Gilbert struggling with his conscience. Out of the corner of his eye, Gilbert saw a flash of Union blue. A Yankee soldier was rushing toward Evan Stryker and brandishing a bayonet-tipped musket, ready to strike. Without hesitation Gilbert swung the revolver away from Evan and squeezed the trigger. The Yankee took the bullet in his head and tumbled into a pile inches from Captain Stryker's feet.

Evan Stryker turned to fend off the assault, but it would have been too late. He turned in time to see the Yankee take the bullet and fall inches short of running him through the back with a wicked looking bayonet. He glanced up at Gilbert, stunned by the turn of events. Gilbert had swung the pistol back toward him and Evan stared into the black void of the smoking muzzle of the gun. Slowly, Gilbert Thomas lowered the revolver and turned away to confront more Union soldiers. Evan blinked in disbelief. In that moment when he stared into the deep, deadly chasm of the pistol barrel, he was sure Gilbert was going to kill him. Instead, he had saved his life.

He was pulled away from his thoughts by shouts from Colonel Jo Shelby. "Look boys, they're on the run!"

The resolve of the Union soldiers hidden in the ditch had been broken by the tenacity of the Rebels and by their sheer firepower. Though the Yankees had the momentum of surprise, their weapons were single-shot muskets. The Rebel cavalrymen carried revolvers and carbines and fired at a much higher rate. Rebel cavalry armed with revolvers were deadly at close range, and instead of one shot between reloading they had five or six. Knowing they couldn't reload so close to the enemy and caught in hand-to-hand fighting, Yankees broke and began escaping toward the Union artillery battery. In their panic many threw down their rifles and ran, their spirits broken.

Captain Gilbert Thomas moved down the ditch and fired a couple more shots at the retreating men in blue. Gilbert cursed his pride and his father, Harlan, for instilling in him such a rigid sense of honor. He had given his word as a Southern gentleman to Colonel Jo Shelby that he would wait until the end of the war to settle his differences and he was bound by it. When he was presented with the opportunity to kill Evan Stryker he couldn't pull the trigger, betrayed by his dammed sense of honor and duty. "Damn!" he thought. "I need another drink." But he knew now was not the time. He turned his eyes to another part of the field.

Colonel Porter led his Confederate mounted cavalry in a column of fours straight as an arrow toward the Union artillery battery like a giant fist ready to strike. The Union artillery had held their fire to the front, afraid they might hit their men concealed in ambush in the ditch. Now, sensing danger, they wheeled their artillery to face Porter's men. As if one, the six-gun battery roared to life and emptied their weapons into the face of the Rebel cavalry charge. The canister and case shot loaded in the cannons turned them into giant shotguns. The front rank of the Rebel charge melted away into a bloody, convulsing heap. It was a hopeless tangle of dead and dying men and horses. The Rebels behind, propelled by the momentum of

the charge, ran over those already down in front, adding to
the confusion. The attack was blunted in a bloody repulse
and the surviving Rebels turned to ride away as a second
round of artillery fire ripped through their packed ranks.
The slaughter angered Gilbert as he watched dumb-
founded. What officer would try to run such a close formation against an artillery battery? The stupidity of it
stuck in his throat and gagged him. He felt a fresh surge
of anger at the mutilation and bloody slaughter. Then he
heard the shouted orders and fell into formation on the
other side of the ditch. The whole Rebel line of dismounted cavalrymen surged forward after the retreating
Union soldiers.

As Porter's men staggered back from their mangled and
aborted charge, the first Union infantry in total rout
reached the Union battery. They fled through the Union
battery's position, disrupting their work and shaking their
resolve. The panic spread as the artillerymen struggled to
save their guns. They managed to hitch their artillery up
and pull them away, but in their haste they left behind
many of their caissons and ammunition wagons. Thompson's regiment, spared the ambush in the ditch and the artillery fire on the right, swept forward, pushing the Union
cavalry out of the woods and pursuing the fleeing Union
army.

Back at the captured hill, Shelby's men paused.
Hartsville lay in front of them, unprotected. Evan Stryker
cast anguished eyes back at the carnage near the fence and
in the ditch. He turned and followed Colonel Shelby back
the way they had come.

When they reached those swept away in the first volley
of the ambush, they found Colonel Emmet McDonald surrounded by his dead and dying men. Colonel Shelby
moved next to him and knelt beside him. "We whipped
'em, Emmet."

Emmet McDonald's eyes brightened for a moment at the news. Wasn't it a gallant charge?" Bloody spittle formed on his lips as the officer coughed. His gaze stiffened as his life slipped silently away.

Colonel Shelby lowered his head as he blinked away his tears. He gently closed his comrade's open eyes before he stood and turned away. So many officers had been struck down among their men in that first terrible volley. Colonel Wimer, Major Kirtley, Captain Charley Turpin, Captain Dupuy, and Lieutenant Royster were dead besides McDonald. The wounded included Captain Garrett, Captain Crocker, Captain Thompson, Captain Jarrett, Captain Burkholder, Captain Maurice Langhorne, and Captain Bob Carlyle.

Colonel Porter, who had led the cavalry charge against the battery, bled to death from his wounds within the hour. They had won the battle, but paid a fearful price. Burial of the dead commenced immediately.

Billy Cahill rode cautiously out of the woods and studied the road in the gathering gloom. He was a part of Ben Elliott's company pursuing the Union army hastily retreating from Hartsville. In the hours after the battle, they had rounded up numerous prisoners and herded them back toward Confederate lines. Now with night closing swiftly upon them, the pursuit would soon be forced to end. He hoped he might spot more Union soldiers to strike, but his gaze fell on an empty stretch of road. Reluctantly he spurred his horse and turned toward Hartsville. He was glad he had been spared from the bloody charge on the Union artillery and had missed the ambush from the dry ditch. This time Elliot's company had been held in reserve, but they were the first to be pressed into service for the deadly pursuit of routed Union soldiers. Panic stricken, the enemy ran. The roundup had gone smoothly. He had personally put a swift end to any resistance by shooting

Union soldiers outright. The others gave up quickly when they saw the result of their opposition. Feeling grim satisfaction, he rode back toward their lines with his friends Riley Crawford, Frank James, and others of Quantrill's band. The dark veil of night put a welcome end to the bloodshed at the battle of Hartsville.

6

A Blanket of White

Captain Evan Stryker eased his horse from the road and into the ditch so he could move past the plodding troopers before him. He set spurs to his jaded mount, whose pace increased only slightly. Evan knew the horse had been pushed nearly to the limits of its endurance. He patted the big animal gently and knew the dark bay was doing his best.

For the last two days since the battle of Hartsville, they had been marching southeast. The raid had met its objective and forced General Blunt to leave his campaign in Arkansas to protect his ravaged supply lines and communications in Missouri. Jo Shelby and his men had disrupted and destroyed many supplies General Blunt needed for his winter campaign. Forced to turn back or face starvation for his men with winter under way, Blunt returned to Missouri to find things in a shambles. Meanwhile, the Confederate army slipped away like a thief in the night.

For their success the Confederates had paid a heavy price. Many of Jo Shelby's finest men and officers were lost in the bloody confrontations at Springfield and Hartsville. Most of the wounded had to be left behind, for the Southerners lacked the ambulances and wagons to carry the wounded south with them. Wherever possible, the wounded were left along the way or near the battle-fields with loyal Southerners who would do their best to heal and protect them from Yankee troops. Many soldiers, fearing falling into the hands of the enemy, or out of loy-alty to the brigade, did their best to ride with the others despite their wounds. All along the trail more wounded troopers fell by the wayside, singly or in pairs, no longer able to keep up with the column. Evan noticed as he rode how exhausted and worn the brigade looked. Since No-vember they had fought four full battles and numerous skirmishes. There was little fight left in the brigade as they struggled south against the bitter cold weather of January 1863.

Up ahead in a gentle bend of the road, Captain Stryker spotted Colonel Jo Shelby and members of his staff ob-serving the passing column from the shelter of a grove of cottonwood trees. He wheeled his horse out of the wide ditch and spurred toward the colonel. In minutes he pulled up beside his commanding officer, who was sitting astride a sorrel mount. Colonel Shelby believed riding a sorrel horse brought him luck and somehow protected him from harm. It might have been lucky for him, but it was unfor-tunate for the horses. So far, at least ten horses had been killed in battle under Colonel Shelby while he remained uninjured. At the battle of Hartsville, just recently con-cluded, Captain Stryker had seen two sorrels killed be-neath the colonel. Jo Shelby was a sure death sentence if you happened to be a sorrel horse.

Shelby gave grudging acknowledgement of Evan's ar-rival as he watched his exhausted troops pass. He scanned the horizon and studied a dark, ominous line of gray clouds racing toward them. Without turning to look at Evan, Colonel Shelby asked, "Captain, did you locate Thompson's men at our rear?"

"Yes, sir, Colonel, I found him."

Shelby twisted in the saddle to study Evan Stryker. "Has he had any contact with enemy troops?"

"No, sir. Colonel Thompson says it is all clear. No enemy pursuit has been encountered, but he will stay vigilant while he is in command of the rear guard."

"I know we can all count on Thompson and his men." A look of satisfaction crossed Jo Shelby's face. "Gentlemen, if we are in no danger of pursuit, then I think we better find a place to camp soon. We all need rest." He glanced back at the bank of clouds relentlessly advancing toward them. "I don't like the looks of that storm front. Captain Stryker, I want you to ride forward and tell Captain Elliott and our advance to find a place to camp immediately, then get back here and report to me."

"Yes, sir." Captain Stryker saluted, turned his horse to the south, and rode toward the front of the column. It took Evan nearly two hours to find Captain Elliott and make his report. By the time he turned to start his search for Colonel Shelby, the storm front had reached them. Dark, low clouds scudding overhead unleashed large snowflakes, driven hard by a frigid wind. Evan wrapped his coat more tightly around him and shoved his free hand into his coat pocket. The snow swirled about the column, making the troopers marching past look like ghostly shapes in the light of day. All along the route of march, the regiments were pulling off into the pine thickets to seek shelter and gather firewood, before the swirling snow covered it all. Captain Stryker, mindful of his orders to report, continued down the road seeking headquarters. After less than thirty minutes, the snow was already two inches deep and falling swift and thick. The snowflakes, driven by a harsh north wind, stung his flesh; his hands and feet were already growing numb. At times the visibility was so poor he lost the road until his horse stumbled in the deeper snow in the ditch. The wind whipped the powder from the ground and swirled it into great, blinding ground blizzards. Evan began to realize he might ride past headquarters in this white veil of frigid snow. Colonel Shelby would just have to understand, he must seek shelter and do it now.

He rode for a while longer and tried to study the encampments springing up along the road. He saw the familiar shapes of artillery, caissons, and ammunition wagons parked in the woods near the road. He rode to the campfire and, seeing familiar faces, dismounted. "Boys, do you mind if I join you? It's getting pretty miserable out."

Corporal Calvin Kimbrough of the battery stepped forward from the shelter and led the captain's horse behind the shelter of some wagons. Together the two men worked swiftly to unsaddle and rub down the big bay. Evan reached in his bags and pulled out some grain he had saved for the horse and fed him. Then the two rejoined the others.

A cheery fire greeted them as they crawled under the protection of some cotton-twill canvas shelter halves tied to wagon and cannon wheels to form a barrier against the storm. On the lee side of the improvised shelter they were shielded from the onrushing wind. The warmth of the fire felt good, as though it might stop the uncontrollable shivering of Evan's body. Evan wrapped himself tightly in his bedroll blankets and thrust his feet near the fire. The wind howled around them through the trees like some dreadful banshee hunting for the unwary. The popping of the canvas against the wind made conversation difficult so the men said little and fought to stay warm.

Evan's feet began to tingle and burn as they unthawed from the cold. The almost unbearable sensation spread to his legs and his hands. He fumbled through his haversack and found some two-day-old biscuits and a little jerky to chew on. When he reached for his canteen, he found that the contents were frozen. He scooped handfuls of the powdery snow and let it melt in his mouth. All the while outside the snow deepened and a fine mist of white flakes sifted under the canvas.

Beyond the warmth of the fire Captain Stryker could make out other campfires with men huddled around them, their meager supplies of firewood carefully protected and rationed. He knew he was lucky to find Collins' battery, for in their wagons they could carry captured shelter halves most of the other soldiers in the command lacked. Most of the troopers had to carry everything they needed on their horses so out of necessity they traveled light. It didn't leave them room to carry tents. Even a few of Collin's men couldn't fit under the shelter of the canvas tied to the artillery and wagons. They, like so many others, were forced to bear the storm huddled around open fire pits as the snow swirled in endless eddies, blanketing them in the cold, wet whiteness.

A soldier approached and squeezed into the overcrowded canvas shelter beside Calvin Kimbrough. Captain Stryker moved over to make as much room as possible, but there was little to spare. "Don't get yer dander up boys, I won't be here long. I just want to talk a spell to Cal."

Evan looked over at the new intruder. He was tall and lean, with broad shoulders. A smile crossed his face as he talked; he looked like a man who could handle rugged surroundings. Calvin turned to Evan Stryker and said, "Have you met Washington Mayes?"

Evan offered his hand and shook it spiritedly, forgetting the soldierly protocol in such dreadful surroundings. "No, I don't believe we've met," he said as he watched the man smiling at him.

The handshake was firm and hurt Evan's tingling fingers, but he tried not to let it show as Mayes said, "Glad to meet you, Captain. Just call me Wash. Everyone does."

Calvin said, "Wash is from Lafayette County and an old friend of mine. When we captured the new cannon at Springfield he was one of the volunteers to come over from the cavalry to help us crew the cannon. He's getting the hang of it pretty well, too."

"I'm sure he is." Evan listened awhile as the two old friends talked. From the conversation Evan learned Calvin had attended Wash's marriage to a woman named Mollie Turnbow last summer. Sitting near the fire after a hard day's ride in the cold had begun to make Captain Stryker sleepy. He listened only a short while longer to Calvin and Wash talk of old times before he drifted off to sleep.

He woke with a start about six hours later when a cold shower of snow fell in his face. He woke up sputtering as he bolted upright in his blankets. Snow had built up deep enough on the canvas cover to collapse it, dropping the snow on their heads. The men grumbled as they cleared away the powdery snow, carefully stoking the fire so it wouldn't go out.

As order in their camp was restored, Calvin looked beyond into the stormy night. He turned toward Evan, who was cleaning out the last remaining snow stuck in his collar. "I think we ought to check Wash's camp. Looks like the fire is out. Those men could freeze to death on a night like this."

They used a long, burning branch as a torch, fighting their way through the foot-deep snow toward the other camp. When they reached the fire they found a soldier sitting upright on a log, leaning on a stick held in his hands. The man was covered in white snowflakes. He sat perfectly still staring out into the face of the storm, seeing nothing. The campfire was cold before him and snow was beginning to settle over black ashes.

Evan reached out and touched the soldier in an effort to

wake him. His efforts failed to get a response. Calvin bent forward holding the torch near the man's face. What he saw startled both men. The soldier sitting there like a stone statue was frozen to death. The realization sent icy shivers down the men's spines. Calvin recognized the man as a new addition to the crew. He began searching frantically through the mounds covered by the snow, trying to stir others sleeping around the frozen camp. Two were found frozen to death in their blankets. Four more were still alive. Among the survivors was Wash Mayes, who had returned to the camp after he finished his conversation with Calvin. When they woke him, he cursed the dead man loudly. When he calmed down he said, "It was Edward's shift to tend the fire. I can't believe he fell asleep and let the fire go out."

Captain Stryker said wryly, "He paid the ultimate price for it."

They got a new fire going after struggling with the snow-dampened wood and, satisfied it would keep going, they returned to their camp with Wash Mayes in tow. Wash was shivering and shaking uncontrollably. "I . . . I can't feel my hands or feet," he stuttered.

They put his feet near the fire and warmed them immediately while they vigorously rubbed his hands to restore circulation. As the blood flow returned to his feet he screamed in agony. In between bouts of fighting the pain, he thanked Calvin and Evan for coming to his rescue. "If you two hadn't checked up on us, we would have all been dead by morning."

After a rough night they arose to a clear and frigidly cold day. The last vestiges of the ten-hour storm passed in the night, covering the exposed soldiers of Shelby's brigade with a two-foot blanket of fresh fallen snow. They met the stark white landscape with trepidation. If they marched today in such conditions, many more would die. Evan wondered if the storm would seal their fate.

* * *

Jessie Kimbrough joined the crowd of people milling about the busy business district of Batesville, Arkansas. He strolled through them aimlessly enjoying the festive atmosphere. Twice he ducked into a bar to brace himself against the cold by downing a shot of whiskey. Each was another excuse to celebrate the arrival of Jo Shelby's Confederate cavalry brigade. Only the day before, one of Shelby's scouts reached Batesville. Sergeant Starke carried welcome news. Jo Shelby and his cavalry were riding toward Batesville and should arrive on the morrow. The word was spread swiftly throughout the county and by midmorning the crowd had grown rapidly. Today was the day of their expected coming.

He was amazed at the variety of people standing around, their excitement building. The arrival of Shelby's brigade was causing as much anticipation as a circus coming to town. Both sides of the street were lined with women and children of all ages. Scattered among them were a handful of young men who had somehow avoided serving in the war and men too old to fight.

Jessie had ridden his horse to town instead of riding in the carriage with the ladies. After being cooped up for several weeks in the company of the women of the family he was anxious for some excitement and he didn't want it cut short because someone was eager to go home.

During the morning, Jessie used a variety of excuses to slip away. The women of Farnsworth House preferred to pass their idle time while they waited for the brigade's arrival by shopping the stores of downtown Batesville. Never one to enjoy shopping, Jessie had wandered through the local bars. Now well fortified against the cold, he moved back onto the streets.

Suddenly, shouts rippled up and down the streets heralding the arrival of the lead elements of the brigade. Jessie pushed his way to the front of the crowd to get a good view. These were the friends he had fought alongside since August of 1862. Among their numbers was his brother Calvin. Jessie had worried ever since he left the brigade over six weeks ago. His older brother, Ross, was seriously wounded at the battle of Prairie Grove and he had used his sick leave to bring Ross to Batesville to recuperate from serious wounds.

Jessie had his own slight wound from the battle of Prairie Grove. He had been hit in the chest by a spent minie ball. Only the luck of the bullet striking a small bible in his breast pocket had saved his life. The result was a cracked rib and a very sore sternum, but it was enough to let him bring Ross here, and for that he was grateful.

Jessie had wanted to return to the command right away, but when his sisters arrived they carried word that Shelby's men were on the march in Missouri. Finding them would be difficult and dangerous for a lone soldier so he had remained in Batesville. Now his conscience would be eased as he rejoined his company.

The first string of campaign-weary soldiers did their best to dress their ranks as they rode down the street, but despite the effort their fatigue was evident. Most had an assortment of clothing wrapped around their boots, hands, and heads to ward off the bitter cold of late January. Blankets were often tied over and around their overcoats and uniforms. If the people hadn't know better they would have thought these were Union troopers by the amount of captured blue overcoats worn by the men. Despite their condition, the men's spirits seemed buoyed by the enthusiastic welcome showered on them by the crowd of well-wishers.

It was beyond the brigade's ability to hide their condition from the people, for the troops were tired and worn beyond endurance. As the numbers of the weary troopers parading by increased, the more intense became the hush from the crowd witnessing their passing. What pitiful few wagons and ambulances that remained with the cavalry troopers were overflowing with the wounded and the sick. Without a word being said, it was evident these men had fought recently.

Jessie knew it had been rough; he could see it in the eyes of the soldiers. He yelled to those he knew until his regiment came along. There were many missing since he last rode with them. Jessie spotted Captain Gilbert Thomas and, after swinging into the saddle of his horse, rode to report to him.

Gilbert smiled wearily at Jessie and Jessie could see the fatigue on the captain's face. "Damn, if you're not a sight for sore eyes, Jess. I heard you found your brother wounded at Prairie Grove. How is he?"

"He's alive, but he's still stuck in bed or on crutches most of the time. He'll be okay once he heals." Jessie motioned toward the men behind them. "The boys look pretty torn up."

"We are, Jess. We fought two battles since you were with us at Prairie Grove. We got caught by a hell of a blizzard on the eighteenth of January. Snow stacked up two feet deep in just ten hours. Wagons with the wounded and sick couldn't move. We didn't have any shelter, damn little food, and we had to use fire to melt water to drink. It's almost impossible to find wood to burn under that much snow. I reckon nearly half the men have a case of frostbite, some of them severe. We had men freeze to death in the cold. Sickness is high, and many of our wounded didn't make it. We had to leave most of them with civilians all along our route. This command has never been overfed, but now we're losing men from starvation."

Jessie swallowed hard as he thought about the suffering the command had been through. He was grateful he had missed it. "Jonas Starke and a few of the scouts came in yesterday, and told us you were on the way. The people here are strongly Southern and they want to help. I think this would be a good central place to set up winter camp. Would you ride with me to talk to Colonel Shelby about it?"

"I'd be for it. I don't think this brigade can handle much more. It seems to me we are all on the verge of total collapse. Let's see what the colonel says."

It didn't take too long for the two men to find Colonel Jo Shelby; he already had made up his mind to set up winter camp in friendly surroundings. He knew his men had been driven to the limit of their endurance and his scouts already reported the favorable conditions in the area. Besides, the geographical position pleased him—Batesville was on the White River in the north central part of the state of Arkansas. From here he would be centrally located to deal with invasions from Springfield in western Missouri by General Blunt or attacks from Helena in east central Arkansas by General Steele.

The people of Batesville responded with generosity. The wounded and sick were taken into private homes, food was distributed, and a temporary camp was set up on the south side of the river. The supply wagons belonging to the brigade were left before the Springfield raid at Lewisburg, Arkansas. Forced to travel light for speed and to save their horses, most of the gear was left behind. Most of the captured supplies that couldn't be distributed among the soldiers were lost on the struggle south. Much of it was thrown out of the wagons to make room for the sick and wounded or lost or used up in the winter blizzard of the eighteenth.

Calvin Kimbrough happily joined his family at the Farnsworth House. The family was together now except for Ross, who chose to stay at Covington Manor until he was healed. His family understood for they realized he was in love with Valissa. Cassandra invited Captain Evan Stryker to stay with the Kimbroughs. She didn't make the same offer to Gilbert Thomas because she was afraid of the friction it would cause. Gilbert felt the rebuff, and his jealousy only intensified. Valissa Covington offered to take Gilbert in at Covington Manor, relieving the serious problem. Other officers were sheltered in homes throughout the town and nearby countryside.

Orders went out immediately to the supply train at Lewisburg to march to Batesville. The men were in desperate need of their camp gear, but the weather refused to cooperate. The supply train remained snowbound in Lewisburg. Shelby knew his men would have to survive as best they could. Fortunately, the local citizens came to the rescue. More soldiers were welcomed into private residences until nearly all were in houses, businesses, churches, and community buildings.

Although the brigade was stationed in the area and Evan Stryker was supposed to stay with the Kimbroughs, they hardly saw one another. As a staff officer, Evan was busy helping the men find shelter and running important errands for Colonel Shelby.

Wash Mayes, a family friend, was weak and suffering from severe frostbite. The Kimbroughs quickly took him in at Farnsworth House. Jessie helped him upstairs to a bedroom and sent Jeremiah to fetch a field surgeon belonging to the brigade.

He returned a couple of hours later with Doctor Spencer, the same man who operated at gun point on Ross Kimbrough. Seeing the familiar face, Jessie recalled the last time they had met, in a field hospital at the battle of Prairie Grove.

Faced with a seemingly endless stream of seriously wounded soldiers, Doctor Spencer had wanted to amputate Ross's leg. Ross wouldn't hear of it and Jessie helped convince Doctor Spencer to fix the leg by aiming a sawed-off shotgun at the doctor.

"Well, I'll be damned!" The man with round wire glasses shifted the stub of a well-chewed cigar to the corner of his mouth. "Your brother still alive or did he die?" The doctor asked the question with no malice, just obvious curiosity.

"He lived, but he had a rough time of it. He's staying nearby at Covington Manor. I'm sure he'd like to thank you proper for what you did for him if you'd stop by to see him."

The doctor grinned, then pulled out a match and lit the cigar. Two good puffs got the glow bright at the tip. He blew out a cloud of smoke that burned Jessie's eyes before he replied. "Last time I said 'Howdy-do' to your brother I was staring into the barrels of a sawed-off shotgun. I can't say as I'm too anxious to see him again, but I'm glad he's gonna make it. If he has that kind of spunk in a battle, I'd hate to be a Yank that has to face him." A worried look crossed the doctor's face as a thought occurred to him. "Hey, this fella I came to check on, he's not one of your brothers too, is he?"

Jessie laughed, then said, "No, he's not my brother, but he is a good friend. I hope you can help him."

"Well, I guess we'd best get to it. Lead the way."

Jessie showed the man to the bedroom where Wash Mayes was resting. Doctor Spencer followed him in and with the aid of a lamp examined Mayes' frostbite.

Jessie noticed the concerned look on Doctor Spencer's face as he inspected the frostbitten skin. He studied the areas on the hands and the feet. Finally, he stood erect and put his hands on his waist. "Soldier, I'm not gonna beat around the bush. You've got a severe case of frostbite on your hands. That right hand is already turning black and the flesh is looking putrid. If we don't remove the hand you'll die of gangrene. It might be too late as it is. I think I can save your left hand but I'm afraid we'll have to re-move the little finger and your ring finger. Your feet are red and blistered from the cold and you're going to lose some skin, but I think they'll be okay."

Wash lay there with beads of sweat glistening on his forehead. "Is there anything you can do except amputate?"

The doctor looked him in the eye and shook his head, no. "I'm sorry, son, but the frostbite is too severe. The flesh is already dead. If we don't operate gangrene could set in very soon. I'd suggest we do it immediately if you want any chance to survive." Wash looked at Jessie, but found little help.

"I don't know what to say; it's your decision, Wash."

Washington Mayes gulped hard. He looked directly at Doctor Spencer. "I don't want to lose my hand and fingers, but I'm not ready to die, either. Do what ya gotta do, Doc."

"I think you're making the right decision, soldier. A chance at life is better than none." Doctor Spencer turned toward Jessie. "Tell the cook downstairs we're gonna need the dining room table to operate on. I'll need hot water and some help getting this man downstairs."

Jessie went to find Cassandra and Fanny. The two women brought Jeremiah and Jethro and, with everyone's help, they carried Wash Mayes to the kitchen. Once they had him positioned on the table they began urging Wash to drink as much whiskey as he could as a simple form of anesthetic. He was very cooperative—it had been a long time since he had free whiskey. As he drank he became more animated in his conversation with Cassandra, who stayed nearby to comfort him.

After thirty minutes the alcohol began to take the desired effect. The slur in Washing Mayes' speech became more pronounced. "Jeez, it's been a long time since I been this drunk. I can't remember the last time I had such a good reason. I sure am lucky I got the help of a pretty woman helpin' me to drink." His movements were becoming less controlled and his eyes had an out-of-focus glaze about them. He struggled to stare in Cassandra's eyes. "Danged if you're not one of the prettiest women I've ever

seen. First time I laid eyes on you it nearly took my breath
away. I've always wondered what it would be like to kiss
a woman as beautiful as you, but I never had the courage
to try. Do ya suppose you'd kiss me?" Smiles passed quietly around the table as everyone realized Wash was getting very drunk.

Cassandra held his head and poured more whiskey into
his mouth. "You drink the rest of this glass of whiskey,
Wash, and I'll be proud to kiss you."

Wash smiled a silly grin and he quickly gulped down
the few remaining swallows. "No problem, Cassie, I knew
I could do it." He threw his arm around her neck and
pulled her down to kiss him. Cassandra didn't resist and
let him have his promised kiss. He was eager and she responded. After a couple of minutes she felt his arm relax
and fall from her. She pulled away, but continued to lean
over him. A confused look crossed his face. "Cassie, do ya
think you could do somethin' about this room spinnin'
around so fast? I don't feel too good." Moments later his
head slumped to the side and he mercifully passed out.

Jessie observed the process of getting Washington drunk
and, if it was needed, he was there to help restrain him.
Jessie smiled at his sister. "You didn't have to kiss him,
you know."

"I know I didn't, but he was scared, Jess. I only wish I
could help him more." She sighed deeply and watched as
Doctor Spencer carefully laid out his instruments to prepare for the surgery. "I know this much, I'm not going to
stay around to watch while Doctor Spencer operates. I
don't think my stomach could take it." Cassandra gave her
friend one more kiss on the forehead and left the room.

Doctor Spencer completed his preparation and his
knives and bone saws were lined up within easy reach. He
had already threaded his needles with the gut he would
need to sew up the wounds from the amputation. "Time to
strap him down, Jessie. I'll need you and one of those

slaves you had in here earlier to help hold him down. You know anyone else who can help?"

"I'll get Jethro and Jeremiah."

"Get with it before he wakes up. We haven't got all day."

The thought crossed Jessie's mind that lately he had seen more operations than he ever cared to. If he never had to watch another doctor work he would be happy.

Calvin Kimbrough stood beside the bed as his eyes studied the sullen face of his friend Wash Mayes. "How's it going, Washington?"

The fatigue of the harsh operation left him looking old beyond his years. "Washington. I haven't heard you call me by my full name in years. Just because they operated on me don't mean you have to get formal on me."

Calvin smiled, then said, "I guess whacking one of your hands off and a couple more fingers didn't make ya any less feisty, did it?"

"It took a powerful lot more out of me than you think, Cal. I can't recall when I've hurt more. It's left me pretty near tuckered out." Wash had his arm with the missing hand in a sling; his other hand was wrapped in bloody bandages over the stumps where the fingers used to be.

Wash studied the bandages. "You know, it's kind of funny, I can see my fingers are gone, but sometimes I'd swear they were still there. Sometimes I think I feel them move, but then I look down and they're gone." He looked up at Calvin, his face turning sad and tears forming in the corners of his eyes. "I don't know how I'm gonna tell Mollie I lost a hand and some fingers. She's a good wife. She deserves more for a husband than a useless cripple." Wash choked back his tears as they spilled down his cheeks. In anguish he cried out, "I can't even wear my wedding ring anymore."

As Calvin sat there and stared at his friend he didn't

know what to say. The mere mention of the word "wedding" brought back memories of the day Wash Mayes married Mollie Turnbow. It was little more than a year ago now, but it seemed like another time and place. Through Calvin's eyes, Mollie was a plain woman and did nothing to fire his blood, but Wash thought she was special and that was all that mattered. Calvin had to admit she had an exception figure. One seldom took the time to linger on her facial features, but many did double takes when she walked by. In addition, Mollie was friendly and outgoing. The kind of woman many men dreamed about because she was a devout Christian, loving and tender, and not afraid of hard work. She loved Washington Mayes and no one who really knew her could ever doubt it.

Calvin felt the crushing weight of compassion for his friend as he sat beside him on the edge of the bed. He placed his hand on Wash's shoulder to comfort him. "I know it's a hard thing to face Wash, but I know Mollie. She'll love you just as much with or without the hand."

"How am I gonna make a living, Cal? What kind of work can a one-handed man do? Hell, even my good hand only has two good fingers and a thumb."

"I know it don't seem so now, but in a way you're lucky. You still got your left hand and you're left-handed. I bet you can find work as a clerk in a store. You'll be a war hero after this is all over."

"Sometimes I wish I'd just died rather than live like this."

"Don't talk like that, Wash. Why, if Mollie was to hear you she'd box your ears. I know it's gonna take a while to adjust to your new situation, but just give it some time."

Wash began to sob again, letting the hurt flow freely from him. Calvin stayed there with his friend until Wash was cried out. "The war is over for you, Wash. You can go home to Mollie with your conscience clear. You've done all you can do in this war and now you can put it behind you and look to the future. Just think about how good it will feel to be back home in Missouri spending your nights sleeping snug beside a good woman in a warm bed. Hell, many a dead man would be plum pleased to be in your situation. I bet many a man alive today would trade places with you and get out of this damn war if they could." Calvin looked down at the floor. "I still have to face the war. I've already seen more of it than I ever cared to. I might not be as lucky as you and live through this war. Even if I do, I don't have anyone who loves me like you do. I don't have anyone anxious for me to come home to start our lives together. You're a lucky man, Wash Mayes, and you don't realize it." Calvin glanced back at Wash. "Mollie will love you no matter what happens. You search your soul, Wash, and you know it's true."

Wash Mayes glanced at his friend as he pondered his words. "I'll think on what you said and I'll do some praying. It doesn't look like I'm gonna be doing much else with my time for a while."

Cassandra strolled into the room in time to hear Wash's words. "How are you feeling today, Wash?"

"I've been lying here feeling real sorry for myself, to tell you the truth, but your brother came by and straightened me out."

"Calvin always was sensible. He has a knack for cutting through the nonsense."

Washington flashed an embarrassed smile at Cassandra. "I want to apologize for my behavior before I passed out. I think I might've gotten a little bold and said and did some things I shouldn't have. If I wasn't dreaming, I believe I kissed you and said some very foolish things."

"Why, Wash Mayes, I will be upset with you if you didn't mean all those wonderful compliments you gave me. It's not every day a girl is so flattered." She smiled at him impishly. "I would appreciate it, Wash, if you'd keep it a secret though. I don't want Mollie mad at me. Any

man who can kiss like that is sure to have a jealous wife."
She laughed softly and Washington smiled shyly. "I know
you'd never do anything to hurt Mollie. You were in pain,
alone, and scared. The whiskey was doing the talking."

His face relaxed. "Thanks, Cassandra, I appreciate the
kind words."

She leaned over and kissed him on the cheek. "Thank
you, Washington Mayes. A girl likes to be flattered now
and then. It makes her feel appreciated. Now, how about
me rounding you up something to eat?"

"I'll try."

"That's all we can ask. I'll have Fanny bring you something as soon as she gets it ready."

"I'm obliged."

She waved as she left the room. Calvin stayed a while
longer reminiscing about the days before the war. When
Fanny arrived with the food, he excused himself and went
on his way. For the time being, it was going to be good to
enjoy this interlude in the war.

7

Confrontation

Ross Kimbrough knew he had a problem when Andrew Covington asked him to come to the parlor alone to talk. Andrew showed all the signs of a man with a lot on his mind; he walked around stiffly, trying to make polite conversation as he fiddled with pouring the drinks while passing time with idle talk about the weather. Ross knew Andrew was building himself up to talk about something important, and Ross figured it had to be about Valissa.

Ross's mind ran like a freight train. Did Andrew know about Valissa's midnight visits to his bed? In the last ten days, she had slept with him four times. Had someone seen her, or had she told her father? Perhaps he knew nothing at all and this was all about something else. Guilt lay heavy on Ross's mind, and he felt a nervous twirl to his stomach.

Andrew lifted a long cigar before him and cut the tip off

with a small pair of scissors before walking over and standing beside the fireplace. He put the cigar in his lips and palmed the tip as he lit the end with a long stick kindled from the fire. He blew out clouds of smoke in three quick puffs. Ross smelled the aroma of the burning cigar and found it unpleasant. He couldn't cultivate an interest in smoking. When he was ten years old, his father caught him smoking behind the barn. His father made him smoke the whole cigar, put the fire out, then chew the butt up and swallow it. He had been sick as a dog for the next two days and lost all desire in smoking. Ross thought it was too bad the same thing hadn't happened to Andrew when he was younger.

"How's your leg feeling, Ross?"

"It's healing nicely. I took my leg splints off. It's been over two months." He patted the leg for emphasis. "Still, the muscles have to heal and grow in strength. I don't need a crutch any longer and soon I won't need this cane, either."

"I'm glad to hear it. I know the South needs every man." Andrew blew out another cloud of smoke as he rested his arm on the fireplace mantle. He plucked the cigar from his lips and began rolling it between his thumb and forefinger. "I guess it's about time for you to rejoin your scouts or join your family at Farnsworth House."

"The brigade is still in winter camp, Mr. Covington. The supply train still hasn't arrived, so the colonel is letting us stay in private homes till our tents arrive. I'd like to stay here if you don't mind."

Andrew looked perplexed. He studied the end of his cigar as if he had never before seen one. He slowly bent down and flicked the length of burning ash from the end of the cigar into the fireplace. He straightened up, then nervously cleared his throat. "I guess there is no easy way to say this ... I would rather you join your family at

Farnsworth House." His words hung heavy in the air between them, filling the room with uncomfortable silence.

Somehow Ross had expected it, though he had hoped it wouldn't come to this. His pride was wounded and he felt his anger beginning to rise. "If that is your wish, sir, I will honor it, though I would like to know why."

"I think you know why, Ross." Andrew hesitated, long enough to let his words take effect. "Everyone here has watched the relationship between you and Valissa grow. She's been smitten with you ever since she met you at the Lightfoot Plantation. Now that you've been here a while and she has spent more time with you, we have watched you both change as your feelings for one another have grown." He looked Ross in the eyes. "I don't want to see my daughter hurt. She's very important to me."

Ross stood slowly and faced Andrew Covington. "I don't want to see her hurt either, Mr. Covington. I love her and I've asked her to marry me."

Andrew didn't bat an eye. He had the cocksure look of a poker player knowing he has an ace in the hole. "When you asked her how did she respond, Ross?"

Ross swallowed hard, choking back the anger and embarrassment. "She said she didn't want to get married till the war was over."

Andrew gave him a condescending smile. "Did she give you a reason?"

Ross paused, not wanting to say more as Andrew shoved him verbally into a corner. "She was afraid she might become a widow."

Andrew smiled, confident of his control of this situation. "You know she's right, don't you, Ross? It isn't right for you to expect her to wait for you and worry about a husband that might come home half a man or not at all."

Ross's anger flared as he rose from the chair. "Nothing in life is guaranteed and you've got to seize any opportunity for happiness you can find. In times like this you must live for the moment and let the rest sort itself out."

Andrew remained calm. "Seems like a selfish, short-sighted way of thinking to me."

"This isn't about the war or what is right for Valissa, is it? You don't want to see me marry your daughter, do you?"

"She isn't going to marry you, Ross. Can't you see that?" Andrew pitched the half-smoked cigar into the fireplace, adding emphasis to his statement.

Ross doubled his hands into fists. He knew he was loosing in this battle of words and he felt the frustration building. "She would if she thought she had your approval."

Red began to color Andrew's cheeks. "You don't want to face the truth, do you, Ross? We're a tight-knit family and she knows we need her with both of our sons gone. I've lost one son and God knows if the other will ever come home again. I won't lose her, too."

So there it was, out in the open for both of them to see. Andrew hadn't meant for the words to slip out like they had, but they did. Now, Ross seized the advantage. "You aren't thinking about what is best for Valissa. You're only interested in what is best for you. You're afraid you'll lose all your children and you'll be left alone."

Andrew's face began to redden with anger and contort with rage. "What's wrong with a father wanting to protect his children?"

"Nothing—if you don't try to run their lives. Let her make her own decisions or she will always blame you for it later. She must decide for herself, right or wrong. If you come between us, she may never forgive you."

"I'll take that chance, Kimbrough." He shook his finger angrily in Ross's face. "What right do you have to come to my home, accept my hospitality, and then insult me? I want you out of here, and right now." Andrew glared at him, his face nearly purple with rage. Ross saw the anger in Andrew's eyes, the throb of blood flowing through the vein bulging in his temple.

"I'll go, but please don't hold this against my family."

"I have nothing against them; this is just between you and me."

Ross wanted somehow to ease the tension flowing between them. Even in his anger he realized this was Valissa's father and somehow, someday, they must reach an understanding if he was ever to marry her. "That's fair enough; I don't want to seem ungrateful. You have been extremely kind to me and my family. I owe you my life. If you hadn't taken me in here at Covington Manor I probably wouldn't be alive today. I am in your debt."

"If you really mean it, then I'll ask you to leave my daughter alone till the war is over."

The words stunned Ross just as much as if someone had smacked him on the head with a two-by-four. He stood there stupidly, searching his mind for the right words. "I won't marry her until the war is over, if that is your wish."

"I'll accept that as your word as an officer and a gentleman."

Ross swallowed hard. He knew he was backed into a corner by his rigid belief in honor and duty, hemmed in by a promise due for a debt owed. Much as he hated it, he would honor his vow. "I give my word on one condition."

Hope sparkled in Andrew's eyes. "Well, spit it out."

"If you'll let me continue spending time with her and won't block her from visiting Farnsworth House."

Andrew looked as if he had a bitter taste in his mouth. "I'll agree, if you'll keep your word."

"I will if you honor yours."

Andrew glared at him as he spoke in a menacing voice. "One more thing, Ross, you do anything to hurt my little girl and I'll kill you! Do you understand?"

"I would never do anything to hurt Valissa, because I love her. She is the only reason I don't challenge you to a duel right now. I know she would never forgive me if I killed her father. If I were you, Andrew, I'd be grateful; it's keeping you alive."

Andrew's eyes were steady and as mean as flint. "Boy, whenever you think you've got what it takes, just bring it on. I'll be waiting."

Ross stood firm but his face relaxed, slowly breaking into a smile. He held out his hand, offering it for Andrew to shake. "I might not agree with you, but I don't doubt your courage. I give my word I won't try to marry your daughter till the war is over."

Andrew stared into Ross's eyes. His gaze shifted slowly to the offered hand. He hesitated a long moment before slowly grasping the hand. Both men squeezed hard, then harder, each expressing his desire to show his toughness. "I accept your word and your conditions."

"Then we'll expect you for Katlin and Jessie's wedding on the fourteenth?"

"I've already accepted an invitation from your sister. I see no reason not to attend."

"I'll see you then in a few days, Mr. Covington. Give my kindest regards to Mrs. Covington, Valissa, Etta, and Henry. I'll be gone in half an hour. Would you please have Henry saddle a horse for me? I'll have it returned."

"I will."

Ross pivoted on his heel, straightened his back, and limping slightly walked proudly to the stairs and up to his guest room. Half an hour later he rode for Farnsworth House.

8

A Time of Bliss

J essie stared at the White River through the window. The green color of the river water contrasted sharply against the crisp, white ice clinging to the banks. The limbs of the hardwood trees near the water stretched over it like bony fingers reaching toward the sky. Patches of snow lay scattered in the shadow of the trees, sheltered from the melting rays of sunlight.

This was the day he had been waiting for, the day he thought might never come, his wedding day. Jessie's throat felt dry and his hands trembled, but he wasn't sure if it was from nerves or from anticipation. He knew he didn't fear marriage, for he wanted to marry Katlin more than anything else in the world. No, his concerns were more of tripping or falling on the way up the aisle, or forgetting the wedding vows. He was as nervous as he'd been the first time he went into battle.

Jessie knew some of his anxiety was due to anticipation

of his wedding night. He had saved himself for Katlin and had even turned down the chance to make love to her before he left for the war. That was a decision he had questioned often in the months that followed. The stupidity of it amazed him, for he could very well have died in battle and been denied the pleasure of knowing the joy of making love to the beautiful woman he so cherished. God, and possibly luck, had been with him. Now, finally he would experience what he had denied himself. They could at last explore the vast mysteries of love and pleasure together.

He fingered the locket around his neck. It had become a special talisman and omen of good luck. Maybe the locket had protected him from harm.

"It's time, Jessie. Are you ready?"

Jessie jerked suddenly, stirred from his thoughts by his brother's words. He turned to face Calvin. "I couldn't be more ready."

"They say it gets better once the ceremony is over. Once she gets her ring in your nose, she can lead you around more easily." Calvin laughed nervously at his joke. Jessie smiled at his brother's attempted humor, but his mind was elsewhere.

They made their way down the tower's winding staircase to the ground floor. There they waited as the minister gave them their final instructions. Jessie glanced down and gave his new uniform a final inspection.

At the proper sound cue from the music, Calvin and Ross swung the doors open for him. Jessie hesitated for a moment as his eyes studied the crowd filling the round ballroom of Farnsworth House. He swallowed hard before he strode briskly down the aisle toward the dais set at the front of the room. A large latticed wooden arch stood behind it, festooned with greens and candles.

The room was full of people and they seemed to press in on Jessie, adding to his discomfort. Among the guests were several soldiers from his brigade and the cream of

the crop of Batesville's society. As Jessie turned and faced
the crowd, he saw many he knew, including his commanding officer, Colonel Jo Shelby. Pride nearly brought tears
to his eyes at the turnout by his friends from the Fifth Missouri Cavalry and the brigade.

His only regret was that his parents were not alive for
his wedding day. He was sure they were looking down
from heaven to witness the event even if he couldn't see
them. Katlin's parents would not be here either because of
the hazards of the journey with the war going on. Wed-
dings were a celebration meant as much for the parents as
the newlyweds. With both sets of parents missing, it
seemed considerably less fulfilling and suffused his heart
with disappointment.

The piano began to play and all eyes turned to watch
the door. The first to enter was Elizabeth, young and beautiful and beginning to flower into womanhood. Calvin
walked to meet her and escorted her to the front of the
room. Cassandra was the second to enter and Ross lead
her to stand beside Elizabeth. Then the piano played the
notes announcing the entrance of the bride. The crowd
rose to their feet as Katlin entered the room on the arm of
her brother, Captain Gilbert Thomas.

Jessie stared at her with awe. Never had she looked
more beautiful than she did as she walked toward him in
her lovely bridal gown of white. She looked at him
through blue eyes filled with promise, while a shy smile
played upon her lips. Gilbert and Katlin stopped before the
dais, facing the minister. Jessie stood to the left of the
preacher.

The preacher began his ceremony, but Jessie heard little
of it as he admired his bride. He was jarred back to reality
by the words, "Who gives this woman to be married to
this man?"

Gilbert responded simply, "I do," then turned and
walked to the first row and sat.

Katlin moved to Jessie's side and joined him as the two of them stood before the minister, who launched himself avidly into the scriptures proclaiming the promises of marriage. Finally, after a monologue that seemed to drag on forever came the words, "Would you please join right hands. Jessie, repeat after me. I, Jessie Kimbrough, take Katlin Thomas to be my lawfully wedded wife."

Jessie said as he lost himself in those wondrous blue eyes, "I, Jessie Kimbrough, take Katlin Thomas to be my lawfully wedded wife."

The minister continued, "To have and to hold, from this day forward."

"To have and to hold, from this day forward," Jessie repeated.

"For better or worse."

"For better or worse," Jessie said as he followed the minister through the vows.

"For richer or poorer, through sickness and health, to love and cherish, till death us do part."

"According to God's holy ordinances, I pledge thee my troth."

Jessie made it through his vows, never taking his eyes off Katlin. When Katlin started her vows she was unable to keep her voice from breaking with emotion. Her heart was overflowing with love as her long awaited dream came true. Tears of joy tracked glistening trails down her cheeks. Jessie squeezed her hand, reassuring her that he understood. Katlin made it through her vows and Jessie knew she meant every word with all her heart. He had never felt so much joy, or ever felt so loved as he did now.

The ceremony continued through the exchange of rings. Jessie's brothers and sisters had voted among themselves and decided the first to wed should have the rings worn by Ellen and Glen Kimbrough. Jessie protested because he felt his mother's ring should belong to Cassandra and his father's ring should belong to Ross, the oldest son. Ross

and Cassandra talked him out of his objections arguing
that it would be a while before they found a need for wedding rings. Reluctantly, Jessie accepted the rings as a wedding gift from his family.

Jessie felt a sense of pride as he slipped his mother's
ring onto Katlin's finger and was equally proud when she
slipped his father's ring onto his hand.

Jessie repeated after the minister, "With this ring I thee
wed and with all my worldly goods I thee endow."

"In the name of the Father, Son, and Holy Ghost,
amen."

Reverend Robert Feldmar smiled as he patted them both
on the shoulder. "I now pronounce you husband and wife.
What God has joined together let no man tear asunder."
He smiled at the couple. "You may kiss the bride."

Jessie leaned forward and lifted the veil from Katlin's
face. She tenderly raised her lips to his as he passionately
kissed his new bride. The crowd broke into applause as
they turned to face family and friends. "I would like to
introduce to you Mr. and Mrs. Jessie and Katlin Kimbrough."

The piano began to play as they strolled down the aisle
lined with family and guests. When they entered the hall
beyond the ballroom they kissed again, lingering in the
embrace. "I'll love you always, Katlin."

"Oh, Jessie, you've made me so happy," Katlin said
with a twinkle in her eye. They were quickly surrounded
by the other members of the wedding party, who shouted
out their good wishes and passed around tears and hugs
aplenty amid the congratulations.

The couple led the guests to the dining room to cut the
white cake lovingly prepared by Fanny. Punch was served
in a superbly crafted silver punch bowl. The newlyweds,
urged on by their gathered guests, cut the cake together.
Amid laughs and jokes, they tenderly fed each other a bite
of cake. The punch was poured next and they toasted one

another. Punch and wine was distributed to the guests so they could join in on the toasts to be offered to the couple.

Captain Gilbert Thomas was the first to salute the newlyweds. "I'd like to propose a toast to my dear sister and my new brother. May God bless and keep you both and fill your life with earthly pleasures."

Ross, as the best man, was the next to offer a toast. "I'm not used to talking before a crowd of people like this, but I couldn't let this moment pass on my brother's wedding day without saying what's on my mind. Jessie, Katlin, I know Mother and Father would have been proud of you both today and I know they'd be here if it was possible." Ross's eyes grew moist and his voice cracked a little with emotion as he continued, "I just want you to remember how much they loved you and I love you, too."

He stopped for a minute, struggling to regain control of his feelings. The silence in the room was absolute as all present listened. "I wish you a lifetime of happiness and a house full of kids." Ross leaned forward and offered his hand to Jessie. Jessie took it and pulled his brother to him, wrapped his arms around his brother's shoulders and hugged him. Katlin, moved by this scene, stepped forward and embraced them both. The crowd broke into applause. After a moment the three of them shyly separated.

The well-wishers passed through the receiving line, each in turn offering small talk and congratulations. By the end, Jessie felt his right hand would never be the same after shaking hands with so many people. His shoulders felt bruised from all the good-natured pounding on his back. His feet were weary from constantly standing.

Dinner followed the reception. The tables nearly overflowed with food prepared by Fanny, Becca, and Etta.

Gilbert Thomas watched it all passively. He had spent the morning sipping bourbon to boost his courage, so walking Katlin to the dais had been easy. In fact, it had been just the right amount to make him downright jovial.

He began drinking again at the reception as he doctored his punch with generous tippings from his pocket flask. As the casual conversations flowed around him at dinner, the wine and the bourbon flowed freely, too. Little by little, Gilbert's attitude became more intense.

He watched Cassandra through the gathered guests, greeting them in the special way that made each one feel important. He couldn't really help himself, although he tried. The old desire and jealousy were still there. He still wanted Cassandra. It galled him to see her slip her arms around that damned Texan, Evan Stryker.

As the dinner was completed and preparations made for the evening dance, he watched the couple drift down the hall away from the crowd. He felt his disappointment and resentment rising. He took another drink and slammed the empty glass on the table. "Damn them," he thought, "damn them both all to hell!" He glanced down at his glass and, with a sigh, moved off to see if he could find another drink. He darn sure could use another.

Cassandra laughed and clung to Evan's arm as they climbed the stairs. All day long she hadn't been able to keep her eyes off of him. She knew it was the dimples in his cheeks that really made her heart pound faster. She loved his smile, which seemed to light up his whole face. A smile that was often followed by an easy laugh. She marveled at how he had been through so much and yet he could laugh at his problems.

She felt happy and content just being in this time and place with Evan. Had she been a cat she was sure she would have been purring. "I know you'll enjoy the view from the observatory. It's really very lovely from up there."

"I'm sure it is, but seeing it with you will make it more memorable." He studied her as a sly smile creased his face. "You wouldn't be trying to get me alone up there, would you?"

Cassandra, amused, gave him a flirtatious grin calculated to offer promise. "You'd like that, wouldn't you?"

His eyes could not hide the answer to her question, but he played along. "Well, I guess it will be all right if you promise to be gentle with me."

She slapped him on the shoulder in pretended anger. "Evan Stryker, I swear you are a tease." She turned and ran up the last flight of stairs with Evan following her.

At the top she stopped and turned, her eyes bright with anticipation. Evan caught her and spun her around, laughing. His smile faded as he looked into her eyes filled with passion. "I've got you." He leaned forward and gave her a light, tender kiss. She returned it eagerly, feeling the passionate crush of his lips on hers.

Cassandra pulled away teasingly and turned her back on him as she walked to the window. She let her eyes linger upon the river as she waited for him to join her.

She took in the rolling green waters of the White River and the rich bottomlands spanning its banks. The naked limbs of the oaks and maples crowding the water's edge stretched high into the sky as if pleading for the return of spring.

Evan moved behind her silently. He put his arms gently around her waist and felt the softness of her blond hair caressing his cheek. He pulled her tenderly to him, pressing his body against hers as he whispered softly into her ear, "It is beautiful up here. I'm glad you brought me here to see it."

Cassandra let her eyes wander over the landscape as she revelled in the feel of his strong arms around her. She felt the soft, seeping warmth of his body pressing into her. "I thought you brought me up here."

Evan squeezed her playfully. "You little devil, you know it was your idea. You kept telling me about the view. Although I must confess, you are the only scenery up here I truly want to see."

She pulled his hands free from her waist and spun to face him as she leaned back against the stone wall. She gave him a long teasing look. "Was it everything I said it would be?"

"Yes, it's beautiful, but it doesn't hold a candle to you." Evan let his eyes roam over Cassandra. He loved the way her long, blond hair cascaded over her slender shoulders and accentuated her figure. She had fine features and a fair complexion, but it was her eyes he couldn't resist. They were blue like morning skies, ringed at the edge of her iris with a darker shade of blue that made them striking. She knew how to use those eyes and could make his heart beat faster with one flirting glance.

The dress clung to the curve of her body and emphasized her firm breasts. His glance lingered there at the soft shadows of her cleavage. Lord, he knew Cassandra was a lady, but she was a woman and she enjoyed the power and allure her charms held over him. His desire for her was nearly driving him crazy. He stepped to her and leaned forward, his passionate lips seeking her, and she responded.

Cassandra felt his hunger build as his breathing became heavier. Reluctantly, she knew this wasn't the time or place. The dance would be starting soon and, as the maid of honor, she would be missed. Still, she wasn't in any hurry to end this time of tenderness together. She pulled away from his eager lips and hugged him to her. "Have you thought what you will do when the war is over?"

Caught off guard by her question, Evan answered evenly, "I haven't really given it much thought. The war seems no closer to ending now than it did a year ago."

"What would you do if the war was to end tomorrow? Where would you want to go?" Cassandra asked suddenly.

Evan pulled back and looked at her thoughtfully. "I might return to San Marcos. It's the loveliest country I have ever seen. My father owns a plantation on the high prairie between the Blanco and San Marcos Rivers and borders a neighbor, Doctor Peter Woods. I think it has the makings of a fine cotton plantation."

"Were you born in Texas?"

"No, I was born in Mississippi in Water Valley. We left there when I was young so I can barely remember Mississippi." Evan tried to kiss her again, but she teased him by turning her head away.

"Not now, tell me more."

Evan looked disappointed, but he continued. "My parents traveled with a caravan of wagons led by Doctor Woods. We settled first near Bastrop, Texas. In December of 1851 we moved near San Marcos. Doctor Woods brought over fifty slaves with him from his old plantation in Mississippi, but my father brought only ten with us. Dad said the land was played out in Mississippi, and he always had a hankering to move to the frontier."

"I've heard so many stories about how wild the land is in Texas and about the dreadful wars with the Mexicans and the Indians. Isn't it dangerous living there?"

"When we arrived, the war with Mexico was over, and for the most part, the Comanche Indians had been driven west. We still have to keep a wary eye out for an occasional roving band of renegade Indians. I suppose with so many men gone to war the Indian problem will increase."

"It's beyond me why anyone would risk their family by moving out near the savages."

"I know it must sound dangerous, Cassandra, but you've got to see it for yourself to appreciate the beauty of the land. It's the most beautiful country I've ever laid eyes on."

Cassandra looked like she doubted his words. "I have a hard time believing San Marcos and Texas is more beautiful than the Missouri River Country or this land right here in Arkansas."

"The San Marcos River is filled by bubbling springs

that constantly flow like a fountain. The water is crystal clear and you can see all the way to the bottom of the river and lakes. Cypress trees line the banks and hang above the river. The plant life is green and abundant and crops grow well in the rich and fertile black soil. The river flows along the hills and scattered here and there are crusty lime-stone cliffs. Trees are plentiful, with pecan, oak, and elm trees the most common. The land and water is so pure and unspoiled it seems like the Good Lord's Garden of Eden."

Cassandra marveled at the excitement in his voice and the twinkle in his eyes as he talked about San Marcos. "It sounds wonderful."

"I can't wait to show it all to you. If there is a heaven on earth, it has to be in Hays County, Texas."

Suddenly, from the head of the stairwell they heard Elizabeth Kimbrough's voice. "There you are. I swear, I've been looking all over for you two. Katlin says to come quick, the photographer is ready to take the wedding pictures."

Cassandra and Evan had been so involved in their conversation and with each other they hadn't noticed Elizabeth as she climbed the stairs. Both of them jerked around to look, startled by the sudden and unexpected intrusion. Each glanced at the other wistfully as they turned to follow Elizabeth. "We're right behind you." Cassandra said.

Downstairs, the photographer was just finishing his first portrait of Jessie and Katlin. Jessie was seated in a chair, sitting stiffly erect. Katlin stood beside him, her hand resting on his shoulder. As Cassandra entered the room, she noticed the photographer, whose head was under the black cloth attached to the camera. The camera itself was mounted on a three-legged wooden tripod. In his left hand he held a pan of flash powder.

"Steady now, hold it." With a whoosh, the powder ignited, causing a bright flash. "Hold it!" It seemed long, but it was over in a minute. "Okay, you can relax now while

I change the plates." The photographer scurried around busily preparing his camera. "Well, if everyone is here, we'll do the entire wedding party."

"There you are, Cassandra. We've been looking everywhere for you." Katlin motioned to Cassandra with her hand, trying to hurry her. The bride then turned toward the photographer. "We're all here now."

The photographer moved quickly as he arranged the group for the portrait. "I want to remind you all there will be a bright flash from the pan, but hold still and try to keep your eyes looking right up here. The camera lens is gonna be open for around a minute, so please hold real still and don't move your eyes." Again the photographer slipped his head under the black cloth and held the pan up, followed by the expected whoosh of the powder.

After the wedding portrait of Katlin and Jessie and the group photo of the wedding party, Cassandra requested a photo be made of her brothers and sisters including her new sister-in-law, Katlin Kimbrough. She knew the chances of getting all the family together again would be slim, if not impossible. After losing her parents she now understood how important photographs could be. She wanted to make sure there would be photographs to keep her memories fresh. The session continued.

Later in the evening at the grand ball, Elizabeth Kimbrough stood near the punch bowl. She took her time as she poured herself a cup, well aware two boys were watching her closely. The wedding dance had been going on for about an hour, and except for one dance with her brother Calvin, Elizabeth had passed the time standing along the walls watching the others swirl around the dance floor.

Elizabeth loved to dance, but so far her activities were mostly devoted to envying and observing other couples. During those moments she had watched with interest the obvious fire and passion between Ross and Valissa Covington. They acted oblivious to everyone about them as though locked into their own swirling, intimate dance.

Jessie and Katlin were full of joy and seemingly unable to get enough of each other, and Elizabeth was surprised to have found Cassandra and Evan Stryker together in the observatory. She felt as if she had intruded on a personal moment. They, too, gave the appearance of being a couple. She noticed it didn't set well with Gilbert Thomas.

Gilbert had been drinking and talking a little too loudly and she was afraid he might cause problems. She felt sorry for Gil, for she knew he loved Cassandra. Elizabeth had liked Gil long before the war started. Gilbert always took the time to include her when he was doing things with Cassandra.

She knew Cassandra never really thought of Gilbert as anything more than a friend, even when she lacked serious interest in any other would-be suitors that came to call on her. Elizabeth had always wondered why, because Gilbert was always nice, came from a good family, and was attractive.

Elizabeth's thoughts were interrupted by a young man beside her. "Excuse me, ma'am, that sure is a pretty dress you're wearin'."

Elizabeth turned to look at the boy speaking to her. He was one of the two boys she had noticed watching her earlier. She guessed him to be around sixteen years of age. His hair was blond and his cheeks and nose were lightly freckled. His brown eyes flashed with an intensity that captivated her attention.

Those eyes had an experienced look about them far beyond his actual age, like someone who had seen too much too early. She recognized that expression, for it reminded her of herself. She responded to his question about her dress. "Thank you very much. It's not new. I brought it with me from Missouri." The dress was a little too short now, because she had continued to grow. But the simple garment of white muslin with tiny pink nosegays of roses still looked elegant on her. "Would you care for some punch?" she asked.

"Yes, ma'am, that would be mighty nice." He watched as she poured him a cup. "Did ya say you were from Missouri? I'm from Missouri, too."

Elizabeth smiled. "Yes, I am. We were originally from Lafayette County, Missouri, and lived near the Missouri River. Have you ever heard of a little town called Waverly?"

"I reckon I never heard of it until we joined up with this outfit. I guess you can't ride with Jo Shelby's boys very long without knowin' about it. That's the hometown of Colonel Shelby, isn't it?"

"Yes, it is. He has a house on Mount Rucker. He built his house halfway up the hill." She hesitated. "Please, I'd feel better if you wouldn't call me ma'am. It makes me feel like you ought to be speaking to my mother." She offered her hand to him. "My name is Elizabeth, but sometimes they call me Liz."

"Please to meet you, Elizabeth." The boy smiled. He took her hand and shook it briskly. "My name is Billy Cahill. I'm from Bates County, Missouri." He enjoyed looking into Elizabeth's pale blue eyes, which were framed by silky strawberry-blond hair that hung midway down her back in soft waves. Her skin was light and dusted with freckles like his. He guessed her to be fourteen or fifteen years old. Her lips were full and shaped like a rosebud.

She sipped her punch after he released her hand. "I'm surprised to hear you're riding with Shelby. I thought most of his men were from Lafayette or Jackson Counties."

"I 'spect you're right, ma'am, I . . . I mean Elizabeth, but I'm one of Capt'n Billy Quantrill's men an' we're just attached to the brigade till Capt'n Billy gets back from Richmond. Are you one of Ross Kimbrough's sisters?"

The remark caught Elizabeth off guard. A look of surprise crossed her face. "Yes, I am. Do you know my brother?"

"Yes, ma'am," he blushed, "I mean, Elizabeth. I know your brother. He came by our farm right after the Jayhawkers came by an' burned us out. Those blue bellies robbed us, an' killed my Pa an' there wasn't nuthin' I could do about it."

Elizabeth saw the anger in his eyes. "I guess we have more in common than I thought. The Yankees burned our home, too, and killed my father. The Yankees were led by Major Benton Bartok and Captain Bob Anders."

"I'm sorry to hear it." He looked down at the cup of punch she handed him and took a drink that nearly emptied it. He studied her. "It might please you to know I've been busy killin' as many Yanks as I can catch. Maybe when we get back to Missouri I can look those two fellers up for ya and make it right. I know I'm lookin' forward to the day we catch Jennison's Jayhawkers. I've got a score to settle with them like most of Capt'n Billy's boys."

"If you ever do catch Bartok and Anders, I'd like to hear about it." She glanced at the dancers on the floor. "Do you dance, Billy?"

He looked embarrassed. "I'm not very good. I danced a little with my Ma, but that's been quite a while back."

Elizabeth grabbed his hands and dragged him toward the floor. "Don't worry, all you need is some practice. I'll help you."

They began awkwardly, but as they continued they showed steady improvement. The longer they danced, the smoother Billy became. "There you go. You're getting the hang of it now."

Billy smiled at Elizabeth. At first he felt embarrassed, but he concentrated hard, and soon they flowed about the room with the rhythm of the music. It felt good to hold this pretty Missouri girl in his arms. At his tender young age he hadn't spent much time with ladies before, but he found this an intoxicating experience. As his confidence started to grow, they began swirling around the edges of the dance floor. He kept stealing glances into those blue eyes. She smiled back brightly at him and sometimes she would laugh softly. He admired the sprinkling of freckles across her nose and cheeks, because they were so much like his own. He felt the soft curls of her strawberry blond hair under his fingers as he held his hand at the middle of her back. When their bodies brushed against one another he felt his skin tingle with excitement and his heart pound until he was afraid she would hear it.

Finally, after the third dance in a row, Elizabeth asked if they could sit one out. As they settled themselves near the punch bowl, she watched as Billy's friend approached.

"You gonna try to keep her to yourself all night, Billy?" the young man asked as he drew near them.

Billy didn't seem happy about this unwanted intrusion. Whether he meant for it to show or not, it was plain to see he wished his friend was somewhere else. "Oh, hi, Riley." Billy glanced at Elizabeth apologetically then back at the intruder. "I'd like to introduce you to Elizabeth Kimbrough, formerly of Waverly, Missouri. She's the sister of Lieutenant Ross Kimbrough. This is Riley Crawford of Capt'n Billy's command."

The other boy gave her a strange, twisted smile that made Elizabeth feel uneasy. She was confronted with a baby-faced youth who stood no taller than her own five foot four inches. Yet, there was none of the childlike innocence she expected to find in the features of the youthful lad. It was his eyes that frightened her. They were hard as flint and filled with hate. They showed not a trace of pity of caring. She sensed they were the eyes of a killer or a madman.

"I'm glad to meet you, Elizabeth." He looked back at Billy. His lips curled, giving him a sarcastic look. "I thought you were gonna hog her all night long." He turned to face Elizabeth. "You sure are a fine looker. Much too pretty for the likes of Billy Cahill. How's about you and me taking a stroll out in the moonlight?"

Elizabeth didn't intend to go anywhere with Riley and she much preferred the company of Billy. Riley's suggestive behavior made her angry. How dare he approach a Southern lady of breeding this way! Her anger flushed vividly across her face. "I'm here to enjoy the dance and I was enjoying myself with Billy until you so rudely intruded. I can see no earthly reason I would want to leave this dance or Billy to go strolling with someone who doesn't know the first thing about the proper way to treat a lady."

The sarcastic smile faded from Riley's face. In its place was a stunned look of surprise and embarrassment. "I don't know how to dance, so I thought maybe we could talk some."

"I really doubt that's what you had in mind, Mr. Crawford, and I find your attitude rude and insulting." Her eyes flashed with fury.

Riley blushed bright red as Elizabeth's voice grew louder. He shot a look of bewilderment at Billy that quickly changed to anger. "I'm sorry." He muttered softly as he turned swiftly on his heels and left the room.

Billy watched it all, amusement dancing in his eyes. He shot an appreciative glance at Elizabeth. "Riley isn't used to a man or woman talkin' to him like that. I've seen him do some powerful fightin' and I think that's the first time I ever saw someone get the best of him." Billy smiled at her.

"He has some nerve if he thinks I'm just going to traipse off into the moonlight with just anyone. He forgets I'm a lady."

"I never doubted it for a minute. It's just that Riley is what you call overconfident and a mite cocky. He's used to shooting his way through situations and I guess he doesn't know how to handle a woman. He always has been kinda blunt, if ya know what I mean. He says what's on his mind and tells you right out front what he wants."

"That might work in the backwoods or with men, but it sure won't get him anywhere with me."

"I reckon you proved it to him quickly, Liz." Billy smiled again in amusement.

Elizabeth started to see the humor in the situation and her anger turned to laughter. She smiled back at Billy, then grabbed his hand. "Come on, Billy, let's dance again," she commanded flirtatiously as the two of them walked back onto the dance floor.

9

Eye of the Storm

February passed swiftly and, with the coming of March, Colonel Shelby crossed his brigade of three thousand men over to the north side of the White River. There, across from Batesville, he selected a camp among giant oaks in an idyllic setting near the river. This would be his new winter camp where his men would be rested and trained for new campaigns to begin in the spring. The camp was named in honor of one of Batesville's most lovely daughters, Camp Nannie Wilson.

The supply train carrying the brigade's camping equipment and tents finally joined the unit in early March. With the arrival of the train, there was no longer a necessity for the men to stay in private homes. The burden of caring for and feeding the soldiers was beginning to tax the food supply and hospitality of the local citizens. Colonel Shelby felt it would be best to require the men to rejoin the camp before they wore out their welcome, and he worried they would become to soft to fight. The men came when ordered, but with great reluctance. After all, life in a real home was much more comfortable than living in a tent in the middle of winter.

In early March, Wash Mayes left Batesville and started for Missouri. For him, life in the army was over and a wife and a new life waited at home.

For Ross, Calvin, and Jessie it was time to return to army life. At least Batesville was nearby and Colonel Shelby was lenient with passes. Weekends would find most of the soldiers free to attend dances and grand balls in the area. No time was wasted in their relentless pursuit of romancing the lovely ladies of Batesville. Those who had family in the area were free to spend time with them. Even during the week, men were allowed to visit their wives if they were on time for roll call the next morning.

For Ross it was doubly difficult. He could see Valissa on weekends, but not during the week because they weren't married. More than anything else, Ross wanted to be with Valissa. She was on his mind constantly. When he went to sleep at night his thoughts would turn to her and he'd recall the nights she tiptoed to his bed. The recollections fired his blood and often made sleep difficult.

Ross had given his word that he wouldn't try to marry Valissa until the war was over. A day didn't pass when he didn't curse the day he had made that promise. He wanted desperately to try to convince her to change her mind. Valissa seemed to enjoy their time together and the romance and passion was still strong, but time to be alone together was practically nonexistent.

Often he worried their time together at Covington Manor might have made her pregnant, but she seemed little concerned about it. At other times, he wished she were pregnant. Her father would be whistling a different tune about waiting to get married if his daughter was expecting out of wedlock.

Jessie thought he was in heaven. He was married to a beautiful wife and life couldn't be better. Oh, sure, he'd rather be home every night with his new bride cuddled up beside him, but he got home regularly. Two or three days a week he'd spend the night at home, get up early, and report at roll call for another day of duty. After duty ended he would ride back to Farnsworth House, have Jeremiah or Jethro put the horse away, then spend the evening in the company of his wife. He felt lucky his marriage gave him special privileges during winter camp.

For Calvin it wasn't so easy. He didn't have a serious girlfriend and didn't see any prospects that captivated him. To be sure, there were many beautiful ladies in Batesville and the surrounding community, but he just couldn't see himself settling down with just one woman. After all, there were so many pretty ones. He supposed his shyness was a factor in moving away from serious relationships. Cal looked forward to the weekends in which endless, mind-numbing drills were replaced by balls, promenades, and picnics.

Calvin recalled rather ruefully the dance he'd been at just yesterday. He had dragged himself back to camp in the wee hours of the morning and he was more than just a little inebriated. When he crawled into his bedroll he lay there with his head spinning, lost in dreams of a dark-haired beauty. His dream seemed so real, so intense, he could feel her lush kisses upon his neck. It felt so warm, wet, and hot, a wide smile crossed his drunken features. Even in his alcohol-fogged mind it occurred to him she had a very rough tongue, but nonetheless he knew she was extremely pretty. He smiled even more broadly as the girl of his dreams moved her wet, passionate kisses to his cheek. Her breath blew moist upon him and felt so warm, so real, he knew he could reach out and touch her.

He felt himself begin to stir, clawing up and out of the clutches of his alcohol-induced dreams. He heard a grunt, or was it a groan? He couldn't be sure. A smile on his lips, he reached to touch her, but the hair was coarse and not what he expected. As he moved from the twilight of sleep to an awakened state, he noticed she had the most putrid breath he had ever smelled in his life!

He opened his eyes a little, then closed them again. What he had seen registered through the sleep and whiskey-soaked brain tissues of his head. Bear! He opened his eyes wide to find himself nose-to-nose with a bear who was licking his cheek. Terror raged through his body instantly sobering him. It wasn't a girl kissing him at all he suddenly realized. It was a damn black bear tasting him before he made a meal out of him! Calvin sat up, kicking his feet wildly as he tried to get them under him. He managed enough traction to fall off the back of his cot. He sprawled in a heap on the floor, trapped in his panic-stricken terror between the cot and the sidewall of the tent. The bear followed, seemingly unperturbed by this man's behavior. The bear strolled over and put his feet on Calvin's chest, driving him flat on the floor. Calvin, his heart pounding wildly, lay still, afraid to anger the bear, who continued to lick Calvin's face. Despite his intention of remaining quiet and calm under this deadly attack, Calvin felt a scream of horror rip from his lips. He was certain at any moment this colossal killer bear would crush his skull with one bite of his gleaming fangs! Charlie Jasper, a member of Calvin's gun crew, rushed into the tent when he heard Calvin's terrified scream.

With a look of disgust Charlie put his fists on this hips as if he were a mother correcting a wayward toddler. "Postletwait! Let the corporal sleep. He ain't in need of a tongue bath so early in the mornin'." Charlie Jasper watched as the bear turned to look at him, grunting a low response and hanging his head like a whipped puppy, while maintaining his position on Calvin's chest.

"Come here, Postie!" After a moment, Charlie walked

over to the bear and grabbed the rope collar tied around the bear cub's neck. "Sorry he woke ya up, Cal." Charlie's face beamed as if he were the proud owner of something precious. "He sure is affectionate, ain't he?" Charlie stepped back enough to keep the bear cub from licking Calvin. Charlies glanced lovingly at the bear cub. He reached over and scratched the bear behind the ears. The bear grunted happily again, then licked Charlie Jasper's hand.

Calvin scrambled to his feet and backed against the wall of the tent. In his haste he nearly pulled the tent down around them. Calvin couldn't believe his eyes. Funny, when Calvin first opened his eyes the bear seemed so much larger than he looked now. Certainly he was big, well, at least compared to a dog. The bear was larger than any canine Calvin had encountered, but he was still just a cub. Calvin felt confused, angry, and a little embarrassed by his rude awakening. "Where in the hell did this bear come from, Jasper?"

"Oh, you don't know, Cal? Shucks, I thought everyone had met Postletwait by now." Charlie took his eyes from the bear and studied Calvin while he continued to pet the big furry baby. "Captain Wave Anderson of the ordinance department bought him from some hunters. They found him wandering around without a mamma in the Boston Mountains. Capt'n Anderson gave him to Dick Collins. Said he'd make a right fine mascot for our artillery battery. Dick named him Postletwait out of some ole book he read. Some of the men have been callin' him Postie fer short, or just Bear."

Calvin stood there, a look of confused amazement on his face. "You mean Lieutenant Collins agreed to this?"

"Sure 'nuff did, Cal. Even Colonel Jo knows about it and don't mind none." Charlie Jasper looked at the bear, his eyes full of the growing affection that he had for the animal."He's a right nice lookin' bear, doncha think? He sure is loveable."

As if to prove a point, the black bear cub turned and raised himself on his hind feet, placing his front paws on Charlie's chest. He licked Charlie lovingly and nuzzled him. Charlie gave him a hug. "Get on down, boy. I guess I better see if'n I can find ya some grub to eat."

"Wait a minute, Charlie, what is the artillery gonna do with a bear? How's he gonna keep up with a cavalry outfit?"

"Don't worry about it, Cal. Lieutenant Collins says he's gonna teach him to ride on the caissons or in the ammunition wagons. The hunters already taught him to ride in a wagon, so's it ain't gonna be such a big deal. Sorry if he scared ya." Charlie looked down at the bear, who was now down on all fours and sniffing the air. "I'm gonna get him somethin' to eat. He sure ain't picky when it comes to chow." Charlie and the bear left the tent together.

As the two walked away he heard Charlie say, "I hope you don't go and get your nose stuck in a bottle again. It took me an hour to pry the last one off."

Through the month of March, Shelby began to intensify training. The men staged two separate dress parades for the benefit of the townspeople and the entertainment of the young ladies of Batesville. Between the dress parades, the brigade put on a mock battle for the town to demonstrate combat tactics. This was followed by a flag presentation, a large picnic, and later, a dance. Although he took the time to train his men, Shelby took care to see his men were allowed plenty of time to rest and enjoy a respite from the war.

During March new men, arriving in small groups from Missouri, enlisted in the brigade. These men filled the gaps in the ranks. Soldiers left behind after the battles at Cane Hill, Prairie Grove, Springfield, and Hartsville rejoined the units as they recovered from their wounds. During these fleeting days, the men enjoyed their escape from the rigors of campaigns and battles. Romance and courtship continued to flourish between the men of the brigade and the local Southern ladies.

Cassandra continued to see Evan Stryker as often as possible. She felt comfortable with him and free to be herself, as if she had known him all her life. He was kind and gentle, rugged and strong. Still, she guarded her heart closely, bracing herself against falling too deeply, or too quickly, in love. This war had already caused her to suffer many heartaches and she didn't want to add to her misery. She realized he was working his way into her heart so deeply she would never get him out completely despite her best intentions. In the back of her mind, she couldn't forget that someday he would be riding away again to war.

Elizabeth found it all exhilarating. For the first time in her life she was finding romance and love. This was her first courting experience and she was enjoying the attention and the heady rush of emotions that battered her. She looked forward eagerly to the time she shared with Billy Cahill. Sometimes she danced with other soldiers from the brigade, but it was always Billy she enjoyed the most. Billy had become an excellent dancer and the two of them moved as if they were one on the dance floor.

She felt a common bond with Billy. Both had lost their homes to the Yankees and both had suffered the death of their fathers at the hands of the enemy. They shared a common, unmitigated hate for the soldiers in blue and anything attached to the Union cause. Elizabeth found herself drawn to this battle-tough young man.

To Elizabeth, Billy was a sea of contrasts. On one hand, he could be gentle and kind, but in battle he was ruthless and unforgiving. He talked often of the men he had killed and the desire to kill more. It sometimes frightened her, but at other times she found satisfaction in knowing Billy and Quantrill's men were gaining revenge against the Yan-

kee invaders. She looked upon Quantrill's men as heroes
punishing a wicked foe with an eye for an eye. These men
were Missourians who had suffered much at the hands of
Jayhawkers and Union men and were eager to settle the
score. They'd been serving with Shelby's command as
regular soldiers ever since Quantrill had left for Richmond. If she were a man, Elizabeth knew she would do
the same.

She knew this time of peace wouldn't last, that it was
only a moment's pause in the hell-fire fury of war. Still,
she tried not to think about it and concentrated instead on
living for the moment.

As April arrived, the restless stirring of the troops and
the increased activity in both supply and dispatches signaled the coming of spring campaigns. The soldiers and
citizens sensed that the lull in the eye of the maelstrom of
war was about to pass, leaving in its wake the destructive
swirl of battle.

10

Mission of Revenge

Billy Cahill tied his chestnut mare to a railing near the steps of Farnsworth House. He moved quickly up the stairs, taking them two at a time. He shifted his weight back and forth nervously as he waited for a response from the raps on the doorknocker. His head was spinning and swirling with uncertainty. He had so much to say and so little time. He tried on the way over from Camp Nannie Wilson to formulate what he wanted to say, but he wondered if he would have the nerve to spit it out. Moments passed slowly until Becca answered the door.

"Is Miss Elizabeth Kimbrough home? I'd like to talk with her."

Becca smiled at his now familiar face. "I know she's upstairs, Mista Cahill. I'll go and fetch her for ya." She motioned for Billy to step inside.

As Billy stepped through the door, he pulled his hat off

and began twisting the brim nervously in his hands as he watched Becca disappear down the hallway.

Billy felt his heart hammering in his chest, and his throat and mouth felt as dry as if he had eaten sand. His chest felt restricted, as if a tightening steel band wrapped around his chest were squeezing the breath out of him. He had so much to say to Liz, he felt like he might explode if he couldn't release the words soon. His breath came in ragged, shallow puffs as he took turns wiping his trembling, sweaty palms on his pants. Billy suddenly realized he wasn't this nervous even in battle.

He didn't know why he was so nervous. Elizabeth had always treated him well and always acted glad to see him. He was certain she enjoyed his company. No, it went deeper than that. It was his realization of his growing affection for her. Never had a girl made him feel this way before, or made him feel so foolish.

Lovingly, Billy recalled the many times he had held her in his arms and twirled her across the dance floor these last two months. Those precious moments had been the happiest in his young life. It was his fear of having her suddenly reject him, or worse, never seeing her again, that twisted at his guts.

He watched as Elizabeth descended the stairs. "Hi, Billy, this is a nice surprise." She smiled brightly at him. "I didn't expect to see you until the dance Saturday night." She saw his eyes soften as he watched her approach, but she could tell he was nervous. Something important was troubling him. A sudden chill of apprehension flowed through her.

Billy's voice broke a little as he said, "Hi, Liz, I was wonderin' if we could talk awhile?" Billy shifted his weight nervously back and forth as he continued to twist the brim of his hat.

"I'm not busy, why don't we go for a walk?" Elizabeth slipped her hands through his arm as she turned toward

Becca. "Becca, I'm going for a stroll with Billy if anyone needs me."

"Yes, ma'am. If anyone asks, I'll tell them."

Elizabeth smiled at Billy as they stepped through the doorway and out onto the porch. Both were silent as they leisurely strolled toward the river. Elizabeth felt Billy's inner turmoil, and although she was curious, she resisted pushing him to tell her why he was there.

They stopped once they were clear of the house and let their eyes take in the natural beauty of the White River. The green water reflected the growth of new buds and harmonized with the freshly opening leaves on the trees lining the riverbank. Billy's eyes scanned the faraway distance; he was uncertain how to begin.

But Elizabeth's curiosity was getting the better of her and she was dying to know what was bothering him. "Billy, you look troubled. What is it?"

He turned toward her and his eyes locked on hers. He smiled shyly. Elizabeth caught herself studying his freckles.

"Capt'n Billy came back from Richmond today. I reckon it won't be long before we'll be headin' north to Missouri again."

Elizabeth knew the return of William Clarke Quantrill from his trip to Richmond probably meant a change in the status of Billy's company. Quantrill's men had been temporarily assigned to Shelby's brigade since last fall when Quantrill left to travel to Richmond seeking a promotion. "So what happens now, Billy?"

"That's why I'm here, Liz. Quantrill says we march in the mornin' and I had to see you again before we left."

"Do you have to go, Billy? Couldn't you stay with Shelby? I could ask my brother Ross to help you get a transfer."

Billy's eyes had a sadness about them and his jaw was tight-set. "I can't ask Capt'n Billy for a transfer. I gave my word when I signed up I'd stick with the boys if they would have me. I've always tried to keep my word once I give it."

Elizabeth felt a sinking feeling, as though something important to her were slipping away. She felt a surge of panic, followed by a sense of dread and loss. "I see," she said, "I guess you have your responsibilities."

"I don't mind returning to battle, Lord knows Missouri needs help drivin' those Jayhawkers away. There's still too many Yankees in need of a quick killin'." He swallowed hard as he tried to maintain control of his emotions. "I don't mind going back to war, but I hate leaving you behind. I don't know when or where I'll see you again." Billy glanced at his feet as a tear spilled from the corner of his eye and trailed down his cheek. "I know every mile I ride away from you is gonna be hard. In my heart I want to be with you."

Elizabeth knew Billy was infatuated with her. They were both young, but she was old enough to feel passion and recognize the love stirring within her. She knew she would miss this blond-haired boy, forced to be a man before his time. "I don't know that we have any choice. In a war, I guess we all have to make sacrifices."

"Liz, I don't want to lose you. I . . . I never felt this way before about a girl and I can't keep you off my mind. I haven't any right to ask, but I want to see you again."

Elizabeth smiled and leaned back against a tree. "I'd like that, Billy. I haven't met anyone I've enjoyed dancing with more. These last few months I've spent dating you have been special to me, too."

A worried frown crossed Billy's features. "Trouble is, I don't know how or when I'll get this way again. I figure we'll stay in Missouri at least until winter and I don't know what Quantrill will want to do then. Only the Good Lord knows how long this war will last. I don't know when I can return, or how I'll find you."

"Is there somewhere I could write to you, Billy?"

"I guess you could send letters addressed to me for general delivery at Independence, Missouri. We get around there pretty often and I could pick them up at the post office. I can give you the address of my aunt, too. That's where Ma is stayin' since we got burned out."

"If you want to write to me, Billy, I'll write back. Maybe if we stay in touch we can see each other again."

Billy smiled. "It would be a help knowing I'll hear from you. I'll try to write as often as I can. Maybe some of the mail will get through."

Elizabeth playfully reached out and grabbed the front of Billy's guerilla shirt and pulled him to her. "Well, before you go I hope you intend to kiss me again."

Billy grinned as he leaned forward and gently kissed her on her lips. She returned his kiss passionately. His turmoil only increased as he felt his passion rise. He whispered softly in her ear, "I think I'm in love with you, Elizabeth Kimbrough." He loved the sound of those words as they rolled off his tongue. "Someday I hope you'll marry me."

Elizabeth pulled herself free so she could look in his eyes, hoping to see how deeply he meant what he had whispered. She saw clearly in his eyes how much he would miss her and she no longer doubted the depths of his devotion. She was uncertain how she felt and wondered if she was old or wise enough yet to make such an important decision. "I think I love you, too, Billy. If I know what love is. We'll just have to wait and see what happens." Billy and Elizabeth lingered there, sharing gentle caresses and soft young kisses under the spreading buds and blooms of spring. A few hours later, Billy rode away.

Ross Kimbrough rolled his bedroll tight with his rubberized poncho wrapped over the outside to protect the contents from rain. He smoothed out the wrinkles and carefully lashed the bundle shut with leather thongs.

Cassandra Kimbrough watched from near the dresser as her brother continued to pack. "Are you sure you're doing the right thing, Ross? You're taking an awful chance going after Bartok alone in Missouri."

Ross didn't look up as he carefully placed extra clothing into his saddle wallets. "I won't be alone for most of the trip. I told you I've received permission from Quantrill to accompany his command to Missouri. Once we reach Lafayette County, I'll go after Bartok."

The plan still sounded dangerous to Cassandra. "What does Colonel Shelby say about all this?"

"He understands how I feel about Major Bartok. He was reluctant until he heard my plan, then he agreed to grant me leave from the scouts. Until I return, Shelby's scouts will continue to operate under the command of Captain Ben Elliott. He's been in charge ever since I was wounded and I'm sure he can handle it a little while longer." He looked over at Cassandra. "This is something I must do."

Cassandra recognized the determined look in his eyes and she knew further resistance would be wasted on him. She felt an overpowering urge to hug her brother and moved over to him. He looked up at her, the agitation showing clearly on his features. When he saw how worried she looked, his expression softened. He stopped packing and stood erect as Cassandra slipped into his arms and hugged his chest, clinging to him tightly. "You take care of yourself up there. I don't think I could stand it if Bartok takes another member of my family away from me."

He wrapped his arms protectively around his younger sister as he patted her on the back reassuringly. "I'll try my best to be careful, sis. I have to do this. All during my recovery I had time to think this through, to think about what Bartok has done to my family. He killed my parents and destroyed my home; I can't rest until I know he's dead and I want to be the one to kill him."

"Killing Major Bartok won't bring Mother or Father back or rebuild even one brick at Briarwood."

Cassandra felt him stiffen at her words and he slipped out of her embrace. "I know killing him won't set things right again, but I'll know he's not inflicting any more pain on innocent people." He moved near the window and gazed out at the blue of the sky. "I can't let this go, I have to finish it. I won't rest until I know he's dead." He looked at his sister. "I've never met the son of a bitch, but in my mind I see him enjoying what he has taken from us and thinking he can do whatever he wishes. I aim to see he doesn't enjoy his success for much longer."

Cassandra knew nothing she could say would keep her brother from going. Deep inside she wanted Bartok dead as much as Ross did. She envied his chance to seek revenge, while she must stay behind. "Then God speed your journey, Ross, and bring you safely home." She looked at him again before she moved toward the door. "I'll see how Fanny is doing gathering your food. I'll meet you downstairs."

"I'm almost finished. I'll be down directly." Ross returned to his preparations. He gathered a cotton drawstring bag from the dresser. From the closet he pulled a Union uniform and carefully placed it in the bag. On top of the uniform, he inserted some ragged clothing. He wasn't sure which disguise he'd use to get close enough to Major Bartok to kill him. Either the uniform of a Union soldier or a drunken derelict should do the trick. This bag should protect his disguises until needed. It would tie neatly to his saddle. He pulled the drawstring tight, closing the bag.

Ross felt gingerly behind his neck, checking to make sure Double Twelve was safely secured in his back holster. He slid one revolver into a holster at his waist and two more into his belt. He knew he would have his hands full as he slung his saddle wallet over his shoulder and picked up the canvas bag in one hand. With the other he reached for his Sharps rifle and headed downstairs. Soon he would be on his way.

This was something Ross knew he must do and only one thing made him reluctant to leave. Things with Valissa remained unresolved. He loved her now more than ever and he knew she would constantly be on his mind as he traveled away from Batesville. Still, their future seemed in doubt. Although her actions indicated she loved him and enjoyed his company, he couldn't forget she had refused his offer of marriage while the war continued. Ross had given his word to Andrew Covington he wouldn't pursue marriage again until the war was over, but it hadn't changed the way he felt or his desire for Valissa. He still fought his nagging doubts about her devotion to him and wondered how a prolonged separation would affect their relationship.

He said his good-byes to her last night and the evening's pleasure would long be remembered. He made love to her near the banks of the White River. Despite the cool evening chill of the early spring weather, their passion kept them warm. He recalled how she clung to him, as if she didn't want to release him, and, remembering, he felt more confident of her love. A short while later, Ross rode away from Farnsworth House, leaving his family behind as he began his mission of revenge.

Orders for the Captain

Major Benton Bartok's Headquarters
Lafayette County, Missouri
May 1863

As Major Benton Bartok breezed through the waiting room of his headquarters and stepped into his office, he noticed the door was slightly ajar. As he entered, he spotted a familiar officer leaning on the two back legs of his chair, his feet crossed on Bartok's desk. Captain Anders was puffing contentedly on the stub of a cigar.

Bartok's temper flared quickly. "Just what in hell do you think you're doing, Captain Anders? Get those damn muddy boots off my desk!"

Anders' boots slid off the desk and thudded to the floor as he lowered the chair down on all four legs. His boots left behind a crumbling residue of dried mud. Anders stood quickly, threw the butt of his cigar into the empty trash can beside the desk, and snapped to attention. "I was ordered to report to your office, sir."

"Did those orders instruct you to make yourself at home in my office, Captain?"

"No, sir!"

"Bob, I swear if you weren't working for me I'd give you every shit detail in the army. If I catch you making yourself at home in my office again, I'll see to it personally. Am I making myself clear to you, Captain?"

"Yes, sir."

"Well, don't just stand there, you idiot. Get that dirt off my desk then get out of my way."

Captain Bob Anders quickly bent forward and swept the dirt from the desk into the palm of his cupped hand as his face flushed crimson. He dusted the dirt from his hands into the trash can beside the desk with a brisk motion. "Sorry, sir."

Bartok moved to his customary spot behind the desk. "I'm not in a particularly good mood today, Captain, and you certainly haven't improved it any." Bartok paused as he glared in anger at his subordinate.

Captain Bob Anders was one of Major Benton Bartok's original Jayhawkers and served with him during the border war days before the all-out war between North and South. The Civil War had come along and given them the opportunity to make their thieving ways legitimate. Both men had welcomed the golden opportunity and seized it. Bartok envied Captain Anders' broad-shouldered, lanky build. Bob's dark eyes had a hardness about them, sharpened by years of fighting and thieving along the border. Anders was used to getting what he wanted by using whatever means were necessary. It was a trait they shared and it drew them together. Benton supposed many women would be intrigued by the mysterious and darkly dangerous captain and found himself envious of Anders' success with the fair sex. Benton turned his attention from his musings to his subordinate, standing at rigid attention before him.

"At ease." As Anders relaxed, Bartok lowered himself into his chair. "Rumors are flying along the telegraph lines that Quantrill might be headed north again. Do you think there is any truth to them?"

"I don't know, Major." Captain Anders shrugged his shoulders. "I wouldn't get too worked up about it. We've heard about the return of the guerillas all winter and they haven't showed up yet. I think they finally got some sense and moved south to Arkansas where things are easier for them. They wouldn't dare ride back into Missouri again."

"I wish I shared your optimism, Anders. I don't think we've seen the last of the Bushwhackers. However, it seems unlikely they will try any attacks on fortified positions or large garrisons. It's not their style; they prefer to hit and run."

"They won't come back, and if they do, this time we'll capture and hang them all. Our operation here is too sweet to let the guerillas mess it up for us."

For the last ten months, the Third Kansas Cavalry under Major Bartok had controlled Lafayette County. During that time the officers had taken, stolen, or coerced whatever they wanted from the hapless citizens under their control. By the generous use of violence, threats, and intimidation they had collected huge sums of money from the citizens for Yankee protection, while Bartok and his officers took advantage of the women of the county.

Benton and Anders understood most women would be willing to do anything to protect their homes and loved ones from harm. Almost any woman could be coerced into submission. They used every opportunity to exploit this advantage. Because Bartok and his cavalry were the local representatives of the Federal government and were responsible for enforcing martial law, the opportunity presented itself often.

Most of their stolen goods and money was shipped to Lawrence, Kansas, for safekeeping under the watchful eye of Benton Bartok's brother, Jacob. After the war, the spoils were to be divided.

Bartok responded to Anders' comments. "I sincerely hope you are correct, Captain." He let out a deep sigh as if doubting Anders could be so sure of himself. "I have a little mission for you."

"Yes, sir. The boys have spring fever. They're itching for a little action. Winter camp can get mighty boring after a while."

"I think a little ride will do your men some good. I want you to take a patrol and locate a man called Washington Mayes. I understand he has returned home from serving with Jo Shelby's Rebels in Arkansas. My informant says Mayes has lost a hand and some fingers in the war and has come home to start over." Bartok pulled himself erect and turned to face his window. He stared off into the mesmerizing deep blue of the spring skies as he clasped his hands behind his back. "I want you to make an example of Washington Mayes. I want the Rebels to understand they can't go off to war against us and expect to come back and resume their lives as if nothing had changed. I don't give a damn if the man's crippled or not. I want it understood by the Southern sympathizers in these parts what will happen to any of those who dare serve in the Confederate army."

"Yes, sir, that's a good idea, sir. Sounds like a task I'll enjoy carrying out."

Bartok turned slowly and glared at his subordinate. "Don't screw this up, Anders. When you return I expect to hear a report on how you've hung Mayes as an example to the rest of the locals."

"Yes, sir! You can count on me, sir," he said as he studied his commanding officer. Benton Bartok was a soldier of average height and a stocky build. His eyes were dark brown and brooding under bushy eyebrows. A large, hawkbilled nose dominated his face. Although well into his thirties, the major maintained a youthful air, but Anders realized what made his commanding officer so dangerous was his cunning mind. Bartok had a knack when it came to getting ahead and taking what he wanted from others. This ability had made them both rich and Anders realized it. It was the main reason he remained so loyal to Bartok.

Bartok's orders broke through Anders' thoughts. "Leave as soon as you get your men organized, Captain. You are dismissed."

Captain Anders snapped off a salute, spun on his heels, and marched out of the office. Bartok watched him go, then looked at the scuff marks left on his desk by the boots of his subordinate. "Damn inconsiderate bastard," he thought. "Does he think I can steal a desk like this from just anywhere?"

12

Deceitful Persuasion

Wash Mayes stooped low over the garden and carefully pulled the young, tender weeds out of the ground. The garden was a new one, and he took pride in the neat, straight rows of green beans, carrots, and peas. It had pained him to watch his wife, Mollie, prepare the garden. She had used the hand shovel to turn the earth as he sat nearby, watching.

It was a humbling experience to be so helpless in so many ways, a blow to his pride to accept the fact he was crippled and would never again be able to do the things he had once taken for granted. Simple little things that before seemed to take little effort were now a major accomplishment. He had changed over to wearing boots a little larger than before because tying shoes was nearly impossible for a one-handed man. He could still tug a boot on with his one good hand if the boot wasn't too tight.

Spading the ground for the garden had been another of

those things he just couldn't do. Mollie had done the work
without complaining. She smiled at him often as she
paused between turning spades of soil. That was so typical
of Mollie, never missing a chance to show him how happy
she was to have him home again. It made no difference to
her that he had just one hand. The only thing that mattered
was that Wash was home and alive and he wouldn't be going to war again.

It was due to his deep love and devotion to Mollie that
he hadn't given up. It would have been simple to surrender
to his melancholy and feel sorry for himself. He could
have hated the whole world for his troubles, but instead he
simply tried to do the best he could with what he had.
Mollie deserved nothing less.

Wash Mayes concentrated on the task at hand, sorting
out the weeds from the vegetables before he pulled out the
uninvited intruders. His concentration was so deep he
didn't notice the patrol led by Captain Bob Anders as it
entered the trail leading from the road to his house. They
were on him so suddenly, there wasn't time to hide. Too
late to run, he decided to stand and face whatever might
come. "Besides, I'm not a soldier anymore," he thought.

Anders brought his men at a gallop and soon the entire
patrol of fifteen men circled the garden, cutting off all
hope of escape. Bob Anders and a sergeant spurred their
horses in close, halting near Wash Mayes. "Well now, Sergeant, looks like we caught us a Rebel spy."

Mollie, with deep concern etched on her face, moved
quickly to her husband's side as the milling Yankee troopers stirred dust up around them and trampled the carefully
groomed garden. "What do you mean, Rebel spy? He's not
a spy, he's not even a soldier anymore. He's no threat to
you."

Anders flashed a wicked grin, knowing he had the upper
hand. "If he isn't a Rebel spy, then maybe he's a Bushwhacker. Either way, he deserves to be hung from the

nearest tree. It will set an example to the rest of the Rebel sympathizers around here."

Washington Mayes stood his ground proudly. He was determined not to show fear in front of these damn Yankee Jayhawkers. "I'm not a spy or a Bushwhacker. I fought as a soldier for what I believed in. I've done my duty as I saw it, just as you've done yours, but now I'm through with the war." He held up his arm with the stump where his hand use to be. "I've given enough. Now all I ask is to be left alone in peace."

"Everyone knows a spy isn't going to admit what he is. A cripple isn't much of a threat as a soldier, but you've still got your eyes and mouth. You can pass on information helpful to the Rebels. We know you will if it will help your precious cause." Anders turned toward the sergeant. "Take him prisoner, Sergeant."

The sergeant swung out of the saddle as he yelled, "Smith, Baker, give me a hand."

Mollie tried to position herself between the sergeant and Wash. The sergeant roughly shoved her out of the way. Mollie hit the ground on her hips and sprawled like a rag doll upon her back, skirts flying. Wash stepped up and threw a powerful left-handed uppercut, catching the sergeant squarely under the chin. The blow lifted the surprised soldier off his feet, spilling him hard on his back. As Sergeant Jones struggled to regain his footing, Smith and Baker moved in and restrained Washington Mayes, holding him by his arms.

Sergeant Jones rubbed his jaws as he growled out in menacing tones, 'Reb, you'll pay for that." Sergeant Jones curled his lips cruelly as he stepped up, balled his fist, and threw it hard in Mayes' midsection. Wash Mayes doubled over as the air whooshed out of his lungs. He struggled to free himself, but it was impossible. A crushing right thrown by Jones hit Wash's nose squarely. Blood gushed from the crushed nose and streamed down his face.

"Stop it, please stop it! Don't let them hurt him anymore," Mollie pleaded.

Anders watched the struggle with amusement. He knew a one-handed man was no match for his soldiers so he studied Mollie as she pulled herself to her feet. The woman was rather plain, but he admired the way her figure filled out her dress. Anders felt a sudden twitch in his loins as he noticed how the dress clung to her hips and he knew instantly how to get what he wanted. He decided to take advantage of the situation since the opportunity presented itself. "Hold it, Jones. Since we're gonna hang him anyway there's no sense in tearing up your hands on the likes of him."

Mollie Mayes felt a rising tide of panic welling up within her as she scrambled near Captain Anders. "You can't mean it! You can't hang him without a trial, he's done nothing wrong!"

Anders felt a rush of power as he smiled nefariously at Mollie's terrified face. "That's where you're wrong, ma'am. The military has local jurisdiction in this area and we're engaged in enforcing martial law, so I can take whatever steps I feel are appropriate to control any resistance in this area. If I decide this man is a spy and want to hang him right now, no one can stop me."

He watched Mollie's frightened, pleading eyes and felt satisfaction as she sensed his power of life and death over her husband. Anders revelled in the dominance he had over her and he knew she would do whatever he wanted if he manipulated her carefully. She would be like putty in his hands. He had never felt more in control.

"Please don't hurt him. Isn't there something you can do to spare him?" Mollie pleaded. Her voice quavered and broke, "He's all I have. Please, don't kill him."

Wash Mayes, the blood still streaming down his face, shouted, "For God's sake, Mollie, don't beg him. I wouldn't give them the satisfaction." Sergeant Jones threw another punch, catching Wash in the mouth. Wash's lip split as it slammed into this teeth and his head reeled back. The only reason he didn't go down were the two Yankees holding him. He heard and felt the crack of bone as one of his front teeth gave way.

"Tie his hands behind his back, Sergeant, and guard him closely."

Jones smiled as he studied Wash's bloodied face with satisfaction. He glanced up at his captain. "Shit, Capt'n, we can't. This Reb's only got one hand. There's no way to hold a rope on his wrists with a stump for a hand."

"Then tie the ropes around his arms and chest. Christ! I wish sometime you'd try to think for yourself, Jones, instead of expecting me to spell it out for you."

"Yes, sir."

Anders leered at Mollie, who had stepped back a couple of paces. "While my men are guarding your husband, why don't we go up to your house and see if we can't reach some agreement."

Wash struggled mightily, but hopelessly against the men tying his arms to his side. "Don't do it, Mollie! I'd rather die here and now than see you give in to these scum!"

Sergeant Jones unleashed a powerful blow to Wash's stomach, followed by another jab to his mouth. Wash's lips were puffed and swelling as the blood continued to flow from his nose and mouth. Dark specks circled before his eyes as Wash sagged to his knees.

"Shut up, damn you! Or we'll kill you right here," threatened Sergeant Jones.

"I'll make the decisions around here, Sergeant. I want the men to hold him here. Private Baker, I want you to guard the door to the house. I don't want anyone coming in there after we enter. Do you understand?"

"Yes, sir!"

"The rest of you take turns watching the horses and guarding the prisoner."

Private Smith asked, "Captain, would it be all right if'n we help ourselves to the chickens?"

Anders smiled. "I'm sure the lady won't mind, do you, ma'am?"

Mollie answered softly. "No, they can help themselves."

Smith grinned, "Thanks, ma'am." He immediately turned and started chasing a chicken across the yard as the hen clucked in terror.

Captain Anders slid from his saddle and handed the reins to a trooper. "I'll follow you to the house, Mrs. Mayes."

Mollie didn't know what to do. The most important thing in her whole life was her husband. She knew she had no other choice. Mollie turned and led the way to the house.

Once they were inside, Anders took a chair from beside the kitchen table. He turned it around so it faced the middle of the room. "Nice little house you have here, looks real cozy."

"We've been happy here. Wash built it himself."

Anders stared openly at Mollie's breasts hidden beneath her dress. "I'm feelin' thirsty. What do ya have to drink in the house?"

"I've got some buttermilk. There's also a bucket of water that's fresh."

"I had my heart set on something stronger than water. Your husband keep any sippin' liquor handy?"

Mollie stood awkwardly before him, clutching her arms. "Yes, we have some in the pantry."

"Well, don't just stand there, go get it and pour some for me." He watched her as she moved over to the pantry, opened the door, and extracted a jug. He loved the way her hips looked as she bent over to retrieve it. He continued to stare as she walked over to the cupboard and returned with a glass. She poured the liquor and handed it to the captain.

He smiled at her as he swirled the dark liquid in the

glass. He tipped the glass and gulped down a generous amount. He felt the burn as it slid down his throat. The warmth grew in his belly. "Not bad sippin' whiskey. He must save this for special occasions. That's real appropriate 'cause you and I are fixin' to have a grand time."

"Please, don't do this." Mollie pleaded with her eyes. "Why don't you just ride out of here and leave us alone? We can't harm you."

He rose swiftly from his chair and slapped her hard across the cheek, spinning her head to the side. Mollie was caught off guard by his sudden movement. She staggered against the cupboard as she fought to regain her balance. She stole a glance at his leering face as he said, "Now, why would I want to do that? I have orders to hang your husband. A good soldier always follows his orders." He enjoyed playing with her, manipulating her. He relished the fear he saw in her eyes. "It would take some powerful persuasion to keep me from my duty."

Mollie tasted the salty tang of her blood trickling from a cut inside her cheek. Her face tingled and ached. Suddenly, Mollie knew what was coming. She had sensed it all along, as she studied his lecherous face, but she hoped she was wrong. "What is it you want from me, Captain?"

"It's nice of you to ask, Mollie. It is Mollie, isn't it?" He settled himself back into his chair. "You don't mind if I call you by your name do you?"

She shrugged her shoulders. "No, I guess I don't mind." She had to force herself to control her anger as her fingers rubbed across her stinging cheek. She knew the safety of her husband depended on it.

"I want you to show me a grand time. I've been away from home for quite a while and I miss the pleasures only a woman can provide, it you know what I mean." Bob Anders licked his lips as he thought about how much fun he intended to have at Mollie's expense. "I want you to do whatever I want without question. If you want what's best for your husband, you better show me a good time. It is the least you can do to keep your husband alive, isn't it?" Captain Anders tipped up his glass and finished off the remaining whiskey. He picked up the jug and poured himself another glass.

Mollie asked, "And if I don't?"

"Then I guess I'll have no choice but to hang your husband."

"If I do what you want, you'll let him live?"

Captain Anders chuckled a high, wicked laugh. When he stopped he looked at her again. "Well, that all depends on how good you are. Make me real happy, make me believe you want it, and maybe I'll let him live. So, I guess I'll think about it."

Mollie felt sick to her stomach as his words sunk into her consciousness. She felt her hands tremble as she smoothed her dress. "How do I know you'll keep your end of the bargain?"

Anders smiled as he gulped down another drink, then set the glass on the table. "You don't. The choice is up to you."

Mollie wanted nothing to do with this detestable, disgusting man. She knew she had only once choice; she would never forgive herself if she didn't do everything possible to save her husband's life, no matter how great her personal sacrifice. All the degradation would be worth it if only her husband would be allowed to live. She nodded her head yes as she agreed reluctantly to his demands. A sudden calm came across her as she made up her mind to do what had to be done. Her voice took on a steady, resigned tone. "What do you want me to do?"

Bob Anders saw the defeat written on her face and heard it in her voice. She would do anything he asked. She didn't dare to do otherwise. He smiled. "I want to see what your legs look like for starters. Lift up your skirts."

Mollie bent down and grasped the edge of her skirt and

petticoats as she lifted them up to reveal her legs and her pantaloons. She felt sick to her stomach as Anders leered at her.

"Not bad, lift them higher." As he stared lustfully at Mollie, he nervously twisted the gold ring back and forth on the little finger of his hand. Mollie had noticed the ring earlier. The bright gold band had a large capital A engraved on it. She supposed it stood for his last name, Anders. From this point on in her life she would forever remember him leering at her as he sat twisting that ring back and forth on his finger while he made her perform for him. Mollie lifted her skirt even higher.

"You've got a nice pair of legs, lady. I know you just can't wait to show me more. I want you to stand right here and take your dress off." He pointed at the floor, just a couple of feet in front of him. "Take it all off slowly. I like a little tease, so give me a good show."

Mollie's face flushed with embarrassment and she felt a shudder flow through her, but she did as she was told. She stood a couple of feet in front of him. She carefully and slowly unbuttoned her day dress, then slid the dress and light petticoat to the floor, exposing her pantaloons and the camisole beneath. Mollie stepped out of the dress.

Anders licked his lips in delight as his palms began to sweat with excitement. He felt a growing stiffness pushing against his fly. In a low, husky voice filled with lust he said, "Take the camisole off."

Mollie began to unbutton it slowly. As each button came loose, more of her breasts and cleavage was exposed. Then she slid the camisole off of her shoulders and let it fall to the floor.

Anders watched in fascination. Mollie's breasts stood firm and proud once freed from the camisole. "Take off your pantaloons." His voice was barely above a whisper as beads of sweat formed across his forehead. "Turn around. I want to watch them slide off your hips."

Mollie turned and, after untying the drawstring, slid the pantaloons down slowly. Anders liked the way her breasts hung full and loose as she bent over, presenting her hips to him while looking back over her shoulder. He studied every move she made. As the pantaloons slid to her ankles, she stepped out of them. He stared at her athletic legs and full, well-shaped hips. He glanced at the narrow waist and admired the lovely curve of her back. "Turn around a couple of times for me."

She turned slowly, feeling his eyes stare at every inch of her nakedness. She felt ill but tried not to let it show.

Anders, captivated by the naked woman at his command, was fully aroused. His desire was even evident in his voice. "Come here," he said huskily.

She moved closer to him.

Anders was still seated in his chair with his knees together. "Straddle my knees and stand facing me. Put your hands on my shoulders."

She did. Anders could smell the soft scent of her as her breasts dangled inches from his face. He lifted his mouth to her breast, licking and nuzzling the deep tan of her nipples as he slid his hands along the outside of her thighs until he reached her buttocks. He caressed and kneaded her hips and felt the cool, soft silkiness of her skin as he pulled her to him and tongued her belly. Anders leaned away as he worked his hands to her waist, then up her flat belly until he cupped and squeezed her breasts. He pulled her down to kiss his eager mouth. Mollie tried not to resist, but she detested the feel of his wet, hot mouth on hers. After a few moments he let her go, pushed her back, and stood beside Mollie as he wrapped his fingers tightly in her hair. Without warning, he pulled her hair backward, tilting her head toward the ceiling. With his free hand he caressed her breasts while he tongued and licked at her neck.

Mollie wanted to cry out from the pain caused by Anders pulling her hair. She wanted to struggle against him, but it hurt too much. Every time she tried to release the pressure on her hair, he would pull harder. Mollie felt his hot breath on her neck as his breathing became quick and ragged. His free hand left her breast and moved steadily downward until Anders was pushing his probing fingers into her womanhood.

Mollie winced even more at the pain from his awkward and careless attempts to invade her. Tears began to well in her eyes and spill down the sides of her face despite her best efforts. She felt degraded and sickened by Anders' manipulation to the point she was near vomiting, but she struggled to control herself. Wash's life depended on her.

Anders stopped licking and sucking on her neck as he tasted a salty tear. He pulled back and saw she was crying. He yanked her hair, forcing her to look in his face. He gave her a cruel, twisted smile. "You're supposed to enjoy this, remember? You want something to cry about, I'll give it to you." With his free hand Anders gave her a resounding slap that rattled her teeth. He shoved her face down on the table while her feet remained on the floor. "Don't move," he growled out. She felt him running his hands slowly down her back and over her hips. He paused there, giving them extra attention with his kneading and probing fingers. His hands continued down her thighs and calves as he explored her long legs. When he reached her ankles he started upward again, pausing once more at her hips.

His breathing was becoming even more ragged and she felt his hand leave her as he fumbled with his pants. Moments later, Mollie felt his awkward attempts to enter her and she had to bite her tongue to keep from crying out in anguish. He grabbed her by her hair again and began to slam himself hard against her hips as he gained his rhythm. In less than a minute she felt him quiver and shake behind her as he grunted and groaned his release and clung to her hips. He laughed when his cruel thrusting finally stopped. The front of her thighs ached from being slammed against the edge of the table by his body. Never in her life had Mollie felt more dirty.

Anders stood behind her for a minute sucking in deep breaths, before he grabbed her hair again and pulled her to her feet. He shoved her roughly toward the bedroom. "Don't worry, Mollie, we aren't done yet. Next time I'll last longer."

13

Horse Dung and Cheap Whiskey

Ross Kimbrough guided his horse along the familiar backroads of Lafayette County. He took a fork in the trail and turned his horse west toward Lexington, Missouri. Kimbrough's face was a picture of grim determination as he worked through his plan of attack. He contemplated several options, discarding those less promising. He was close now, so close to his enemy his hands itched with anticipation. After months of suffering through pent-up anger and remorse over the death of his parents, Ross knew he would soon have his chance for revenge.

Yesterday he separated from Quantrill's men shortly after crossing the Lafayette County line. He had a mission to accomplish and it was one better done alone. This attack would require careful penetration deep within the enemy compound. More men would only complicate and increase the chance of failure.

He camped last night near the ashes of his beloved Briarwood. Only after he had seen the destruction for himself and visited his father's grave did it all seem real to him. Somehow, a part of him didn't want to believe it was true. He had hoped his parents and Briarwood might still be there waiting for him, untouched and happy as he remembered them. His arrival shattered any illusion or hope. If he hated Bartok before, now the hate was all-consuming. He would not rest until Benton Bartok was dead.

Ross would use his experience as a scout to pull this off. Often he had used disguises to penetrate enemy camps or travel through enemy-occupied territory to gather information. In the bag tied to his saddle, he had two such disguises.

One was a complete Union cavalry uniform for a private trooper. He was thankful most of the Union's companies in this theater of operations used the same uniform and lacked any designation for regiment. One uniform looked pretty much like another when it was from the same branch of service.

The other disguise he would use first. It was a set of ragged and dirty clothes like those one would expect to find on a beggar or drunken derelict. In the sack was a bottle of cheap whiskey to complete the outfit. His plan was deceptively simple. First, he would use the drunk outfit and wander through the town to familiarize himself with the layout. Once he located Benton Bartok's headquarters, he would use the trooper's uniform on his next visit to get close enough to make the kill. The plan was the best he could devise and he settled upon it.

As he neared the town of Lexington, Ross Kimbrough pulled his horse off the road and guided it deep into a dense thicket. Once he found a suitable location he tied off his horse and stowed his weapons and equipment under a brush pile. Once sure everything was well hidden, he dressed in his derelict outfit.

He sloshed a generous amount of the whiskey around in

his mouth, then spat it out. Ross poured some on his shirt, then slid the cork back into the bottle. He carefully folded his Confederate uniform and placed it in hiding with the rest of his equipment.

This time he wouldn't take Double-Twelve. He tucked a pistol in the small of his back, stuffing it into his belt and hoping his large, loose-fitting shirt would cover the weapon. He slid his knife into the top of his worn-out boots. Ross started walking toward town.

It was late afternoon when he reached the outskirts of Lexington. As he neared the sentry post guarding the entrance to the county seat, Ross ducked into the bushes. Using the cover of the dense foliage, he moved away from the sentry post until he reached a bend in the road which effectively hid him from view.

His hair was long and his beard untrimmed and bushy. Ross pushed his hands through his hair to make it even more unruly. He had let his hair grow long as he rode from Arkansas to Missouri with Quantrill's men. Long hair and a stringy beard would make his disguise believable. Carefully he rubbed some dirt on his face and exposed skin to make himself more convincing. He knew what he needed, the one thing that would give him an edge. He saw it lying at the edge of the road. He hesitated a moment, then reached down and put his hand in a fresh pile of horse dung.

Ross choked back bile in his throat as he felt the sticky, warm dung in his hand. He carefully wiped some on his shirt then threw the rest away. He wiped his soiled hands on his pants. Ross gagged on the pungent odor of the horse dung clinging in the fibers of his tattered and filthy shirt. If he could stand the smell, he just might make it. He took a small drink of the whiskey.

When Ross came around the bend in the road, he walked directly toward the sentry post. He staggered just a bit to make his act more convincing.

"Hey, you, come here," shouted a burly private with a thick coal-black walrus mustache almost covering his upper lip.

Ross staggered to a stop just a few feet away from the Union sentry. He gestured to himself. "Do you mean me?"

The Union private stepped forward with his carbine held firmly across his chest. "Where in the hell do you think you're goin'?"

Ross did his best to look puzzled as he wove on his feet and took a pull from his bottle of whiskey. He let some of the dark liquor run down his chin and beard. Ross slurred his speech as he talked. "Hell, I'm on my way to see my sister. She lives in Lexington. I thought she might take me in." Ross leaned forward and exhaled in the sentry's face.

The soldier wrinkled his nose in disgust as he smelled the cheap whiskey on Ross's breath. He caught a whiff of the pungent smell of horse dung reeking from Ross. "Jeezus Christ! What did you do, pass out in a barn?" He shot Ross a look of disgust. "You worthless bastard, get away from me!" The Union sentry kicked Ross firmly in the butt. Ross staggered past the sentry before falling in the dirt. "I'd arrest you and haul you off to the jail if you didn't stink so bad. You get your sorry carcass out of my sight before I decide to shoot you."

Ross crawled to his feet and stumbled toward town as he furtively glanced over his shoulder at the soldier. "Yes, sir, sorry I bothered you." Ross let out a deep sigh of relief as he moved away from the Union sentry and into Lexington. He let a smug smile cross his lips as he realized his plan had worked, so far.

Ross explored the town carefully as he stuck to his drunken derelict act. Once soldiers or civilians moved near him the rank smell of his clothes and his filthy appearance were enough for most to give him a wide berth when passing. Ross felt satisfied his disguise was effective. The farther people kept from him the less likely was his discovery and the greater his margin of safety.

After two hours of searching, Ross walked past the white, columned courthouse of Lafayette County. He was amazed to see a six-pound cannonball firmly lodged in a column high above the ground. He knew it must have been fired during the battle of Lexington earlier in the war, but the sight still astonished him. He continued to work his way down the street.

Two blocks farther he noticed what appeared to be a local Union headquarters. Staff officers and personnel moved in and out of the building at regular intervals. He wondered if this might be the headquarters of Major Bartok.

Earlier in the day he had examined the outer perimeter of the Union fortifications on the large hill above Lexington. From there the big guns could defend the city against attack, although the city itself lay at the foot of the hill below the main Union fortifications. The Union fort also commanded a view of the Missouri River and could protect Union shipping along the waterway.

Ross supposed the headquarters in town was used by the soldiers to control the local population. Ross leaned back and slid down the wall until he settled firmly on the boardwalk in front of the building across the street from the headquarters. There he pretended to nurse on his bottle like a common drunk as dusk began to settle on the city.

Ross listened carefully to the passing conversation of soldiers moving by him in the street. His ears perked up at once when he heard a young lieutenant cursing Benton Bartok under his breath as he spoke to a sergeant on their way past Ross. Apparently the young Union lieutenant was upset because he was ordered to take charge of the night patrol guarding the city because another officer was sick. His resentment showed clearly in his voice and demeanor.

Ross watched alertly until he spotted another Union officer exit the building. This soldier strutted across the boardwalk with an arrogant swagger. The officer's uniform was impeccably clean and pressed, but his expression was clearly agitated. In the yellow lantern light spilling through an office window, Ross could make out the officer's features. He wore the uniform of a major, was stockily built, and of average height. He slapped new leather gauntlets against his thigh as he took in a deep breath of evening air. The major fished a large cigar out of his pocket and struck a match on the wooden post nearest him. As he cupped the burning match to the end of the cigar, the light cast from the match illuminated his face, revealing a rather prominent hawk-billed nose.

The major contorted his face into an angry snarl as he shouted, "I don't give a damn what your men heard, Captain Shay. Captain Anders and his patrol should have arrived tonight. If they don't show up soon I expect you to send out a patrol to look for them at dawn. Do I make myself clear, Captain?"

"Yes, sir, Major Bartok, I'll see to it personally."

"See that you do, Elias, see that you do." Bartok strutted to his horse, untied it from the hitching rail, and swung into the saddle. He rode at a gallop toward the Union fortifications.

Ross Kimbrough smiled in grim satisfaction. He now knew what his adversary looked like and where to find him. Ross slid slowly away from the wall and pulled himself erect. His legs felt stiff as he took his first few steps. His eyes scanned the surrounding street and he spotted a stable situated just two buildings down and across the street from Bartok's headquarters. A smile crossed his lips as he studied a hay door in the loft, facing the street. The door stood slightly ajar.

Moments later, Ross cautiously entered the stable. He halfway expected to find someone in there, but it was empty except for the cavalry mounts filling most of the stalls. Saddles, blankets, bridles, and other equipment hung from the walls and saddle racks. The piquant smell of fresh hay and leather mixed freely with the harsh odor of dung in the stalls. Ross noticed a ladder leading to the loft. He began to climb. He carefully tested the floorboards as he moved to the door of the hay loft. Peering through the crack in the partially opened loft door, he had a clear view of Bartok's office. He slid the door, forcing the rusty hinges to give as he opened it a little more. When he was satisfied with his angle of view, he climbed down and examined the possible exits from the stable. When he was finished, he left Lexington and returned to his horse and hidden equipment. "Tomorrow will be the day," Ross thought. "Tomorrow Major Benton Bartok will die."

14

At the End of a Rope

An hour and a half passed before Anders, now fully dressed, emerged from the house. He left Mollie struggling to dress herself.

Captain Bob Anders felt fully satisfied and cocky as he swaggered out of the house. "Baker, I want you to see to it the woman doesn't come out of the house. I don't want any interference from her."

"Yes, sir!"

Anders walked quickly to the barn where his soldiers were gathered. "Sergeant Jones, get the prisoner on a horse. We're gonna have a hangin'."

Jones smiled as he bit off a chew of a plug of tobacco. "Yes, sir, be my pleasure. Come on, boys, let's get a rope over the beam on the barn." While others hoisted Wash Mayes onto a horse, Jones fashioned a hangman's noose out of a rope. He threw it over the beam and tied it to the handle of the barn door. They led the horse beneath the dangling rope and Jones gleefully slipped the noose around Wash Mayes' neck.

"Is that tight enough for ya, Reb? If it ain't, we'll adjust it a mite." Jones flashed his tobacco-stained teeth as he smiled.

Wash was scared, but he wouldn't give them the satisfaction of knowing it. He knew it wouldn't make any difference if he pleaded for mercy. He'd spent the worst two hours of his life as he waited for time to pass while Captain Anders was alone in his house with his wife. He knew Anders didn't take her up there for tea and cookies.

Wash knew whatever she had done had not been enough to satisfy Anders' need for blood. Wash was determined to die like a man if that was the way it had to be. His only regret was that he couldn't take Anders with him.

Captain Anders remounted his horse and rode up beside Wash. Wash's arms were still tied to his sides.

A blood-curdling scream echoed from behind the house as Mollie emerged from a window. She was dressed now, but hurriedly. Free of the window, Mollie ran as fast as she could, screaming at the top of her lungs.

Private Baker, who was watching the preparations for the hanging, was surprised as Mollie raced past him toward the barn. Baker started in pursuit. Before she could reach the men gathered around Wash on the horse, two of the troopers caught her and wrestled a large kitchen knife from her hands. "I did what you asked!" she screamed. "You said you'd let him live!"

Anders laughed. "I didn't promise, Mollie. I said I would think about it. I have my orders and I intend to follow them. I don't want to seem ungrateful. I do want to thank you for the fine entertainment you provided. Next time I'm in the neighborhood I'll drop by again. A new widow is gonna be in need of manly comforts."

"I'll kill you, you lyin' son of a bitch!" Mollie screamed.

Anders continued to laugh. A crazed, mad look came into his eyes. "You shouldn't have threatened me, Mollie. Because now I'm gonna let you watch him swing. Hold her, boys, I want her to watch him die."

Anders pressed his horse up next to Wash Mayes. He wanted to see the fear in the man's eyes, but he was disappointed, there wasn't any. He knew what it would take to hurt this man and he used it. "That wife of yours moves pretty good in bed, doesn't she? Why there wasn't anything she wouldn't do for me. Some of it I bet she never let *you* do." Anders smiled wickedly.

Wash felt a seething anger rise within him beyond his control. He was powerless to do much, but there was one gesture he could make to retaliate. He spat upon Captain Anders' face.

Anders was surprised by the audacity of Wash's sudden move. He felt the slimy wad of spittle mixed with blood from the cut in Wash's mouth as it slid down his cheek. He wiped it off quickly with his hand onto Wash's pant leg. Anger raged like a runaway forest fire within Anders. "Your wife has a cute little mole just below her belly button, doesn't she, Reb?" His voice became louder as he continued. "I want you to think about me makin' love to your wife, her doing anything I wanted. You think about it on your way to hell!"

Anders reached over and slapped the horse hard on its rump. The horse jumped from the blow and, as the horse pulled away, the rope tightened until it swung Wash free of the saddle. Wash arched his back, his feet dangling in space, trying to touch something, anything. His head was thrown to the side by the knot as it tightened. His face turned red, then purple as he gagged. His eyes began to bulge and his tongue protruded grotesquely from his mouth. His body swung back and forth on the rope, his legs kicking wildly. Wash's body began to spasm as his life was strangled out of him.

The men stood silent as they watched the hanging in stunned fascination. Mollie's horrified screams broke the stillness. For God's sake, cut him down! I'll do anything you want. Just let him go." She collapsed to her knees as they restrained her. Mollie's grief and anger slipped beyond control as sobs racked her body. The soldiers restraining her relaxed their grip as they sensed her giving in to her grief.

When they let go of her she twisted herself free and ran to her husband, still swinging back and forth on the rope. She struggled to grasp his legs and lift upward, trying to take his weight off the rope. The Jayhawkers moved to stop her.

Anders shouted to his men, "Let her go! There's nothing she can do now to save him. She can't bring him back from the dead." He motioned to the patrol. "Mount up."

"What do ya want to do with him, Captain?"

"Leave him hangin' as an example to others. Let's march; we've got a long ride back to Lexington." Anders rode near Mollie. "Thanks for the good time, lady. I'll give you a couple of weeks to get over this then I'll be back. You was so good I want to do you again. Maybe next time I'll let you work to save your house." He let loose a rolling belly laugh as he sat there, taunting her.

Mollie turned red with rage and found herself staring into his mocking face. She was struggling to no avail. There wasn't any feeling of life left in Wash's legs. Mollie turned loose of Wash and attacked Anders' leg, pounding her fists into him. "So help me God, I will see you dead, Anders!" she screamed.

Anders laughed at her and spurred his horse forward as he led his men from the yard. She ran back to where her husband was dangling and tried to lift him again. Her mind raced through her limited options. She must get him down quickly. She darted through the open barn door to the haying scythe. She grabbed it, and ran toward his swinging body. Mollie leveled a hard swing at the rope. The scythe cut through. Wash's body collapsed into a heap as he thudded against the ground.

She dropped the scythe and knelt beside the body of her husband. Mollie tried to slip the rope from his neck, but his weight hanging against the rope had made it bite deep in the flesh of his neck. It took her several desperate minutes working with the rope and the knot to slip it free. She put her head on his chest and listened, but there was nothing. She felt for a pulse, but he was cold and lifeless. Mollie collapsed in sorrow, giving herself over freely to her grief.

15

Reap What You Sow

Mollie Mayes lay sobbing as she clung to the chest of her dead husband for forty minutes before she heard the sound of approaching riders. Fear filled her. Was it Captain Anders and his Jayhawkers returning for her?

Mollie stood quickly as she listened to the sound of horses approaching. Her eyes were red and puffy from crying. She strained through her tears to identify the horsemen. Mollie saw over one hundred heavily armed men riding magnificent horses and, at a glance, she knew these were not Anders and his Yankee Jayhawkers. These men wore the distinctive guerilla shirts adorned with fancy stitching in a variety of colors. She had only seen these shirts worn by Quantrill's raiders. Raiding at the head of the column and under a snapping black flag rode William Clarke Quantrill. Quantrill had packed his colonel's uniform away and now wore the same uniform as his men. He halted the column as they neared her.

Mollie noticed for the first time the outriders patrolling the flanks of the column and scouts that had ridden past her. She had been too involved at first with venting her grief to notice them. Two of these scouts were already examining the tracks of Anders' patrol.

Quantrill swept his hat off, and held if before him. "What happened, ma'am?"

Mollie teetered on the edge of complete hysteria, but she told them as much as she could. The words gushed out of her like a raging torrent as she tried frantically to tell her story. Quantrill swung down and tried to comfort her. He urged her to slow down so they could understand her.

Her story gradually unfolded as she told them how the Union soldiers had surprised them. How Anders had abused her and forced her to do his bidding while holding out the hope he would let her husband live. He had laughed at her grief as she struggled to save her husband's life. She began to tremble as she clutched at her arms, hugging herself as she recalled his threat to return to abuse her again.

She supposed their only excuse for hanging her husband was that he had been a soldier in the Confederate army. She told Quantrill how they accused Wash of being a Confederate spy and suggested he might be tempted to help Quantrill's guerillas as an excuse to hang him. Captain Anders had said Wash Mayes' hanging was to be an example to other Southern people living in the area.

Quantrill quickly took charge of the situation. "Lieutenant Gregg, take thirty of our best mounted riders and catch that Yankee patrol."

Billy Cahill had listened carefully to Mollie's story. When he heard the name Captain Bob Anders, it struck a nerve within him. That was the name of one of the two men Elizabeth Kimbrough had mentioned were responsible for the burning of her home and the death of her father. Billy said, "Capt'n Billy, I know this area. If the Yankees take the main road to Lexington, I know a shortcut where we can get ahead of them and ambush them. The main road twists and winds around often before it reaches Lexington. I know a back trail that is quicker and less traveled. If we ride hard, we might get ahead and surprise them."

Quantrill ignored his men calling him Captain Billy; even though he called himself a colonel now, he didn't bother to dispute it with his men. "Lead Lieutenant Gregg to the back trail, Billy. I'll stay here with a few of our men and see this man properly buried."

Billy swung down from the saddle. He studied the dead man's face. The face looked familiar and Billy realized he had seen him a couple of times around Farnsworth House back in Arkansas. Billy had only met him a couple of times, but he seemed a likable sort. Billy glanced up at Mollie, touched by this woman's grief.

Billy felt his old memories flooding back as he recalled how the Jayhawkers had tortured and hung his father while they forced him to watch. Billy felt a renewed rage burning in him until he felt as if his blood might boil. He grit his teeth and doubled his hands into fists. It was time, high time, to pay the Jayhawkers back with some of their own medicine. He snatched up the rope they had used to hang Wash from the barn. He coiled it carefully, then slipped it onto his saddle. Billy quickly swung into the saddle and spurred his horse forward.

Lieutenant Gregg followed Billy at a gallop and in his wake rode over thirty of the best mounted and most experienced of Quantrill's guerillas. Among them rode Frank James, Andy Blount, Fletch Taylor, and Riley Crawford.

The guerillas pushed their mounts hard and made excellent time. Billy had been in the area the previous fall and had used this trail to escape a Union patrol. He was fortunate a local farmer had shown him the way. Now he would use it to deal a blow against the Yankees.

Billy knew they had a few advantages over the Jay-hawkers. First, they were mounted on the finest horse flesh the South had to offer. Quantrill believed if you were to stay one step ahead of the enemy you needed to move quickly and, if necessary, outrun them. He always insisted his men trade for better horses at every opportunity.

They also knew the numbers of the enemy they were facing, and the direction they were heading, and they had them outnumbered. Even better, the enemy wasn't expecting them.

Two hours later, Billy Cahill led Quantrill's men to a point overlooking the road where the Yankees should pass. Billy spurred his horse down the hill and angled toward the road. As they worked themselves closer he pulled his horse to a halt. He turned toward Lieutenant William Gregg. "I'll ride down there and see if I can tell if the Yankees have passed this point yet. If they haven't passed by, it looks like the perfect place to set up an ambush."

"Good idea, Billy, check it out, and I'll set up the ambush."

Billy reached the road and swung out of the saddle. He walked slowly across the trail as he carefully examined the tracks. Except for a few wagon tracks, there were no signs indicating the passing of a Yankee patrol. Billy let loose a sigh of relief. If the Jayhawkers had taken this road, he was sure he and his companions were ahead of them. He remounted and rode into the thick cover of the brushy hill overlooking the road.

Quantrill's men didn't have long to wait before the arrival of Anders' patrol. Two riders led the main body by two hundred yards. The men, dressed in Union blue, moved cautiously. Each kept his eyes scanning the road, as they moved along at a steady pace. Even from the hill,

Billy saw pairs of dead chickens tied by the feet and slung over the Yankee saddles.

An officer wearing a captain's uniform and a sergeant led the column as they came around a bend in the road. The rest of the troopers followed in columns of twos, except one trooper who was trailing behind as a rear guard.

Billy smiled to himself as he realized how easy this was going to be. The guerillas waited patiently until the lead riders came abreast of their position.

On Lieutenant Gregg's signal, gunfire rolled down the length of the column. Temporarily, Billy's vision was obscured by the clouds of blue-black powder smoke. The firecracker sound of the pistol fire reverberated and echoed across the hills. Screams of men blown out of their saddles and cries of terrified and dying horses mixed in a deadly milieu of sound. Billy smiled with satisfaction as he spotted the empty saddle of the trooper that had been his target.

The firecracker rattling of shots continued as horses' hooves pounded against the road. Billy jumped from his hidden position in the brush and darted out into the road. Before him, sprawled in the deep dust of the road, lay the soldier he had just shot. The Yankee was gasping out his last breath. Billy glanced down the road and saw three Yankee riders, bent low over the necks of their horses and moving at a fast gallop back the way the Yankee column had come. He watched with satisfaction as out of a brushy gully rode a group of guerillas, cutting off their escape. He watched Frank James leading the attack, a pistol in both hands and the reins in his teeth. Beside Frank rode Riley Crawford. In a matter of seconds it was over. The last three Yankees tried desperately to surrender, but their attempt was in vain.

Riley smiled his strange, twisted smile as he aimed his pistols into the faces of the terrified soldiers. Two of them, still with their hands in the air, fell from pistol shots between the eyes or in the forehead fast as you can snap your fingers. The third rider went down from a bullet in the back as he tried to ride away from Frank James. As always, Quantrill's men did their job with bloody efficiency.

Billy immediately began his search for the officer leading the column. He wanted to be certain the man was dead. As he moved down the line he spotted the dead horse he believed belonged to the officer. As he approached he heard the officer struggling to pull his pinned leg from under the side of the dead animal. Billy moved at an angle so he would have an unobstructed view of the soldier. He stared into the Yankee's terrified eyes as he lay there, wide-eyed and trembling.

The officer studied him and his eyes fell on the smoking pistol still held in Billy's hand. "Please help me?" His eyes were pleading. "Don't shoot, I surrender!"

Billy seethed with rage. He stepped in closer and carefully disarmed the officer. Billy could barely contain himself, but he needed to be sure. He jammed the barrel of the pistol under the chin of the Yankee officer. "I want some quick answers and they better be damned straight."

Anders swallowed hard. He could feel the hot muzzle of the barrel burning into his flesh. He nodded, showing he understood.

"What is your name and your unit?" asked Billy.

"Captain Bob Anders, Company A, Third Kansas Cavalry," he said shakily. "Please help me, my leg hurts. Can you get me out from under my horse?" Anders didn't like the deadly look of hate in the eyes of the youth standing before him.

Billy drew his free hand back and slammed home a punch. The blow caught Anders squarely in the face, smashing his lips into a bloody pulp against his teeth. Billy stood over the prostrate officer.

William Gregg moved alongside and gave Billy a grin.

"I was hopin' we'd catch him alive. I told the men to aim for his hoss."

Billy stared hatefully at Anders as he said, "This is the one that done it, Bill. Says his name is Anders."

"Just what I figured. Since this Yankee surrendered I guess we ought to be hospitable and get him out from under the animal."

Billy nodded as he understood what William Gregg had in mind. Riley Crawford spurred forward, moving his mount into position. In short order a rope was thrown around the dead horse's neck and the carcass was moved free of Anders' leg. When Anders was freed, two of the Bushwhackers grabbed him and tied Anders' hands behind his back.

Billy Cahill saw Andy Blount ride out of the brush leading Billy's chestnut mare. Billy removed the rope he had found at Mollie's house from the saddle. He dangled the noose before Bob Anders' frightened face. "Do you remember this, Anders?"

The Jayhawker's face turned white as a ghost. His eyes widened in terror. "I . . . I don't know what you're talkin' about."

Billy enlarged the loop, slipping the rope through the thirteen knots. It slid smoothly. He placed the noose around the neck of Captain Anders, who tried unsuccessfully to duck his head away from the rope. Billy tightened the knot around Anders' neck. "Try again to remember, Capt'n Anders. Try real hard. I bet you remember this rope. We found it just a couple of hours ago wrapped around the neck of a helpless crippled farmer named Wash Mayes."

Anders began to tremble. "I didn't want to do it. I had my orders," he whined. "Don't you see, it's not my fault? I had to do it. You've got to believe me."

Billy smoldered with pent-up anger. "Yeah, someone

stood there and held a gun to your head and forced you to rape his wife, you son of a bitch!"

Billy rammed his fist deep into the pit of Captain Anders' stomach. Anders doubled over and grunted loudly as he fought to suck air back into his lungs. Two of the guerillas pulled him upright. When he could speak again he said, "No! You got it all wrong. I didn't force her, she wanted to do it. We went into the cabin just to discuss things. She had a couple of drinks and then threw herself at me. I guess she needed a real man after livin' with a cripple. It wasn't my idea."

Billy couldn't stomach any more of this damned Jayhawker's lies. He took a step forward and grabbed Anders in the groin. Billy gave Anders a hard-eyed look as he started squeezing his hand tighter on the man's privates. Billy growled, "You lyin' son of a bitch. I ought to rip these off and stuff 'em in your mouth."

Anders cried out in pain. Sweat beads spread across his forehead as his face contorted in distress. "Please, I only did what I was told. It was Major Bartok's idea. He thought it would set a bad example if we let an ex-Confederate get away with livin' in the country. He said if we'd hang Mayes and leave him for the other locals to see, we'd have more cooperation and less trouble from the locals. Aaaah . . . Oh, God, please let go." Anders began to sob and cry. Between gasps he continued, "Ya gotta understand. I was just followin' orders. I didn't wanna do it."

The guerillas watched the disgusting spectacle of the cowardly Union officer begging for his life. Bob Anders in his efforts to escape death blamed everyone but himself for his actions. Billy relaxed his grip. Then out of frustration he cocked his arm back and delivered a solid blow to the teeth of the sobbing hull of a man. He felt the solid impact of his fist striking him and the satisfying crack of bone as Anders' front teeth gave way. Blood spurted and gushed down Anders' chin.

"That's enough, Billy, I can't stand to listen to this coward whine any more," said William Gregg.

"Let's hang him just like he done to Wash," Riley Crawford yelled.

William Gregg looked deadly serious. "Let's do it, boys, and get on the road. Quantrill will be waitin' for us back at the Mayes place."

Anders stood between the guerillas as they began to shove him onto a horse. He could no longer control himself and a dark, wet stain spread over his crotch. Frank James looked at the spreading moisture.

"Look at that boys, we scared the piss out of this Yankee." The guerillas laughed loudly at Anders' expense. They led his horse over to a tree that draped its branches over a turn in the road. A quick loop was thrown over the branch and the rope secured to the tree.

"You got any last words, Anders? Better say 'em now if ya got 'em."

"I'm sorry! Dear God, I'm sorry. I was just followin' orders. Please don't kill me. I . . . I don't want to die." Tears poured down Anders' trembling face.

William Gregg leaned forward in his saddle. "Anders, you're a piss poor liar. I hope for your sake ya don't meet up with Wash Mayes in the next world. He was a real man, not a spineless yellow belly like you." Disgust was plainly visible on Gregg's face. "I hope you rot in hell." Gregg nodded his head and Billy slapped the rear of the horse.

The horse leapt away and left the Yankee swinging in the wind. Anders' legs kicked and pawed the air for a minute as spasms ran through his body. Streaks of blood trailed from his nose, flattened and stained his broken front teeth. As Anders' body swung like a pendulum, Billy heard the creak of the rope as it moved slowly back and forth, grating against the limb and sounding like an old rocking chair with a creaky rocker.

Billy stepped forward and stopped the body from swinging. He reached inside the uniform jacket and removed a wallet from the body. He ripped the captain insignia from Anders' uniform jacket and stuffed them and the wallet into a large pocket on the guerilla shirt he was wearing. He glanced down and noticed the ring the man had on his little finger, a gold ring with a large letter A. Billy pulled out his Bowie knife and sawed off the finger. He removed a handkerchief from his pocket and wrapped the finger and ring in it before adding it to the collection in his pocket.

William Gregg watched it all solemnly. "What ya fixin' to do with all that, Cahill?"

"Reckon it would comfort the widow to see proof that we killed the man who hung her husband. I figure it will have plenty of meanin' for her." Billy thought, "There's a girl in Arkansas that will be mighty glad to know justice has finally caught up with Captain Bob Anders. Elizabeth, this one is for you and all his other countless victims."

They left Anders dangling from the same rope he had used to murder Wash Mayes. Just a few yards down the road lay the slaughtered remains of his patrol, stripped of anything the Bushwhackers might find useful.

Shortly after nightfall the band of Missouri Bushwhackers returned to the Mayes place, where Billy proudly presented his grisly gifts to Mollie Mayes. The captain insignia from Bob Anders' body he would soon mail to Elizabeth Kimbrough with a detailed account of the deadly ambush.

16

The Blood of a Tyrant

I t was after midnight before Ross Kimbrough relocated his horse and hidden supplies. He immediately changed to the Union uniform and discarded his smelly and dirty disguise in the bushes. He felt a wave of relief as he was finally free from the reeking, dung-encrusted garments—even wearing Yankee blue was better.

As Ross buckled his belt and holster around his waist, he thought about the consequences should he be caught wearing a Union uniform. They would shoot or hang him on the spot it he fell into enemy hands. He clenched his teeth in grim determination as he thought about his mission. It was a risk worth taking if he could kill Benton Bartok.

Moments later, he slid his Sharps carbine into its scabbard and slung the saddle onto the back of Prince of Heaven. The black stallion snorted and pranced, showing his eagerness to move after spending the day tethered in the brush, as he tightened the saddle girth. Ross patted the stallion lovingly before he gathered the rest of his supplies.

He carefully checked Double-Twelve to make sure she was loaded before he slid the weapon into his specially designed back holster. He placed the weapon into the cotton bag. He tied the bundle tightly to the bedroll behind his saddle. As much as he would like to, he knew he couldn't wear the double-barreled sawed-off shotgun. The weapon was too distinctive and was nonregulation equipment for Union soldiers.

It had always perplexed Ross when he considered how rigid the Union army was about keeping arms and equipment standard. The Confederate army was much more freewheeling and would use nearly any weapon they could lay their hands on. He supposed it would be different if the Southern army had as much equipment available to its soldiers as the Union army.

Ross swung aboard and guided Prince of Heaven toward the trail. As he rode under the dim light cast from a glowing sliver of moon, he strained to see his way through the dark shadows. When he neared the road he waited.

Ross knew he couldn't just ride into town alone. A single rider would cause too many questions, and he didn't know the answers. His best bet would be to wait for a patrol or supply train to pass by and slip in under cover of darkness. With a little luck he might blend in and no one would notice.

He waited impatiently for over an hour before he heard the sound of a Union supply train plodding its way toward Lexington. After the lead wagons passed by, Ross eased the black stallion from the brush into the road. He fell in behind an outrider protecting the side of the wagon train. After a few minutes Ross began to relax; no one had noticed him joining the guard. He studied the rider directly in front of him. The horse seemed to follow alongside the wagons out of habit; his rider rode with his head down and weaved in the saddle like a man asleep. Ross had seen many soldiers asleep in the saddle on night rides during the war and recognized the signs when he saw it. He smiled to himself as he silently thanked Lady Luck.

Ross pulled his Union blue overcoat more tightly around him as he felt the evening's chill seep through his clothing. He scanned the sky and reckoned the time to be somewhere between two and four in the morning. He would have to work swiftly to be in position by daylight. An hour later the supply train rambled past the guard post at the edge of town and rumbled toward the Union fortifications.

Ross slipped from the formation as they passed an alley in the business district. He guided Prince of Heaven into the deep shadows alongside a brick building as the remainder of the column and guards plodded past. When he was certain it was safe he spurred Prince forward and rode toward the stable near Bartok's headquarters. He would use the back way he'd discovered earlier in the night while playing derelict.

Ross tugged his hat down over his eyes and rode cautiously toward the stable. Earlier, the stable had been empty except for the cavalry mounts standing in the stalls, and he hoped it was still vacant. He swung down from Prince of Heaven and led the stallion through the back door facing the alley.

Ross stepped inside and struck a match on a post. From the weak light cast from the match, he located a lantern and lit it. He hung the smoky lantern on a nail in a post near an empty back stall and threw some grain into a small trough in the stall for Prince. He knew when he was ready to ride he would be in one hell of a hurry, so he left Prince of Heaven saddled and ready to go. He slid the Sharps carbine from its boot and slipped the bundle holding Double-

Twelve from behind the saddle. A quick glance around the stable revealed mostly empty stalls. The night before they had been filled with cavalry mounts. Ross knew with the dawn of a new day the soldiers working at headquarters and in town would refill the now empty stalls with their horses. He hung the lantern near the front entrance and silently slipped up the ladder to the loft.

Ross retraced his steps to the open hay door, carefully noting the squeaky floorboards. A man never knew when such information might save his life. He opened his cotton bag and slipped Double-Twelve onto his back. He then checked the Sharps carbine carefully and aimed his weapon at the door to Bartok's headquarters. He smiled in satisfaction when he realized his view was still unobstructed. Now all he had to do was wait for Major Benton Bartok to appear.

Two hours later, Ross carefully stretched his leg to improve the circulation. His leg began to tingle as fresh blood poured into cells deprived of their natural supply. Ross grimaced at the pain. All morning long, staff personnel had arrived at the stable, then crossed the streets to the headquarters. He waited with bated breath as he listened to the soldiers put away their equipment and horses, fearing his discovery. Despite his hopes and expectations, Major Bartok had not made his appearance. A nagging fear that, for some reason, Bartok might fail to appear tugged at Ross. Just when his hope was beginning to ebb, Ross spotted Bartok approaching astride a dappled gray.

The major rode directly for his headquarters at a trot. Ross moved to a kneeling position and stayed in the inkiness of the shadows of the loft as he swung his Sharps carbine up, tracking the officer's progress. Ross felt a surge of adrenaline as he saw his chance to even the score. He figured his best shot would come when Bartok dismounted and stood momentarily beside the horse. In that brief moment, he would be standing still. "I must make my first shot count," Ross thought as he squinted down the gun barrel and aimed the gun sight on the center of the major's chest.

Ross was concentrating so deeply on aiming the carbine, he didn't notice the approach of a carriage traveling down the street toward headquarters. Just as Major Benton Bartok swung down from his saddle, the four-wheeled carriage and horse team pulled between Ross and his intended target. Cursing under his breath, Ross urged the carriage to move more swiftly. When his view cleared, Bartok had handed his reins to an orderly and was strolling toward the office door.

Ross quickly aimed his carbine as Bartok approached the door, desperately trying to steady his bead as the major slipped from view through the doorway. Ross cursed his luck, the words escaping from his lips harshly when he realized he had failed in his first attempt.

Suddenly a booming voice echoed through the loft floor. "Say, is someone up there? Come down here immediately."

Ross swallowed hard. Damn his temper; in his anger he's let himself be discovered. Not wishing to be caught, Ross moved silently to the ladder. He waited there, thankful he had checked for squeaky boards earlier.

Ross listened to the movement coming from down below. Again he heard the voice. "I said, is there anyone up there?" A pause followed. "If I have to come up after you it will only make matters worse. I'll not ask again, get down here!"

Ross remained silent, crouched beside the hole in the floor leading to the stable below him. He quietly eased the carbine down and pulled Double-Twelve from its scabbard. After a prolonged silence Ross saw the ladder begin to wiggle and heard the scraping sounds of someone ascending the ladder. Ross waited patiently. A gun and a hand protruded through the hole followed by a head. Ross kicked out his foot, pinning the gun hand against the ladder, while simultaneously bringing Double-Twelve in a swinging arc against the intruder's head. The intruder grunted harshly as the blow bounced off his skull. Ross felt the man's falling body weight rip the pinned hand from beneath his foot as the man crashed to a heap on the floor. Ross lowered his head through the opening and quickly scanned the stable. He didn't see any other soldiers so he stowed Double Twelve into its holster and scurried down the ladder.

At the base of the ladder, Ross found the intruder lying unconscious. He stuffed the man's revolver into his belt and slung the Union trooper over his shoulder. Any moment now, the orderly sergeant across the street might bring Bartok's horse to the stable and put him away. Ross felt his breath coming in quick, shallow gasps as he felt failure and discovery closing rapidly in on him. Ross glanced around the stable and, seeing no place to hide the body, decided to take the man to the loft.

Ross struggled to hang on to each rung as he climbed, precariously balancing the dead weight of his victim. Upon reaching the loft, he shoved the man roughly out ahead of him. Regaining the safety of his perch, Ross strangled his prisoner until all signs of life ceased. As he slowly crawled back to the loft window, Ross felt remorse and guilt for murdering the young lieutenant. He hated to kill the soldier in such a brutal manner. "Better him than me," he reminded himself. Ross sat silently brooding about the past as he renewed his vigil at the loft door.

Benton Bartok sat restlessly at his desk, pouring over paperwork. His thoughts were not on the reports lying scattered on the desk before him, but on the absence of Captain Bob Anders—his patrol was long overdue. Captain Elias Shay had led a fresh column out to search for the missing patrol at dawn's first light.

Benton Bartok slid his chair back and pulled his pocket watch from his vest. He studied the face, checking for the fifth time today. The watch read ten minutes after three o'clock in the afternoon. Bartok clicked the lid closed and deposited the watch back into his pocket. He knew he should be hearing something soon, unless Elias was having a difficult time. He stood and stretched as he yelled through the door, "Sergeant Dirks, come here!"

Sergeant Dirks, a wiry man with wire-rim glasses and a lanky body, strolled into the room. "Yes, sir!"

"Have you heard anything from Captain Anders or Captain Shay yet?" Bartok already knew the answer.

"No, sir, we haven't heard a word," Dirks said as he saluted before Major Bartok's desk.

"I want to know immediately if anyone brings in news about either of them."

"Yes, sir," Sergeant Dirks replied.

As the tall, painfully thin sergeant spun on his heels, Bartok heard a horse sliding to a stop outside the headquarters. In moments, Captain Elias Shay stepped through Bartok's office door. The captain looked tired and dusty from his early morning ride. Shay's face looked grim and pale and his eyes had a terrified look about them. He halted in front of Bartok's desk and stood at attention.

"Well, don't just stand there, Captain. Did you find Anders and his patrol?

Shay's hand seemed to tremble as he finished his salute and lowered his arm. He looked at Major Bartok. "Yes, sir, we found Anders and his men about four miles east of Lexington. The patrol was ambushed and all the troopers are dead." Elias paused as if reluctant to continue. "We found Captain Anders hanging in a tree. His body was mutilated. Someone cut off his ring finger and left this note pinned to his body." Shay reached into his pocket and extracted the folded note. He handed it to Benton Bartok.

The major stared at the blood-tinged note and read:

This coward murdered a crippled man and raped his wife. He died at the avenging hands of Quantrill's men. He deserved worse than he got. All Jayhawkers we catch will suffer the same fate. Quantrill's Raiders.

Bartok felt fear clutch at his throat as he read the words scrawled across the paper. The reports were true, William Clarke Quantrill and his hellions had returned. He knew that they would give him little rest in the coming months. He was glad he had sent Anders instead of taking care of Wash Mayes personally. It might have been him swinging from the tree. Bartok rose to his feet. "Did you see any of Quantrill's men?"

"No, sir, but their signs were everywhere. Our entire patrol was killed and left stripped naked where they fell. The only horses left behind were dead. It looks like they got away clean, sir."

Benton Bartok's throat suddenly felt very dry. What he needed was a drink to calm his nerves and dull his pain. There would be one less man to share the wealth, but Anders had been a dependable officer—it would be difficult to find another as devious and black-hearted as Bob Anders. Bartok looked up at Elias Shay. "Did your men pick up their trail?"

"Yes, sir, we found their tracks leading down the backroads. My patrol wasn't much larger than Anders' and we saw what happened to him. We knew we would need more troops to capture Quantrill and his men. Besides, we thought you'd want us to return with our dead."

Bartok slammed his fist into his desk out of frustration. After a moment of silence he said, "You probably did the right thing, Captain. I'm afraid we're in for a tough sum-

mer." Benton yelled around Shay, "Sergeant Dirks, have
my gray mare brought around front immediately."

Bartok walked over to the window and gazed out at the
skies. "I'm feeling the need for a drink, Captain Shay.
From the look of you I think you could use one, too." The
major turned to face his junior officer. "I think we have
suffered enough surprises today, don't you agree?"

Ross Kimbrough watched the officer arrive from his lofty
perch. He waited as the man disappeared into the office. All
day long he had kept up his vigil. It had been over two
days since he had last slept and he fought to stay alert as
he bit his lip until it nearly bled or pinched himself to stay
awake. After a while he watched a lanky sergeant appear
from the headquarters and hustle to the barn. He kept silent
as he heard the man saddling a horse. He led it to the hitching rail in front of headquarters. Ross caught his breath in
excitement as he realized the horse the sergeant was leading
was the dappled gray Bartok had rode in on this morning.

Ross swung into position. He watched quitely, gun at
the ready. The sergeant disappeared into the headquarters.
Moments later, two officers strolled through the door. Ross
cursed under his breath as he realized the captain was between him and Major Bartok, unwittingly shielding him
with his body. Ross kept the carbine aimed at the two
men, hoping for his chance.

When the two officers reached the horses, Bartok stood
on the far side of his horse, effectively blocking any killing shot. Ross knew his best chance would come when
Major Bartok swung into his saddle and he waited, poised
for action.

The moment came as Bartok stuck his foot into the stir-
rup and swung his leg over the saddle. Just as his hips settled into the saddle, a carbine shot echoed across the
street. Major Bartok never realized what hit him as pain
pulsed through his head. Everything swirled and faded to

black before Major Benton Bartok rolled from the pitching horse and fell face first into the dusty street.

Ross studied his shot as he jacked another paper cartridge into the Sharps' breech. He felt a surge of joy as he watched his shot strike home and Major Bartok pitch from his horse into the street. Bartok's body was like a sack of potatoes hitting the ground. He showed no movement or sign of life after his rough landing. Ross raised the carbine and fired another shot, but Captain Shay was running toward the protection of the headquarters' door. Wood splintered from the doorjamb as the shot missed its target. Ross swung away from the loft door. If he had any hope of escape he must move swiftly.

Ross hurled his gun through the opening in the loft and, putting his feet on the outside of the ladder, slid to the ground. He threw open the stall door and slammed the carbine he had hastily gathered from the stable floor into the waiting scabbard. He hurled himself into the saddle and spurred Prince toward the open stable door and the alley beyond. Angry voices swarmed behind him. His shots had been heard and the soldiers in town would be alert for trouble.

Ross ducked low in the saddle as he cleared the stable door. Prince seemed anxious to show his stuff, as if he sensed how grave the situation had become. Ross reached behind his head and filled his hand with the smooth handgrip of Double-Twelve. As Ross approached the street, a Union soldier holding a rifled musket jumped in his path to block his escape. He leveled the musket at Ross while yelling, "Stop or I'll fire!" Ross urged Prince on at a faster clip as he pointed the black stallion directly at the soldier.

A flash blossomed from the Yankee soldier's rifle and Ross heard the bullet whir past his ear like a mad hornet. He was just a few feet from the soldier now and closing fast as the Yankee's eyes widened. As the soldier danced out of danger Ross leveled Double-Twelve at point-blank range. The shotgun bucked in his hands as the blast turned the soldier's face into a mask of twisted flesh.

Prince jittered to the side as he turned. Down the street they raced at a breakneck pace. Three blocks later a pair of Union cavalry troopers moved to block his path. Ross bore down on the two and as he drew near cut Prince of Heaven to run behind the rear of one horse and the storefronts on the right. He felt Prince lurch onto the boardwalk and felt his hooves slipping on the hard boards. Miraculously, he skated the stallion safely around the blocking riders. As he drew abreast of the riders, Ross touched off the second of Double-Twelve's barrels. One soldier pitched forward falling dead in the street as his heart pumped pulsating blood through the sieve-like buckshot holes punched through his back.

The other trooper whirled his horse in pursuit as Prince of Heaven turned on his power. On they raced through the streets while Ross stowed Double-Twelve back into its special scabbard. Ross drew a pistol from his holster and returned fire at the chasing bluecoat. Both shots missed. Behind him he heard the echo of yet another shot. He watched a pistol ball splinter a shop sign near his head. Involuntarily Ross ducked his head from the shot. On he raced until he approached the sentry post at the edge of town. By now the soldier pursuing him was falling back, his horse unable to keep up with the raw speed and power of Prince of Heaven.

Ross pulled up hard on the reins and pitched Prince into a tight turn around the barricade. As he spurred past the Sentry he heard a surprised shout, "Halt! Halt I say!" A loud boom from a musket sent another minie ball whizzing dangerously close to Ross's head.

They were past Lexington's outskirts now and galloping into the country—his country. Ross Kimbrough was raised in this area and he knew it like the back of his hand. If they didn't catch him soon they never would. He guided the horse into the woods and onto a little known trail.

He had done it! He had killed Benton Bartok and made good his escape. It wouldn't bring his parents back, but it was satisfying to exact revenge against the black-hearted tyrant and end his terrifying harassment of Lafayette Country.

17

Assault on Helena

Evan Stryker knew something big was brewing as he watched the arrival of the department commander of the Trans-Mississippi region, General Theophilus Holmes, at the Jacksonport headquarters of General John Marmaduke and Colonel Jo Shelby. During the morning, Generals James F. Fagan, Sterling Price, and Marsh Walker joined their commanding general.

Captain Evan Stryker knew these developments pointed toward a new campaign against the enemy. The realization did nothing to ease his mind as he shuffled slowly along toward headquarters. For the last three days he had been constantly in the saddle delivering orders and dispatches to the scattered commands asking them to concentrate near Jacksonport. He still felt worn-out from the hard-riding raid on Cape Girardeau in Southeast Missouri and he had enjoyed precious little time to recover his rest.

During the Cape Girardeau raid, Marmaduke and

Shelby's men had fought a small battle, and were nearly cut off by superior forces. By a daring escape in the night, the Confederate cavalry had managed a river crossing on a hastily erected floating bridge across the St. Francis River. The quick ingenuity exhibited by the Rebel cavalry had allowed them to return intact to Jacksonport, Arkansas. The raid had proved to be both exhaustive and ineffective and they had been lucky to escape a dangerous trap.

All this was fresh on his mind as Captain Stryker joined the generals at the staff meeting. When the generals finished haggling out the details of the new campaign it was a sure bet they would need Shelby's staff officers to deliver dispatches and orders. Evan was ushered into the conference room and settled himself into a chair near the back wall. Hopefully, he wouldn't draw too much attention at the back of the room.

The meeting was called to order by General Theophilus H. Holmes, the regional commander. The heavy, slow-moving old soldier stood stoop-shouldered before his high-ranking officers and their gathered staffs. "Gentlemen, I know you've been pushing me for a long time to attack Helena. I have been reluctant to do so for fear we would fight overwhelming numbers." General Holmes' voice seemed unnaturally loud as it echoed off the walls of the room. The general was hard of hearing and he spoke loudly to compensate for his loss. The old soldier clasped his hands tightly behind his back as he spoke, which exaggerated the immense girth of his stomach. "The situation has improved over the last few months and I have decided to attack. If we can capture Helena, we can interrupt navigation of the Mississippi River and lower the supply of Union troops available to attack Vicksburg."

General Holmes let his eyes sweep over the officers gathered in the room as he continued, "If we can open a third front, perhaps we can draw attacking troops away from Pemberton's battered Vicksburg defenders." He paused to listen for a response.

General Shelby rose from his chair. "General, I've been pushing for this attack for months, but Vicksburg is on the edge of surrender. I seriously doubt they can hold out much longer. I don't see how an attack at this late date will change anything." Shelby glanced around the room at his fellow officers. "As you know the rains have been incessant. They will hamper our movements and Helena is heavily fortified."

"I agree with you, Colonel Shelby, the road conditions are poor at best and it may very well be too late to save Vicksburg, but we must do something."

Shelby glared at his commanding officer. For months he had badgered the old fool to attack Helena, and now when it was nearly too late to do any good, Holmes was considering the attack. Shelby replied, "I just want it on the record that I advised making this attack months ago when it could have really made a difference for the Vicksburg defenders. I fear an attack now will be too little, too late. I am forced to agree we must do something—even if our odds of success remain low. General Pemberton and his command deserve any support we can give them."

General Sterling Price, recently returned from commanding Missouri troops east of the Mississippi River, rose from his chair. "I agree with your comments Colonel Shelby, but we can't change the past. I think we all agree an attack should be attempted even if it might fail. What we must do now is formulate our attack and get on with it."

Evan listened carefully while the officers debated the routes of attack. They finally hammered out a plan which, if followed carefully, might have a chance of success. Once the decision to attack was made, the officers gathered around a large map laid out on a table. There they planned their attack routes.

According to the reports brought in by the scouts and the Southern spy network, the town was well fortified. To the south of town on Hindman Hill, a fort armed with four large Parrott cannons guarded the approaches. In front of the fort, the Union forces had dug rifle pits and filled them with infantry. The plan specified that General Fagan would attack from the south against the fort and rifle pits protecting Hindman Hill.

The Graveyard Fort, named after the hill it was situated on, held three large siege guns and commanded the center of the Yankee defenses. Rifle pits covered the approaches to Graveyard Fort. General Sterling Price's command would attack the center and try to capture Graveyard Hill.

Fort Soloman, armed with three large-bore Parrott rifled cannons, guarded Helena from the north. Fort Soloman's defenses were also strengthened by a net of interconnecting rifle pits and trenches. General Marmaduke would lead the attack against Fort Soloman from the north. The plan called for General Marsh Walker to place his men between Marmaduke and the banks of the Mississippi River. Once in position, General Walker would lead the attack on Fort Soloman's rifle pits while Marmaduke's men concentrated on Fort Soloman.

Coordination of the attacks would be necessary if any of them hoped to succeed. All units were to attack at sunrise and continue until the victory was complete. Success depended on a coordinated attack. Once the outside defenses collapsed, a secondary attack would be launched from all sides simultaneously against Fort Curtis, located in the center of Helena, Arkansas.

Fort Curtis, a large square redoubt armed with twenty large Parrott cannons, stood in the center of the city. From its brooding walls, bristling with large bore cannons, it could hammer out massive fire support to all the adjacent outlying forts. Concentric rings of casemates, rifle pits, and wooden spiked abatis surrounded and protected Fort

Curtis. To succeed, the Rebels would need a carefully coordinated attack on the outer forts and a bit of luck to even
reach Fort Curtis. Marching orders were issued and the officers disbursed to return to their commands.

Ross Kimbrough stared across the muddy, swollen stream.
It was his job as head of the scouts to find the best and
quickest route to Helena, Arkansas, and this stream was
just one more of the many obstacles they had crossed today. Ross studied the skies overhead and watched thick,
gunmetal gray clouds scudding across the skyline, dump-
ing fresh rain to slow their progress. Ross felt a shiver run
through him despite it being the middle of summer. Everything he owned was wet and he was soaked through to the
bone. He eased his horse into the raging torrent until the
muddy water swirled around his saddle and filled his boots
again with water. He held his cartridge box and ammunition as high as he could, trying to keep his gunpowder dry.
After a few harrowing moments Prince of Heaven found
purchase in the muddy bottom and climbed out on the far
shore. Ross pulled aside and watched other troopers cross.
   They had fought these rains for three days. Twice they
had set up campsites only to have them flooded by morning. Little creeks and streams were becoming as wide as
rivers and treacherous to cross.
   The infantry fought its way through mud and water, at
times walking chest-deep in the muck. The cavalry fared
better only because they rode their horses and didn't have
to walk in the sticky, clinging mud. Despite their advantage, the cavalry troopers were coated with the mud
thrown up by the horses' hooves directly in front of them.
   Water ran down the spines of the soldiers, soaking beneath slickers and coats and chilling the men. Rain stung
their eyes and filled their boots, adding to their discomfort.
Blisters quickly formed where the wet leather rubbed
against their feet.

Ross ducked his head involuntarily as a loud thunderbolt cracked across the sky and lit the scene like a photographer's flash powder. The sky rumbled and rolled as the sound echoed off the countryside. The din reminded Ross of a great artillery duel, only fought in the sky.

As he rode, his mind wandered and he recalled his trip of revenge to Missouri. He remembered with satisfaction watching his shot strike home and Major Benton Bartok falling out of the saddle. The escape had been dangerous. He had ridden until exhaustion had overtaken him. He holed up in the wilds of the Sniabar region for two days and slept. Once rested, he began his travels south to rejoin Shelby's brigade. He regained his command of Shelby's scouts after the army returned from the Cape Girardeau raid.

Ross knew they must fight the elements and the enemy if this attack on Helena was to succeed. Riders toughened by months of campaigning found themselves blistered and sore from the constant friction of wet wool rubbing against the saddles. The troopers rode, shoulders hunched against the sheets of rain, silent in their misery.

For Calvin Kimbrough and the artillery it was much worse. The cannons became mired in the mud. Often the artillerymen would have to dismount to help push or pull a cannon or ammunition wagon out of a mud hole. At times the horses would have to be double-teamed to pull each cannon through a particularly tough stretch. Progress was slow and, because of it, the enemy knew they were coming and were prepared.

Ross led his troopers cautiously along the route of march. He had to guard against leading Shelby's men into an ambush. As they neared a bend in the road, Ross noticed movement. He pulled his hand up and motioned for a halt. Jonas Starke and Rube Anderson swung around the bend, riding hell-bent-for-leather toward them. The two scouts slid their horses to a stop near Ross.

"What's up, Jonas?"

"We've been up the road apiece, Ross, and the Yankees have been busy. They've felled trees across the road for a couple of miles."

"Can we get our columns through?"

"I reckon we can, Lieutenant, but it's gonna be slow goin'. We'll need to get some squads up here towin' and choppin' trees out of the way. I don't see how we're gonna get wagons and artillery through that mess."

Ross looked at his soggy scouts sitting before him. They were already pushed to the limit, but they would have to do more. "I'll take the lead with the rest of the scouts. Jonas, I want you to ride back and let General Marmaduke and Colonel Shelby know what we face ahead of us. Ask them to send engineers and men equipped with ropes and axes up here right away. We need help to clear the roads. If I know Colonel Shelby, he'll work us all night to reach our attack point on time."

Jonas nodded his head, understanding the importance of the information he was carrying, and spurred toward the rear.

Ross led his scouts forward. He set to work immediately trying to find ways to move around obstructions, while clearing those that could be moved easily. In a short time they were joined by the advanced units of Shelby's brigade. The added manpower was helpful, but the going remained slow and tedious. Jo Shelby reached the front and held a quick conference. Captain Waters, the leading engineer, studied the tangle of trees blocking the road to Helena. "Colonel, maybe we should leave the artillery behind. If we try to bring them through this mess we might be late for the scheduled attack."

Shelby's face contorted in rage. "I'll be damned if I'm going into battle without my artillery. I want these cannons on the battlefield in time for the fight. I don't care how you do it. Do you understand, Captain?"

Waters looked at his commander. "Yes, sir! We'll get them there if we have to carry them."

"See to it, Captain. When we attack at sunrise I want to see Collins' battery shelling the enemy."

The men worked all night, but it was impossible to clear all the obstructions. Many ambulances and extra ammunition wagons had to be left behind. Postletwait, the brown bear cub, stayed with those left behind, napping under the protection of a convenient ammunition wagon.

Calvin Kimbrough felt bone weary from the long night of pushing and pulling his cannon over obstacles and mud. He leaned against the cannon, one hand resting on the steel rim of a cannon wheel and the other on the cannon breech, as he studied the battlefield. False dawn cast new light across the terrain. Little by little, he was beginning to make out the panorama stretched before him. Shelby's brigade was situated on a narrow ridge running directly toward the earthen casemates of Fort Soloman. As the light began to filter through the vast veil of fog whirling and twirling off the mighty Mississippi River, Calvin could see the foreboding network of rifle pits, casemates, and cannons awaiting them. He felt a shiver run through him as he stared at the fortifications. As the sunrise broke through, he noticed the dark shape of a Yankee ironclad as it drifted down the river, escorting a Union troop ship. Out of the ironclad's stacks poured coal black smoke hung low and drifted, swirling along the water. The ship's deck swarmed with troops wearing Union blue.

From across the battlefield to the south, musketfire and the boom of Union cannons from the fort on Hindman Hill echoed to the men on the ridge as General Fagan opened his assault.

Colonel Shelby, standing near Collins' battery, issued his order. "Lieutenant Collins, open fire on the troop transport."

"Yes, suh!" Richard Collins turned toward his men. "Collins' Battery, prepare to engage the enemy. Fire at will at the troop ship."

Calvin stepped forward and quickly aimed the cannon, leading the bow of the troop ship. He stepped back from the barrel. When the piece was primed and Delmar Pickett nodded he was ready, Calvin gave the order, "Fire!" Delmar yanked the lanyard, and the cannon roared to life. Flames leapt from the end of the barrel as the acrid black powder smoke drifted on the wind. Calvin kept careful sight on the flight of the cannonball. The other guns from Collins' battery opened within seconds of Calvin's crew. He watched as a geyser of water gushed upward from the impact of their cannonball, barely missing the ship. They continued to load and fire as fast as possible.

In minutes, the men on the tinclad gunboat, *Tyler*, opened with return fire. Ross could hear the distant booming echoing off the water as the *Tyler* opened with its first salvo. He flinched as the shells from the *Tyler* shrieked overhead, leaving a dreadful whine behind in their passing. The large-bore projectiles rocked the earth and tossed dirt and debris into the air. Calvin pulled his head down into his hunched-up shoulders. He felt like a startled turtle trying to pull his head into his shell. Only problem was he didn't have a shell to hide inside.

The duel continued. At least one shot struck the troop ship before she turned her bow to run with the river's flow and drift out of range. The men shifted their fire to Fort Soloman. The uneven duel continued.

Above the roar of battle, Shelby's brigade heard the attack of General Price's command commence on Graveyard Fort on the west side of the battlefield. The three large cannons in the fort mowed large gaps into the line of onrushing Confederate soldiers. The Confederates attacked only with musket and pistol fire because their cannons had been left behind on the obstructed roads. Despite the noise and roar of battle, Calvin felt **proud**. Collins' battery stood alone as the only Rebel artillery battery upon the entire battlefield.

The attack was commencing south and west at sunrise, but on the north side General Marmaduke's command stood in line, waiting for orders to advance. They stood and watched the duel between the Union forts and ships and the Rebel attackers supported by Collins' lone battery.

Evan Stryker tried desperately to keep up with Colonel Jo Shelby. Shelby already had one horse shot out from beneath him, and was mounted on his second sorrel of the day. Evan followed his commander as they approached General Marmaduke and his staff at a gallop. The general stood near his horse while observing the battlefield through binoculars. Shelby reined his horse in before General Marmaduke. "General, when will you issue my order to attack?" Shelby asked.

Evan pulled his horse alongside Colonel Shelby. He looked down at the general and snapped off a quick salute. Evan sat silently as he listened to the conversation.

General Marmaduke lowered his field glasses. His face showed the fatigue of the night. "Colonel Shelby, I will give you the order to advance when I feel it is the proper time to attack and not a minute before."

Jo Shelby's sorrel sidestepped as a cannon shell from Fort Soloman ripped through the trees behind them. "Generals Fagan and Price have begun their attacks. They need our support."

The muscles along Marmaduke's thin cheeks tightened as his face flushed with anger. "I am well aware of the attacks, Colonel. We can't begin our attack until General Walker advances along the river. If we march in there without his support, my men will be flanked. They'll shoot enfilading fire down our ranks. No, sir! It would be a massacre to advance our men without support from General Walker."

Shelby tried to remain calm. The battle light glowed in his eyes and he desperately wanted to join the attack. "If we don't advance, General Price will be flanked and the Union army will concentrate all the guns in Fort Curtis on the attackers." His anger and frustration rising, Shelby shouted, "They will be repulsed, sir!"

"Damn you, Shelby! I know we need to attack. I've already sent two of my staff officers requesting Walker to attack immediately. They have not returned. Until I give the order, I want your men to wait."

Shelby's eyes narrowed as he listened to his commanding officer. "I want it shown on the official records and I will place it in my battlefield report that I personally requested permission to attack at sunrise."

"You shall have it, Jo. If Walker doesn't advance soon, I'll kill him myself. By heaven, I'll not destroy my entire brigade on a useless attack because we lacked proper support."

Shelby saluted briskly. "I'll be with my men, General." He pulled the sorrel around and dug his spurs deep. Urged on, the horse sprinted toward the lines of dismounted Confederate cavalry.

Colonel Shelby rode to the ridge near Collins' Battery. Anxious to attack, he ordered Ben Elliott's company to advance a skirmish line in front of the brigade. A six-gun mounted battery of Union troops rode out from Helena to silence Collins' battery. Calvin watched as the horses raced down the road then turned out into the field. Quickly the Union soldiers worked to place the cannons.

Shelby issued orders for Dick Collins to direct his fire at the field battery instead of Fort Soloman. Calvin made the necessary adjustments to his piece, then fired. The first shot fell short, kicking a rooster tail of dirt into the air. The second shot shattered a wheel on an enemy cannon, taking out several crew members. A shout rose from Calvin's crew as they celebrated hitting the target. The celebration was short-lived as the remaining guns of the Yankee battery began to return fire.

Another horse was killed beneath Jo Shelby. Quickly, another sorrel was brought forward for the commander, who, as soon as he was mounted, positioned himself near Dick Collins.

Evan Stryker watched as suddenly Colonel Shelby lurched in the saddle. He reeled, nearly falling, before regaining his seat. Crimson blood flowed down his hand and dripped on his horse. The horse rolled its eyes at the smell of blood and skittered sideways before Shelby got him under control. A minie ball shot by a Union soldier had shattered Joe Shelby's wrist.

Evan spurred his horse near Shelby and helped him regain control of his horse. "Colonel, I need to take you to a surgeon."

"No, Captain, I won't leave my men."

"Colonel, you're hit bad in the arm and, if we don't do something, you'll bleed to death."

"We could be ordered to attack at any moment. I'm needed here."

"Beg your pardon, sir, but if you let yourself bleed to death, this brigade is gonna have to do without you anyway."

Shelby looked down at his arm. The pain was intense, but he was reluctant to leave his post. "I suppose you have a point, Captain. I'll go see the surgeon, but I'll be back." He looked over at Dick Collins. "Get word to Colonel Thompson. Tell him I've been wounded. He's in command of the brigade until I return."

"Yes, suh, I'll send a man to tell him. Take care of yourself, Jo."

Jo Shelby overlooked the use of his first name. "Give 'em hell, Dick. I'll be back."

Evan rode close to the colonel, ready to support him should he faint, escorting him to a hastily set up field hospital to the rear. At their arrival, hospital attendants helped their commander carefully from the saddle.

Doctor Webb, chief surgeon of Jackman's brigade, began his examination. "This wrist is in bad shape, Colonel. I need to operate on it and set the bones."

"When the battle is over, Doc, you can do with me what you will, but I've still got a brigade to direct and a battle to fight."

"Colonel Shelby, with this wrist shattered like it is, you have no business trying to do anything. The bullet went clean through, and by some luck the bullet missed your main artery, but it is a serious wound. You could lose your hand. If you don't take care of it, you could bleed to death."

"Look, Doc, there's a battle going on. I've got men up there dying or wounded worse than I am. They need me to lead this brigade, and by heaven, I'm gonna do it."

"All right, I guess there's no use tryin' to talk sense into you. You're bullheaded enough to do what you want anyway. I'll try to stop the bleeding by applying a tight bandage. We'll have to make you a sling for that arm." He paused as he looked Jo Shelby in the eyes. "Jo, I need to operate on this arm soon."

"It'll have to wait until the battle is over." Jo Shelby fidgeted. "Hurry it up, Doc, that's an order!"

Doctor Webb shook his head sadly. "You're a stubborn man, Colonel, but you're the boss."

Evan watched as the doctor carefully wrapped Shelby's wrist with bandages. He noticed the colonel clench his teeth as he fought off the pain.

Calvin Kimbrough continued to work feverishly at his cannon. The melding sounds of battle filled his senses. It seemed the entire Yankee army was shooting at them.

Calvin understood, for being the only Confederate artillery on the field made them a high priority target for the enemy. The duel with the Union field battery on the plain below continued. The *Tyler* had rejoined the fight and opened up with her massive shells on Price's troops assaulting the Graveyard Fort. The guns of Fort Soloman added their strength to the Union field battery dueling with Collins' guns. Union infantry kept up a continuous musket barrage from the rifle pits at Marmaduke's division and Collins' battery.

Calvin lost all sense of time. They might have been fighting for two hours or for four. The crew next to his already had most of its members down, either killed or wounded. Acting quartermaster Major Smith of Marmaduke's brigade had just delivered more ammunition for the little battery. At the next cannon the gunner was wounded and Major Smith took his place. Calvin glanced over and smiled in appreciation. The major returned his smile, then turned and aimed. Calvin was still watching when a minie bullet struck the major in the chest. The blow sent him reeling as he pitched over onto his back.

Calvin wanted to leave his gun to see Major Smith, but kept to his duty. Lieutenant Collins bent over the major, shook his head after a few minutes, and walked away.

Calvin caught the arm of Dick Collins as he walked by. "Lieutenant, how is the major?"

Lieutenant Collins pulled his arm free and glared solemnly at Calvin. "He's dead. shot clean through the heart."

"You gonna leave him there?"

"There isn't anything we can do for him. He damn sure won't be the last man to die today."

Calvin turned back to his cannon. He sighted the reloaded piece on the Union battery. "This one is for you, Major." Calvin looked over at Delmar. "Fire!" The cannon bucked upward.

The heat of the summer day was building quickly. Calvin wiped a dirty hand across his sweaty brow. He squinted into the sun, nearly straight above him. It occurred to him it must be nearly noon. The sun was partially obscured by clouds of black powder smoke drifting across the sky from the battle raging below. The whole scene took on a surreal appearance as the sun fought its way through the haze, casting a ghastly hue upon the land.

Calvin watched as Price's men, in a triumphant charge, carried the works of the Graveyard Fort, sweeping the rifle pits before them. They immediately began to attack the dark citadel of Fort Curtis. The fort concentrated its cannons on General Price's brigades. The joy of the moment quickly turned to agony. Calvin watched as General Fagan's attack was repulsed by the fort on Hindman Hill. As the survivors of the attack streamed to the rear, Fort Hindman opened fire on the flanks of General Price's Confederates now engaging Fort Curtis. The combined crossfire from the two forts blew huge gaps into the ranks of the proud Rebel soldiers. Calvin felt his stomach tighten as he watched the slaughter on the hills and plains of Helena. Moments later, as his crew was reloading the cannon, Calvin felt the force of a great concussion as he was hurled head over heels through the air. He hit with mind numbing force: the air crushed from him. The sunlight dimmed and the sounds of battle seemed far, far away as everything faded to black.

18

Safe Haven

Ross Kimbrough spent a harrowing day in front of the brigade searching for any weakness the Rebels could exploit when the order to attack finally came. He traveled all around Rightor Hill within the shadows of Fort Soloman. Still General Marsh Walker's men did not advance. Without their support attack would be a disaster. Ross had seen enough to know the extended rifle pits and trenches would leave them open to flanking fire. The whole brigade had sought whatever cover they could find as they lay on the ground and waited in ranks for the order to attack the ominous fortress before them. Ross had watched the progress of the battle and, before the attack even began, he knew it was doomed to failure. Generals Price and Fagan's men were being slaughtered in their wild attack upon the fortifications. His only joy all day had been observing General Price's men carry the Grave-yard Fort and seeing them turn the big Yankee cannons on

Fort Curtis. Still, three cannons were no match against the twenty in Fort Curtis. He watched in dismay as General Marsh Walker began to withdraw his command from the field without an attempt at attack.

Ross knew there was nothing to do but try to work his way back and report to Colonel Shelby. He moved cautiously, tree to tree and rock to rock, until he regained the Rebel lines.

Ross crossed through the ranks of Shelby's dismounted troopers when he saw Colonel Shelby, accompanied by Evan Stryker, riding behind the lines and shouting at his troops. Ross was surprised to see that Colonel Shelby's arm was in a sling, from which protruded a hand wrapped in blood-soaked bandages. Even wounded, Shelby handled the big sorrel horse with ease. "Volunteers to save the battery. Shelby's brigade has never lost a battery, and with God's help it never shall! Volunteers, come forward," the colonel shouted above the din of battle. Ross, and more than a hundred others, stood to volunteer.

"Fifty, only fifty," ordered Shelby. "You go with them Colonel Gilkey. Bring the battery safely with you or remain yourself."

"Yes, suh," replied Colonel Gilkey.

Ross followed Colonel Gilkey to the battery. As they approached, Ross could see how much abuse the battery had taken. Men were scattered on the ground like so many broken dolls. Dead men, horribly mangled by cannon projectiles and bullets, lay in bloody confusion. Wounded were left where they fell, while some managed to crawl away. The carriages and wheels of most of the cannon were heavily bullet riddled. All the horses used to pull the cannons were dead in their traces. The survivors of the battery were working as if they were machines. Black powder grit and grime streaked their faces and hands. They were a ghastly looking crew, lost amid the murky, swirling powder mist. Above it all, flapping defiantly in the wind, stood the tattered, bullet-rent flag of Collins' battery.

The first men to reach the battery attempted to remove the harnesses from the dead horses. In most cases the traces simply had to be cut because they were pinned under the carcasses of the dead animals.

Ross's heart began to pound and he felt fear rising within him when he could not spot Calvin among the active members of the battery. Ross moved toward a battery member he recognized and shouted above the roar of battle swirling around them, "Delmar, where's Calvin?"

He's over there I think, Ross." Delmar pointed to the side and rear of the battery. "Last time I saw him, we took a hit from an exploding shell fired from Fort Soloman. Blew the bloody hell out of us! When the dust settled I didn't see Calvin."

Ross moved quickly among the many bodies lying to the rear of the battery. The first body he turned over had its guts hanging out of a bloody hole in the abdomen. Ross felt sick, but was relieved to see it wasn't Calvin. The next one he tried was his brother.

Calvin lay limp as a rag doll as Ross flopped him over onto his back. Ross tried shaking him, but there was no response. Relief flooded through Ross when he felt a steady heartbeat throbbing against his fingers, resting against Calvin's neck. Ross searched Calvin for wounds, but could only find a trickle of blood from his ears. Ross grabbed one arm and one leg and slung Calvin over his shoulders in a fireman's carry. He moved steadily under his heavy burden toward the horse holders hidden behind the battery's position. He lifted Calvin into the saddle of Red Roses with the aid of one of the horse holders. Ross swung himself up behind Calvin and held him in the saddle.

He rode Red Roses toward the position where he had left Prince of Heaven. He was glad to see the powerfully built black stallion was still okay. He'd ridden Prince of Heaven since Katlin Thomas had offered the use of the horse for the duration of the war back at Batesville, Arkansas. Ross recalled his own wounding and the loss of Sultan at the battle of Prairie Grove. No horse would ever take Sultan's place in Ross's heart, but he trusted Prince.

Ross carefully tied the lead reins of Prince of Heaven to Red Roses' saddle. He wheeled Red Roses around and headed toward the road away from the battle. General Marmaduke had issued orders to retreat and hundreds of mounted soldiers swarmed over the road. The confusion of milling horses and wagons filled the road as the troops fled the disaster behind them. Wounded soldiers were strung across their saddles or were leaning low over the necks of their mounts. Few wagons had made it this far, and the few that had, were quickly filled by wounded soldiers.

Ross's arms began to ache from the fatigue and strain of keeping Calvin from falling. Still, Ross rode onward, balancing his unconscious brother in the saddle. In his mind he tried to formulate a plan. He couldn't continue this way much longer, but he refused to abandon Calvin.

As Ross rode, the area began to look more familiar to him. The farther he went, the more sure he became of his location. Not far from this road should be the home of Dee Ann Farley.

Ross thought back on the last time he had seen her. Ross and his scouts had caught a group of guerillas busy raping the women in her home. Those surviving Ross's fury had been shot by firing squad. He wondered if she would remember him now when he needed help.

Ross spurred Red Roses forward as he turned off the main road and headed for the cabin. The deepening gloom of a sweltering summer evening pressed in upon him. Fatigue from battle and the long struggle of the night march before the battle closed in on him.

Finally, Ross sighted a cabin that looked familiar. He halted for a few moments to study the house. Smoke poured from the chimney and a few of the windows stood open to allow the escape of the summer's heat. In other circumstances Ross would be more cautious, but this time he rode Red Roses directly to the front gate and halted. He had barely stopped his horses when the barrels of a shotgun protruded through the window. A woman's voice boomed out clearly, "Halt right there, mister. Move and I'll empty your saddle."

Ross strained his eyes against the gloom. "Are you Dee Ann Farley?" Ross asked.

"Might be; who wants to know?"

"I don't know if you'll recognize me, ma'am. I was here about a year ago. I rode with Shelby's company."

There was a pause, then the barrel retracted from the window. "Stay there, mister. I'm a-comin' out so I can get a better look at ya."

He sat motionless as he watched her move slowly from the cabin, holding the shotgun waist-high and aimed at him. Standing in the doorway he could see the form of a boy about eight years old covering him with a pistol. "Ma'am, I trust you not to do anything foolish while you're aiming that shotgun in my direction, but I'd feel a sight better if you'd tell your boy to point his gun somewhere else."

The woman edged slowly toward him. Dark brown hair flowed over her shoulders and her day dress hugged her body closely. "My boy knows how to use a gun, mister, and he'll prove it to you if ya try anything."

"Mrs. Farley, I'd appreciate it if you'd help me with my brother. My arms feel like they're about to fall off."

"You hold it right there until I get a good look at ya." As she moved closer, she halted. A slow grin of recognition broke across her face. "I remember you. You're the fella with the sawed-off shotgun that saved me." She set the shotgun down and leaned it against the weathered picket fence. "Jimmy put the gun down an' give me a hand out here."

She moved forward and grabbed Calvin. Jimmy ran up and tried to help as they lowered the limp body to the ground. Mrs. Farley stared at Calvin as he lay immobile before them. "What's the matter with him?"

"I'm not sure. He was near a large explosion on the battlefield at Helena. When I found him, he was unconscious. I can't see any wounds on him, but I did find blood coming from his ears. He might have internal injuries we can't see."

She felt his wrist, then lay her head on his chest. "His heart sounds strong and his pulse feels good. That's a good sign."

Ross swung stiffly out of the saddle and handed the reins to Jimmy. He walked around the horses and knelt beside Calvin.

Mrs. Farley looked up at Ross. "I'd appreciate it if you'd call me Dee Ann. It won't sound so formal." She squinted one eye as she looked at him. "Your name is Ross, ain't it?"

Ross smiled as he looked at her face. She was not pretty; in fact, she was rather plain looking. She had the look of a farmer's wife, no stranger to a harsh life. He was pleased she remembered him. "Yes, Lieutenant Ross Kimbrough of Jo Shelby's brigade. This is my brother, Calvin."

"Well you sure 'nuff saved my bacon the last time you came along. Now it's my turn to repay the favor. Let's move him inside."

They lifted Calvin between them, each of them putting one of his arms around their necks. "Let's put him in my bed," Dee Ann said as she lurched toward the door to her bedroom. "Over this way."

Ross began to protest, "Dee Ann, where will you sleep if we put him in your bed?"

Dee Ann strained to support Calvin's weight. "I'll sleep with him. He ain't gonna try nothin' in his condition. Besides, we don't have extra beds."

Ross hesitated as he resisted the move toward her bedroom. "I'm not sure this is proper."

"If'n ya don't mind, I'd like to lay him down before we talk about it. Danged if he ain't gettin' heavy!"

Ross stopped fighting her as they carried Calvin to the bed, where they laid Calvin on his back, his feet still touching the floor.

"Best start gettin' those boots off him. I don't allow men wearin' boots in my bed," said Dee Ann as she tugged at his belt. "We need to get these filthy clothes off him before I tuck him under my clean blankets."

Ross was stunned. "You aren't gonna take his clothes off, are you?"

She looked at Ross as if he were crazy. "You don't think I can clean him up with them on?"

"I . . . I guess not. But do you think you should?"

"Hell, Lieutenant, I'm a grow'd woman. I got two children, and you don't get them without bein' familiar with men. He don't have nothin' I ain't seen before." Her face grew tense. "Besides, he ain't in any shape to try anything." She yelled over her shoulder. "Jimmy, fetch me some water and put it on the fire to warm. I got some cleanin' to do."

Ross and Dee Ann worked as a team to remove Calvin's clothes and clean the dirt and grime from him. Once they were done she tucked Calvin beneath clean sheets and closed the door. Calvin's six foot three inch frame was so much longer than the bed his toes dangled over the edge.

Ross walked over to the fireplace and watched the flames dance on the logs. Dee Ann dried her hands on her apron. "How long has he been like this?"

"Just since I found him this afternoon."

"Well, I couldn't find any wounds on him, except the dried blood near his ears."

"One of his friends said he was near an explosion. I figure he has a concussion and probably ruptured eardrums. I just hope he doesn't have any internal injuries."

"It's in God's hands now. One thing for sure, he's gonna get better or he's gonna die, an' there ain't much we can do about it but wait an' see."

"I suppose you're right, but I don't draw much comfort from it."

"I wouldn't worry too much. He looks like a strong young man. How old is he?"

"He'll be twenty-one come August eighth."

"He looks as old as my husband Robert looked. The war has a way of aging a man." Dee Ann turned her gaze to the floor as a sad expression crossed her face.

"Pardon me, ma'am, but I'm not sure your husband would appreciate my brother in his bed."

"Don't worry yourself, Ross. My husband was killed at the battle of Corinth. He was dead when you were here before, but word hadn't reached me yet." Ross saw Dee Ann blinking away tears. "I hadn't seen him for a year before he went and got himself killed. I tried to talk him outa goin' to war, but he said it wouldn't be right lettin' others fight his fight for him."

"I'm sorry to hear your husband is dead, Dee Ann. I didn't know."

"That's all right, you had no way of knowin'." Dee Ann turned and faced him. "There wasn't any stoppin' Robert once he made up his mind. He talked about how the war was gonna be grand and glorious an' how he'd chase the Yankees clean outa the South in the first good fight. I guess it all was more excitin' to him than workin' on the farm and starin' at the backside of a pair of mules every day."

"I guess most of us expected the war to be different than it is."

"It musta seemed mighty important 'cause he didn't have any problem walkin' away an' leavin' me here alone to take care of this farm and the two youngin's, but we're still here. This place ain't much, but you an' your brother are welcome to such as I got."

"We surely appreciate your hospitality, Dee Ann. I don't know what to do about Calvin. I need to rejoin my brigade as soon as possible, but I hate to leave my brother."

"If you need to go on back, you just go on ahead. I'll hide your brother here an' look after him. If'n it wasn't for you, me an' my children would most likely be dead. I'm pleased to do what I can for him."

Ross listened as the door creaked open and the boy, Jimmy, walked in carrying his mother's shotgun. "Ma, I got the horses rubbed down and in the barn. I got your shotgun here, too. You left it by the fence."

"Thanks, son. I plum forgot all about my gun when we were takin' care of Mr. Kimbrough."

"He's a fine lookin' boy, ma'am."

Dee Ann smiled proudly. "He's been a mighty big help to me. He's the man of the house now that his daddy is gone. I guess he's had to grow up faster than most."

Ross watched as the boy hung the shotgun over the fireplace. "Yeah, I reckon you're right. This is the real tragedy of this war—what it does to the children."

"Before you came I was fixin' some stew. It oughta be done by now. If you'll pardon me, I'd like to clean up an' change before we have supper. I'll have Jimmy show you where you can wash up." Dee Ann turned to her son. "Jimmy, show Ross where he can clean up. Then get your sister up from her nap and clean yourself up for supper."

Jimmy smiled shyly at Ross. "Sure, I'll show him, Ma, but can't you get Debbie up? You know how she gets mad at me when I try to wake her up."

"If she give ya any trouble, you just tell her I'll paddle her little fanny.

'Yeah, Ma." Jimmy led the way to his room, where he had a pitcher of water and a washbowl on the dresser. Beside it lay a towel. "You can clean up in here. I'll go wake up Sis, then I'll clean up after you're done."

Ross washed as much of the grime off himself as he could. He took his uniform off and, with a washcloth, gave himself a good cleaning. A bath like this was better than none, and that's what he'd had for far too long. It amazed him how filthy the wash water became as he cleaned up. Later he joined Dee Ann and her children for supper.

When Ross stepped out of Jimmy's bedroom, he was amazed at Dee Ann's transformation. She was wearing a clean new dress. Her hair was freshly brushed and she looked better than he had ever seen her. She had the table set an she motioned for him to sit at the head of the table. Ross took in the fresh-baked aroma of bread and stew as he looked at the food spread before him. "That sure looks and smells better than what I'm used to in the army."

Dee Ann smiled. "It's a meat stew with fresh vegetables from our garden. I baked the bread this mornin' an' I just warmed it a little. I've got some butter an' a little honey you can spread on it."

"Ma'am, you didn't need to go to all this trouble."

"It wasn't any trouble. Besides, we don't get much company nowadays. It feels nice to have a man in the house again. I'd prefer it, Ross, if you'd call me Dee Ann."

Ross looked a little embarrassed as he helped himself to the stew and bread. He had to admit Dee Ann Farley cleaned up real nice. He realized he was enjoying himself. Here he was away from the war, in a comfortable home, and eating a good meal. It seemed he was a world apart from the death and destruction he had witnessed earlier in the day. The contrast between the two situations made them both seem unreal in comparison.

Ross still could remember how good Dee Ann Farley looked last time he was here and had stopped those men from raping her. He had tried not to notice, but after all, he was a man and it had been a long time since he had been with a woman. Try as he might, he was unable to keep himself from appreciating her body even as he watched her stab that butcher knife, over and over again, deep into the back of a rapist. The vision of her nude before he covered her up had burned its way into his memory like a picture. To this day, he could still recall those shapely legs, well muscled and toned from a life of work. If he closed his eyes, he could still picture her full but firm breasts and the soft, feminine curve of her back. He looked at her now, and tried to blink those visions out of his mind.

Dee Ann was obviously enjoying his company. She smiled often and chattered on about her life and the farm; much of it he let go in one ear and out the other. Now that his belly was full and he was sitting in a comfortable chair, the fatigue of the battle and the night march the night before came crashing down upon him. An uncontrollable weariness began to engulf him. He jerked awake and felt embarrassed for nearly falling asleep at the table.

Dee Ann started clearing away the dishes. At one point he was sure she deliberately rubbed her breasts against his shoulder as she reached for his empty plate. She lingered there longer than Ross felt was necessary, and he noticed a twinge of pleasure in his groin. "Ma'am', I . . . I mean Dee Ann, I'm sorry, but I'm very tired. Do you suppose you could show me where to sleep?"

"I guess you can sleep here on the couch. I hope you'll stay up a little longer. It's been so long since I enjoyed company."

Ross moved himself wearily to the couch and pulled his

boots off. He put them on the floor, then he leaned back for just a moment and closed his eyes to rest them. Soon he was snoring.

Dee Ann kept chattering away until she heard him snore, then realized with disappointment he was asleep. She shrugged her shoulders and went to fetch him a blanket, which she spread over the exhausted soldier. After putting her children to bed she slipped into her white, soft cotton nightgown. She studied the unconscious face of Calvin Kimbrough. Dee Ann found his lightly freckled face and his sandy, blond hair attractive. She leaned over and softly blew out the lamp beside the bed, then slipped in next to Calvin, turning her back to him and scooting back until they barely touched. When she closed her eyes it felt like the days before the war when she had her husband sleeping beside her. She liked the feel of a man in bed next to her, even if it was a stranger. She felt contented as the heat of his body seeped through her gown, warm against her skin. She listened to his breathing. It had been so long. . . . She felt contentment as she drifted off the sleep.

Calvin stirred. He heard a loud ringing in his ears and his head ached. It was pitch black when he opened his eyes. His eyes fought to adjust, but still everything remained black. He tried to figure out where he was, but his thinking was muddled. He moved his fingers and felt the unaccustomed softness of a bed beneath him. He listened, but could hear nothing over the ringing in his ears. "Am I dead?" he wondered. He tried moving his toes and he felt them wiggle. He tried to move his hands and one of them touched something soft and warm beside him. He stopped moving his hand and squeezed softly. The material was cottony. Beneath it he felt something warm and pliant. He rolled over quickly, straining in the darkness to see what was lying beside him. He yelled as he jerked around, startled and unsure of his surrounding. His hands quickly went to his temples as if to keep his head from exploding and he lay back in pain.

Dee Ann Farley was startled from a good dream by Calvin's yell and the sudden movement of the bed as Calvin jerked up, then fell back. She slipped from her side of the bed and moved around to the nightstand. Near the base of the lamp, she felt for matches. As her hands closed on one, she struck it on the lamp. She turned up the wick, spreading a soft, warm light throughout the room.

"I see you finally woke up, Calvin."

Calvin squinted his eyes as they tried to adjust to the light. "Where am I? Who are you?"

"I guess it would be surprising to wake up and find yourself in a strange bed. My name is Dee Ann Farley."

"Do I know you?"

"No, but your brother Ross does. He brought ya here."

"I don't understand. Is this a dream?" He rubbed his temples. "I don't think it can be, I hurt too much." He watched as Dee Ann shook her head no. Calvin said, "The last thing I can remember I was with my cannon crew firing on Helena. Where are they?"

"Last I heard, they were retreating toward Jacksonport. We heard they were marching to defend Little Rock."

"How long have I been here?"

"This is your third night." She walked over and sat next to him on the bed. "Your brother brought you here when you were knocked-out. He stayed all the next day, then left lookin' for your army this mornin'. My boy, Jimmy, hid your horse and has been takin' good care of him for you. He'll be ready to ride when you're up to it. Your brother saved my life once and I promised him I'd take real good care of ya and I will."

"It's very kind of you, ma'am, but would you mind if I ask you a personal question?"

She looked at him and smiled. "No, I don't mind."

"Well, I was kind of wondering how I got into this bed with you."

Dee Ann tried to control herself, but she began to smile before breaking into a laugh. She couldn't help herself once she saw that lost-little-boy look on Calvin's face. Here was a grown man who could stand up to a hail of bullets in a battle, yet was frightened to find himself alone with a strange woman. Once she regained control she explained, "We don't have any extra beds in the house. When Ross brought ya here, you was in bad shape. I thought it was best to put you in here. So, I took your clothes off, cleaned you up, and put ya to bed."

Up till then, Calvin had been so concerned with the pounding in his head he hadn't taken time to consider what he might be wearing. He pulled the blankets back a little, and looked down at his naked body. Embarrassed, he quickly pulled the blankets back up again. "Where's my clothes?"

Dee Ann smiled again. "Don't worry, I've washed 'em and put 'em in a drawer for ya." She chuckled again and said teasingly, "Don't worry, I ain't gonna hurt ya."

Calvin studied the woman more carefully. She was neither pretty, nor ugly. At best he would call her ordinary, a plain looking woman he guessed to be in her mid to late twenties. He knew from the deep suntan on her face she was no stranger to working in the fields. He admired the way her thick, brown hair cascaded over and around her shoulders. Whenever he didn't think she would notice, he let his eyes stray to her nightgown. He admired the way her body filled out the gown and he liked the nice jiggle to her breasts as she laughed and moved about the room. The gown she was wearing was a simple ankle-length cotton nightgown. There was just a small bit of lace around the collar.

If Calvin hadn't been in so much pain, he might have found his situation more stimulating. For now, he just felt dizzy. Everything she said had a strange echo to it as it she were speaking from within a barrel. "I'd feel more comfortable if I had some clothes on."

Dee Ann smiled again. "You are a shy one, ain't ya. Well, I suppose it would be more respectable if you had somethin' on." She walked over to a set of dresser drawers. She opened one and extracted a man's nightshirt. She turned and tossed it to him. "Here, wear this. It belonged to my husband. I figure it'll be a little short on you, but it should fit."

Calvin grabbed the nightshirt and then looked at her. "Did you say this is your husband's shirt?"

She smiled again. "Don't worry. The nightshirt belonged to my husband, but he won't be comin' back for it. He was killed over a year ago at the battle of Corinth." She paused as she noticed Calvin wasn't changing into the nightshirt. "I'll turn so I won't see you." She turned her back to him. "I don't mean to be forward, Calvin, but you ain't got nothin' I ain't seen before. After all, I was the one who bathed you. Besides, I got two kids an' I spent a few years bein' a wife to my Robert before he went an' got himself killed."

Calvin wriggled as quickly as he could into the nightshirt before she turned around.

"Are you ready?"

"Yes."

"Good," she said as she walked to the lamp and blew it out. As she moved around the bed in the dark she continued to talk. "It's late and we're both tired. We'll talk more in the mornin'." She pulled the blankets up around her again as she settled into the bed. "I'm glad you're awake. I 'spect it will take a few days before you're ready to travel again. Gonna be real nice to have someone around to talk to for a little while. It gets mighty lonely out here sometimes." She rolled over. "Good night."

Calvin lay still as the throbbing in his head continued.

In the dark of the room he could feel the soft heat of her body near him. There was a part of him that wanted to touch her, but the part of him in pain overruled any such notion. Never in his life had Calvin found himself in a similar situation. He supposed it would be better to handle it when he felt better. He knew he was lucky. Who would believe him if he told them that instead of being in a Yankee prisoner-of-war camp or field hospital he would be sharing a comfortable bed with a strange woman intent on taking care of him? He closed his eyes and drifted back to sleep.

Evan Stryker kept an eye on the wagon before him. Inside rode his commanding officer, Jo Shelby, and Doctor Webb. If he remembered this stretch of road correctly, they should be nearing Batesville, Arkansas.

Jo Shelby had enjoyed his stay in the small city during winter camp and when it was obvious he would need time to heal, he decided to return to Batesville.

All during the battle of Helena, Evan, as a staff officer, had accompanied the colonel. He had been there when Shelby had been wounded and there again as Jo Shelby personally directed the removal of Collins' battery from the field. Evan felt pride, as did the other soldiers of the brigade, that they were the only Confederate unit to get their artillery into the attack on Helena. Shelby had made sure they didn't leave Collins' battery when they left, too.

Now the beaten Confederate army was marching toward Jacksonport to lick its wounds. To make matters worse, in the last town they passed through they had received the sad news that Vicksburg had surrendered to the Yankees on the Fourth of July, the same day they tried their disastrous attack on Helena.

Evan could still picture the horror in his mind as he recalled how the attack of Generals Fagan and Price had failed. Nearly all Lewis' Confederate brigade under Price

was either killed or captured in the attack. Although they
had taken heavy fire, Marmaduke's command had never
charged because of lack of support from General Walker.
The waste of it all weighed heavily on Evan's mind. If he
could have somehow taken the wound in Jo Shelby's place
he knew he would've done it gladly. He was glad when
the colonel ordered him to accompany him to Batesville. It
would give him an opportunity, he hoped, to see Cassandra
again. The thought of her alone was enough to make him
smile. "Soon, Cassandra," he thought. "Soon I'll see you
again."

19

The Evil Still Lurks

Major Benton Bartok felt an intense, throbbing pain as though someone had driven a nail into his head. He opened his eyes slowly and stared up at the ceiling above him. He fought to focus his eyes, but the effort took nearly all of his concentration. Gradually the ceiling began to sharpen in detail as his eyes adjusted.

"I see you're awake, Major," an unfamiliar voice said, off to his left.

Benton heard the voice, but it had an echo to it, as though someone were shouting down an immense hallway. Bartok turned his head toward the voice. As he did, a wave of dizziness swept over him and the room seemed to spin. The major closed his eyes, took a deep breath, and prayed the room would quit spinning. Slowly he opened his eyes again and the world settled down. Lying on a cot near him was an unfamiliar Union soldier. "Where am I?" Benton asked.

"You're in the military hospital in Lexington."

"How did I get here?"

"Captain Shay and a few of your men brought you here. I'll get an orderly to fetch a doctor. I'm sure they'll want to know you're finally awake." The soldier turned his head and shouted at the door. "Orderly! Come Here!"

Moments later another soldier looked into the room. His clothing was slightly rumpled; he looked overworked and nearly worn out. "What is it now, Sergeant Adderly? I have other things to do than check on you every ten minutes."

"Get Doc Bradford, Major Bartok is awake."

The orderly standing in the door was so agitated by Adderly's shouting he hadn't noticed Bartok was conscious. The orderly studied Bartok for a moment. "How are you feeling, Major?"

Benton tried to swallow, but his mouth was too dry. "My head throbs." As if to show where it hurt the most, Benton reached his hand up and touched his head where the pain was the worst. He felt thick cotton gauze bandages and was momentarily surprised. For the first time, he realized he was injured. This was more than a simple headache.

"Take it easy, Major. I'll go get Doctor Bradford. He left instructions to let him know if there was any change in your condition."

A few minutes later Doctor Bradford sauntered into the room. "Major Bartok, I'm glad to see you've regained consciousness. You had us worried for a while." He approached the bed. "How do you feel?"

"I've got a splitting headache and when I turn my head I become dizzy. Would you please tell me how I ended up in here?"

"Captain Shay brought you into the hospital three days

ago. Someone tried to kill you. Fortunately for you, they didn't finish the job. When you first arrived you were losing a great deal of blood. A bullet passed through the right side of your scalp and cut a groove starting from the back of your head and stopped before it reached your temple. You were lucky it was a near miss and didn't penetrate your skull."

The doctor gave him a patronizing smile. "It looks like you will be left with a permanent scar. The blow to your head was powerful. The concussion caused by the bullet caused us serious concern."

"Why is my nose bandaged?" asked Bartok.

"When you fell off the horse you apparently landed on your face. Your nose was broken. I did my best to straighten it."

"I thank you, Doctor, for your efforts. May I ask you to send someone for Captain Shay? I would like to talk to him."

"Certainly, Major, I will send someone immediately. Is there anything else we can do for you?"

"Yes, I'd like something to drink and eat if you think it is all right."

"Very well, I'll check on you again later in the day. I'll go make the arrangements." The doctor turned and left the room.

Major Bartok had plenty of time to contemplate his situation as he tried to remember the events leading up to his waking up in the hospital. Despite his best efforts, he couldn't recall much.

Later Captain Shay arrived. "Good to see you awake, Major."

"I guess I'm lucky to be here, Elias. Please tell me what happened. I'm afraid I can't remember much."

"It all began when I brought you the reports of the ambush of Captain Anders' patrol. Do you remember it?"

A sickening feeling swept over Benton Bartok as the

words clicked in his mind. Now he remembered how shocked he was to hear about the death of Anders at the hands of Quantrill's men. Bob Anders was as close to being a true friend to Benton as anyone he'd ever known. "Yes, I remember. What happened next?"

"I believe we were on our way to get something to eat and drink. At the time we were both shook up."

"Then what happened?"

"Then someone opened up on us with a carbine from the hay loft in the stable across from your headquarters. You went down from the first shot and a second shot nearly hit me, but plowed into the door frame instead. Our soldiers rushed the stable, but by the time we arrived a man dressed in a Union cavalry trooper's uniform made his escape on a big, black horse. We tried to catch him, but with little luck. The assassin killed one soldier in the stable and two more as he dashed through the streets of Lexington. I organized a search party to hunt him down but we lost his trail in the region along Sniabar Creek."

Benton Bartok clenched his teeth and fists in anger at the news. It made him all the more angry when he realized how close the man had come to completing the job. "Did anyone recognize him?" Bartok asked.

"We questioned several people. One local thought he looked like a citizen named Ross Kimbrough, but he said it couldn't be because the last he had heard Kimbrough was serving with Shelby's brigade. The man he saw was wearing a Union trooper's uniform."

The name clicked in Bartok's mind. He had heard of Ross Kimbrough. It was the name of a brother of Jessie Kimbrough. The knowledge that Jessie had managed to escape his wrath after punching Benton in the nose over a dispute with Jessie's sister, Cassandra, still nagged at him. It was a great disappointment that he hadn't placed Jessie in front of a firing squad for his imprudent actions. He recalled with satisfaction how he had burned the Briarwood

Plantation and killed Jessie's father. Still the plan had not gone quite as he had hoped. He had planned to reduce Cassandra Kimbrough to poverty and then, when she was destitute, force her to submit to his wishes. Unfortunately, the girl escaped and headed south.

Certainly, Ross Kimbrough had a motive. He wouldn't know what the man looked like if he walked up to him and shook his hand. He was the only member of the family he had never met. If it were true, Ross had succeeded in penetrating the Union defenses. But Ross Kimbrough wasn't his only concern. Bob Anders and his patrol were ambushed and killed by William Clarke Quantrill and his men. Danger lurked all around him. He would have to make doubly sure no one got to him. If nothing else, he intended to come out of this war in one piece, rich beyond his wildest dreams. He could still reach his goal, but he must be cautious, very cautious indeed.

20

Like an Angry Wind

Billy Cahill smiled as he watched George Todd lead a band of heavily armed riders into camp. The men were a rugged, dangerous looking crew. He easily recognized many faces. There were men who had stayed the winter in Missouri and others who left Arkansas early and reached Missouri before Quantrill's return from Richmond. Ruthless fighters like Cole Younger and his brother Bob, Fletch Taylor, Archie Clements, David Poole, and Dick Yeager rode among them.

There were two more he recognized and they held his attention more than the others. The first was Bill Anderson—he was wearing a hat with the brim pinned back with a star. Bill was powerfully built, black bearded, and fierce looking with a darkly handsome face. Billy guessed him to be in his early twenties. Billy had fought alongside Anderson at Shawneetown, but there was a new twist to the man he had never seen before. His jaw was set with grim purpose and his pale blue eyes were those of a crazed killer.

The other rider was a thin, smooth-faced youth named Jesse James. Billy knew this younger brother of Frank James was near his age. He had seen him often. Jesse had wanted to join Quantrill for a long time, but his mother kept him home. Billy knew something must have happened for him to be riding with George Todd.

Frank James stood near Billy, joy spreading across his face as he watched his brother Jesse approach. It had been several months since last they had seen one another. When Jesse swung down out of the saddle, Frank embraced him. "Man, you're a sight for sore eyes, Jesse," Frank said as he pounded his brother on the back. "God, I've really missed ya, Jess. Looks like ya growed a foot, boy."

"Glad to have ya back, Frank. It's been a tough winter in these parts." Jesse pulled himself back so he could look in his brother's eyes. "Yankees have come to call several times. They nearly beat me to death tryin' to make me tell them where you were hiding. Next time they come callin' they tried to burn us out."

Frank's smile faded to a worried expression. "How's Ma? Is she okay?"

"Yeah, she's doing as fine as can be expected for all the blue bellies have put her through. She's stayin' with friends."

"When I saw you with Todd I knew there must have been trouble. I know she's always been dead set against you ridin' with the boys."

"She don't like it, but she told me it'd be better for me to hide in the bush than to get beat to death, or hung by the Jayhawkers or the militia."

"It's getting that bad, little brother?"

Jesse nodded in response. "General Thomas Ewing and his damn Yankee militia have been arresting mothers, sisters, and wives of anybody they suspect of riding with Quantrill. Hell, it doesn't even have to be true before they haul the women away and lock 'em up."

Anger burned in Frank's eyes as he followed Jesse over to the fire. They sat on a log next to Billy Cahill. Frank asked, "What do they intend to do with the women?"

Jesse prodded the fire with a stick, then looked up at his brother. "All kinds of rumors are floatin' around. Some say Ewing will ship the women to Arkansas hopin' the men will follow the women and leave Missouri. Others say they intend to hang the ladies or lock them in prison until the war is over. It's most likely they intend to use 'em for bait, trying to lure us into a trap when we try to rescue them."

"Does George Todd know where they are?"

"They shipped a few to Fort Leavenworth. They have another group locked in an old warehouse in Kansas City."

Billy Cahill had listened quietly to the exchange between the James boys, but now he had to ask, "Have you heard if they have my Ma under arrest?"

"I'm afraid so, Billy. I heard she's among the ladies kept prisoner in the warehouse in Kansas City."

"Is she all right?"

"Last we heard they were okay, but the building is really in bad shape. It should have been torn down a couple of years ago."

Frank stood nervously, his concern reflected in his face. "They haven't got Ma, have they?"

"Nah, I told ya she's hidin' out with friends."

A relieved expression flooded across Frank's face. He glanced about the camp till his eyes fell on Bill Anderson. "What's the matter with Bill? He's got a crazy look in his eyes like he's gone plum loco."

"Steer clear of him, Frank. Ever since they arrested his sisters Josephine, Mary, and Jennie and locked 'em in that warehouse he's turned into a killin' machine. Says he's gonna kill every Federal soldier and every Union man he can catch. He's surefire been doin' it, too. Him and David Poole went through the German settlements in Lafayette County about a week ago shootin' down any Union men they could find. The fellas are startin' to call him Bloody Bill."

"Is he crazy?"

"I don't think so. The boys I've been ridin' with think he's a natural born leader. He's been leadin' our band out of Clay County since he came back from Arkansas. George Todd has shared the leadership with Bloody Bill and he's earned it. Bloody Bill seems to have a knack for finding Yankees. He's come up with some great ideas, too. Hell, we ambushed a patrol of the Ninth Kansas Cavalry back in June in the very shadows of Kansas City. We killed over twenty of them and chased them clean into town, an' we didn't lose a man. He's plenty smart. He has us wear Yankee uniforms sometimes an' we approach Union patrols like we are on their side. When we're right on top of 'em we cut loose with our revolvers. Works slicker than snot." Jesse laughed. "Wait till you see the surprised look on their faces when we start killin' 'em."

"I hate to be the one to tell you, but Capt'n Billy Quantrill come up with that tactic long before Bloody Bill."

Billy Cahill listened to the brothers' conversation, but his thoughts were still on his mother and the women being held prisoner with her. When the conversation slowed, Billy asked, "Jesse, have you heard who else they have as prisoners in that warehouse?"

"Yeah, I know some of them. I heard they were holdin' Mrs. Charity Kerr and Mrs. Nannie McCorkle, sister and sister-in-law of John McCorkle; Susan Vandiver and Armenia Gilvey, cousins of Cole Younger; Bill Anderson's three sisters; and your Ma."

"So what are we gonna do about it?" asked Billy.

"I don't rightly know. Some of the boys want to ride in there and bust 'em out, but Todd and Anderson say it'd be pure suicide. The Yankees are just waitin' for us to ride into their trap."

Billy felt frustrated. He gestured wildly as he spoke. "Well, we have to do somethin'! We can't just let 'em get away with this."

Jesse saw the anger on Billy's face. "I know how you must feel, Billy. Now that we've got all the gangs together, Quantrill, Todd, and Anderson will come up with a plan."

"Ever since we came back, Quantrill has kept us up in Lafayette County, and here lately around Blue Springs, chasin' after Bartok's Third Kansas Cavalry and Pennick's Missouri militia. If we'd been closer to home maybe we could've stopped 'em from takin' the women."

"Thinkin' about might-have-beens won't change nothin'," said Frank. "We'll hit 'em. Tonight we'll make plans. Let's fix somethin' to eat while we got the chance."

Later that night under the warm, yellow glow of the campfires, William Clarke Quantrill proposed to his gathered chieftains his response to Union General Ewing's plans to ship southern families out of the state.

"Boys, let's go to Lawrence." He paused, letting his words sink in, before he continued. "Lawrence is the center of abolitionism in Kansas. Most of the plunder stolen from Missouri goes there. We can get more revenge and do more damage to the Jayhawkers and Red Legs there than anywhere else." His eyes looked wild in the glow of the campfire as his voice rose in intensity. "Boys, there's money there for the takin' beyond our wildest dreams."

A loud murmur coursed through the group as the Bushwhackers reacted to the proposal. William Gregg stood and spoke. "Capt'n Billy, you know I'd like to hit Lawrence more than any other town, but ya gotta be reasonable. Lawrence is forty miles inside Kansas and has nearly three thousand people. They'd be warned of our coming by the border outposts along the state line. Besides, Yankee militia and Federal troops are probably stationed to defend the city. Hell, even if we were successful in raidin' the town, we'd never make it back to Missouri." Loud murmurs of agreement rose from the group.

William Quantrill remained calm as he stood before the men. "I know you have doubts about our success, but hear me out. Dick Yeager, sittin' right here beside me, led two dozen raiders clear to Council Grove in Kansas. That's one hundred and thirty miles into Kansas. They raided Diamond Springs, and the Yankees couldn't do a thing."

Bloody Bill Anderson stood. "I was on that raid with Yeager and what you say is true—but you left out what happened coming back. We got hit by General James McDowell and his Kansas militia near Emporia. They captured a dozen of us and the rest of us had to scatter and make a run for Missouri. Course, you know what happened. The Yankees claimed all our boys were killed tryin' to escape. We know they shot all their prisoners."

"The point is, Bill, we can go forty miles faster than we can go one hundred and thirty. We can get in and out before they can catch us. Besides, all we have to do is split up and scatter and they'll never catch us all." Another murmur went through the crowd. Quantrill continued, "I've had many men scouting and they rode nearly to Lawrence. The border outposts are weak and scattered. The country between Lawrence and the border is lightly populated so's there's not much chance of them knowing we're comin'. If we move fast and at night we can attack at dawn. The Yankees don't think we would try to strike a town so large or so deep inside Kansas. Surprise will be on our side."

William Gregg mulled it over in his mind. The sheer audacity of it could make it plausible. He said, "If we can pull enough men together it just might work."

"I'll send a couple of them into Lawrence to scout the town. If they bring back information to confirm what I've said, will you men ride with me?" The proposal was met with murmurs as the Bushwhackers argued among themselves.

"There's rich banks, well-stocked stores, and warehouses filled with goods stole from Missouri just waitin' for us. This is the home of Jim Lane, head of the Jayhawkers. This is the headquarters of the Kansas Red Legs. These men have been killin' Missourians and burnin' us out for years. It's time to pay 'em back, boys! It's high time we show them how it feels to be robbed and burned-out and have their men shot down like dogs in the streets. Their banks are swollen with money stolen from our people. Let's get it back. Burn Lawrence, boys! Burn her to the ground!"

A wild cheer went up among the men as waves of Rebel yells filled the night skies. Their blood was running hot now and all the Bushwhackers dreamed of loot and revenge. Not all the men were ready to risk it, but they were willing to consider it; and for now, that was enough to satisfy William Clarke Quantrill.

The leaders of the various gangs and factions of Missouri Bushwhackers filtered back to their respective commands where they waited for word to gather and prepared to move.

Quantrill's men cleaned and oiled their pistols and guns, repaired harnesses, molded bullets, and prepared thousands of cartridges. While they readied themselves, Quantrill sent out scouts as he had promised. Fletch Taylor and a negro named John Noland were sent to spy on Lawrence.

The news they brought back was helpful and encouraging to the guerillas. Surprisingly, there were no pickets stationed on the road to Lawrence. The town's small Union garrison had been withdrawn to the north side of the Kansas River. No one in Lawrence seemed to believe Quantrill would ever dare to attack the town. The news was just what the eager Bushwhackers wanted to hear. They began to believe Lawrence could be taken. Word was sent to all the Bushwhacker gangs.

Billy Cahill was among those who believed the raid had possibilities. Jayhawkers had burned his family home and killed his father. Yankees at this very moment held his mother prisoner in a dilapidated warehouse in Kansas City. He wanted revenge—he wanted to deliver the same kind of pain he had suffered at their hands.

Still, many in the Bushwhacker bands were unwilling to risk the attack and resisted the plan. Important news arrived on the fourteenth of August 1863 that would forever seal the fate of Lawrence, Kansas. It alone was enough to erase any lingering doubts any of the Bushwhackers might have had about the raid being justified. Billy was there when a rider rode into their secret camp near Blue Springs, Missouri, bearing the news. He watched as the courier hastily handed Quantrill a note.

Quantrill unfolded the note. His jaw tightened as he read. He paused and looked around the camp. "Have the men gather, Billy. I have some news that's mighty important."

Billy hustled and soon the men gathered around their leader. Quantrill began, "Boys, one of our riders just brought in this note sent to us by Bloody Bill. The warehouse in Kansas City where some of our women have been held prisoner has collapsed."

Billy heard the words and he felt his heart sink. Fear clutched tightly at his stomach as if it were in a vise.

"The building fell down yesterday, on August thirteenth. From the rubble the rescuers have pulled the dead bodies of these women: Josephine Anderson, Susan Vandiver, Charity Kerr, Armenia Gilvey, and Betty Cahill. Mary

Anderson has been severely injured in the building's collapse. For those of you who have lost family, I'm sorry."

Billy heard the words, but the reality of it was hard to swallow. Could it be true his mother was dead? First Pa and now Ma was gone and he never felt so alone in the world. Would there be no end to his misery? He felt a rage burning in him like a coal-stoked fire. He hated the Yankees before, but now he was filled with bloodlust. Revenge was what he wanted, and by God, he would have it! Billy vowed there would not be one Jayhawker, not one Kansas Red Leg, nor one Yankee soldier he would allow to escape his guns alive. "I'll take no prisoners. I swear they'll think they're eye-to-eye with the devil when they meet me!"

Quantrill was still talking, and even through Billy's shock and rage, the words penetrated. "You know they planned it, don't you, boys? They made the building fall down on purpose to kill our women. They wanted it to happen and they wanted it to look like an accident. Well, are you gonna stand here and let them get away with it?"

Loud cheers and yells greeted him. "Hell no! Burn Lawrence!"

"That's right, boys. It's time we gave them some of their own medicine. Let's hit 'em like we never hit 'em before. We'll give them something they'll never forget and while we're at it, we're gonna make ourselves rich, boys!" A wild cheer filled with raw anger and bloodlust met his words.

On the morning of August eighteenth, Quantrill's band broke camp at Blue Springs and moved southward. They crossed Sniabar Creek and moved on until they reached the home of Captain Pardee on the Blackwater River, where they camped for the night.

Here Quantrill was joined by Bloody Bill Anderson with forty men, including Jesse and Frank James. Andy Blount rode in leading over one hundred men.

The next day the band of guerillas moved westward behind a screen of scouts intently looking for Union patrols. At noon they camped near Lone Jack, Missouri, on Potter's Farm.

Quantrill gathered his men around him. "Boys, do ya want to continue the raid on Lawrence?" His question was met with a resounding, "Yes!"

"We'll have to go through some tough dangers. There will be Union troops and militia everywhere. There may be very few of us who get back alive, but I believe we can strike a blow against our enemies they will never forget." Quantrill paused. "If there is any among you that don't want to go, now is the time to fall out. None of us will think the less of you, 'cause we're facin' terrible odds. After we leave here there will be no fallin' out or turnin' back. We will continue until we destroy Lawrence."

After his statement, babble coursed through the gathered Bushwhackers. Around a dozen men returned to their horses and mounted up to ride away. Only two were from Quantrill's own band; the rest were from Blount's guerillas.

After dark the raiders continued moving west. South of the Blue River the raiders crossed paths with one hundred new Confederate recruits under the command of Colonel John Holt. Holt made the decision to join Quantrill on the raid, because Holt felt it would be good experience for his men. The Missourians camped at daylight on the middle fork of the Grand River, only four miles from the Kansas line.

All along the route Billy Cahill had been amazed at the large gathering of guerillas. He had seen large groups of men before in the Confederate armies and fought with them at Cane Hill and Prairie Grove. This was a different command entirely. This band was a trained pack of heavily armed killers with revenge on their minds and hate in their hearts gathered for a common cause. These men would not be held back or restrained by any vague rules of conduct as they pertained to war. These men had suffered at the hands of the enemy and had been wronged. They would expect no quarter and would give none in return. Soon they would ride like an angry wind, whipping a path of destruction and death across the land.

21

Eye-To-Eye with the Devil

At three in the afternoon Quantrill's men saddled up and headed for the border. The column of Missourians moved across the prairies two and a half miles south of Squiresville, where they halted until nightfall. The command had already penetrated ten miles inside Kansas. As darkness approached the men swung back into their saddles. They traveled west to Spring Hill, then northwest toward Gardner.

Billy was riding with the scouts in front of the main body. As they were riding through Gardner, they rounded a corner and found themselves standing before a Yankee picket post. William Gregg was in charge of the guerilla scouts.

A large Yankee sergeant stepped out into the road. "Whoa there, boys! Where do you think you're headin' this time of night?"

Billy fought to rein in his chestnut mare, which was

dancing in the street. Before Billy could speak Bill Gregg said, "Howdy-do, boys. We're on our way to Lawrence."

"What kind of business can you have in Lawrence this time of night?"

"Hell, Sergeant, we ain't gonna do no business there at night." Bill Gregg smiled in the dim lamplight. Billy kept his hand hovering near his pistol. Bill Gregg continued, "You see, we're a new outfit and the capt'n wants us there bright and early in the mornin'. These horses are in dire need of some horseshoes before we can go into active duty. The capt'n is mighty fired up about getting us in the war. He says we'll show them Rebs how to fight."

The Union soldier studied the two soldiers. Billy was grateful Quantrill had suggested the scouts wear blue uniforms before they left Missouri. The Yankee seemed partially satisfied with the answer. "What's the name of your company?"

"The Thirty-third Kansas Militia. We were recruited near Coffeeville."

"Well, ya better route your men around the outskirts of town. The colonel won't take it lightly if you disturb him from his sleep. We don't need a regiment marchin' through the streets of town at this hour."

"No, sir, we don't wanna wake the Colonel. We'll just ride back an' tell our regiment to go around town." Bill Gregg snapped a salute to the sergeant and the two privates standing guard with him.

The Yankee sergeant returned a lazy salute as he watched the two riders turn their horses around in the street. They set spurs to their mounts.

"That was fast thinkin', Bill. I thought for sure we was caught. How did you know about the Thirty-third Kansas Militia?"

"I didn't. I just made it up and hoped they wouldn't know the difference. We gotta let Quantrill know so we can ride around this outfit."

Soon the band of guerillas had cleared Gardner and continued west. Three miles later they veered north toward Hesper, Kansas.

The night was pitch black without a hint of a moon. The terrain was difficult and dangerous. Quantrill ordered the scouts to take prisoners from the local German farmers and use them as guides. Whenever the guides were of no further use, they were shot. The column slowed as the Bushwhackers looked for prisoners. Most of the captured men didn't know the country except near their homes. It didn't take long to go through ten different guides.

The raiders continued through the little town of Franklin. As the first rays of light began to break, Billy noticed many of the guerillas were tied into their saddles so they wouldn't fall out while they slept. Billy had long ago rejoined the main body of riders as other men now led the column, snaking its way northward. As Billy and the column passed by Quantrill, who was watching them from a small rise, he heard Quantrill shout, "Push on, boys, it'll be daylight before we get there."

As they left the sleepy community of Franklin, the Bushwhackers spurred into a gallop. In a few miles they reached a summit overlooking Lawrence from the southeast. Quantrill ordered the men to wait while he sent five men under Bill Gregg to check out the town. Billy remained with the column.

The men peered down at the city of Lawrence. It was bigger than they had imagined and looked formidable. The streets appeared deserted because most of the people were still asleep at this early hour. A few of the guerillas began to lose their nerve as they stared down upon the city. One of them shouted so they all could hear it, "Let's give it up, it's too much!"

The mere suggestion they quit now when they had come so far, at the very moment they were on the verge of their attack, angered Quantrill. He stood in his stirrups and looked down the line at his Bushwhackers. "You can do as you please. I'm going into Lawrence." Without waiting for the return of Gregg and his men, Quantrill gave his order, "Follow me, boys!" as he rode toward the town.

Billy guessed the time to be near five o'clock in the morning as he readied himself for the charge. He leaned forward over the neck of his horse. They rode swiftly through the empty streets of Lawrence using vacant lots to speed them toward the center of town. Billy heard Quantrill order Colonel Holt and his men to the east side of town, Andy Blount's men to the west, and the remainder toward the center of town.

Rising out of the cool morning shadows before him, Billy spotted a military tent camp. He leveled his revolver and released a vicious yell as they charged the tents. A few of the Union soldiers were awake and stirring, but they were caught totally by surprise. Quantrill's riders charged among them with pistols blazing. Billy felt his horse plow through a tent, nearly tripping in the process. A man with Union blue trousers stood among the canvas, his mouth hanging open in fright and his eyes large as saucers. Billy fired at the man and watched with glee as the bullet ripped through the Yankee's forehead and blew out the top of his head. The Yankees seemed unable to respond, frozen in their tracks by fear and surprise. Billy saw some Union soldiers trying to escape by running down the street. Billy pursued two of the soldiers. As he closed in on them he held his revolver scant inches from the back of the first soldier he reached. He pulled the trigger and felt the gun recoil in his hand. The soldier pitched forward on his face, rolling in the dirt of the street. The second soldier looked behind him, his eyes full of terror. He veered to the right and tried to cut across the boardwalk, but stumbled and sprawled. Billy pivoted his mount and fired twice into the chest of the soldier. The Yank slammed onto his back and lay still.

Billy wheeled the big chestnut mare in the street as he looked for more soldiers. He could feel the blood lust pounding through his veins. As he scanned the scene, he saw the small camp was destroyed. Dead Yankees littered the street.

He watched as a man named Larkin Skaggs ripped the Union flag from its staff and tied the stars and stripes to the tail of his horse so it would drag through the dirt of the streets. Larkin spurred away as he hooped and hollered his delight. A Rebel yell ripped involuntarily from Billy's lips.

Billy was swept up in the continuing charge down the street. As they approached the next tent camp, they saw it was mostly empty. The soldiers there had heard and witnessed the slaughter of the recruits of the Fourteenth Kansas. These colored recruits knew they stood even less of a chance. They ran as fast as they could.

When the camps were destroyed, Quantrill led his men at a fast gallop up Massachusetts Street. The street was filled with hard-riding, long-haired, wild-eyed killers; as unstoppable as a tidal wave. When they reached the river, Quantrill yelled to his men, "Surround the Eldridge House." Billy moved to follow his commander's orders. The hotel was a large brick structure standing four stories high. Iron grilles covered the windows on the ground floor. If there was to be any trouble, it would be here. The Bushwhackers moved cautiously.

Suddenly, a gong began ringing in the hotel. Surprised by the noise, the guerillas scurried to cover. Billy rode his horse around the corner and tied her to a hitching rail. He quickly returned and glanced around the corner. From here he could cover the entrance to the hotel. The quiet in the street seemed oddly out of place after the screaming charge through the tent camps.

After a short while a man appeared at an upper window waving a white bedsheet. "I want to talk to your commander."

Billy watched as Quantrill rode forward. He had cast off his Union overcoat and now wore his elaborately stitched guerilla shirt. His gray cavalry pants were tucked into the tops of high cavalry boots and four revolvers were stuck into his belt. His face was streaked with dirt after a hard night in the saddle and the stubble of his reddish beard showed clearly under the slouch hat he was wearing.

The man holding the sheet wore a Union captain's uniform. He shouted down to Quantrill in the street. "My name is A. R. Banks. Why have you come to Lawrence?"

Quantrill stared up at the man at the window. His answer was simple and direct. "Plunder."

The Union officer looked down on the men surrounding him. "We are defenseless and at your mercy. We will surrender the hotel, but we demand protection for those inside."

Quantrill studied the situation. After a pause he answered. "Surrender and I promise those inside will not be harmed." Quantrill raised himself in his stirrups and shouted to his men. "Spread out over the town. Check every store and house. Kill!" He paused. "Kill and you'll make no mistake. The town must be cleansed, and the only way is to kill!"

With wild shouts of exaltation and glee the guerillas poured through the streets to carry out their commander's orders. A large number, including Billy Cahill, stayed with their leader.

Billy rushed through the front door of the hotel with two of his revolvers pulled. Inside, the other Bushwhackers forced the captured guests to shell out their money and their valuables. Other raiders marched upstairs to ransack the rooms. Shots were fired on an upper floor. Billy rushed to see who was doing the shooting. He asked a Bushwhacker what was going on.

"Three Easterners locked themselves in a room and wouldn't come out. A few shots through the door was all it took." He laughed at their audacity. "We wounded one of the fools."

His curiosity satisfied, Billy returned to the ground floor. After the guests were marched outside and the hotel was thoroughly looted, the raiders set fire to the structure. Billy stood in the streets and watched with satisfaction as flames danced in the windows. Black columns of smoke twisted and drifted on the wind as the fire spread.

Quantrill left a small group of Bushwhackers to guard the prisoners and moved on to lead his men. When he was gone, a few of the guerillas who'd helped themselves generously to the liquor from the hotel bar threatened to shoot the prisoners. A Bushwhacker fired his revolver into the milling captives. The bullet struck a prisoner and killed him.

Quantrill heard the shot and returned just in time to prevent a massacre. "I gave them my word if they surrendered they would not be harmed. I'll kill the next man who tries to shoot one of them." Quantrill shouted from his horse, "Todd! Take these people to the Whitney House for safekeeping." Quantrill followed his men and the prisoners to the Whitney House, where he set up his temporary headquarters.

Years before the war Quantrill had stayed in this hotel when he was living in Lawrence. The owner, Nathan Stone, had befriended him; and once when Quantrill had been ill, Stone's wife and daughter nursed him through it. For this kindness from another time, the Whitney House was spared. Quantrill made it clear to his followers no one from this hotel was to be hurt and the building was to be left undamaged.

While Quantrill ate breakfast at the Whitney House and discussed old times with Nathan Stone, Billy Cahill walked out of the door of the hotel and stood on the boardwalk. He heard the echo of gunshots in the streets and watched black and gray smoke winding its way into the skies from burning buildings. As he leaned against a post, Bill Gregg stepped up beside him.

"This has gone a lot smoother than I thought it would, Billy," said Gregg.

"We caught 'em with their pants down fer sure, Bill." Billy stared across the street at a store that still looked untouched. The building was nice but nothing extra special. It was the sign above the door that caught his attention. It read JACOB BARTOK — AUCTIONS, LIVESTOCK, AND DRY GOODS. "Hey, Bill, see the shop across the street?"

"Yeah, I see it."

"I think we should look in there."

"Why, Billy? I'd rather rob a bank."

"Look at the name on that store." Billy pointed at the sign. "It says Bartok. It might be a coincidence, maybe not, but a name like that ain't real common."

"So?"

"Well, there's a Major Bartok back in Lafayette County, Missouri. We've been chasin' his troops for months. Maybe this guy is related, maybe he isn't, but I hate his name enough it doesn't make much difference. Hell, we're in Lawrence to clean 'er out. Why not start there?"

William Gregg looked over at the young Bushwhacker beside him. What he had said made sense, and what the hell, he had nothing better to do. "Let's go, youngin'."

The two raiders moved cautiously as they dodged other guerillas riding wildly down the street with their loot and stolen goods, shooting their pistols into the air as they passed. Billy led the way as they approached the door of the building. Billy tried the door, but it was locked.

"Stand back," Bill Gregg said. He fired two shots into the lock. Both men slammed their shoulders into the door and it gave way with the sound of splintering wood. They entered quickly with guns at the ready.

The lamps were lit in the office, connected by a narrow hallway to a larger room where goods were stored and indoor auctions held. They worked their way back to the office. On the desk sat a still-warm cup of coffee, but the chair behind the desk was empty. Billy noticed it was pushed back farther than it should be. He moved cautiously around the desk until he saw the feet and the butt of a man hiding under the desk.

"Get out from under there, pronto!" shouted Billy.

"Don't shoot! I'll come out." The man slid from under the desk. "I'm not armed."

Billy watched the portly gentleman with amusement. The stranger held his hands high. "Please ... Please, don't shoot." The man wore muttonchop sideburns touched with gray. Wire-rim glasses were perched on his hawk-billed nose. He looked soft from years of easy work behind a desk.

"Who the hell are you?" asked Billy.

The man's eyes were wide with terror. His hands trembled as his breath came shallow and rapid. "My name is Jacob Bartok. Please ... don't hurt me."

Bill Gregg laughed at the trembling wreck of a man standing before him. "Give us one good reason why we shouldn't kill ya right now."

"I got money! I got lots of money I can give you if you'll just promise you won't hurt me."

Both men quit smiling at the mention of large amounts of money. "Where's this money, Bartok?" asked Bill Gregg.

"If you'll allow me, I've got a wallet in my pocket."

"Don't bother, I'll get it. Just keep those hands in the air, pilgrim." Bill Gregg stepped forward as Billy Cahill covered the man. Gregg slipped his hand inside the man's coat and extracted a long, thick wallet. He opened it to show a stack of Union greenbacks. "Well, now, looks like you've been doin' real well."

Billy couldn't resist asking, "You any relation to a Major Benton Bartok?"

The man looked even more nervous. "No ... I don't think I am. The name doesn't sound familiar to me," Jacob Bartok lied as he swallowed hard.

"The name ain't too common, and this Benton Bartok is from Kansas. Seems unlikely you wouldn't be related to him," said Billy.

The sweat glistened heavy on Jacob's brow. "I suppose we could be distant cousins or something. I'm originally from a large family from Ohio," Bartok lied. He watched as the two Missourians glanced at one another. He knew they doubted his story. He watched Billy thumb back the hammer of his Colt Navy. "Wait, don't be hasty! I've got more money than what I have in my wallet."

"Hold it, Billy," Bill Gregg said in a low growl. "Where's the rest of it, Bartok?"

"It's over at the bank. I'm a partner and owner of the bank. If you'll take me over there I can open the vault. But ... first promise you won't kill me."

"I ain't promisin' you nothin' till I see if you're tellin' the truth. You open the vault without any tricks and we'll see about the rest."

Cahill and Gregg followed the portly gentleman out of the office with their pistols nudging him in the back. While they walked toward the bank Billy asked, "How'd you make all this money, Bartok?"

"I've made most of it through selling at auction livestock and used goods and the rest through investments. My business is all perfectly legal."

Billy didn't like Bartok's response. "Just cause it fits neatly under the protection of the law don't make it right. I'm guessin' that most of the stuff you been sellin' has been stolen in Missouri and brought here for sale."

"It isn't my business to ask where my customers get their goods. My job is to sell it."

"Yeah, I bet it is, you fat son of a bitch." Bill Gregg gave Bartok a rough shove through the doorway. "That stuff you been sellin' was stolen from our people, but you don't have time to worry about it, do you? Nah, you're only interested in how much you can get out of it to fatten your wallet."

Billy reached for Gregg's shoulder. "Easy, Bill, this gentleman wants to repent and make things right. He's gonna give us all that money back, isn't that right, Jacob?"

"Yeah, I . . . I didn't know. I'll get the money for you."

"Damn right you will," shouted Bill Gregg.

It took just a few moments for the men to walk down to the bank. They found other Missourians had made it before them. Cash drawers lay empty, strewn across the floor. The bodies of three men lay scattered around the room. Two of the men, judging from the clothing they wore, appeared to be bank tellers. The other body could have been an owner or loan officer. All were past talking. As they entered, two of the guerillas were trying desperately to force the door on the vault. Luckily, the two Bushwhackers knew Bill Gregg and Billy Cahill. One of them asked, "Who you got with ya, Bill?"

"Someone who can open this vault; if you haven't messed up the tumblers on the lock."

"We tried to slip the dead bolt with a bar, but it didn't work. We wanted to do this the easy way, but hell, these boys wouldn't cooperate at all. The big boss over there went for a gun so we pumped him full of lead. Damn shame though, 'cause these other two didn't seem to know the combination. We shot the first one figurin' it would convince the other one to talk. Guess he was stubborn or he didn't know 'cause he couldn't tell us either. Charlie here got so pissed about it he jammed his pistol barrel through the teller's front teeth and pulled the trigger." The Missourian looked down at his blood-splattered shirt. "Damn fool got blood all over my best shirt."

"Quit yer whinin', Red. I didn't miss 'em an' get you instead, did I?"

Red studied Jacob. "You say this dandy can get this open?"

"That's what he claims. How about it, Bartok, you willin' to open this vault, or do you want to be like your friends?" Bill Gregg motioned to the bodies scattered about the room.

Jacob Bartok's face turned ashen. "If I open it will you give me your word you won't shoot me?"

"Yeah, I give you my word," said Bill Gregg impatiently.

Jacob Bartok put his trembling hand on the vault's tumbler. He spun first to the right, then to the left, then slowly back to the right. He gave a twist to the door lever and the dead bolt slid free. Slowly the heavy door swung open. Bill Gregg and Red rushed through the door and stared at the loot stored inside. Billy wanted to follow, but someone had to keep an eye on Jacob.

"I got it open like I promised. Take whatever you need. You can have it all. Just . . . let me live," pleaded Bartok.

Charlie stepped behind Bartok and Billy heard the muffled blast as he watched Jacob arch his back. Bartok's eyes stared vacantly at Billy as he coughed up blood before he slumped to the floor, his hands helplessly clawing the air. Billy couldn't believe what he had seen as his eyes moved up to stare into the smiling face of Charlie, still brandishing his smoking gun. "That's one less of these Jayhawker sons-a-bitches."

Bill Gregg bolted from the vault when he heard the shot. One look was enough. "What the hell ya shoot him for, Charlie? I gave him my word I wouldn't kill him if he opened the vault."

Charlie smiled wickedly at Bill Gregg as he stuffed his pistol into his belt. "I heard your promise and you kept your word. You didn't kill him, I did."

Bill Gregg was mad when he first saw what happened, but he couldn't stay mad. "I guess ya have a point, Charlie. I didn't kill him an' Billy didn't either." Gregg motioned back to the vault. "Since we don't have a prisoner any longer how about gettin' in there and helpin' load some bags with greenbacks."

Billy stared at Bartok's body, face down on the floor. Blood pooled near his mouth and a burnt hole was visible between his shoulder blades. When he thought about how this vulture had lived off the pickings stolen from the hapless in Missouri, he was glad that Charlie had fewer qualms about promises than he did. Billy stepped into the vault and began shoveling money into cloth sacks.

"Leave the silver. It weighs too much and will slow us down. It's a long hard ride back to Missouri. If ya must have a jingle in your pockets make 'em gold pieces," ordered Bill Gregg.

The four raiders hurried to their horses and tied the money bags to their saddles.

"Wait just a minute, fellas." Bill Gregg ran back into the open doorway. He smashed a lamp in the entrance, then bent down and struck a match. With a whoosh the oil lit and fire began to spread across the floor of the bank. "I guess they don't need this bank anymore." The boys laughed as the flames spread. "Let's find Quantrill." The riders spurred their horses as they galloped away toward the Johnson House, the known hangout of the infamous Kansas Red Legs. Billy saw men lined up unarmed against the wall of a building in the alley. Facing them stood a group of Bushwhackers with leveled guns. They reined in their horses just in time to witness a fusillade of pistol shots mowing down the unarmed Red Legs. Missourians moved forward among the bodies and finished off those still moving with pistol shots to the head.

Billy knew he should feel some remorse for those killed so callously, but he knew that had things been reversed the Red Legs would have done the same thing. His group of four Bushwhackers continued down the street.

Around him, Billy watched scenes of men gone totally berserk. He saw men shot down unarmed in front of their pleading wives and children. He watched his fellow gueril- las weighted with stolen booty as they staggered away from private homes. Women and children wept as they clung to dead sons and husbands shot down in the streets as if they were nothing more than bothersome stray dogs.

Billy felt sick to his stomach. What were they doing? Were they no better than the Jayhawkers and the Red Legs they had come to seek revenge against? Had they turned into nothing more than cold-blooded killers, no longer left with any sense of right or wrong? He never imagined it would be like this. Sure he wanted to come in and clean out the Jayhawkers and Red Legs. He wanted to help cap- ture and kill their leaders, but he wanted no part in killing men before the innocent eyes of their children and wives.

Fighting a war against invaders in Missouri was one thing, but to ride in here and shoot down men like animals in the street was another matter entirely. Billy felt as though he'd stood eye-to-eye with the devil. It had changed him. One glance at William Gregg riding beside him and Billy knew he felt the same way. Disgust showed clearly on Bill Gregg's face. Red and Charlie joined the melee while Cahill and Gregg rode on. Fires from burning buildings heated the streets to almost unbearable tempera- tures. Smoke stung Billy's eyes as they rode; hot cinders rained down on them, glowing and winking. Up ahead of them they spotted Quantrill and a squad of his men cross at the intersection. Bill Gregg and Billy pivoted their horses at the corner and followed Quantrill.

Gregg spurred his horse alongside Quantrill. "Where you goin', Capt'n?"

"We're about to pay a call on Senator Jim Lane. He's a leader of these Jayhawkers and I want him bad."

"I thought Noland and Taylor said Lane was out of town."

"I hope he's back now. Even if he isn't, we'll burn down his house for him. Time for him to get a taste of his own medicine." They rode to the big house in the northwest part of town. Mrs. Lane met Quantrill and a squad of his men at the front door.

Quantrill asked with mock politeness, "Mrs. Lane, I would like to speak to the distinguished senator. Is the senator home?"

"No, I'm sorry to disappoint you. The senator is not home to greet visitors."

Quantrill was clearly disappointed. The information squared with the information his spies Fletch Taylor and the negro Noland had brought to him so he figured there was no sense making a search. Instead Quantrill turned to John McCorkle, Bill Gregg, and Billy Cahill. "The senator isn't at home, boys. It's a damn shame we missed him. Torch the place. I want the esteemed senator to come home to a pile of ashes." Two other men removed Mrs. Lane from the house and forced her into the yard.

Billy walked through the house and into the parlor. John McCorkle stared at the elaborately furnished home filled with rare treasures. His eyes fell on two grand pianos sitting in the parlor. Anger burned in John McCorkle's eyes. He had lost family in the warehouse collapse in Kansas City. "These two pianos belong to Missourians from Jackson County. I've been a frequent visitor to the homes where these pianos belonged before the war, before Lane's Jawhawkers stole them. We can't take 'em back, but I'll make sure no damn Jayhawker ever enjoys them again." McCorkle poured oil from a lamp on the pianos and set them ablaze. Other guerillas hurriedly ransacked the house, stealing jewelry and silverware. Some like Billy hurriedly piled expensive drapes and rugs in the center of the rooms and set them on fire. The boys didn't ride out until they were sure the house was in flames.

Unknown to them, Senator Lane had returned to Lawrence and was hiding in a nearby cornfield in his night-shirt. Had they not paused to hit the Eldridge House and lay waste to most of Lawrence first, they might have caught him in his house. They had come close to capturing the hated Jim Lane, but he escaped with his life.

The only organized resistance to the raiders came from a few soldiers and surveyors stationed on the opposite side of the Kansas River. They fired across the river and wounded three men—Jim Bledsoe, a member of Quantrill's gang, and two of Holt's recruits.

Holt's Confederate recruits refrained from the killing. They were not regular guerillas and had not been previously exposed to this kind of warfare. They were shocked and took little part in it. Some of them showed their unfired guns to women in Lawrence to prove they hadn't killed anyone, others helped the Lawrence women remove furniture from burning homes. A few admitted they were sorry they had been ordered to join this raid by Colonel Holt.

When Quantrill and his small band rode back from the Lane House things were totally out of control. Many guerillas had broken into saloons and were now savagely drunk. The destruction had been systematic. Almost every business and home had been robbed, looted, and set ablaze. Most of the men living in Lawrence were now dead. Despite the killing frenzy, no women were injured or raped by the Missourians. Despite their brutality they still clung to tattered remnants of a once proud Southern code of honor. A southern gentleman must honor and defend women; men must take their chances.

By nine o'clock, word was passed to Quantrill by a lookout posted on Mount Oread. He had seen the dust of approaching Union troops from the east. Quantrill ordered his raiders to reassemble.

Billy joined the hastily formed column of fours in the south part of town as the guerillas regrouped. They galloped away leaving a smoking and battered Lawrence in ruins.

They left fiery monuments to mark their passage. Nearly every business and over one hundred homes were in flames. Another one hundred homes were damaged. Bodies of men and boys littered the streets, sidewalks, and yards. One hundred fifty soldiers and townsmen had been killed, and thirty more were wounded. Many of these would later add to the death toll. As they rode south the Bushwhackers continued to murder, loot, and burn farms. After crossing the Wakarusa River they set the bridge ablaze.

Near the bridge Frank James joined Quantrill. "I heard sixty Red Legs just rode into Lawrence. Should we go back and kill 'em?"

Quantrill shook his head no. "Boys, we haven't got the time. Word is out and the Yankees will do their best to keep us from returning to Missouri. I'm gonna need all of you if we're gonna make it. We did enough in Lawrence, now it's time to ride."

22

Recovery

Calvin had never in his life been more surprised than when he awakened from the black void of unconsciousness to find himself in bed with Dee Ann Farley. The next day and night flew by swiftly. Calvin frequently lapsed into unconsciousness for hours at a time. He awoke each time to find Dee Ann taking care of him. At night he could feel the warmth of her as she cuddled next to him in bed.

By the second day he began to regain his strength and no longer passed into periods of unconsciousness. Even his headaches were decreasing in intensity.

That night as he lay on his back in the darkened room he felt Dee Ann as she rolled over to him. She lay her head and hand on his chest and her leg slipped up over his. "Calvin, are you awake?"

"If I wasn't I'd think I was dreamin'."

"Do ya mind?" she whispered.

Calvin could smell the fresh-washed scent of her and he felt the heat of her body as if flowed through the thin nightshirt he was wearing. "No, I don't mind. I can't remember a time in my life I felt so good."

Dim moonlight filtered into the room, gently lighting her face with a soft glow. Calvin saw her smiling as she coyly looked up at him. "Are ya married, Calvin?" she whispered softly.

"No," he answered swiftly, caught off guard by her sudden question. "No, ma'am, I don't even have a girlfriend." He talked softly, afraid he might wake the children.

"That seems so strange to me. A good lookin' man like you and you don't have a girl."

Calvin felt himself blushing. "I was going to college at the University of Missouri when the war began. I guess I just put my total concentration on getting an education rather than chasing girls."

"There's more than one kind of education, Calvin, and some are more fun than others," she said teasingly in a low, husky whisper. "It wasn't schoolin' kept you from findin' a girl. I know your problem; you're shy."

Calvin knew she was right. "I admit I've never known what to do or say around the ladies. I've always been afraid it would be the wrong thing."

"I bet you never slept in a bed with a lady before, have ya?"

Calvin hated to admit it, for it would show his inexperience. Somehow he realized it would be useless to lie, for Dee Ann would see right through it. "No, I can't say as I have."

She gave him an understanding smile. "It ain't nothin' you should be ashamed of. I got married to Robert when I was sixteen and I had Jimmy 'bout a year later. Robert met me in the hill country an' decided we'd be better off to move down to some good farmland. We settled here in fifty-eight. We built this cabin ourselves."

Dee Ann glanced around the room. "Rob was a good husband. He never hit me or nothing'. He was kind and gentle. He taught me all about good lovin'. He always said good lovin' was the best gift a person could give on this here earth an' the only thing that made life worthwhile. Pleasurin' each other makes the hard times easier. If you have good lovin' it eases your troubles, Robert always said. I reckon he was right cause it sure has been hard since he's been gone."

Calvin saw the sadness in her eyes. "I guess it must be difficult for you to be left alone to raise your kids."

"At first it was hard for me to accept Robert bein' dead an' all. It was really hard for me when he left. A gal gets used to havin' a man to cuddle with at night and to share your troubles with durin' the day. Suddenly, I found myself alone night after lonely night with no one to talk to and no one to hold me." She sighed deeply, then continued, "Sure I got the kids an' I love 'em, but they can't fill all a woman's needs. I'm mighty lonely, Calvin."

Dee Ann propped herself up on her elbow. He felt her hand caress his cheek and he felt a tingle as she traced the outline of his jaw with her finger. She looked deeply in his eyes and he could feel her breathing quicken. She leaned forward and he felt the tender touch of her lips on his. He enjoyed the velvety feel of her warm, passionate mouth as her lips parted and her tongue gently probed against his. Instinctively he opened his lips to receive hers as he slipped his arm around her and tangled his fingers into her hair.

Calvin felt himself becoming aroused as she awakened new passions within him. He felt her hand gently and slowly trace a path down his stomach with her fingers. She didn't stop until she cupped his rising hardness as it pushed against his nightshirt. She squeezed gently.

Calvin's breathing quickened as his pulse began to pound. Boldly he lifted his right hand to caress her breast.

He sensed her nipple as it became taut and strained against the nightgown. He was startled as she suddenly pulled herself away from him and brought herself to her knees facing him. She reached down and hooked her fingers in the material of her nightgown and slowly pulled it up and over her head until it was free from her body. She dropped the still-warm nightgown on the bed before her.

Calvin couldn't believe his eyes as he stared at her naked body kneeling beside him. She might not have been the most beautiful woman he had ever seen, but no other woman had stirred such passions in him. His eyes drifted over her luscious body. She had firm, full breasts with large nipples. Her stomach was flat and her legs were athletic.

Dee Ann studied him as his eyes took her in. She could read the appreciation in his eyes. She smiled as he swallowed hard. She leaned forward and kissed him again as her breasts slid across his chest. Calvin clutched at her and rolled her over on her back. He lay beside her and looked down into her eyes.

"Tonight, Calvin, love me tonight and then just hold me. That's all I ask." She closed her eyes as his lips found hers.

Dee Ann Farley wiped her hands on her apron. She had just finished the last of the dishes and they were draining near the washpan. She turned to look at Calvin who still sat with his feet propped on the edge of the table. She could tell by his expression he was lost in his thoughts. She walked over and stood behind him, then put her arms around his neck. She leaned forward and whispered in his ear, "Penny for your thoughts."

Calvin moved his hands up and gently grabbed her arms. "I was just thinking I ought to be rejoining the brigade. I'm not dizzy anymore and I can hear good again."

Dee Ann felt her heart catch in her throat. She knew the

time would come when Calvin would leave, but she had
hoped it would not be so soon. The war was still trudging
along and she knew he was a man bound by his strong
sense of duty. She had tried to avoid thinking too much
about the time he would leave. Calvin filled a void in her
life that desperately needed filling. Living in a dangerous
land alone with her children had become difficult. Though
she loved her children she was still lonely, until Calvin
came along. She hadn't been aware of how hungry she had
become for companionship until Ross had brought Calvin
into her life. The thought of his leaving was almost more
than she could bear. "How long before you go?"

"I should leave tomorrow morning."

"I'm gonna miss ya, Calvin." She answered sadly.

Calvin lifted her arms away from his neck and pulled
her around in front of him. He held her hands in his as he
looked into her face. "Dee Ann, I've never lied to you,
and I don't want to mislead you. You knew all along I
couldn't stay."

Dee Ann was on the verge of tears as she looked down
at his upturned face. "Yes, I knew you'd have to go."

"Dee Ann, you're a very special woman and you've
been very good to me. You've given me pleasure, sensa-
tions, and joy like I've never felt before, and made me feel
real passion. I'll admit it has all been sudden and I'm confused. I don't know if this is what I want or if I'm ready
to settle down and take on the responsibilities of a ready-
made family. I'm also torn by duty. I am enlisted in the
army for the duration of the war and people are counting
on me. I must return. I won't lie to you. I don't know
when or if I'll come back."

She read more in his eyes than he was willing to say,
and she saw his confusion. She knew in her heart what
was troubling him. "Don't worry, Calvin. I knew I never
had any claim on ya. What I've done was what I needed
and I ain't sorry. I'm just glad for our time together."

Calvin looked into her brown eyes as a tear tracked across her cheek. He knew how much she loved him. It all had taken such a short time. Still, he wasn't ready to accept what she had to offer, at least not yet. He pulled her close and wrapped his arms around her waist, hugging her to him. He felt her soft breasts press through the dress against his cheek as he held her.

Calvin thought about how different they were. He had been raised on a plantation in luxury and she had lived a life of poverty in the backwoods hills on small farms. "Dee Ann, the time with you has been very special and I'll never forget you, but I've got my duty. I can't just walk away from the army. If I were to desert, then I would be a criminal and a wanted man. Besides, I can't live knowing I turned my back on my family and friends."

"Now ya sound just like my husband, Robert. He was always talkin' about duty, an' how he had to fight. All duty got him was dead."

"When you're fightin' in a war it's always a possibility. I live with danger everyday. I don't want to make any promises I can't keep."

Dee Ann cradled his head to her bosom as she ran her fingers through his hair. "Hush now! You don't have to explain to me. I just want you to promise me one thing, Calvin."

Calvin glanced up at her. "Sure if it's possible, Dee Ann."

"Just until ya leave, love me. That's all I ask. When it's time to leave, go knowin' I don't expect ya to come back."

He looked up at her, then pulled her down to sit on his lap. "You're one hell of a woman, Dee Ann Farley. I know there's no way I'll ever forget you." He kissed her passionately and her lips felt warm and wet. Her breath was faster, coming in shallow little gasps as she pressed herself against him. Calvin lifted her up in his arms and carried her to the bed. He dropped her on it and jumped in beside her. "What about the kids?"

"Debbie is still takin' her nap and Jimmy is out workin' in the garden. He won't come into my bedroom without askin'."

"Then I guess we've got the time," Calvin said as he started to undress.

The next morning Calvin said good-bye, mounted Red Roses, and rode off to rejoin his brigade. It had not been easy riding away from Dee Ann Farley. A man never forgets the first, and although he had known prettier women and ones who came from better families, he had not met one with more passion or character. Deep within him, Calvin knew he wasn't yet ready for the kind of commitment Dee Ann Farley deserved. Yet, he was grateful for the things she had taught him and the time they had shared.

23

The Cornfield Ambush

Quantrill's column traveled east along the Santa Fe Trail. At the town of Brooklyn, they left the Santa Fe Trail and turned south on Fort Scott Road toward Ottawa. Soon, Yankee pursuit became troublesome and shots were exchanged without loss of life. Quantrill's raiders felt increasing pressure from the relentless pursuit of Yankee troops angry over the destruction of Lawrence. Somehow, their pursuit had to be checked.

The running skirmish took them through a narrow lane bordered by large cornfields. As they rode out of the confined area, the guerillas began to spread out in panic on the prairie. George Todd, sensing disaster if action wasn't taken to stem the panic, stopped in the middle of the road and flagged down riders. Billy Cahill and William Gregg were among the first to join Todd. Others, seeing a gathering knot of determined fighters, stopped to join them.

Among those who gathered in the road were the James brothers, Cole Younger, and Bloody Bill Anderson.

Todd spoke rapidly to those around him, shouting above the noise of retreating guerillas who streamed past them. "Boys, we've got to stop them or we're gonna lose the whole outfit. I want some of you to ride on both sides of the cornfield and flank the road. I'll take the rest and charge the lane when you are in position. We gotta stop 'em, boys!"

Billy guided his horse as best as he could through the standing corn. The going was tough; the stalks slapped and scraped at him and his mount. Near Billy rode Frank and Jesse James. Once in position, hidden behind a green curtain of cornstalks, the raiders readied themselves for combat. It wouldn't take long for the advancing Federals to funnel down this narrow lane, moving fast on the heels of the Rebel retreat.

The Yankees, sensing the disorganization and panic among the raiders, galloped down the road at full tilt, ignoring the danger their reckless behavior was causing as they rode right into the middle of the trap. Todd waited patiently until the Yankees were drawn deep within the ambush. He set spurs to his horse as a shrill Rebel yell shrieked on the wind behind him. Guns blazing in both hands, he led the charge directly at the surprised Yankee troopers leading the pursuit. In their confusion under a heavy fusillade from the onrushing Missourians, the Yankees stopped their advance in the middle of the road. Uncertain what they should do and cowed by this sudden resistance, the Union troopers began milling in the road like cattle, unsure of which direction to stampede. Those in hot pursuit piled into those who had stopped, further adding to the confusion.

Billy and the other raiders hiding in the corn opened fire on the tightly bunched, confused Union troopers. It was like a turkey shoot at point-blank range. Meanwhile, the charge led by Todd swept down on top of the hapless Federals. The front rank of Union riders dissolved in the hail of gunfire.

Amid the curling blue-black smoke of discharged weapons and the shrieks of dying horses and men, Billy and his friends laid down a curtain of lead in the killing zone. The scene became a hopeless blur of movement as Billy emptied both revolvers into the mass of milling soldiers in blue. Saddles emptied before his eyes, the bodies falling to be trampled beneath the spinning hooves of the confused horses.

Yankee riders pressing in from behind went down in the tangle of bodies and horses piled in the center of the road. Billy shifted to a third pistol and emptied it into the mass of flesh in the chaotic melee. The mission accomplished, the raiders turned and prepared to gallop away.

Billy watched as George Todd and his horse went down in a sprawl in the middle of the lane. Todd's favorite horse had been shot from under him. George immediately cast aside the Union overcoat he was wearing in fear that his men might mistake him for a Yankee. Billy veered toward George, but he saw Fletch Taylor rein in and help George swing on behind his saddle.

Billy slowed a little as he exited the field and rode into the lane. He galloped beside Fletch Taylor and George Todd as they rode double on the horse. Slowly they put distance between them and the enemy. Suddenly, Billy heard George Todd utter a string of black oaths.

"What's the matter, George?" Fletch asked.

"When I took that damn coat off back there and left it, I plum forgot I had over four thousand dollars stuffed into the pockets!"

Fletch Taylor grimaced at the news. "Well, we damn sure ain't goin' back for it."

When the rear guard caught the main body of guerillas, George Todd obtained another horse. The Missourians continued their steady retreat through the morning and afternoon.

Billy felt hot and sweaty under the August sun. His body ached with fatigue after the night ride, the raid in the early morning hours, and now the retreat. He was not alone. He saw the same exhaustion stamped on the dirty, grimy faces of the riders around him, and the horses were pushed to the limit.

After the raiders had checked the Union pursuers, the Yankees followed much more cautiously and, for the moment, were not pushing Quantrill's men. Billy noticed as he rode that many riders had begun to lighten their load along the way. The side of the road was cluttered with discarded bolts of cloth, women's dresses, hats, saddle gear, and extra items no one wanted to carry any longer.

As far as Quantrill could tell, only Larkin Skaggs had not made it out of Lawrence. None of the men seemed to care, for Larkin was very unpopular. They had lost two more guerillas killed on the retreat and during the battle in the cornfield. Three more wounded had to be left and they were killed by the Yankees. Quantrill's men had stolen hundreds of horses from Lawrence. They were riding these to rest their favorite horses, while sacrificing the captured horses to speed their escape. The fresh horses gave them an edge against their pursuers.

Late in the afternoon the raiders swung east again. Just before sunset Quantrill's band came within sight of Paola, Kansas, and Quantrill saw at least one hundred mounted soldiers standing in battle line to protect Paola from the raiders.

Just as Quantrill was taking stock of the situation, his rear guard was driven back on the main body by a fresh assault from behind. A unit of Kansas militia had caught them and attacked. Quantrill quickly formed his men into a line of battle. The Yankees, seeing the standing array of battlehardened veterans, decided not to attack. The guerillas still outnumbered those who would be close enough to give battle. After the impasse, as both sides studied each other's positions, the Rebels continued their withdrawal. This time they moved north around Paola. It wouldn't do to stay between the two Union forces.

The Yankees, sensing the danger of continued pursuit, rode on into Paola. They were physically exhausted and had seen the disaster at the cornfield. All decided it would be better to leave the active pursuit to others.

About five miles north of Paola the raiders stopped for a brief rest. Billy Cahill, Bill Gregg, and Quantrill rode straight into a small farm pond. Billy tumbled from his saddle into the shallow water. He washed his face and arms, drank heavily from the cool water, and refilled his canteens. When he rode his horse out of the pond, he slid into the grass under a tree and quickly fell asleep.

He was awakened less than an hour later. The Yankees were coming again. Billy swung his tired, stiffening body into the saddle.

Shortly after midnight the raiders crossed the border back into Missouri. By dawn Quantrill's men reached heavy timber along the Grand River.

Billy knew they were home and he doubted the Yankees could catch them. The guerillas called a halt and the men unsaddled and began to prepare a meal for the first time in a long while. All the loot was pooled and divided during the rest. Just as they were sitting down to eat, word came that the Kansans were crossing the border and would soon be upon them. A friendly farmer, sympathetic to their cause, brought word that the Missouri militia was gathering just on the other side of the ridge.

Quantrill wasted no time. He swung into his saddle, then rode among his followers. "Boys, we got to saddle up again and get goin'."

Bill Gregg, tired and hungry, looked at him like he was crazy. "Hell, we ain't had time to eat yet."

Quantrill turned in his saddle and pointed toward the horizon. "See those Kansans coming toward us?"

Bill looked at the column of riders still some distance away. "So what? We whipped them yesterday, we can whip 'em again."

Quantrill leaned forward as he stared into the lieutenant's eyes. "Yes, I know you can whip the Kansans, but what are ya gonna do with the twelve hundred Yanks in the Union Missouri militia over the next ridge?"

Bill Gregg swallowed hard. "I see what yer sayin' there, Capt'n. I reckon it is time to saddle up. Hell, I wasn't too hungry, anyway."

By now the three men wounded at Lawrence and hauled all this way in the back of a stolen wagon were unable to keep up with the riders. They tried to hide the wagon at a local farm. Those left without good mounts or horses that had gone lame were ordered to hide in the brush as best they could. If they waited until nightfall they might slip away. The rest of the command saddled up and headed east to face the Missouri militia.

As it turned out, the farmer had exaggerated and the militia only numbered a hundred and fifty men. They had little desire to face Quantrill's men and were easily brushed aside. Once clear of them, Quantrill split his command into smaller bands and disbursed them to hide out in the countryside.

The Kansans, led by a Red Legs leader named George Hoyt, caught the wounded men and killed them. A farmer whose misfortune it was to have them dropped off at his farm was also killed. An Indian traveling with the Red Legs scalped the three dead prisoners. Several other guerillas were found hiding in the brush during the day and were hung by the Red Legs. Many of them were strung up so high they could not be cut down. Their corpses hung in the trees for months, slowly rotting away, unburied.

Larkin Skaggs had gone back and killed Nathan Stone

at the Whitney House after Quantrill left the hotel. This would have angered Quantrill but justice was swift. Skaggs was caught by the people of Lawrence and killed. His dead body was dragged through the streets behind a horse and left to rot in a gully for months before finally being buried.

The raid had changed Billy Cahill. Although he hated all Red Legs, Jayhawkers, and Union soldiers and would not hesitate to gun them down without regret, he saw a new side of the guerillas he didn't appreciate. He feared they were becoming no different from the very men they were fighting. Deep inside, Billy knew his allegiance to Quantrill and his band was fading as his mind resisted justifying this new kind of warfare. He decided it was time to fight a more honorable war. At the first opportunity, he intended to rejoin Shelby's cavalry brigade as a regular trooper. Billy still wanted to fight, but he'd had enough of this kind of war. He suspected William Gregg felt the same.

A great sigh of relief coursed through him as he felt the weight of uncertainty drop from his shoulders. He now knew what he must do and was glad the great raid on Lawrence was over.

24

From Rich to Penniless

enton Bartok stood at the window in his office in
Lexington, Missouri. His mind wandered as he
stared through the rainstreaked panes into the gray
skies. Tears blurred his vision like the rain beating against
the windows. In his hands he held the crumpled telegram
he had received an hour before. Lawrence was nothing
now but a smoking ruin destroyed by Quantrill's raiders.
Buried within the ashes of Lawrence was the dream of
riches he had carefully gathered from Missouri. "Damn!"
he thought. "All that work and effort snatched away from
me in one day. It isn't fair." His mind reeled as he considered the news the telegram carried. He clenched his jaw
and fought against the racking sobs that were trying so
desperately to spring forth from his body. He would not
surrender to his emotions and he would remain strong. He
would not allow himself to give way to grief.

Benton had worked hard to gather a fortune for himself

from these traitors. He had planned carefully and shipped his spoils of war out of Missouri to the one place the guerillas and Missourians would never dare to approach—Lawrence, Kansas.

What had gone wrong? he wondered. He thought surely the Union army would judiciously protect a target so important to the Missourians. How could his army have been so stupid? Benton brushed away the tears that came despite his efforts to stop them. He rubbed his forehead as he absentmindedly stuffed the telegram into his pant's pocket.

It was all gone now. The money they had saved in the bank, the bank itself, and the auction house his brother had operated. All burned to the ground. Benton Bartok had made the quick transition from very wealthy to nearly penniless in one day.

The money wasn't all—he had lost his brother, Jacob. The telegraph said his brother's remains were found in the ashes of the bank. Apparently Jacob had been shot before his body was burned. Benton gained little satisfaction from this news. They hadn't been very close during their childhood, but Jacob was family.

"It was Jake who took care of Ma after Pa died," thought Benton. He took good care of her and saw to her burial. Benton had been too involved in his own life to worry about his parents he had left behind. It had all fallen on Jacob's shoulders. Jake did what needed to be done, while accomplishing the task of turning the goods Benton stole into money. Now Jacob was gone, and Benton Bartok realized there wasn't anyone left in the world that would care one way or the other what happened to him.

"If I still had my money I could use it to forget Jacob," Benton thought. "Money can buy friends and be mighty comforting."

A loud rapping sound of knuckles on wood reverberated through the door, stirring Benton from his thoughts. "Yes, what is it?"

"Major, it's me, Captain Rodgers."

"Come in, Captain."

The door swung open and in stepped the officer. "Sorry to disturb you, Major. I heard about the bad news. I'm sorry about your brother."

Benton cleared his throat carefully. "Thank you, Captain. Get on with it."

"Yes, sir, I have a dispatch from General Kessington. It says the guerillas that raided Lawrence have been chased back to Missouri and have broken into smaller bands. We're to send out patrols to look for them."

Benton Bartok stepped away from the window and slumped down into the chair behind his desk. "Is Kessington some kind of fool? Isn't he aware we've been trying to fight Quantrill's men since May? He massacred Captain Anders and his whole patrol. They've blasted Captain Shay on numerous occasions and killed nearly half his company, while threatening the entire county.

"Why, Bloody Bill rode through the German settlements just a short time ago leaving a trail of corpses in his wake. Yet, the army has refused to give me any replacements though I have repeatedly requested more men. No, our hands are tied. We will not venture outside our fortifications until we are strengthened."

"What about our orders, sir?"

"Damn the orders, Rodgers! If Quantrill can take his guerillas clear to Lawrence, destroy the town, whip the armies, and bring his men back out, then how can we stand against his raiders in their territory? I'm not a fool and I'll not risk any more of my men until we are reinforced."

"Major, if it's true they've split into smaller bands, we might be in better shape to hit them than ever before. They're gonna be tired and sore after the raid. We can hit them while they're weak."

"Shut up, Rodgers! I swear you would believe anything you hear. I simply don't believe Quantrill would split his forces. He just wants to make it look that way so he can lure us out and trap us, but I'm too smart to fall for his shenanigans."

Captain Rodgers shot his commander a look of disgust. "What if you're wrong, Major? What if we miss this opportunity to track them down? If General Kessington finds out he'll hang us both."

"He isn't gonna find out 'cause you're gonna keep your mouth shut. I want you to fake some reports. Make it look like we've been attacked, or the guerillas are in large numbers in our area, and ship those reports by telegraph. Then, by God, they'll send us more troops. I'll destroy Quantrill's plans."

"Quantrill's plans? I don't understand what you're talking about, sir. What plans?"

"Don't you see, Rodgers? Quantrill has been out to get me from the start. It's really me he wants, but he hasn't got me yet. He killed Anders and his patrol, but he didn't get me." Bartok's eyes had a wild, crazy, scared look in them. "He went to Lawrence just to kill my brother and clean out my money. They're out there waitin' for me like a pack of wolves, but they won't bring me down. No, sir, I won't let 'em. I'm too smart for them. No, we're gonna stay right here in the fortifications till help comes."

Captain Rodgers studied Bartok. The man had been drinking and a nearly empty bottle sat on the desk before him. Rodgers knew Bartok was pushed to the edge by his paranoia, fear, and grief. Nothing could be gained by continuing the conversation. Since he wasn't in command, the fault would not fall on his shoulders. Who could blame him for following his commander's orders? Rodgers pulled himself erect and saluted. "Very well, Major, I'll send the telegram and tell the men to be vigilant at their posts. Is that all, sir?"

Benton looked up from the rye whiskey in the bottom of his glass. "Yes, Captain, you're dismissed."

"Very well, sir." Captain Rodgers spun on his heels and marched through the door, shutting it behind him.

Benton Bartok picked up his glass and swallowed the last of the whiskey then set it down, grabbed the bottle, and refilled the glass. "They won't get me, by heaven. I'm too smart for 'em," Benton said to himself aloud.

25

Man Proposes, God Disposes

General Shelby sat in the chair, studying the flames dancing along the logs in the fireplace. He pondered all the bad news of the last few days. As he nursed his wounds received at the battle of Helena, word had come of the depth of the disaster on July Fourth to the Confederate cause. Lee's army had been defeated at Gettysburg the same day Vicksburg surrendered in Mississippi. This coming on the heels of the defeat at Helena meant Union victories in all three theaters of war on the same day, and all on the Fourth of July.

Word had arrived of Quantrill's raid on Lawrence. Shelby reflected on the days he himself had been involved in the border war with Kansas. He had always hated Lawrence and saw it as a haven for those Free-Staters who would destroy Missouri and his way of life. He knew the reports of the destruction of Lawrence would inflame the enemy to even sterner measures and greater retaliation.

While he was glad to see the blow struck, he knew the consequences would be severe.

His fears were justified when reports came in of Ewing's Order Eleven, issued on August the twenty-fifth of 1863. In brief, it ordered all people living in Jackson, Cass, and Bates Counties, with the exceptions of those living within one mile of Independence, Hickman Mills, Pleasant Hill, Harrisonville, and Kansas City, to leave their homes by September ninth. Those who established their loyalty to the Union to the commanding officer of the nearest military headquarters would be permitted to move to a military post in the district, or to any portion of Kansas except the border counties. All others were ordered out of the district of the border.

It didn't matter whether you were loyal to the Union or not, you must leave your home and property. It amounted to an even more drastic removal policy than the one already underway under Order Ten. Tens of thousands of people were forcibly uprooted and found themselves homeless refugees. Wives left alone with their children while their husbands were away at war were forced to leave their homes behind, and take only what meager possessions they could carry in wagons or on their backs. The mass exodus from the Missouri counties flooded the roads with the disenfranchised.

To add to the misery, marauding Union troops burned out the empty homes and forced out those who refused to leave. Bands of Kansas Red Legs swarmed into the areas looting, burning, and murdering indiscriminately. Quantrill had destroyed a town; in retaliation the Federal government, in league with the Jayhawkers and Red Legs, destroyed most of three Missouri counties.

Even Jo Shelby's family were being forced to leave the Rebecca Redd Farm, where they had been staying. Fortunately Jo had called on an old friend before the war, Union General Frank Blair. With his help and the help of Benjamin Gratz, Jo Shelby hoped his family could be safely moved to Kentucky. He had written them both and was anxiously waiting for their replies.

Still lost in his thoughts as he stared at the fire, he didn't hear Fanny enter the parlor in Farnsworth House. "Colonel, I got some good chicken soup here."

Shelby glanced up at the big black woman approaching with the lap tray filled with food. He waved his left hand at her, signaling for her to remove it. "Take it away, Fanny, I'm not hungry right now."

"Jo Shelby, you gonna stop this foolishness right now and eat this chicken soup if'n I have to feed it to ya a spoonful at a time."

Surprise mixed with a touch of anger at her impertinence, showed clearly on his face. "I've never taken orders from a slave and I don't intend to start now."

Fanny set the tray down on an end table near the colonel. She raised her meaty hands and balled her fists on her hips as she stared eye-to-eye with the colonel. "I ain't no slave. I'm a free woman workin' for the Kimbroughs. I was hired to take care of this house and everyone in it. I ain't in your army, Colonel, but you're darn sure in this house, an' around here I give the orders. Now, are you gonna eat this soup or not?"

Jo Shelby melted under the housekeeper's glare of determination. He admired her spunk and, despite himself, a smile broke across his face. "Well, since I appear to be outranked I guess I better eat the soup."

Fanny flashed her white toothy smile broadly as she realized she had won. "That's more like it, Colonel. You an' I both know it's for your own good. This here soup is real good an' it'll put meat on your bones."

"Spare the lecture, Fanny. Just give me the tray and I'll eat the soup."

The big woman turned and grabbed up the tray and set it across Jo Shelby's lap. "You got to take care of yourself.

Our boys need you to lead the brigade against them damn Yankees. How am I gonna get you well if'n you don't eat?"

Shelby spooned up a generous amount of the soup and tasted it. After his first two swallows he looked up into Fanny's watchful eyes. "I'm eating it, all right?"

She nodded her approval.

"Will you find Captain Stryker for me?"

"I think he's with Miz Cassandra." Fanny smiled in triumph. "I'll go fetch 'em though I got other things need doin'." Fanny proudly lumbered out of the room.

Jo Shelby scooped in another spoonful of the soup. He was hungrier than he thought and the soup was tasty. He had to admit his time at Farnsworth House had been restful; and under the care of his doctor and the good people here, he had begun to recover. He shook his head in amazement as he considered Fanny's grit. "If the Yankees had to face Fanny, they'd have already surrendered. I have to admit, she sure can cook," he thought.

Moments later Captain Evan Stryker strolled into the room. He smiled as he watched his colonel finishing off the soup. "I heard you lost a skirmish with Fanny."

"It's darn hard arguing with the woman when you know she's right." He looked up at Evan. "Besides, the soup is really very good. I hope I didn't tear you away from anything too important," Jo said slyly.

"I'd have to say Cassandra is a mite more enjoyable to look at than you, Colonel, but I'm here when duty calls. By the way, I picked up this telegram for you from town a little while ago. I thought you'd like to read it." Evan handed it to the colonel.

"Well, I guess you haven't allowed the ladies to distract you too far from your duties."

Evan Stryker smiled at the remark. "No, sir." Stryker waited while his commander read the telegram.

A look of relief spread across Jo's face as he read.

When he glanced up, Evan could see tears welling in the corner of Jo Shelby's eyes. "It's good news. It's from Benjamin Gratz. He says he has made arrangements for safe passage through Union lines for Rebecca Redd, my wife Betty, and the children on a riverboat bound for Lexington, Kentucky."

"That's great news, Colonel."

Shelby looked back into the fire. "Did you hear anything else while you were at the telegraph office, Captain?"

"Yes, sir, I have these dispatches as well, Colonel."

Evan reached into his pocket and pulled out several telegrams. He handed them to his commander.

Jo held them in his left hand. "Here, Captain, remove this tray. I'm done anyway." He tried to unfold the first telegram with his one good hand. After a moment he gave up in frustration. "Just report what they say, Captain."

"Yes, sir," said Evan. "One of them reports General Marmaduke has killed General Walker in a duel fought over the disaster at Helena. General Marmaduke has been arrested."

"I was afraid it was going to come to that. Marmaduke was really upset when Walker refused to advance. Was Marmaduke injured in the duel?"

"No, sir, reports say he is fine," Evan answered. "Another telegram says General Steele is pressing his attack on Little Rock. He isn't attacking the fortifications head on, but rather encircling his armies in the hope of cutting off Price and Holmes and our entire army. Holmes fears if he doesn't abandon the city, it will be another Vicksburg. Price wants to abandon the city to the Yankees and Holmes is slowly being convinced. Another telegram asks you to return to command the cavalry as soon as possible."

"What do you think they'll do to General Marmaduke, Evan?"

"I don't know, Colonel, but I know our army needs every good commander it has right now, especially with you injured. I hope they'll restore General Marmaduke to his command. We need him."

"I hope you're right, Captain. He's too good an officer to lose." Shelby shifted in his chair and said, "If Little Rock falls, then Batesville won't be far behind. Batesville will be too far behind our lines to protect and the Yankees will seize it. It's time to inform the locals of the bad news. They should consider evacuating the area."

"I know you're right, but it's gonna be hard on these people. This will be the second move for the Kimbroughs. I know they don't want to do it again. Emotions don't seem as tense here in Arkansas as they were in Missouri. Maybe the Yankees will treat the civilians better here."

"I hope those who have experienced Yankee occupation will share their experiences with those that haven't."

"I'll do what I can, sir."

"Thank you, Captain. I think it is time for me to rejoin my command. Make the arrangements, will you, Evan?"

"Yes, sir, but your arm . . . it's not healed."

"I know, Captain, that's what my doctor keeps tellin' me. The war is not going to wait until I am one hundred percent. It seems clear of infection and that is good enough for me. You have my orders."

Evan felt concerned about the condition of Jo Shelby's wrist. It was a long way from healed and the colonel was still weak from loss of blood. Aside from the condition of his commander, he was also enjoying his time spent with Cassandra here at Farnsworth House and hated to see it all end. His concern ran even deeper as he realized Batesville would soon be at the mercy of Union armies if Little Rock fell. He feared for Cassandra's safety and for those living in this house. He knew he must tell her.

"If you'll excuse me, Colonel, I'll inform the others and begin making arrangements." Evan pulled himself up and snapped off a salute.

Shelby returned it with a left-handed salute. "By all means, Captain. You're excused."

Evan Stryker left Jo Shelby in the parlor and started down the hallway toward the ballroom.

"Capt'n Stryker, Miz Valissa Covington is here and asked me to find you. Says she'd like to talk to you for a few minutes, if she could," said Jethro.

"Thank you. Where is she?"

Jethro smiled widely. "She's in the ballroom."

"Thanks." Evan picked up his stride. When he entered he saw Valissa standing near a window. He noticed her mind was somewhere far away.

Valissa turned to face him as she heard the sound of his boots on the wooden floor. She flashed him a quick smile. "Captain Stryker, I hope I haven't come at a bad time."

"No, Valissa, this is as good as any. How can I help you?"

"I was wondering if you've heard anything from Ross Kimbrough?"

"No, I haven't seen him since the battle of Helena. I'm sure he is okay, or we would have heard something."

Evan could see a flicker of disappointment cross Valissa's face. "Oh, I had hoped someone might have heard from him. I know he must be very busy and the mail is so disorganized because of the war." She hesitated a moment. "Well, I was hoping you had some news, but that's not the reason I've come. Father has just returned from Little Rock. He says the city is in danger of fallin' to the Yankees. They closed congress and are ready to evacuate the city."

"Yes, I know. The news rolls in off the telegraph and I updated Colonel Shelby just minutes ago."

"Oh, I should have guessed Colonel Shelby would be staying aware of developments. Father received a letter from Joseph Farnsworth before he left Little Rock. He says the blockade is growing tighter, but he still can slip his ships through their patrols. They take the cotton they haul to the islands in the Caribbean then transfer it to ships heading for England and France. On the islands the blockade runners load up with guns, powder, medical supplies, and other essentials for the war effort then run them back through the blockade."

Evan listened to the news carefully. "Is Joseph Farnsworth sailing the ships himself?"

"Oh, heavens no! He lives in England and keeps busy selling the cotton and buying supplies to ship to the South. Father says he invested wisely when he joined Farnsworth in his shipping business. They're making handsome profits. Father has his share stored in banks in England."

Evan swallowed hard as he choked back a harsh response. He knew the South needed as many supplies from Europe as it could get, but it galled him to hear some men were getting exceedingly rich off the war while others were dying and losing everything they owned. He tried to hide his true feelings. "I'm glad to hear it's going so well."

"Father says they've lost one ship off Mobile Bay in Alabama. Federal gunboats caught her and sunk her, but she had already paid out her cost many times over. Joseph has three more blockade runners. One of them makes regular runs into Texas ports to help our cause west of the Mississippi."

Evan kept his thoughts to himself. He knew Farnsworth and the other blockade runners landed in Texas because the ports were easier to enter and the Union blockade wasn't as tight. Out of politeness, he asked, "What else did your Farnsworth say?"

"He says he fears he will be unable to return to Farnsworth House until the war is over. Since the Yankees control the Mississippi River there's no easy way to travel home. The trip overland would be too slow and arduous.

Joseph says if the war gets too difficult we can take our family to England on one of his blockade runners."

Evan could not conceal his contempt at the suggestion of abandoning the Confederacy. "I suppose there are some that lack the will to stand up against the enemy. I, for one, could not abandon the South."

Valissa noticed the irritation in Evan's voice, but seemed anxious to avoid an argument. "Father says if Little Rock falls this area may become unsafe. He is considering moving us away from here. What do you think?"

"I've discussed this with Colonel Shelby. He agrees with your father. I think the safest place to go for now would be East Texas. I think the Yankees are concentrating their efforts on capturing Arkansas next."

"I suppose you're right. Should I tell Father you agree we should leave?"

"Yes, I would, Valissa. Anyone with the means to evacuate this area in my opinion should do so. I hate to tell Cassandra because she seems so happy here, but I'm going to tell her she should leave for Texas. I couldn't live with myself if anything should happen because I didn't warn her. I just hate to see her move so far away."

"You won't have to tell me, Evan. I overheard your conversation."

Evan turned, startled by the sound of Cassandra's voice. "Cassandra, I'm sorry, I didn't know you were here." He held his hands out to her.

She took his hands in hers. "I understand. It sounds like Little Rock might fall."

"I'm afraid Little Rock is hovering on collapse. The Yankees have us outnumbered and they have a river fleet of ironclads, gunboats, and transports that can move quickly against us. It doesn't look good."

Cassandra could see the genuine concern on Evan's face. She knew he was worried not only about the fall of Little Rock, but about her safety. She wanted to ease his concern. "I like Batesville and it's started to feel like home. I know the tortures of the road, but if it becomes necessary we'll move again, even if it requires going to Texas."

Evan smiled at the way she replied. "You make it sound like Texas is right next door to hell! Believe me, most of Texas is very beautiful. Besides, you might as well get used to Texas because after the war I hope you'll live there with me."

"Why, Evan Stryker, you do presume a lot, don't you? Am I to consider this bit of news a proposal?"

"I had hoped to propose more romantically later, but the war won't wait. Colonel Shelby is planning to leave to rejoin the brigade by tomorrow. I'll be goin' with him. I'm afraid I haven't the time to be more indirect." Evan gazed into her eyes with hopeful expectation.

Cassandra was not surprised by the proposal, merely by the timing of it. She had known from the beginning that this big, gentle Texan was special. The time she had spent with him over the winter in Batesville and during Shelby's recovery only served to deepen her love for him. She felt his hand warm in hers and her eyes began to fill with tears. She was so overcome with joy she couldn't speak immediately.

In the awkward moment that followed as Cassandra and Evan stared into each other's eyes, Valissa discreetly cleared her throat. "I can see you two need some time alone. If you'll excuse me, I'll see myself to the door. My best wishes and congratulations." Then Valissa left the room.

"Will you marry me?" Evan asked again.

"Yes, I'll marry you, Evan Stryker. I've heard you talk so much about San Marcos and Texas and how beautiful they are. I guess I'll just have to marry you and see for myself."

Evan beamed with joy and pulled her to him. He

hugged her tightly as his lips found hers. After their kiss he held her in his arms. "I was so afraid you might turn me down."

"If I had any sense I probably should have. Here I am promising to marry you and I've never met your family, or even seen Texas."

"I'll promise you this: if you don't love Hays County after a year, then I'll move wherever you want me to go, just as long as I'm with you."

Cassandra pulled back and studied his eyes. "Wherever you are, darling, is where I want to be."

Evan kissed her again. As he held her in his arms, she asked, "When can we be married?"

"I don't know. I don't see any way we can be married before morning. By tomorrow I'll be gone and on our way back to the brigade. We'll have to keep in touch. When the brigade goes into winter camp I'll try to get marriage leave, or maybe you can join me in camp long enough for the ceremony."

"Whenever it is, I'll be waiting for you," vowed Cassandra.

26

Shelby's Missouri Raid

Evan Stryker followed Jo Shelby into the headquarters of General Theophilus Holmes, commander of the district of Arkansas, presently at Arkadelphia. Jo Shelby had made the trip with the expressed intention of asking permission to make a raid into Missouri. When they entered the room Evan Stryker positioned himself near the door. Although he was a staff officer, he knew that when the big brass held the floor it was best to make oneself as unobtrusive as possible.

Before Shelby could utter a word General Holmes attacked. "Colonel Shelby, your men are nothing more than thieves. The thieving must be stopped. They steal all the best horses, live off the land, and drink up all the whiskey they come across. They give me more trouble than the rest of my army put together." The general paused, then in exasperation his shoulders sagged as he let out a tired sigh. "Despite the thieving you lead my best fighters."

Shelby's eyes flashed cool anger as he sized up the old man standing before him. General Holmes was suffering from acute depression ever since the failure at Helena, and now the Yankees held Little Rock. Obviously, he was looking for somewhere to vent his anger. Shelby responded quickly and loudly enough for the nearly deaf Holmes to hear. "Sir, whoever told you my men are thieves is a liar."

General Holmes puffed up his chest and glared. "I believe it is true."

"Why?" asked Shelby.

"Because everyone says so, sir—everybody, do you hear?"

"Do you believe everything you hear, General, just because everyone says it?"

"I certainly do."

"Well, General, I don't believe everything I hear and I'll give you an example. Do you know what everybody says about you?"

"No, sir, I do not!" General Holmes snapped.

A sly smile crossed Shelby's lips and a bold twinkle came into his eyes. "They say you are a damned old fool, but I don't believe it. In fact, I invariably deny it, sir."

Anger flashed in General Holmes' eyes for a moment, then realizing Shelby had outwitted him, he broke into a smile. "You have a point, Colonel Shelby. Perhaps I have been too quick to listen to idle gossip. You have a fine command, sir, and I'm sure your men haven't taken a thing they didn't need."

"General, my command from its earliest beginning has supplied itself from the captured stores and horses of our enemies. If my men have stolen, it has been from the enemy, not from our people."

General Holmes smiled again. "Then you haven't taken even one horse too many. Since the Yankees are so willing to equip your command, tell your men to help themselves."

"That is why we're here, sir. I wish to make a raid into Missouri."

Holmes' smile faded as he clasped his hands behind his back.

"No, I need every man I have. We don't know when General Steele will begin to advance again. Besides, the fall is upon us and winter will be here soon. It's not a good time to start another campaign."

"My men will ride and fight despite the weather, General. We need to stir up things behind the enemy lines. We can take the attention away from Arkansas and direct it on Missouri. I believe I can disrupt enemy communications and supplies and pull enemy troops away from the lines facing you. That, General, could do more to turn the war in our favor than sitting here waiting for the enemy."

"Indeed, Jo, sometimes I feel our army of the Trans-Mississippi is nothing more than prisoners at the whim of the Union army and self-supporting at that. At every turn it seems we are on the defensive."

Jo Shelby sensed the general weakening in his arguments. He moved to seize the advantage. "That's what I've been saying. It doesn't have to be this way. We can go on the offensive and make them respond to our moves for a change."

"I'm short of men now. I can't spare a large command to attack Missouri."

"I'm not talking about a large command, General. All I want is the independent command of my brigade of eight hundred men."

Holmes began to pace slowly as he pondered Shelby's request. "I don't know if it would work. They might cut you off and I can't afford to lose your men."

"If it's men you are worried about, sir, I think I can return with more soldiers than I have now."

Holmes stopped his pacing and snapped up his head to study Shelby. "Just how do you suppose you can do that, Jo?"

"You know what the Federals have been doing to Missouri. I believe if you give Missourians a chance to join a Missouri command, they will flock to our colors."

"I have no doubt you can find the men. What are you going to do with the untrained, unequipped men you recruit? Supplies are very tight. I don't have the horses, the guns, or equipment to outfit even so much as a company if I had them."

"You don't have to worry, General. I'll arm and equipment them from my regular supply depot."

Holmes looked at Shelby incredulously. "And just where the hell is this magical supply depot of yours?"

"The Union army, sir. We'll take what we need from the enemy." Shelby showed his sly smile again. "If you don't mind me setting loose my band of thieves, sir."

Holmes smiled back. "If anyone can do it, Jo, I believe it would be your boys. I've already heard from Governor Thomas Reynolds. From the way he talked I'm sure you've already convinced him. He has expressed his wishes that I let you go on this raid. As you know it would be very difficult for me to oppose the wishes of the Confederate governor of Missouri. I've been against this raid from the moment I first heard rumors of it. Tonight you have given me the reason to wonder if I've been wrong." General Holmes turned to face Colonel Shelby. He offered his hand which Jo clasped firmly. "Godspeed, Jo, and good hunting."

Jo Shelby allowed himself to smile. He pulled to attention and snapped off a salute. "Yes, sir, General." He spun on his heel and marched out the door without so much as a pause to see if Evan Stryker was following him.

Evan felt relief at the outcome of the meeting. Jo would have been impossible if he had been refused the right to

make a raid. Evan stepped quickly behind the colonel, trying valiantly to keep pace. "Besides," Evan thought, "it's
been a while since I've seen Missouri."

Captain Ross Kimbrough scanned the area before him with
binoculars. Near him lay many of this dismounted scouts.

"Can ya see who they are, Ross?" whispered Jonas
Starke.

Ross tried to ignore the fact his sergeant didn't refer to
him by his new rank. He was now a captain of the
scouts—promoted by Colonel Jo Shelby just before the
column moved north. "I can see 'em, Sergeant. God,
they're a ragged lot. The men are mostly in civilian clothing. There's many women and children in the wagons traveling with them."

"Do ya figure them to be friends or enemies?"

"Hush up, Jonas! You nag me like some old woman.
Soon as I see somethin' that'll give us a clue I'll let you
know." Jonas didn't respond, instead sulking like a repri-
manded eight-year-old.

Ross studied the column. Riding in front of the wagons
was a large group of men. They rode in loose and ragged
groups suggesting a dearth of military training. He guessed
more men were guarding the flanks and the rear of the
slow-moving caravan of wagons. Ross swung his binoculars on the man he thought might be the leader of the
group. The soldier wore a uniform of some sort but it was
so heavily covered by trail dust he couldn't make out its
color. Beside the officer rode a flag bearer, his banner
hanging limp against the staff, concealing its design. Ross
wished the wind would come up a little and straighten out
that banner; then they would have clue to the identity of
this group. He strained to see anything that might identify
the men approaching; and as the riders topped a rise, a
slight breeze unfurled the flag revealing a somewhat crude
Confederate banner.

Ross smiled. "Jonas, I do believe they're ours."

"Well, who the hell are they, Ross?"

"I don't know, but I think it's time to find out. Saddle up, boys, we're gonna meet this bunch." Ross paused a moment. "Sergeant, I know it's hard for you, but would you try to call me Captain, or sir? You know I don't really care, but Colonel Shelby would skin us alive if he heard us ignorin' soldierly protocol."

Jonas glanced at Ross. "I hope those captain bars ain't gone to yer head, youngin'."

"No, Jonas, I'm still the same. I just don't want either one of us in trouble if we get around higher brass."

Jonas grunted in acknowledgement as he swung into the saddle. "Yes, suh, Captain, suh!" Jonas said sarcastically.

Ross chose to ignore Jonas' attitude as he mounted Prince of Heaven. He rode ahead and motioned for his men to hold back and block the road.

As he approached the column Ross noticed that the officer and his men spread out across the road, then Ross saw the officer hold up his hand. The column shuddered to a halt. Flanked by two of his men, the commanding officer rode to meet Ross.

Ross watched the advancing men carefully, praying he hadn't made a mistake about the flag he had seen. Ross held his hand up to greet them. "Good morning, gentleman. May I ask the name of your command?"

The officer made a haphazard salute. "I'm Colonel David Hunter. Who might you be?"

"I'm Captain Ross Kimbrough of Jo Shelby's brigade."

The colonel smiled as he recognized Jo Shelby's name. "We're mighty pleased to meet you, Captain. I've got over a hundred and fifty new recruits for Confederate service."

Ross studied the pitiful wagon train trailing the new recruits. "Looks to me like you have more than some new recruits."

Hunter's expression became serious. "I'm afraid so.

We're escorting a couple hundred Southern refugees south to Arkansas. Most were forced from their homes by the Yankees in the areas surrounding Kansas City. They're tired, hungry, and have nowhere in particular to go. As we marched south they just kept joining our column. It's a hard thing to say no to women, children, and old people left with nothing in hostile country."

Ross didn't say it, but he admired the colonel for helping these people. "I'm surprised the Federals didn't find you and attack."

"I couldn't refuse these people—although it *has* caused us a few problems. Between Cassville and Fayetteville, we had to set up an ambush for a Yankee detachment doggin' us. My boys are armed mostly with shotguns and squirrel rifles so we waited until they rode right up under us. They were so busy concentrating on raiding the wagon train, they never spotted us. We counted eighty dead, and many more wounded. They haven't given us anymore trouble since."

Ross looked skeptical. "That's a mighty effective ambush for new recruits."

"These men may not be regular soldiers, but many have fought from the bush, or seen hard times at the hands of the Yankees. They had a score to settle and they did what I told 'em."

Ross glanced at the hard, pitiless expression of the two riders accompanying the colonel. Both had tied double-barreled shotguns to their saddles. "I didn't mean to offend you. I was just surprised."

"No offense taken. Where's Shelby's brigade?"

"They're comin' through Caddo Gap now. They should arrive soon. It's our job to scout ahead of the column."

"Why don't we pull off the road and let the wagons keep movin' south, Captain?"

"Sounds good to me. I'll send word for Colonel Shelby to ride forward."

The soldiers moved off the road and Ross watched in morbid fascination as the wagon train flowed past him down the dusty lane. Some of the wagons were nearly full of household goods others held only a few meager belongings. The majority of the wagons were driven by grim-faced women, hollow eyed and tired. Most looked like they had cried themselves out miles or days ago and now were struggling to cope. Small children filled nearly all of the wagons while the older children walked along behind. All were lean and hungry. A generous amount of trail dust coated their tattered clothing.

The wagons looked little better than the people. Many were nothing more than buck boards or hay wagons pulled by a variety of oxen, mules, and horses. The luckier ones rode in regular wagons covered sparsely by patched canvas. Ross choked back tears as he watched these proud but tattered refugees stream past. It angered him to see these women struggling south toward an uncertain future and an unknown destination. Their meager hopes lay before them.

Soon Jo Shelby and his column joined them. After a short conference, Colonel Hunter decided one hundred of his best men would join Shelby's raid and the other fifty, consisting of the less healthy and the older men, would continue south to protect the refugees. Ross and his scouts moved out ahead of the brigade.

27

Katlin's Plight

Katlin laid the opened letter on the table. Her hands trembled as she felt cold talons of fear clutching her stomach. She was confused, hurt, and surprised all in one wild mix of emotion, but she knew she only had herself to blame. Her curiosity had finally gotten the best of her, and giving into it, she had opened and read the letter in the sealed envelope her father had given her before they left Missouri. Her father had instructed her not to open the letter unless something happened to him. She felt guilty for betraying his wishes.

At least now she understood why he had insisted she never sell Becca. And she thought about her childhood years, suddenly she understood her father's actions more clearly.

She recalled the many nights she had lain awake in the Great House and listened to her parents fight. It had always been about the same things. Her mother was cold and while her father's nature was warm and loving. No, if she were honest with herself she knew her mother constantly shoved her father's attention and affections away, preferring to keep him at arm's length. It wasn't all her father's fault. Perhaps her mother ignored the late night indiscretions because it took pressure off her. Maybe Caroline Thomas knew what was going on.

Katlin considered this for a few moments, then sprang to her feet. She would face this problem head-on. Right or wrong, it was the only way she knew. Like it or not, she would follow her father's wishes.

She found Becca working alone in an upstairs bedroom. Katlin still held the letter in her hands. She closed the door quickly, then watched Becca spread a clean blanket on the bed. "Becca, I have some important news that I must share with you."

A mixture of fear and concern crossed Becca's features as she studied Katlin's worried expression. "What is it, Miz Katlin?"

"I have a letter from my father that concerns you. It also includes some documents that rightfully belong to you. I was instructed to open this letter only if Father died, but I let my curiosity get the better of me and I opened it anyway.

"Massa Thomas ain't dead, is he?"

Katlin glanced down at the papers she held in her hands, then lifted her eyes to Becca. "No, the last we heard Mother and Father were doing fine." Katlin's eyes pleaded for understanding. "I just had to know what was in the letter. Now that I do, I feel I must share it with you."

Becca could tell whatever was in the letter must be important. She stopped making the bed and moved near Katlin.

Katlin's chin trembled. She tried to speak, but at first the words would not come. Finally, she managed to say, "I have a letter granting your freedom."

Becca was stunned by Katlin's words. Her expression twisted in surprise and disbelief. Suddenly, her knees seemed to go weak and she sat on the edge of the bed. "Miz Katlin, did you say I'm free?

Katlin studied Becca's face. She saw the joy in Becca's eyes and the fear that it all might be some sort of terrible joke. Katlin said, "There is more in the letter."

"What else does it say, Miz Katlin?"

"It says we are sisters." Katlin paused as the words lay heavy between them. Katlin began to pace. "My father admits he frequently made love to your mother, Callie, in this letter. He says your mother was his secret lover until her death. He admitted he knew it was wrong, but my mother was not interested in love makin' and rather than constantly arguing with her over it, he let Callie fill his needs.

"He fathered all Callie's kids, but only you survived past childhood. He felt he could not rest in peace if he did not acknowledge you as his child. He only wanted to wait until after his death, because he didn't know how he could ever explain it to my mother. He couldn't stand to see the hurt this news would bring to her. He said in his letter he is sorry for the hurt and shame he has brought upon Mother, Gilbert, and me and for lacking the courage to tell you the truth himself."

Katlin stopped pacing and stood staring out the window into the blue skies beyond.

Becca sat stunned. She tried to think back over her younger years and it all began to make more sense now. Her mother had been treated far better than a common slave. Master Harlan Thomas had always shown an interest in Becca as a child and frequently held her on his lap. She never imagined he was interested in her because he was her father. She had always thought he paid attention to her because he was a good, kind master. Nothing more had ever crossed her mind.

She wondered why her mother had never discussed her father, and she remembered how her mother had looked at Master Harlan with special devotion. "Massa Thomas, he ain't dead?"

"No, he is still alive."

"Does that mean I'm still free?"

"I can't keep you in bondage knowing you are my half sister. I know I shouldn't have read the letter until my father's death, but I did and nothing can change that. You will have your freedom."

Becca smiled in relief. "What else does the papers say?"

Katlin resumed her pacing. "My father admitted he loved Callie. She filled a void in his life that my mother was unwilling to fill. Callie provided him with the love and affection he so desperately needed and my mother was afraid, or unable, to give. Mother was always afraid she might become pregnant again. At least that is what she claimed.

"Father wrote that the world would never have understood if he openly acknowledged his relationship with a slave. For the sake of Gilbert and myself and for the safety of his children born to Callie he kept his indiscretions a secret. It was the only way he could continue to operate Riverview Plantation."

Katlin returned to the window. "He says he wants you to know he loves you every bit as much as he does Gilbert and me." Katlin tried to control the pain she was feeling, but she began to sob as the tears spilled down her cheeks.

Becca's mind was a jumble as she mulled over the shocking news. She was a Thomas? A half sister to Katlin and Gilbert? She had been a personal servant to Katlin since she was a small child. Her mind recalled those long years of servitude and how she often wished she were white like Katlin and free to come and go. Becca didn't feel elation, she felt only anger. "All these years I been takin' care of you an' pickin' up after you an' we were sisters? All because my mother happened to be a slave an' your mother happened to be white?"

Anger propelled Becca to her feet. She stood quickly and approached Katlin, still sobbing by the window. "What's the matter, Miz Katlin. Does it hurt to know you got a nigger for a sister? Your mother couldn't satisfy your daddy so he used my mother. He ain't the first white man to satisfy his urges with his slaves. Lord knows they can't turn him down," Becca taunted.

Katlin's cheeks flushed with anger. She unleashed a resounding slap, striking Becca across the cheek with the back of her hand. The blow caught Becca off guard and she staggered back a few steps. Anger flashed in Becca's dark eyes, but years of training to submit kept her from responding to the blow.

Katlin said, "You speak about our father with respect. What he has done is shameful, but at least he told the truth in his letter. He not only wanted you to be free, Becca, he wants you to share equally in his estate upon his passing. It's all written right there in his letter. I know you must feel pain, but you can't possibly feel more hurt or anger than I do." Katlin turned away. "The past is behind us. We must now face the future."

Katlin stared at the floor and chewed on her lower lip, thinking. After a few moments she looked again at Becca. "Now that you know you are a Thomas you must stop seeing Jeremiah."

Becca rubbed her stinging cheek. "Just because you found out I have a white daddy I'm suddenly too good for a nigger? If I'm truly free, like you say I am, I can do whatever I want an' you can't stop me. I love Jeremiah. He's a good man and the first one to treat me right. I ain't gonna stop seein' him just 'cause he's black."

"Don't you understand, Becca? You'll have a right to claim a portion of Father's plantation when the war is over. You'll be a landowner and worth far too much to spend time with a common slave."

"You forget, I'm also half black. That's the part you don't wanna accept, ain't it, Miz Katlin? You don't want to think your lily-white daddy would prefer to sleep with a nigra than your momma," Becca drawled out derisively. "Well, I've been treated as a slave all my life, an' just because I suddenly find out my daddy was white don't change the way I feel none inside."

Katlin could see the anger in Becca's eyes and the truth of her words slapped Katlin like a bucket of cold water in her face. Shaken, Katlin replied, "Yes, I suppose I can see how you feel, but don't you see you have a stake in a new future?"

"One thing I know is money don't always bring happiness. I'll take my chances with Jeremiah."

"Jeremiah is a slave and he belongs to Andrew Covington. He isn't free to leave whenever he wants. Besides, where would you go and what would you do?"

Katlin saw the confusion in Becca's mind. She hadn't had the time to think it through that far and she hesitated before she answered. "I don't know. I just know I love Jeremiah."

Becca needed to think. It was still too risky to run away through Rebel lines. If they were caught, Jeremiah might be killed, and she couldn't risk losing him. Becca reached down and picked the pillows up off the floor where she put them while making the bed. She arranged them against the headboard. "I'll make a deal with you, Miz Katlin. You buy Jeremiah away from Massa Covington and we'll just let the news in your daddy's letter be a secret for a while. You can tell everyone you gave me my freedom. I'll keep doin' what I'm doin' now and you can pay me a little for my work. You give me the freedom papers on Jeremiah and I won't tell nobody about our daddy."

"I understand how deeply you must feel about Jeremiah,

but it wouldn't be right to keep treating you like you are a slave. You are my sister."

"You been doin' it all my life. I can't see no reason it has to change right now. 'Sides, I need your help with Jeremiah." Becca paused as she moved away from the bed and stood looking into Katlin's face. "How you think your brother Gilbert is gonna take this news? How is your new husband gonna like findin' out his wife has a half-black sister?"

Katlin felt her fear of those same unanswered questions gnawing away in her mind. She had struggled with these thoughts since she first read her father's letter. How would people she considered friends react if she acknowledged Becca as her sister? Would they scorn her? It was one thing for a man to use his slaves for pleasure, but another to claim the children that resulted. Society would ostracize any man bold enough to attempt it.

Katlin laid her hand on her swelling belly and rubbed it. How would Jessie feel if he knew his wife had a half-black sister? She knew the baby she carried must be nearly five months along. She hadn't told Jessie yet—she wanted to share the news with him in person instead of by letter. At first she had waited until she was certain she was pregnant. By then, Jessie had returned to the war. Now it was beyond any doubt and everyone could see for themselves as her belly continued to swell. She would soon be forced to let Jessie know by letter as it became more unlikely she would see him soon. She was planning to send a letter bearing the good news with Evan Stryker when Evan returned to the brigade. All this ran quickly through her mind. Wouldn't it be better for the baby to keep the secret a little longer?

Her mind made up, Katlin said, "All right, it's a deal. I'll try to buy Jeremiah and for the time being we'll keep this a secret. I'll inform everyone tomorrow I've given you your freedom and now you're working for me, agreed?"

"Yes, ma'am!" Becca felt a fresh surge of joy. In one bold move she might secure Jeremiah's freedom and assure the two of them would not be separated. Becca's fear had always been that eventually Andrew would call Jeremiah back to his plantation, forever separating them. Now, perhaps it would never happen. This meant more to her than anything else. For now, it was all that mattered.

28

Captured Union Blues

Corporal Calvin Kimbrough sighted down the breech of his cannon at the brick courthouse in Neosho, Missouri. He felt satisfied with his aim as he prepared to fire the first shot into the Yankee fortress.

As he worked, Calvin thought about the morning's events that had brought them to this point. They had hit the Yankees hard on the road to Neosho. Outnumbering them two to one, Shelby's men encircled the town like Indians against a lonely wagon train. The Union resistance was spirited and they refused to give up. Those still fit to fight holed up in the brick courthouse, turning it into a fortress. The rest of the Union soldiers settled into nearby buildings, intent on making this fight a house-to-house, street-to-street contest to the end.

Colonel Shelby knew from previous experience the futility of fighting in the open against heavy fortifications.

He instructed Lieutenant David Harris to bring the artillery forward and to set up out of rifle range of the courthouse. His intention was to bombard those inside until they surrendered and thus spare his men. Calvin admired the colonel's good judgment as he reported his piece ready to fire.

"Fire at will," ordered Lieutenant Harris.

"Fire!" yelled Calvin.

Delmar Pickett yanked hard on the lanyard. Black smoke and searing flame leapt from the muzzle as the cannon bucked into the air. Calvin's ears rang from the sound of the blast from his cannon, followed closely by the roar of the second cannon beside them. He saw the courthouse clearly now, easily the most prominent building in the town. He listened to the shriek of the shells as they cut their way through the air, and he heard the echoing slap as the first cannonball found its mark. Fragments of bricks and dust filled the air as the shot carried through an upper floor and continued out through the other side.

Quickly Calvin and his crew bent to their tasks. The cannons continued to roar as fast as they could be reloaded. The range was set now and the accuracy was terrific. Nearly every shot found its mark and great gaping holes began to appear in the side of the building. Soon a white flag of truce began to flap in the breeze from the highest steeple on the building.

"Cease fire," shouted Lieutenant Harris. "Stand by your cannons, men." Calvin repeated the order, though he knew his men had heard the lieutenant. Calvin glanced over at Harris. He was no older than himself and yet there he was, commanding the two pieces of artillery they had brought along for the raid.

Calvin didn't resent Harris's ascendency; he admired him. He would have preferred to have Captain Collins leading the battery, but he was left behind at Arkadelphia with Holmes and the rest of the army. Richard Collins had been promoted to Captain and given command of Collins' battery, which was named for him as was the custom. He hadn't joined the raid because of illness. It was the first time Calvin and the battery had fought without Dick Collins at the helm. The battery had suffered greatly at Helena and there were many new faces among the cannoneers.

The battery until recently had been considered a part of Bledsoe's battery, but with Bledsoe now long departed, command fell to Collins. When Collins recovered from his illness it would again be his battery to command. Two of the artillery pieces belonging to the battery remained behind with Captain Collins and the Confederate Army of the Trans-Mississippi. There weren't enough healthy men left to crew all four cannon, and besides, Holmes didn't want to give up any more artillery than necessary for this raid.

Calvin's attention returned to the present as he watched four Union officers ride out from the courthouse for a parley. "Your terms, Colonel?" asked the Yankee leader.

"Unconditional and immediate surrender," answered Jo Shelby.

The Union officer had little choice but to accept, and in less than a half hour the town was in Confederate control. Calvin went with Delmar to explore the courthouse. Both were anxious to see the amount of damage their artillery caused. In the upper floor of the courthouse the evidence of destruction was more vivid than they wished to see. In the room where their first shot had penetrated, the men found the grisly, bloody remains of five dead Union soldiers. One had been decapitated and the remains of his head had been generously splattered on the walls of the room. Another had been disemboweled and the entrails scattered.

Calvin felt his stomach convulse as he stumbled into the

hallway. The stench of death and gore mixed with the smell of his fresh vomit. He vowed not to be so curious in the next battle. The two men proceeded downstairs, where they ran into Calvin's brother Jessie.

"What's the matter with you, Calvin? You don't look too well."

Delmar laughed. "He's seen a mite more'n he intended upstairs. Our cannonballs sure done something terrible to those boys."

Jessie studied Calvin's deathly pale face. "Sometimes war isn't pretty, but remember they'd have done the same to you. Be grateful it's not you up there." Calvin nodded, still feeling too weak to risk responding.

Jessie's face relaxed a little. "Cheer up, Calvin, I've got a few presents for you. We scored a great haul here. I've helped gather the supplies and distributed the wealth while you were busy with your cannon and going sightseeing." Jessie handed his brother a heavy bundle. "I got you a new forty-four caliber Navy revolver and a Sharps carbine. There's a brand new Yankee uniform that's never been worn and a brand spankin' new overcoat."

Calvin stared down at the bundle in his hands and felt like a young child at Christmas. His eyes nearly brimmed with tears. "I shouldn't take more than my share."

"Don't worry, just take it. We captured four hundred good horses, four hundred new Colt Navy revolvers, four hundred Sharps carbines, four hundred new cavalry overcoats, with pantaloons, boots, spurs, hats, underclothing, medicines, blankets, socks, not to mention commissary supplies."

Calvin's eyes widened with enthusiasm. "Did you say new boots?"

"Yeah, we have them in several sizes."

"My boots are paper thin. A new pair of boots would make my life more comfortable."

Jessie beamed. "I'll even throw in a pair of new socks to sweeten the deal."

Throughout the command, Shelby's men were lost in celebration as they put the new uniforms to good use. The discarded, tattered rags of their old Confederate uniforms were left behind. Yankee prisoners were quickly stripped of their weapons and in some cases forced to trade their uniforms for worn-out scraps of clothing worn by the Rebels. Once the Yankees signed parole papers promising not to fight again unless they were exchanged for Southern parolees, they were released unarmed to find their way home. Meanwhile, the Rebels feasted on the newly captured commissary supplies.

Ross and his men were pleased to be issued captured uniforms. A good Union uniform might offer an advantage for scouts traveling through enemy-occupied territory. The three Kimbrough brothers shared a joyful evening together as they gathered around a new campfire to enjoy the spoils of war. While they ate, the sounds of gunfire drifted down from the north.

They heard later that a large Federal scouting party was sent out from Newtonia to investigate the sound of cannonfire. The Yankee captain and fifteen of his men were killed and the rest chased back to Newtonia after they stumbled into Confederate lines.

As he sat at the fire, Ross reflected on the success of the raid. Along the route of march they had destroyed a band of Jayhawkers led by Captain McGinnis. Seventy-nine had been killed outright and another thirty-one executed by firing squad the next day after a military courtmartial. Included among the executed was the infamous Captain McGinnis. Only three of those captured were spared by the military tribunal.

Near Roseville they struck the First Arkansas Regiment. The regiment was composed of Rebel Arkansas deserters and runaway negro slaves. The First Arkansas was now in the service of the Union army. Accompanying the First Arkansas were detachments of a few Illinois companies. The command melted away under fire and surrendered to the Southern army. Those known to be deserters were executed, and the runaway slaves were thrashed and sent home to their masters. The true Federals were treated well, paroled and released after being disarmed.

Near Ozark, Shanks' company hit another band of Jayhawkers and killed fifty-four of them in a running fight. At Huntsville, Arkansas, a group of men led by Colonel Horace Brand left the column to recruit new Confederate soldiers in northwestern Arkansas. After recruiting, they were to march toward Rolla, Missouri, to create a diversion.

After Huntsville the brigade traveled through Bentonville. The town had been burned out just months before by Union general Siegel and his hessian troops. The fire-blackened bricks and the naked walls struck deep chords of sympathy within Shelby's men. Around them lay the bare bones of a once proud Southern town, stripped bare of its dignity. At Bentonville more troops were dispatched north toward Springfield, Missouri, to disrupt Yankee communications by destroying telegraph lines. Now, they were twenty-five miles north of Bentonville in Neosho, Missouri, and enjoying the fruits of victory. It was a sweet start to a good homecoming.

That afternoon as the men rode out of Neosho, Shelby made sure each man wore a single red sumac plume in his hat to identify him as a member of the brigade. Jessie found it fascinating to observe the smart new lines of the Rebel troopers riding out dressed from head to toe in Union uniforms. The column looked blue as indigo and as loyal as troops from bleeding Kansas. Only the red sumac in the hats and the proud flowing banners of the Confederacy floating above them showed their true identity.

Jessie kept an eye on Captain Gilbert Thomas. Among the captured supplies were a few demijohns of good bourbon. Gilbert always had a nose for such things and sipped away from a pocket flask as they rode north toward Bower's Mill. Jessie prayed he wouldn't drink so much it would impair his judgement if they should run into the enemy.

Bower's Mill was a militia outpost left for the amusement of Union troops. What few houses were not full of stolen goods taken from Southerners were the houses for the numerous prostitutes plying their trade among the local Union troopers. The soldiers fled without a fight, leaving the whores behind in Shelby's hands.

The Southerners helped themselves to any supplies they needed. What could not be brought away easily was burned. As the last of the rear guard left Bower's Mill, flames licked at the skies. The prostitutes stood in the harsh glare of the firelight huddled in small groups and watched their brothels burn.

The brigade rode all night in the chilling cold. By morning, white frost coated the hats and coats of the riders. At daybreak Greenfield was surrounded and another fifty militia were stripped of weapons and paroled. The courthouse had been fortified by the Yankees; to deny them any more use, the building was burned. The rest of the town was left intact. Supplies were again plentiful and more of the Southern soldiers received new uniforms.

The march continued to Stockton where twenty-five more militia who had remained to guard the courthouse where captured and paroled. Again the courthouse was set to the torch to deny the enemy the use of their fortification.

As the brigade rode between Bower's Mill and Stockton, the men were surprised to pass house after house where belongings had been removed and stacked outside.

This was an area populated by those loyal to the Union. Shelby was expected to burn and destroy as he advanced. Not one private home was entered and none put to the flame. Not a stick of personal property was touched as the brigade rode by mile after mile.

The people were stunned when Shelby's men didn't burn them out in retaliation for the Southern homes torched by Union loyalists in this region. It had not been easy for Shelby to restrain his men. There were many who wanted to vent their anger on the Unionists. There were some among his troops who had lived here before the war. Many a Rebel soldier clamped his teeth in anger as they passed the burned-out homes and farms scattered among the Unionists. These had been Southern homes.

At Humansville another seventeen Union calvalrymen were killed and one hundred thirty more were captured. Now every man in the brigade was fully uniformed and equipped with the best the Union army could offer.

At Warsaw the Federal garrison attempted to make a stand, but they were surrounded and chased in a running fight. Seventy-nine more prisoners were taken and the dead and dying were strung out for miles along the road. Once more vast quantities of supplies were available to Shelby's men. So plentiful were the supplies that new wagons were pressed into service to haul the military bounty.

After Warsaw, Missouri, Shelby ordered the Confederate banners cased. Since the entire brigade looked like they belonged to the Union army, Shelby decided to take advantage of it as they approached the German settlement of Cole Camp.

Shelby's brigade were treated as Yankee heroes as they entered town. Seeing the Union blue of their uniforms, the German people thought Shelby's brigade were Union troops. Shelby let them make their false assumptions. The

Rebel soldiers, enjoying the deception, dined on delicious apple cider and ate sauerkraut, German sausage, and cheese offered freely by the German immigrants. A few of the troopers made love to willing local beauties in the hay-stacks. The girls were eager to show their support to the soldiers they thought were fighting for the Union cause. With the entire brigade outfitted in Union uniforms and gear and a good many riding horses branded with U.S. on their hip the deception was easy to maintain.

Cattle and commissary supplies were eagerly offered and accepted by the brigade. New Conestoga wagons and strong workhorses to pull them were taken and notes signed for the promise of payment by the Federal govern-ment for the new goods. When the Rebels rode out, the German settlers waved at them from every house. The ruse continued to work as mile after mile furloughed Union mi-litia came out to the road from every haystack and brush patch to have one good shout for Abe Lincoln as the blue-coated soldiers rode by. These men were quickly subdued by grinning Confederates in disguise, who relieved them of their weapons and cartridge boxes while taking them prisoner. They signed parole papers before their release.

Evan Stryker, as was his custom, rode near Jo Shelby at the front of the main column. Suddenly, a tall, thin individual jumped from the brush into the middle of the road. He stood defiantly before Colonel Shelby.

In his hand the newcomer held a new Mississippi rifle. A Colt pistol was stuffed into his waistband. "Well, boys, I'm mighty glad to see ya." He obviously had mistaken them for Federal troops. "I heard that ole Jo Shelby him-self was headin' this way and I told my girl, Nancy, that I oughter have a pop at him with my gun." He tapped the end of the barrel with his hand for emphasis.

"Ah," said Colonel Shelby as he motioned his men to be quiet and suppress their mirth. "What is the name of your command?"

"Well, General ... I guess yer a General, from the feather in yer hat and the big crowd ridin' behind ya. I ain't exactly in any regiment, but I'm as good a Union man as there is. Me and some of the boys up and formed our own little guerilla company fer home service. We been drawin' our guns and ammunition from Warsaw."

Shelby studied the man standing before him. "I don't suppose there are any Rebels around here, so who do you fight?"

"Hell, general, there's plenty of 'em around here, and damn bad ones, too." The man smiled proudly. "We've been workin' them over though. Just two days ago we killed Old Man Beasly, Tom Mayes, and two of Price's men home from the army."

Shelby's expression turned stern and ominous. "Did these men resist you or were they fightin' out of the bush?"

"Nah, nothin' like that, General. They were just Rebels is all."

"It sounds to me like they were true Rebels like the ones that stand before you now." Shelby raised his voice as his anger grew. "You are nothing but a common murderer and a thief. Captain Stryker, arrest this man and take him to the rear."

The Unionist now realized his terrible error. His face turned a ghastly white and his entire body began to tremble in fright. He tried to speak, but words failed him. He handed over his pistol and rifle without resistance and gave a deep sigh as he faced sure and sudden death.

Evan Stryker held the prisoner's weapons as other Rebel troopers prepared to escort him to the rear. "Allow me to introduce Colonel Jo Shelby," said Stryker. "Instead of you getting him, he bagged you."

The man stared in awe, his mouth wide open at his own stupid blunder. "I ... I never figured on no Union uniforms."

"I don't suppose your victims figured on being killed in their homes by the likes of you, either," said General Shelby. "Get him out of my sight."

The hapless man was taken to the rear and shot by a firing squad. After a brief delay the column continued the march.

29

The Great Egg Feast

The weathered sign proclaimed the name of the town: WELCOME TO FLORENCE, MISSOURI. Ross and his men advanced cautiously, eyes watching for movement as they rode slowly down the street. Florence lay silent except for a gentle breeze that blew through the town swirling little whirlwinds of dust on the wind. Not one man, woman, or child was sighted in the ominous, silent streets. A complete town devoid of any signs of life seemed unnatural; Ross felt a cold shiver run down his spine. He couldn't recall having seen a town *totally* abandoned before. Fearing a trap, Ross signaled his men to search house by house.

Ross tied Prince to a hitching rail in front of a general store. He pulled Double-Twelve from its sheath and held it firmly in his hands as he started his search. He kicked open the door of the general store. The wood splintered and gave way as the door slammed open. No one was there. Then, Ross heard something move behind the counter, but he couldn't see what it was. "Come on out of there before I blow you in half," Ross growled.

Only silence greeted him.

Ross edged forward, legs spread for balance as he moved like a prizefighter. Beads of sweat broke on his brow as he heard soft sounds stirring behind the counter. With one final leap he swung the twin barrels of the sawed-off shotgun on the area behind the counter.

He saw a blur of motion and a flash of orange as he heard the startled cry of a tabby cat. Ross leaned back and tried to calm his shaking knees. "Damn! Nothin' but a cat! Nearly scared the devil out of me. Where is everyone?" he wondered. His eyes scanned a store full of goods left unattended.

Ross moved on. Every house and store was the same, full of possessions, but not a human to be found except Shelby's scouts. It was as if the earth had opened and swallowed the town's inhabitants whole.

Not a soul living or dead had been found. All the scouts reported something else that seemed peculiar. Vast quantities of fresh eggs were found stored in every house, store and barn. Hogsheads, boxes, baskets, and barrels in every direction were filled with eggs.

Jonas said, "I figure they heard we were comin' and cleared out lickety-split. Didn't take time to take nothin' with 'em. They must have thought Quantrill's boys were a-comin' the way they left here in such a hurry."

Ross looked at the scouts gathered around him. "Have you boys ever seen more eggs in your whole life?"

"I can't remember the last time I ate fresh eggs," said Jonas. "I can't wait to fry some up."

"There's plenty for everyone. Gentlemen, I predict tonight the brigade will feast on omelets and fried eggs. I doubt if there is a way to eat eggs that won't be tried before this day is over. Hey, Jonas, let's make french toast.

I saw a fry skillet, some bread, and some pure maple syrup in the general store."

Jonas's eyes gleamed with delight. "Sounds mighty good. I bet we could make a stack of flapjacks to go with the eggs, too."

"I found some hickory-smoked and sugar-cured hams and bacon. I reckon they would go mighty fine with the other fixin's," added Rube Anderson.

"I can round up a sack of spuds I spotted in one home. Hash browns would top things off nicely," said Terrell Fletcher as he licked his dry, cracked lips.

Ross grinned. They were about to share the best dang breakfast any of them had enjoyed since they left Batesville, Arkansas, months ago. "Let's find the makin's for some biscuits and round up a little jam or honey to go with it, boys, and I'll think I died and went to heaven!"

With a wild Rebel yell the men split up to gather the food for their feast. Word was passed down the line and the lean Confederates of Shelby's brigade rode into town to share the wealth of eggs. Soon Confederate campfires blossomed around the town, busy with the preparations for the meal. Many an empty Confederate belly would be filled tonight.

Early the next morning Ross and the scouts were back in the saddle again. Ross felt the swell of a belly stuffed to capacity. He rode like lead in the saddle, but he felt content. It was a feast for soldiers who suffered through long months of short and poor rations.

Ross eyed Jonas, who was particularly happy that morning. He asked Jonas why he was feeling so chipper.

"Ya see the rucksack on my back?"

"Yeah, I see it," replied Ross.

"Well, the next time we stop long enough to build a fire we're gonna eat fresh eggs again. I found some newspapers and some soft cloth an' I loaded up two dozen fresh eggs in my ruck. Ain't nothin' in the world like a good fresh egg breakfast, an' I aim to have them again. Fletch has some ham and bacon, an' Rube is carryin' some extra biscuits, bread, and honey."

"Lordy, sounds good to me, Jonas. Reckon there's enough for me?"

"I reckon we could spare some for a fellow scout, even if he does wear captain's bars." Jonas gave him a smug smile.

The scouts pressed on toward Tipton, Missouri. Ross knew they should intersect the Missouri Pacific Railroad tracks at Tipton. There were very few railroads operating in Missouri and Jo Shelby had made it clear he wanted to destroy as much of the track as possible. The railroad ran west from St. Louis through Jefferson City, Tipton, Sedalia, and on west to Pleasant Hill, ending just short of Kansas City. The war had stopped all new construction of the railroad. Still, it was important to the Union for moving troops and supplies westward from St. Louis.

The scouts galloped ahead with the brigade close on their heels. As they approached the town, a volley of musketfire shattered the quiet. The volley came from behind a white frame house. Ross heard the whine of minie balls shrieking through the air around him and cringed at the sickening sound of one slamming into Jonas. Jonas lurched hard in the saddle as if he had been slugged by a two-by-four. Ross watched in horror as Jonas slowly slipped from the saddle and sprawled into the road, rolling this way and that like a broken rag doll.

There was no time to spare to check on Jonas. The first volley's powder smoke still drifted on the wind, followed by a second round of ragged gunfire coming from around the building ahead. Ross pulled Double-Twelve from its holster on his back as Prince of Heaven surged forward. Ross leaned low on Prince's neck as he urged the charger to jump the low fence standing before them. The jar of the landing nearly unseated him, but Ross held on.

Around him, Ross saw his fellow scouts. On the near side he saw Gordon's Rebel troopers removing the rails from the very fence he had just jumped. Anger and the excitement of battle propelled him forward. Before him, the cohesion of the Union troops was disintegrating. Many of the Yankees broke for the rear. Some even threw away their muskets in their headlong flight.

Ross rode directly at a small knot of men clustered around a flagbearer. As he approached, the nearest soldier squeezed off a quick shot that went wide of the mark. Ross held Double-Twelve level with the soldier's face from ten yards away and tickled the trigger. The blast slammed the soldier onto his back, his face bleeding from a half dozen holes. Ross swung past the remaining soldiers and spun Prince to face them. The soldiers were now firing at more Confederates following his charge. Ross pulled another trigger and the hammer tripped on the second barrel of the gun. The blast caught Prince by surprised and he reared from the terror of the blast so near his head as the gun discharged. The shot caught a broad-shouldered soldier square in the back. A blood mist lingered in the air where he had stood as the man pitched onto his face. Ross stuffed Double-Twelve back into the holster and pulled a Navy Colt from a saddle holster, methodically blazing away at the fleeing Union soldiers. He had run down and shot nearly half a dozen men by the time he finished emptying his third pistol. He allowed Prince to slow as he studied the scene around him. These Yankees were dead or totally routed. They would give no further resistance this day.

Worry forced its way into Ross's mind as he felt the adrenaline of battle starting to subside. He could still picture Jonas blown from his saddle. He spurred Prince back into a gallop toward the road. Prince was winded from the chase, but seemed to sense the urgency of his rider and rode on without complaint.

Ross anxiously glanced about him, trying to spot his friend. Around him surged more advancing soldiers of the brigade as they pushed forward to the receding sounds of battle.

"Jonas!" Ross yelled.

From a stand of trees near the road he heard a weak reply. "I'm over here."

Ross dismounted quickly and rushed to his friend. Jonas lay belly down over a large log sitting near the road. "Jonas, how bad is it?"

"I don't rightly know. I felt the bullet slam into me and it knocked me out of the saddle. I tried to get out of the road, but I got stepped on by horses following me. My back hurt something awful, so I crawled over here to catch my breath." Jonas paused. Ross saw the fear in his friend's eyes. "I know I'm bad hit. I can feel the blood runnin' down my back. I'm afraid to move. Lordy, I'm sure glad ya came back, ole friend. A man sure hates to die alone."

"Jonas, let me see how bad it is. I'll take you to the brigade surgeon."

"I doubt he can do anything for me. I hurt somethin' awful and I know I must have lost a lot of blood. I can feel it trickling and oozing down my back."

Ross ignored Jonas as he cut the straps to the rucksack from Starke's back. A sticky, yellow mess oozed from the pack. Eggs! It was the fresh eggs Jonas was carrying in the rucksack. They had run from the pack and the thick goo had spread down his back. Ross examined the sack carefully. He saw where a large-caliber minie had ripped into the side of the rucksack and exited out the other side. He examined his friend's back and couldn't find a bullet hole. Relief flooded through Ross as he helped his friend remove the Union jacket from his back, and saw there were no holes.

"You're wastin' your time, Ross. Leave the shirt on me.

If I'm gonna bleed to death, then I sure don't want to freeze, too."

Ross smiled as he ignored his friend and lifted the shirt. Beneath the cloth Ross found a deep, dark bruise in the shape of a horseshoe in the area below where the rucksack had been.

"Jonas, you're not going to bleed to death, but I reckon you're gonna be plenty sore for a while. Looks like you got stomped on by a horse."

Jonas snapped his head around quickly to stare at Ross with disbelief. "You don't have to lie to me, Ross, I know I've been hit bad. You can tell me the truth, I can take it."

"You damned old varmint! I am telling you the truth. You haven't been hit. The bullet hit your rucksack and knocked you out of the saddle. That blood you feel runnin' down your back happens to be the fresh eggs you were savin' for a feast. You have one hell of a nice bruise on your back where you were stepped on, but there isn't a hole in you anywhere. I suspect the horse broke the eggs the bullet missed and your fall didn't destroy."

Jonas studied Ross's grinning face and from the genuine tears of joy in his eyes, Jonas finally believed him. "Ya mean I ain't shot? I'm gonna live?"

"You might even outlive me if this war keeps on," Ross assured him.

Relief flooded Jonas's features for a moment before anger replaced it. "Those damn Yanks ruined my dinner!"

Ross laughed as he saw the angry expression on the face of his old friend. Jonas soon joined in. "I guess I'm lucky. They could have scrambled more than my eggs if they'd hit what they aimed at."

Ross helped Jonas recover his horse. Besides the bruise he found on Jonas's back there was another on his leg. When they reached the riders at the lead of the brigade, the smoke was already rising in hot swirling clouds from the depot and railcars along the sidings of Tipton, Missouri. Detachments of cavalry were busy tearing up rails and stacking them over piles of railroad ties. When the rails glowed red-hot in the middle of the flames, the troopers bent them around telegraph poles until they were well twisted. Other troopers were busy destroying and ripping down telegraph lines.

Troops led by Colonel Crittenden appeared briefly from the direction of Sedalia, but after one good charge the Yankees fled the field. Captains Wave Anderson and Charley Jones led two Rebel companies after Crittenden as far as Otterville.

The rest of the command turned away from the intended target of Jefferson City. Dispatches captured at the Tipton depot showed clearly the Union army had set a trap for Shelby if he moved on the capital of Missouri. Turning sadly away from his goal, Shelby ordered his troops north toward Boonville.

As the brigade approached Boonville the scouts were met by a delegation of citizens from the city. The town was a Southern city in sentiment and the people showered the Rebels with gifts of food, horses, and supplies. Ladies turned out in droves to cheer them as they marched through the streets.

The peace was to be short-lived as Union general Brown pursued the Rebels from the direction of Jefferson City. Hunter's battalion, covering the rear of the column, nicely executed an ambush at the Lamine River leaving eighty-nine Yankees to be buried. They suffered the loss of only one wounded Rebel soldier in return. After the ambush, General Brown's troops were less eager to push the rear of the column.

30

Trapped at Marshall, Missouri

The march continued as Shelby's brigade moved northwest toward Marshall, Missouri. Ross Kimbrough delivered bad news to Colonel Shelby when he located him near the Salt Fork Bridge. Blocking their path to the west was Union general Ewing with four thousand soldiers lined up on the outskirts of Marshall. As the first flames stretched into the sky from the torched bridge spanning the Salt Fork River, Ross made his report to Colonel Shelby. The thick cloud of black and gray smoke twisted its hot tendrils skyward, signaling those in pursuit they would have one more obstacle in their path.

Colonel Shelby had not expected this. Ewing was the same hated adversary who had personally written Order Eleven forcing so many families from their homes in western Missouri. Behind Shelby was General Brown with another four thousand soldiers. Shelby's brigade was trapped between two enemy armies pressing him from both sides.

Jo Shelby turned to Major Shanks who was in charge of the rear guard. "Major, General Brown will be here in approximately a half hour. How long can you hold this crossing with your two hundred men?"

"As long as you wish it, Colonel. With the bridge gone, they'll find hell to pay trying to cross this river against my troops. Just tell me how long you want me to hold it and I will."

"I'm going to go ahead and lead the attack against General Ewing in our front. I'll do my best to dislodge him from our path. I don't have time to worry about my backside, Major. If you must sacrifice every man in your company and yourself—do it. Don't let Brown get past you. Don't leave this post until I order it, then ride for all you're worth."

"I'll hold them, Colonel. How should we face them, mounted or dismounted?"

"I'd fight them on foot with the horses safely away from the battle. You'll have need of your horses if I can cut us a path."

Shelby mounted his sorrel and galloped to the front accompanied by Evan Stryker and Ross Kimbrough.

The scene that greeted Colonel Shelby only caused him added despair. The battlefield stretching before him was broken ground with many rugged gullies covered thickly with hazel bushes and undergrowth. It was not the kind of terrain that would allow a quick cavalry charge toward Marshall. His brigade would be forced to fight on foot.

The brigade stood in battle line with Hunter and Coffee on the extreme right, Hooper in the center, and Gordon on the left. Ewing's men formed a V formation with the town of Marshall at the apex and the sides of the V wrapping around Shelby's position and blasting into the flanks of the Rebel brigade. Eighteen pieces of Union artillery opened up against the Rebels and Lieutenant Harris's two-gun battery.

Calvin led his crew as they feverishly worked his cannon. Shells exploded around their position. Calvin's ears rang from the incessant sound of cannonballs tearing and slamming through trees. Others gouged great holes into the earth. Geysers of dirt leapt into the air on both sides of their position. Not believing his eyes, Calvin watched Jo Shelby order the brigade forward against that storm of shot and shell—twelve hundred men, counting the green recruits, against four thousand with heavy artillery support.

The overconfident Federal troops were caught off guard by the sudden charge. What they hadn't considered was that Shelby's men were fighting for their very existence. If they failed they faced certain death or imprisonment. They were facing a Union general they hated as much as any in the whole Union command system. They would not be denied and they would not surrender to Ewing's men.

The Rebels began to make gains. Two of the field batteries belonging to the Yankees had to be removed from the field to save them. Hunter and Coffee drove the batteries back toward the town of Marshall. Hooper flanked to the left and swept General Ewing's left wing, forcing them back. The retreating Yankees left a long line of dead and bloodied troops strung across the battlefield.

Union soldiers with their single-shot muskets were no match for crazed Southerners with pistols and shotguns blazing. Each Rebel carried several pistols and they could lay down a constant barrage of firepower as they advanced, while the Yankees had to reload laboriously between each shot. The fighting spilled into the very streets of Marshall.

The attack stalled as fresh Union troops replaced those that were killed, wounded, or scattered. The battle raged for two hours with both sides suffering terrible casualties.

Ewing extended his lines until his cavalry reached the banks of the Salt Fork River. Now the encirclement was complete. The battle was not fought only on the front

lines. General Brown heard the fighting across the river
and knew Union forces must be attacking Shelby's men.
Brown drove his troops forward. Wave after wave of soldiers attacked Major Shanks' Twelfth Missouri Cavalry as
they tenaciously held the rear along the riverbank. General
Brown brought up his artillery and lined them up across
the river. From there he fired a constant barrage into
Shanks' defenders.

Shelby sent Evan Stryker with orders for Major Shanks,
which read: "Major Shanks, you must hold the line for at
least half an hour so I can mount my men."

Calvin stood near his shattered gun. The woodwork on
his Parrott Cannon had been shot to shreds, both wheels
were broken and the trail piece was cut in two. It was a
miracle that he was unhurt. Most of his crew were dead or
wounded. Delmar Pickett, Billy Jo Paxton, and Calvin
were the only ones who remained healthy. Charlie Jasper
had been wounded by a chunk of wood that had splintered
from the carriage and entered his leg. The crew tried to
save the cannon barrel by lifting it into an ammunition
wagon, but it was heavy and the barrel was so hot from
constant firing they burned their hands. When they completed the task, the wagon was blasted apart by the enemy
artillery. Eight more Rebel artillerymen died needlessly
around the wagon. Billy Jo Paxton was nearly ripped in
half by an enemy cannonball. He never knew what hit
him.

Meanwhile, Brown extended his lines three miles down
from the burned-out bridge where he could cross some of
his regiments over to join with Ewing on the other side of
the Salt Fork.

During this lull in the action, Shelby ordered his men to
mount up. Shelby had the wounded loaded carefully inside
the wagons, and an extra driver assigned to each wagon.
He was determined to drive through the enemy lines. On
the extreme left Shelby watched as a Union Missouri in-

fantry regiment formed in ranks on the other side of a cornfield. Shelby made up his mind to drive his entire force upon this one regiment and crush it, or double it back on the center, even if it cost him half the brigade.

To Evan it seemed like a desperate measure, but one worth the risk. If they didn't move soon they would surely be captured. Evan Stryker realized, as did many of his fellow Southern troopers, that these Federal soldiers weren't interested in prisoners. Most of the Confederates would likely be shot trying to escape long before they would ever see a prison camp. Shelby sent word to Shanks, but the major was so hard pressed by Brown's troopers that he had difficulty joining up with the rest of the brigade.

Shelby waited, but still Shanks did not arrive. With every moment lost, the more their chance of escape ebbed away. Colonel Shelby could wait no longer, and led the charge in double column. The stampede of the charge was too much as the Rebels fired their devastating barrage of close-range pistol fire into the faces of the enemy. The Union regiment began to waver, then broke.

Union troops on both sides of the fleeing regiment tried to move to fill the hole, but it was too late. Yankees who were too slow were either shot down or run over by the Rebel charge. Supply wagons rolled close on the heels of the charging cavalry. Fear spread at the sight of the destroyed Union regiment. What had been merely a trickle of hightailing Yankees became a torrent. Trepidation filled the Federal troops and the entire left wing was routed in panic. Only the timely arrival of Brown's army could stem the tide of Union soldiers fleeing the battle.

Shelby paused once clear of the battlefield in hopes that Shanks would soon follow. It was not to be, for Shanks could not fight his way through the same way Shelby had gone. Major Shanks gathered his remaining troopers from the Twelfth Missouri Cavalry, picked up the one remaining cannon and the surviving artillery crewmen, and marched east at the point where Shelby had cut to the west. Shanks drove his men toward the heavy timber using the same tactics Shelby had used.

Shelby saw General Brown drive his division between the two Southern forces, cutting them apart. Jo knew he could not save Shanks so he turned west toward Waverly, Missouri, and his old home.

The pursuit continued, but the Rebel rear guard held off the Yankee cavalry. The well-mounted Southerners easily outdistanced the enemy infantry. Once they were sure they were clear, the brigade stopped for a short, three-hour rest to feed the men. Ammunition was redistributed and all the remaining empty wagons were sunk in the Missouri River to deny their use to the enemy. Only those still carrying captured supplies and the wounded were kept. As the sun broke its bright colors on a cold and dreary new day, the column passed through Waverly.

Ross could not resist. He fell back until he located Major Gordon's Fifth Missouri Cavalry and was relieved to find Jessie alive and well. "Jessie, I know this isn't pleasant, but I want you to see Briarwood. It will never seem real until you see it for yourself. I want to visit Father's grave again. Will you ride with me?"

Jessie nodded solemnly. "I know you're right. No matter how much it hurts I must see it for myself." He swung his horse out of line and followed his brother. Other boys from the old neighborhood left the column to search out homes, friends, and family.

Jessie and Ross rode silently along the familiar road, each struggling with his feelings. Cold, hard silence rode with them as they neared home. Neither knew at this point if their brother Calvin was alive or dead. They knew none of the artillery crews had made it out with Shelby's column. They could only hope Calvin might be with Shanks. They found little comfort from this, for it was highly likely Shanks' regiment was either destroyed or captured.

Still they prayed a few Rebels might somehow slip through enemy lines to safety. Maybe one of them would be Calvin. Their thoughts remained on their brother, until they reached the lane leading to Briarwood.

The two brothers rode to where Briarwood's Great House once stood so proudly. Now the stark brick chimneys reached cold, lifeless fingers to an amber sky. Piles of burned timbers lay in heaps among the black ashes. The outer walls and foundations had collapsed from the heat of the fire into irregular rubble piles. Tears stung his eyes as Ross looked around. Only the slave cabins were left standing and no one dared show himself at this early hour in an area overrun with roving guerilla bands and thieving Jayhawkers. Ross tried to picture the majesty of Briarwood. Gone . . . all gone in the searing flames of war.

With a heavy heart, Ross rode toward the cemetery. He remembered Cassandra had told him they had buried his father near his grandparents' graves. He had visited the graveyard once before when he came to kill Bartok. Ross and Jessie swung out of the saddle and stood near the mound of soil and sod covering their father, Glen Kimbrough. The grave was marked by a crude wooden sign with Glen's name carved into it. Ross felt an anger building within him he could not contain. He screamed in renewed pain at the wide-open skies as he sunk down to his knees. The sound echoed off the dark, rolling waters of the wide Missouri. His fingers clutched cold handfuls of dirt from the grave.

Jessie stood, rubbing his locket slowly with his fingers. He started talking as he stood before the grave as though his father stood before him. "Hi, Father, it's me, Jessie. I don't know if you can hear me, or see me from heaven or not, but I want you to know I married Katlin. I sure wish you could've been with us, but I bet you saw it from up there. I got a letter before we left on this raid and Katlin says we're expectin' a baby. She said the baby should be

born sometime in January. It's gonna be your first grand-
child if everything goes right.

"I guess Mother is up there with you and it gives me
comfort to know you're together. If you can, you might
keep an eye out for Calvin. We don't know if he's okay or
not. If you can watch over the girls I surely would appreciate it." Jessie paused as his eyes filled with tears. They
streaked down his face until they fell on the dust of his father's grave.

"There's one more thing, Mother, Father. I should have
told you more often when we were together, but I didn't."
He paused. "God, how I love you both and miss you." His
voice broke with emotion. "I wish I had told you more
when you were alive to hear it. I sure could use one of
your hugs now." Jessie stood silently, his head down, as a
gust of wind swirled across the grave in a little dust devil.
It swept over him, lifting dust in little puffs, then quick as
it came it was gone.

Ross looked up at Jessie, his face filled with anger. "Do
you really think they can hear you?"

"I don't know and you don't either. I hope they can. I
know I believe in heaven and life after we leave this old
world. Maybe in heaven they can hear us, like God hears
our prayers."

"Yeah, maybe they can, little brother, maybe they can."

Their discussion was interrupted by a familiar voice.
"Massa Jessie, Massa Ross is that you?"

Ross drew his gun in a blink of an eye and spun around,
stopping himself when he spotted Old Jack. Old Jack was
the eldest of the slaves at Briarwood before the war. He
had first moved to Briarwood when Glen Kimbrough decided to build his plantation along the Missouri. Old Jack
had been retired before the coming of the war and was
given a cabin of his own to live out his last days on the
lands of Briarwood Plantation.

Jessie stepped forward as Ross lowered his gun. "Old Jack, is it really you?"

The balding old man stood rail thin and frail in the morning light. His hands looked worn as he leaned on his cane, but still he flashed a weak, nearly toothless smile at the brothers. "Good to see you gentlemen come back to pay your respects to your daddy. He was a fine man. Sure did hate to see him go."

"It's good to see you, Jack. How have you been?" asked Jessie.

"Times been hard, and food is always hard to come by, but I'm still here. Briarwood is the only home I ever knowed. No, suh, I just wouldn't be happy nowhere else. I been tendin' the graves for ya."

Now both boys understood why the grave looked cared for. Ross said, "Thank you, Old Jack. It's mighty kind of you."

"Your daddy, he always looked after me and the missus." A sad look glistened in his yellowed eyes. "She been gone now almost a year. She's buried near my cabin."

"I'm sorry to hear she's gone, Jack. She was the best seamstress I've ever seen."

"That's mighty kind of you, Massa Ross, to say so."

Ross glanced down at his father's grave. "Well, at least I have the satisfaction of knowing I killed the man responsible for my father's death."

"You talkin' 'bout Major Bartok, suh?" A puzzled look crossed Old Jack's face as he pointed his bony finger at Ross. "So it was you tried to kill him. They came lookin' round here for ya. I was gone fishin' when it all happened, but I heard about it when I came home."

"Yes, it was me and I'm glad he's dead."

"Oh, he ain't dead, suh—not at all."

Jessie and Ross stared at each other in amazement. "What do you mean, he's not dead? I shot him myself and I saw him fall."

"Oh, you hit him all right, but it only creased his skull, the way I hear it. I know he's all right cause I seen him ride by here less than a week ago. No, suh, he ain't dead. Lord knows I'd recognize the nose on that evil man."

Ross felt stunned at the news. He had assumed his mission was successful and his shot was true. How could he have missed? He had no reason to doubt Old Jack. Somehow, Bartok must still be alive. Ross asked, "What can you tell me about Major Bartok?"

"Oh, the major, he's up to his old tricks. He's been busy collectin' money from folks so they won't be burned out. Widow Johnson couldn't come up with enough, so he burned her out nearly three weeks ago. I seen him once up close when he led his troops here. He got a nasty scar runnin' down the side of his head 'cause of you. Made him meaner than ever."

"I'm this close, I've got to go after him again, Jessie."

"Don't be a fool, Ross. Every Yankee outfit within two hundred miles is converging on this area to capture Shelby's brigade. Bartok is well aware Shelby is in the area and he'll be taking extra precautions to defend himself."

"I can't let him get away with all he's done. He has to be stopped."

"I know you, Ross, and I know you are a man who would not turn his back on his duty. Our brigade is in extreme danger. Shelby is counting on you and your scouts to lead us to safety. The brigade needs you now; Bartok can wait."

Ross slammed his fist hard into his hand in desperate anger; he kicked at the dirt in disgust. He hung his head and after a moment he said softly, "I know you're right, Jessie. It just pains me I didn't do the job right the first time."

Jessie walked over and put his hand on his brother's shoulder. "There will be another time, Ross. Justice has a way of catchin' up with men like Benton Bartok. We'll get him, sooner or later."

"Yeah, I suppose so."

The boys didn't stay long. There was no point to it, and they didn't want to be left behind in enemy-held territory. Shelby would need the scouts to lead him back to the safety of Arkansas. The boys said good-bye to Old Jack and left him a little food.

It didn't take long to find the trail of Shelby's brigade and soon the men rejoined their command. Upon leaving Waverly, Shelby pointed his troopers toward Arkansas, and they moved south rapidly. Ross and his scouts led the vanguard.

Three days later, some of Ewing's men finally caught the brigade, but were easily thrown back by the rear guard. As the troops entered Southwest Missouri, a company of men belonging to Coffee's command wanted to spend the night at Carthage. This was their hometown and Shelby allowed it. This pause was a mistake, because with the new dawn, Ewing attacked Shelby at Carthage. After a battle lasting an hour, Shelby continued south toward friendlier territory. Seven days after the battle at Marshall, Shelby's men camped on the White river near Berryville, Arkansas. Various detachments sent out to recruit and destroy telegraph lines at the beginning of the raid rejoined Shelby's command at Berryville. Still the brigade waited with worried anticipation for news of the fate of Major Shanks and the remainder of the brigade.

Before long, word came in from the scouts. Shanks had escaped! Shanks and his men were camped within five miles of Berryville and he had the rest of the brigade and the one cannon that survived the battle with him. The other barrel had been spiked and left behind at Marshall. Shanks and his command had fought skirmishes at Florence, Osage, and Humansville—all on the hurried trip south. Somehow they had made it and so had Calvin. That night, and on many nights thereafter, the soldiers and officers would sit by their campfires and tell the stories of the raid and their daring escape.

They had ridden fifteen hundred miles to the Missouri River and back in thirty-four days. A small band of eight hundred men had added and equipped four hundred more on the march against a state filled with fifty thousand of the enemy. The Rebels left over six hundred Yankees dead in their wake, but not without cost. Shelby's brigade lost nearly as many men as they had recruited. Many of those lost were good, loyal veterans and hard to replace. During the raid they fought over a dozen battles and skirmishes. They captured forty stands of colors from the enemy. They took whatever they needed from Union supplies.

Ten thousand Union troopers were sent to capture or destroy Shelby, but they failed and Shelby had defeated them at every turn. Jo Shelby led what perhaps was the most daring single cavalry raid of the war. His men wondered what would have happened had he been given a cavalry division instead of a brigade for the raid. How much more could they have accomplished? The great raid was over, but its legend would remain forever.

31

Order Eleven

Billy watched as firelight illuminated the hanging man, painting him with grotesque shadows in the growing dusk of late evening. He stared in horror as the man tried desperately to relieve the pressure around his neck by clinging to the rope above the noose. He kicked like a swimmer in water, straining to get tension off the rope biting into his neck and choking the life out of him. His legs swung helplessly in the air scant inches above the ground.

Billy felt the hairs rise on the back of his neck as he listened to the rope creaking against the tree limb as the man swung and struggled in the wind. The Jayhawkers' coarse laughter filled the air around him. He strained to see the face of the hanging man, but the man's back was to him. The ruddy glow of firelight brightened as the fire flared from the burning building behind Billy. The smoke wrapped its ash gray tendrils around him, choking the air from him like the dying man swinging on the rope before him.

He heard a Jayhawker yell, "Look close, boy! The next fire you'll see will be the fires of hell!" Billy swallowed hard as sweat beaded on his face and panic overpowered him. The hanging man was slowly twisting to face him, his struggle ending as he sagged lifelessly from the noose. Billy could see the blackening face, the protruding eyes, and the tongue lolling from the mouth of the dead man. He knew the face . . . for it was the face of his murdered father.

He screamed as he sat upright, his hands feeling for his gun beside him. He tried to focus his eyes, but everything before him was black as ink. His scream echoed in his ears as he felt a hand clamp tightly onto his arm.

"What's the matter, Billy?"

The sudden grip on his arm and the voice startled him and Billy jerked toward the sound. He hollered as goose bumps covered his skin.

"It's okay, boy, relax, you're safe here." Billy tried to blink the face into focus. Slowly, in the faint glow of the coals of last night's fire, he made out his friend William Gregg. His breath slowed from the quick, ragged gasps as his senses began to return and he recognized his surroundings.

"You have another bad dream, partner?" asked Bill Gregg.

Billy nodded his head yes as he dropped his gun and ran a trembling hand through the locks of his hair, smoothing them out of his eyes. He wanted to speak, but he didn't trust his voice.

William Gregg studied him carefully before softly observing, "It was the death of your father again, wasn't it?"

Billy's nod told William he was correct. "Can I get you anything?"

Billy's voice sounded strange to him, distant and shaky.

"No, I'll be all right, Bill. Go on back to sleep. I'm sorry I woke you." He looked around the campfire at the other Bushwhackers still in their bedrolls. Some were awake looking at him. In some eyes he read worry and in others, anger at being disturbed. He said to no one in particular, "Sorry," as he rolled himself back into his blankets and turned onto his side away from those watching eyes. The sweat on his brow dried quickly, leaving him chilled. Winter was approaching earlier than it should for October in Missouri.

Billy wanted to go back to sleep, but a part of his mind was reluctant. Fear of reliving the nightmare of his father's death still haunted him, so instead he lay there thinking about the last few days.

After the raid on Lawrence, they returned to their old stomping grounds in the Blue Springs region of Missouri. The raid had stirred up a hornet's nest among the Yankees and they had increased their patrols in response. Quantrill's men simply went into hiding and enjoyed the plunder taken from the Lawrence raid. For a while they stayed near Bone Hill, then moved down into the Sinabar region when things got hot. Later they drifted back into the Blue Springs area again. Once a Yankee patrol stumbled onto them and killed a couple of the guerillas, but it was a minor irritation. The Federals lost far more. Quantrill spent most of his time romancing his new girl, Kate King, from near Bone Hill. Meanwhile, his gang rested and waited.

Billy and William Gregg profited from the Lawrence raid thanks to the money taken from Jacob Bartok's bank vault. Some money they hid, some they spent in wild celebration, and the rest they carefully saved to see them through the winter. There was much speculation among the Bushwhacker camps on just who had profited most from the raid, but it seemed to Billy that George Todd's men garnered the lion's share. Despite promises of splitting the money equally among the raiders, it wasn't done, and now it appeared it would never happen.

In fact, two of the Bushwhackers, Charles Higbee and a man named Woods, split with a large cache of cash and deserted the command. Quantrill was fit to be tied when he discovered their escape. Billy heard later the two men headed for Canada.

Billy's thoughts often turned to the raid. Attacking Lawrence—the home of the hated Jayhawkers—was in some ways satisfying. He didn't feel a bit of guilt over any of the soldiers killed in the streets. After all, it was Jennison's Jayhawkers who murdered his father before his eyes over a year ago. It was Yankees who were responsible for killing his imprisoned mother in Kansas City when the warehouse collapsed. Yankee terrorism justified the raid in his eyes. A small payback to those who raided Missouri from the safety of the Kansas border only to hustle back to the protection of the United States government. But somehow the whole raid got twisted and it was no longer a war just against soldiers, but against civilians as well. The raid left doubts and set uneasy on his mind.

What bothered him the most was the trouble they had brought on their own people. In retaliation for the raid, Union General Ewing, under the insistence of Jayhawker Jim Lane, issued Order Eleven on August 25, 1863. During the next two weeks a mass exodus of Southern people fled the district. Thousands loaded up the few meager possessions they could carry or load in wagons and headed for northern Missouri or south toward Arkansas. Those who resisted were forced out by Federal soldiers who torched their homes before their eyes while stealing anything of value. Behind the fleeing columns of civilians, dark rolling columns of smoke marked the burning and destruction of homes in their wake.

Billy had personally witnessed this mass destruction against innocent people. His home in Bates County was burned out by the Jayhawkers. Now the homes of his neighbors who had escaped earlier attacks joined the ashes of his home. It galled him to witness Kansas soldiers seeking vengeance by enforcing the order. Gleeful Kansas Jayhawkers and Red Legs swooped down and began to loot, burn, and indiscriminately murder the hapless civilians with the guarded blessing of their government.

By the end of September, Jackson, Cass, and Bates Counties were one vast wasteland. The Bushwhackers had destroyed a town; the Jayhawkers completed the ruin of an entire region all in the name of preserving the Union. The destruction served only to deepen Southern resolve and add to the hate between the two factions.

Now Billy found himself in this camp along the Blackwater, on Captain Pardee's land. Last night the guerilla bands of Bloody Bill Anderson and George Todd joined them. The soldiers under Colonel Holt had ridden in before the others. The Union patrols had kept Holt's men from moving south toward Arkansas after the Lawrence raid. Holt's men were not guerillas and they simply wanted to join the regular armies of the Confederacy. Now they realized they would need Quantrill's help to escape Missouri.

All the bands were gathering for the trip south for the winter. The departure had nothing to do with Order Eleven, or the effectiveness of Union patrols. Instead the Bushwhackers sought to avoid a harsh winter climate and take a break from the constant fighting. Some Missouri guerillas chose to stay and most of these would ride that winter under the leadership of Andy Blount.

Billy Cahill couldn't wait to leave. Each mile south would bring him closer to Elizabeth. She was on his mind constantly and he missed her terribly. He had given serious thought over the last few days to leaving Quantrill and joining Shelby's brigade. Billy discussed it with William Gregg and found Bill felt the same.

The action at Lawrence hung heavy at times on Billy's conscience—it was one thing to fight a war against soldiers, another to kill civilians and destroy homes and businesses. It made him wonder if he was any better than a Jayhawker. The memory of the burning town, the fathers and sons murdered in the streets while their women wept, left a bad taste in his mouth. Perhaps by serving in the regular army with Shelby's brigade he could find a more honorable war.

Time seemed to inch by slowly, but soon the first streaks of dawn creased the sky. And hour later the guerilla army led by Quantrill moved south, four hundred men strong. They moved by way of Lone Jack and Harrisonville, then turned west close to Carthage. Soon they picked up the Fort Scott Road leading into Indian Territory.

32

Kansas, Bloody Kansas

Billy rode relaxed in the saddle. This was the fifth day on the march and his body was adjusting to the rigors of the trail. He felt lighthearted and free as he rode alongside William Gregg. Every mile traveled carried him farther from the destruction in Missouri. As they rode through southeastern Kansas Billy knew they were closing in on the border of Indian Territory. They would be that much closer to Texas.

Billy steered his horse off the road and into the ditch. Once free of the column he could see ahead and the dust wasn't as heavy. He noticed a rider approaching the head of the column and he recognized him as one of Dave Poole's men. Billy knew this could be significant because Poole was scouting ahead of the column.

Sure enough, the column halted while the guerilla consulted with Captain Quantrill. The rest of the Bushwhackers remained in column behind them. Quantrill yelled for

William Gregg to come forward and Billy rode beside him.

"What's up, Capt'n?" asked William Gregg.

"Poole captured two teamsters and a wagonload of lumber earlier this mornin'. The prisoners said they were haulin' the load up to the Union fort at Baxter Springs, Kansas. It's just a few miles south of here. After Poole finished interrogating them he killed 'em and rode on ahead. John says the lumber wagon is just over the next rise."

Quantrill looked thoughtful for a moment. He turned and looked directly at William Gregg. "I never heard of a fort around here before. Bill, I want you to take about a hundred men and catch up to Poole and give him a hand. We might capture the fort if we play our cards right."

Bill Gregg gave Quantrill a lazy salute. "All right, who do you want me to take?"

"Take some of our boys and a few of Anderson's men. I'll bring the rest along directly. Ride hard, Bill; Poole might get himself in over his head." In a matter of minutes the hundred men led by Bill Gregg thundered off to the south.

They passed by the dead teamsters lying near the abandoned lumber wagon at a gallop. Billy's first glance told him the traces and harnesses were cut and the horses stolen. "Poole probably has them," he thought. He leaned forward in his saddle as if by doing so it would make his horse run faster.

They found Poole's men in the woods to the south and east of the fort. Using the cover of the woods the raiders studied the fort before them. It was constructed of logs with dirt banked up against them. The walls looked to be about four feet high and one end stood open. Two hundred yards south of the opening in the fort, a stark, white officer's tent caught Billy's eye. He saw an officer seated in a camp chair, bent over a plate of food. Watching the man eat made Billy aware of the growl in his stomach. His eyes looked longingly at the unprotected fort's kitchen station directly south of the officer's tent. His mouth watered as he watched the cook serve food to the soldiers standing in line.

Beside him he heard Bill Gregg whisper, "Caught 'em at noontime. Can you believe it? Here they are, eatin' outside the protection of the fort's walls and not a guard posted in sight. Mistakes like that'll get you killed."

They moved cautiously back to the line of mounted Bushwhackers. Bill Gregg walked over to David Poole, sitting astride his horse. Dave was busy helping the raider next to him unfurl a Union flag. Poole looked at Bill Gregg as he approached. "Well, did ya get a look at 'em?"

"Yeah, it's just like you said. They're out in the open and no guards. Looks like half of 'em are nigger troops to me." He paused for a moment as a puzzled expression clouded his face. "What's the flag for?"

"I'm hoping it might fool 'em. When they figure out who we really are we'll be all over 'em." Dave smiled devilishly as he shifted his lit cigar to the other side of his mouth. "You put your boys on my right and we'll ride right over 'em."

Bill Gregg smiled. "Let's do it."

Moments later the line of Bushwhackers broke at a walk from the cover of the woods. Bill Gregg and David Poole rode in front and watched over their shoulders as the men straightened out their line. Billy kept his eyes on the Union soldiers as the wind snapped the fake Union flag out to its full length. The approach of the Bushwhackers did not go unobserved. A few soldiers stood up slowly, eyeing the approaching line less than an eighth of a mile away.

Billy heard Poole's high-pitched yell above the drumming roar of the warhorses' hooves as they moved forward. "Give 'em hell, boys!"

Billy felt a smile crease his face as he slipped the reins

in his teeth and filled both of his hands with revolvers. Out of the corner of his eye, Billy watched the faked Stars and Stripes flutter to the ground as the raider carrying it cast it aside. Many Union soldiers stood, mouths hanging open in shock. Others dropped their plates and ran for the protection of the fort.

Poole's men swung around in a large loop, trying to cut the Yankees off from the fort while Gregg's boys charged directly at them. The Union officer abandoned his tent and sprinted at full tilt for the protection of the fort while shouting for his men to follow him.

Billy lost sight of the officer as he neared the first of the Union soldiers. He smiled gleefully as he leveled his revolver and squeezed off a round into the back of a white soldier, pitching him on his face. Another soldier turned to face him, and all Billy could see were the whites of his eyes, large and round and full of fear as he stared into the muzzle of Billy's gun. The black face erupted into crimson red as Billy pulled the trigger.

He swung past the slumping body as he pivoted his mount to avoid the cook's campfire. The stark white tent suddenly loomed out of the chaos as the momentum of the mare carried him forward. Billy's horse lurched suddenly as she skittered to the side, trying desperately to avoid the tent ropes and pegs.

Billy lost his balance with the sudden change in direction and found himself cartwheeling from the saddle. He lost all sense of direction as the canvas tent swallowed him whole and turned his world to white. One of his Remingtons roared near his ear as the shock of the collision tripped the trigger. His progress came to a screaming halt as the impact slammed the wind out of him with a whoosh.

Disoriented, Billy fought down his fear as he struggled to free himself from the suffocating canvas. His arms were trapped in the collapsed folds of the tent and he felt rising waves of panic in his throat. Billy could face death without a whimper, but having his hands pinned or tied terrified him beyond all reason. He screamed in fear and the sound of his muffled cry only added to his panic.

Billy wasn't even sure which way was up as he fought to get his feet under him. The sound of gunfire and running horses seemed to fade as he wrestled for control. He heard a horse slide to a stop and a high-pitched laugh from outside his white world. "Just what I'd expect from a lazy, no good bum like you, Billy. Here we are smack dab in the middle of a fair-sized fight an' you decide to pile into a Yankee tent for a nap." More laughter followed as Billy heard the ripping sound of a knife slicing through the canvas.

Billy recognized the familiar voice of Riley Crawford and knew he would be freed. He began to relax as Riley worked to cut him from his entanglement. Riley pulled Billy to his feet. Billy reached for one of his revolvers he'd lost in the fall and when he looked up again the battle had swept past them.

"If you hadn't stopped to take that nap, I might've killed me a couple more of them blue bellies."

"Shucks, Riley, I wasn't after a nap. My hoss just thought I oughta get a jump on stealin' that Yankee loot 'fore you all thought of it."

Riley laughed again before he replied, "That was one of the prettiest cartwheels I've seen. I'd have never thought to enter a tent by flyin' through the air and landin' on my head like you did. It was original, but next time it might be easier if you decide to enter through the tent flap."

Billy couldn't help it; he smiled and then burst out laughing as he pictured himself flying through the air. The roar of a cannon blast shook them both from their mirth as a geyser of dirt flew into the air fifty feet behind them. Instinctively they ducked their heads. Billy looked toward the fort and saw smoke still curling from the mouth of a howitzer as a Union officer worked alone to reload the piece.

Surrounding them on the grassy plain lay the scattered bodies of Union troopers killed by the charging Bushwhackers. Many lay in twisted positions like so many broken rag dolls left behind by some careless child. By now most of the soldiers had reached the meager protection of the fort and their stacked weapons. They moved to the outer walls to defend themselves. Most of the guerillas swept past the fort, carried to the north during their mad charge.

Riley moved to his horse and swung into the saddle. He offered Billy his arm and Billy slid on double behind him. Riley touched his spurs to the horse and near the woods they caught Bess, Billy's mare. They paused only long enough to grab the free reins as they trailed the mare behind them into the protection of the woods.

The muffled roar of the howitzer boomed again in the distance just as they entered the tree line. They heard the whir of the cannonball as it passed overhead, showering them with splintered wood from severed limbs. They came to a halt and Billy jumped down and swung into his saddle. The two young Bushwhackers kept low as they pointed their mounts toward Gibson Road, running northeast to southwest north of the fort. Maybe there they could join with Quantrill's column or circle to the north to rejoin Gregg's and Poole's men.

As they crested the ridge, Billy looked down on Quantrill's men arrayed in line of battle just east of the road. He felt a sigh of relief as he realized they were no longer alone.

Suddenly, Billy jerked his eyes up at the unmistakable sound of a martial band playing. Beyond Quantrill's line a column of Union soldiers were marching toward them, lines smartly dressed, flags flying, and band playing as if they were on parade. Trailing behind the Union soldiers

stood a wagon train carrying supplies. Billy quickly esti-
mated the Union numbers at around a hundred men. It appeared to Billy the Yankees thought the guerillas were a
welcoming committee from the fort. Billy spurred his
horse forward down the ridge. He caught up with Riley at
the base of the ridge as they neared Quantrill's men.

When the two lines closed within two hundred yards of
one another it became apparent to the Union soldiers that
this was no troop sent out from the post to welcome them.
Despite many of the guerillas wearing captured Union blue
there were enough variations in the uniforms to distinguish
this group from regular Union troops. The Union line fal-
tered to a halt and the band sputtered to a stop in an awkward staccato. They hastily formed their column into line
of battle facing the rapidly closing Southerners. Quantrill
ordered his black flag unfurled on the wind leaving no
doubt among the Yankees what troops were before them.

Before a shot had been fired two Union soldiers broke
from the line and started to run away. An officer forced
them back into line. No sooner were they back in line
when again they broke away, eight more soldiers following them this time. Quantrill noticed the lack of
confidence among the Yankees and ordered a charge.

The company of Union soldiers riding under the regi-
mental banner of the Fourteenth Kansas bolted and fled
before the wrath of the Missourians. A company of Union
soldiers flying the battle flag of the Third Wisconsin Cavalry held until Quantrill's men were within twenty feet.
Their resolve weakened by the departure of their comrades, they too broke before the swarm of charging devil
riders.

Billy and Riley joined the second file of Bushwhackers
just in time to join the charge. Billy slipped the reins in his
teeth again and filled his hands with two fresh revolvers
taken from his saddle holsters as he touched spurs to his

horse. He felt the muscles bunch in Bess as she leapt forward, her hooves digging for traction.

In moments they closed the distance between the lines. The guerillas held their fire until they were directly upon the Wisconsin troopers. The Bushwhackers merged with the men in blue. The first volley of shots echoed off the hills as the guerillas unleashed their fury. What remained of the Union line, nearly forty men, disappeared to a man in the onslaught. All were gunned down in a matter of seconds in Quantrill's relentless charge. The Yankee carbines were useless after the first volley because it was virtually impossible to reload the muzzle loaders while astride a running horse. The guerillas, armed with several revolvers apiece, had them outgunned.

Somehow in the chaos, a Union major miraculously slipped unharmed through a gap in the Missourian line. Instead of running like the others, he laid low against the neck of his powerful charger and rode toward the fort at Baxter Springs. Billy noticed the escape, but decided to let the man go. With Poole's men still harassing the fort the chances the Wisconsin major would get through were slim at best.

Billy Cahill spurred forward after the retreating fugitives and put Bess in a long, ground-covering lope. He watched as the race became every man for himself. After a quarter mile of pursuit he caught his first soldier. His second shot caught the man in the back. The victim pitched forward and slid off the side of his horse to the ground. Billy didn't slow down as he passed the tumbling body in a blur, already his eyes searching for the next target.

In front of him, looming out of the dust, Billy could see what appeared to be a deep ravine blocking the path of the Yankee retreat. He watched the Union troopers pulling up at the edge, afraid to try the jump. They milled frantically, searching for some hope of escape.

Billy smiled with grim satisfaction as he picked out his next target. A Yankee officer on a magnificent charger loomed in front of him. Billy fired once and his shot went high. They were nearing the ravine and the Yankee urged his horse into a full-out run. Instantly Billy knew the officer would try to make the leap. In one last desperate attempt to stop his escape, Billy fired another round. The big horse started to gather himself for the leap when Billy's shot caught him in the hip. Billy aimed for the Yank's back but the rough ground threw his shot low. The charger stumbled from the shot and tumbled into the ravine taking his rider with him.

Billy pulled up Bess as he looked to his right. To his amazement he saw a one-horse buggy bouncing over the prairie at full tilt directly at the ravine. The woman driving it was standing up and whipping the horse to a frenzy. Behind her a man fired a pistol at the pursuing Bushwhackers. Spellbound, Billy watched the impending disaster. To his utter surprise the speed of the horse and buggy was so great they cleared the ravine smoothly and continued on. If Billy hadn't witnessed it himself he would never have believed it possible.

He redirected his attention to the officer and his mount at the bottom of the ravine. The officer was hopelessly pinned by his horse, so Billy let his eyes stray. On his left he saw a Union general just as his horse leapt the wash. The charger landed roughly on the other side and stumbled, throwing the general onto the horse's neck. Billy fired at him once with each revolver but missed him in all the confusion. When last he saw the officer, he was still clinging desperately to his horse's neck as he sped away.

The guerillas swarmed over the remaining Yankees in the ravine area. In a matter of minutes those who had failed in their attempt to jump the deep wash were killed. Billy passed his reins to Riley as he slipped down the bank of the ravine. Three shots later he killed the wounded Yankee major, his injured horse, and another Union trooper dragging a wounded leg. A few Bushwhackers continued their pursuit of routed Yankees both to the north and south along the ravine.

Billy searched the pockets of the dead officer and found a set of orders. When he read them he found the officer's name, Major Henry Z. Curtis, General Blunt's chief of staff. Instantly, Billy realized the identification of the general who had managed to jump the gorge and escape. It was the despicable Major General James G. Blunt, the abolitionist commander of the district of the frontier. Billy felt his stomach twist as he kicked the saddle of the dead horse in anger. General Blunt was one of the most hated enemies of the Bushwhackers and he had slipped through their fingers.

Billy continued his search and found a letter written by General Samuel Ryan Curtis to his son, Henry. The letter made the death of the officer all the more significant, for General Curtis was an important Union commander stationed in Missouri. He stripped the weapons and items of interest from the slain around him and returned to Riley with the waiting horses. There he split the loot with Riley. In the canteen taken from the killed trooper, Riley discovered whiskey. He tipped the canteen back and swallowed some of the amber liquid. Billy swung into the saddle and pointed his horse toward the abandoned wagon train.

As the two teenagers rode east they spotted a lone wagon pulled several hundred yards to the southwest of the wagon train. Roiling black smoke and the sight of dancing red and yellow flames attracted the Missourians' attention.

Riley gestured toward the wagon and both rode to see the cause of the excitement. Several guerillas gathered around the burning wagon and pitched dead Union soldiers upon the flames. Scattered in the dust and catching sparkling glints of sunlight lay various abandoned band instruments. The boys approached a grim-faced Cole Younger watching the fire consume and blacken the bodies.

Billy asked, "What the hell is goin' on, Cole?"

"Damn Yankees killed William Bledsoe when he asked the wagonload of musicians to surrender. We lit out after 'em when we saw Bledsoe go down. They broke a wheel on the wagon and most of them spilled out on the ground. We rode up and shot 'em. A few idiots were wavin' white handkerchiefs like that would save 'em, but after they killed jolly old Will we weren't in the mood to take prisoners."

The news hit Billy hard. William Bledsoe was a jolly, older guerilla and the others took delight in teasing him about his immense weight. Will took the ribbing well and always had a smile or a laugh ready. Billy knew he would miss him. "Where's Will's body?"

"He's lyin' between here and the wagon train."

Billy nodded as he looked around at the somber men. The smell of the roasting flesh from the burning wagon sickened him. The cloying odor filling his nostrils reminded him of the burning wounded at the wintry battle at Prairie Grove last December. He swept his eyes away from the grisly scene. As he did so he noticed Bill Gregg searching through a large leather valise.

Inside the pouch were many pen-and-ink drawings and sketches. Billy looked at some of the sketches and noticed a signature on many of them, James O'Neal. He glanced up at Bill Gregg. "Where did you get these?"

"I took this pouch off a man we killed in the wagon. According to the papers in his case, he's an artist-correspondent for *Leslie's Weekly.*"

"Yeah, I've read some of his work in copies of *Leslie's Weekly*. He's very pro-Union."

"I guess he won't be writing any more war stories about masses of frightened Confederate soldiers routed by a few noble lads in blue," said Bill Gregg dryly.

"What did ya do with his body?"

"We threw it on the stack with the others, why?"

"Just curious; I wondered what he looked like."

"Dead! Just like the rest of 'em, and good riddance, too."

"Do you mind if I keep a couple of these for souvenirs?"

"Hell no, suit yourself. The ones you don't want we'll burn in the fire anyway."

Billy pulled a few of the better ones from the stack and folded them carefully. He slipped them in his haversack for safekeeping. He handed the stack to Riley when he finished and waited for him to pick through the remaining drawings.

Riley hurried his search and put a couple away for himself. He walked over and pulled a trombone from a busted case, then lifted the horn to his mouth and blew a few raucous off-key notes before stopping to laugh. "Do you think I'm ready to join a brass band?"

"Not if they expect you to play in tune," said Billy. "The way you play you're gonna wake the dead."

Riley put the horn to his mouth again and blew more discordant noise. When he stopped playing he looked up. With taunting, laughing eyes he said, "Did you see any of them move?"

"Come on, Riley, forget the horn and let's see what's in the wagon train." The two boys mounted and headed for the wagons. On the way they passed by four Bushwhackers loading William Bledsoe's body into a captured ambulance wagon taken from Blunt's supply train. The boys stopped for a minute to pay silent tribute to their friend before they continued to the wagon train.

33

Apparition From Hell

The scene at the wagons was one of wild abandon. The Bushwhackers gleefully tore through each wagon searching for treasure. Their search rewarded them with a variety of fine foodstuffs. Quantrill himself was carrying around a five-gallon demijohn of whiskey taken from Blunt's buggy. Whiskey was plentiful among the captured supplies. Indeed, many Union soldiers had whiskey in their canteens. The guerillas helped themselves to the canteens stripped from the dead and began their victory celebration.

Billy sipped a little of the dark, foul-smelling liquid. The raw whiskey burned his throat and made his eyes water. He wondered how anyone could enjoy drinking this stuff. He'd tried beer once or twice and found it much more to his liking.

Billy continued his search. He took a smoked ham from a wagon and joined a few Missourians cooking over an

open fire. He cut off some thick slices and pierced the
meat with a sturdy twig. This he held over the fire to
warm.

He'd fought hunger pangs all day and now the smell of
the roasting ham made him all the more ravenous. When
the meat was warm he pulled it off the stick and devoured
it. He ate five large slices before his hunger lessened. The
honey-cured smoked ham melted in his mouth and he revelled in the taste.

Riley discovered a tin of biscuits and a jar of honey. He
shared the find with Billy and the others gathered around
the fire in exchange for some of Billy's ham. The honey
dripping off tender biscuits was a perfect finishing touch
to the meal and served as a fine dessert. As he ate Billy
kept his eyes on William Clarke Quantrill. Billy had ridden with the guerilla chieftain for over a year and this was
the first time he'd ever seen him drunk.

Quantrill stood near the fire and said in his whiskey-
soaked voice, "By God, Shelby couldn't whip Blunt, and
neither could Marmaduke, but I whipped him." He looked
around the fire at his men and smiled. "I believe I'll take
a ride around the battlefield and enjoy my victory." He
staggered away and struggled into his saddle, all the while
retaining possession of the keg of whiskey. Once in the
saddle he placed the demijohn across his lap.

Just for fun, Billy decided to follow Quantrill. They
moved west toward the area of the great skedaddle executed by the running Yankees earlier. When they had gone
less than a quarter of a mile they came upon John
McCorkle, who had been among those who first discovered the post at Baxter Springs. During the morning's battle he participated in the attack on the fort. Quantrill
decided to have some fun with him.

"John," Quantrill shouted in a rough voice, "I thought
you knew that whenever a pilot leads me into trouble, I always shoot him."

McCorkle drew a revolver and pointed it at Quantrill while shouting, "If you think you can shoot faster than I can then go right ahead."

Quantrill let loose a long, rolling laugh and said, "Put that thing up, you damned fool; I'm going to shoot you in the neck." He offered McCorkle the keg of whiskey.

A smile crossed John's face and Billy thought he saw a look of relief, too, as the man slid his gun back into its holster. McCorkle took a swig from the keg and smiled as he handed it back to his leader. "You better slow down on that, Capt'n, 'fore the ground comes up and smacks you in the face."

Quantrill wove slightly in his saddle with a silly grin plastered on his face. "I suppose you're right, John. Let's ride back to camp; I need to confer with Bloody Bill and Todd on our plans." His look became more stern as he searched his old comrade's face. "Tell me, John, would you really have shot me?"

"If you'd gone for your gun, Capt'n, I wouldn't have had any other choice."

Quantrill pondered his words for a moment. "I bet you would, John, and if I'd been that much of a fool I'd have deserved to be blown to kingdom come." He turned his horse around and Billy followed the two men back toward camp. The joke had nearly gone too far and disaster had almost occurred. He was glad to see things return to normal.

When they reached the wagons, Quantrill ordered his lieutenants to report. He gathered Bloody Bill Anderson, George Todd, Dave Poole, Bill Gregg, and Captain Holt.

During the attack on Blunt's command the guerillas lost William Bledsoe killed and John Koger wounded. Dave Poole reported Robert Ward and William Lotspeach killed in the attack on the fort. Wounded in the fighting were Toothman and Thomas Hill. The Bushwhackers lost a total of three killed and three wounded in the day's fighting.

Bloody Bill read the report on the enemy losses. His men counted six Union dead scattered on the plains in front of the fort. Seventy-four more fell in the attack on General Blunt's headquarters column. Several Union soldiers managed to escape, including General Blunt. Several others got away, but carried bloody wounds. Quantrill took delight in capturing General Blunt's personal possessions, which included his personal sword, his general's commission, personal papers, and a headquarters' flag. These prized souvenirs would go south with the guerillas.

David Poole spoke up. "Capt'n, the Yankees still hold the fort on the other side of the ridge. I think we can take them if we try."

"You ought to know better by now than to try to attack a fortified position."

Bloody Bill spoke up. "Poole an' Gregg hit 'em earlier and we killed more than we lost."

"We also caught them by surprise. We won't catch them unprepared again. This time they'll be ready and we could lose many men."

George Todd scratched at the dirt with the toe of his boot while the others talked. When the conversation paused he said, "Dave says the fort is open on one end. These Yankees look green to me. They're so scared they're peein' in their pants. I think we could roll right over them."

"Forget it, men. We've done enough for one day. We've managed a great victory with few casualties. Why risk more? Remember, we've got a long way to go to reach Texas and we already have wounded to haul."

Bloody Bill had his battle blood up and his eyes had that kill-crazy glaze to them. "If you won't let us attack, at least let us send a flag of truce in to ask for their surrender. Then if we can get them out without a fight we can kill 'em all."

Although Quantrill was drunk, he wasn't crazy. Still, it

was early in the afternoon and Bloody Bill's plan might work. "Okay, you can try to get them to surrender, but if it doesn't work, no attack."

The others in the circle reluctantly agreed. "We'll wait here until we hear if they accept our demands." Quantrill turned toward Todd. "I want you to lead the detachment to the fort and ask for their surrender." George Todd left immediately to carry out his orders.

As the meeting broke up, Billy Cahill and Riley Crawford drifted toward the wagons. As they walked, Riley picked up a Union cavalry saber lost in the brief struggle fought earlier near the wagons. He playfully slashed the air with numerous sword strokes as though he were killing a vast multitude single-handed. Billy laughed good-naturedly at Riley's awkward attempts to use the sword. Neither boy had any training in the use of a cavalry saber and Riley's attempts clearly illustrated it. After a few minutes of playful maneuvers, Riley stopped before the body of a dead Union soldier lying facedown in the dirt.

Riley slapped the flat side of the blade across the hips of the Union trooper. As he did so he announced loudly, "Get up, you Federal son of a bitch!" He shot an ornery smile at Billy as he stood in mock triumph.

Riley's eyes went wide in terror as the dead man rose slowly to his feet. Billy and the others stepped back, caught off guard by this unexpected occurrence. The sword fell limply from Riley's fingers as fear clutched at his heart. He staggered back a couple of steps, his fingers clawing for the revolver at his side. Riley's face went slack-jawed as his eyes studied the apparition from hell in front of him. The Federal soldier stood his ground silently.

As far as Billy could tell, the man was uninjured and unmarked. Billy realized the trooper had been faking death in the hope of escape. Riley's blow with the sword convinced the Yankee his ruse was over. The roar of a revolver shattered Billy's thoughts. The pistol ball struck the

Federal soldier in the chest. His hands went to his wound as he staggered back. A second shot followed quickly on the heels of the first as the man toppled over on his back.

Billy swung his eyes off the Federal lying in the dirt and glanced over at Riley. Smoke still curled from the pistol muzzle as it shook in the boy's trembling hands. Billy walked over to the man and toed him gingerly with his boot. Encouraged by the lack of response, Billy bent cautiously closer and felt the soldier's neck for a pulse. The silence around him was nearly as deafening as the echoed reports from Riley's pistol moments before.

Billy looked up. "He's dead for sure this time." Only then did Riley, still staring silently in disbelief, slowly lower his smoking gun.

"Well, if that don't beat all. A Yankee playin' possum smack dab in the middle of us all. He lay right there while we looted the wagons and ate dinner and not one of us even noticed him. If ole Riley hadn't slapped him on the ass, he'd have gotten away with it, too," said Bloody Bill Anderson. "Don't it beat all?" He walked away, slowly shaking his head in wonder.

The men waited till nearly four-thirty in the afternoon for the response from the fort. The officers inside wisely refused the offered surrender. Anderson and Todd briefly pleaded to resume the attack on those still in the fort, but Quantrill overruled them. Lacking the momentum of surprise, an attack on the fort could be disastrous. He ordered his men to march south.

Before the column departed, Quantrill ordered the two prisoners to be brought before him. Two black civilians, trembling in fear, were forced to face the wrath of the guerilla chieftain. One of the men was a barber from the Kansas City area. In fact, several of the guerillas knew him and Quantrill offered to spare his life in exchange for becoming a company orderly. A man with barbering skills would benefit the command. Zach wisely accepted the offer.

The other prisoner was identified as Jack Mann. One of Bloody Bill's men knew him from Jackson County. Jack was wanted in Missouri for crimes against Southern people, but had escaped to Kansas to seek Yankee protection. Quantrill ordered his hands bound and kept the prisoner with the column. Another wagon was pressed into service to carry captured supplies and food. It joined the ambulance carrying Bledsoe's body and the wounded Koger. As the sun began to color the western skies, the Missouri Bushwhackers turned south on Gibson Road.

34

A Traitor's Grave

Billy listened to the soft, muffled sound of a shovel biting into dirt. He shifted his position as he sat with his back to the abandoned house and watched another spadeful of dirt land beside the hole. His eyes shifted away from the grave and dirt pile to the vista stretched out before him. The land in this valley was fertile and rich, but lay abandoned and overgrown. The war had left its imprint on this place as it had on so many others.

He let his eyes gaze at the far horizon and slowly move up into an azure blue sky flecked with wisps of cirrus cotton. Billy thought the sky blue matched perfectly the color of Elizabeth Kimbrough's mischievous eyes. A smile creased his weary face as he thought about the Missouri girl he'd left behind in Arkansas. He hoped he would see her again soon, but little could be counted on in these turbulent times.

His concentration was broken as he heard Bloody Bill Anderson's approach. Anderson strode past him as if he wasn't there and walked over to the hole in the ground. He looked down at the forbidding pit as he spoke. "Jee . . . zus Christ, Riley, you gonna let that nigger dig all the way to China?"

"Lighten up, Bill. We're gonna plant Will in there for a long time; I want it to be good enough for him."

"Hell, he's long past caring about anything of this world."

"Maybe so, but all the same, he was my friend."

Anderson nodded his head in understanding, but his impatience at the delay was evident. "Jack, drag your ass outa that hole, I got more work for you to do."

Billy watched as the shovel sailed out of the hole and landed on the pile of dirt beside the grave. Moments later, the sweaty and grimy face of Jack Mann appeared above the hole in the ground as he pulled himself out of the depths of the grave. Weariness showed clearly on the features of the man. Jack brushed the dirt from his clothes as he flashed a nervous smile at Bloody Bill. "I done a good job 'cause I know'd he was your friend."

A sardonic smile crossed Bloody Bill's face. "I'm glad. You did such a good job I want you to dig another one right beside it, but don't make the next one so deep or so wide. We ain't got all day."

The black man's eyes widened in fear as he glanced nervously around. "Pardon me, Masta Anderson, but why we need another grave? Ain't nobody else dead except the fella in the wagon, is there?"

"You just concentrate on diggin' the grave and I'll worry about who goes in it. Unless you'd rather fill the one you just dug."

The statement was more a threat than a question and the black captive lowered his eyes in understanding as he reached with trembling hands for the handle of the shovel. "Yes, suh, I'll get right on it."

"See that you do." Bloody Bill Anderson looked over at Riley Crawford. Riley was sitting on the pile of dirt beside the first grave while he kept the carbine pointed in the general direction of the black prisoner. "Riley, don't let Jack waste time. We're burnin' daylight and I don't want to spend all winter in the Indian Territory." Bloody Bill didn't wait for a reply as he walked toward the ambulance. He glanced at Billy Cahill, still resting against the outside wall of the house. He hardly slowed as he said briskly, "Why don't you give Zack and the boys a hand with Bledsoe."

Billy nodded in acknowledgment as he reluctantly left the shade of the house and approached the wagon. Zack and Koger were both wearing bandanas over their noses. Immediately the rich, sweet smell of ripe, rotting human flesh assailed Billy's nostrils. He felt his stomach turn as he gagged back the bile from his stomach. William Bledsoe's face was blackened and his arms and legs protruded grotesquely from his swollen body. Zack tried to smile as he watched Billy approach. "Hey there, youngin', you're just in time to give me a hand. Try to lift him up so I can wrap a blanket around him."

Koger glared weakly at him. "I've complained all day he was too ripe, but nobody paid any attention until he puffed up and stunk so bad even the riders ahead of us could smell him when the wind was right. I tried last night to get someone to do something, but all you wanted to do was kill those Yank Indian soldiers from Fort Gibson."

The evening before, they caught a wood detail made up of Indian troops at dusk, just south of the Kansas state line. Quantrill ordered the execution of the Indian prisoners and the bloody task was carried out.

The odor emanating from Bledsoe's body brought Billy back to the present. He flinched, not wanting to touch the swollen carcass of his friend. The body reminded him of the dead horses and cows he had seen as a boy back on their Missouri farm.

He grabbed a carbine and used the stock of the gun to pry the body up enough to allow the blanket to pass underneath. It took a bit of maneuvering to complete the job. Halfway through Billy had to make the others wait while he stepped to the side and emptied the contents of his stomach. The bile still burned in his throat as he returned to the job at hand. Finally they finished sewing the blanket closed. Koger looked satisfied. "Boy, go get the other nigger to help Zack carry the body to the grave. Be quick about it. I can't stand much more of this."

"Sure, John, I'll get him. You try to rest."

"I'll rest a damn sight easier once you get this stinkin' corpse away from me; hurry, boy!"

Billy took off at a run. It didn't take him long to reach Riley. "I need Jack to come down and help tote Bledsoe's body up here for burial."

Riley Crawford's look showed marked resistance to the suggestion. "Bloody Bill told me to keep him diggin' another grave. I don't want to get in trouble."

"Look, Riley, I'll stand guard and you can help Zack carry the body."

"Hell, no! I ain't touchin' him." He looked down on the black man digging in the hole. "I guess it won't hurt nothin' if it don't take too long."

"Thanks, Riley." He turned toward the sweaty negro standing shin-deep in a new grave. "Take a break and give us a hand."

Minutes later they lowered William Bledsoe's body into its final resting place. Zack went to clean up and start fixing something to eat while Jack Mann returned to digging in the new grave.

Two hours later the Rebel raiders gathered around William Bledsoe's grave. A few hasty words were spoken in prayer for the deceased before Jack Mann was instructed to cover the body. Already tired he moved slowly about his work. Arch Clements watched the negro's slow movements for a couple of minutes. He pulled a revolver from his holster and fired off three quick shots in a circle around the black man standing on the dirt pile. Jack flinched in fear and Arch laughed heartily at his discomfort. "You better dig faster, Jack."

The black man bent to his task with renewed vigor as the dirt started flying into the pit. Arch winked mischievously at Billy, standing near him, and said, "Amazing how fast a man can move with the proper motivation." Billy should have felt some sympathy, but the man was wanted in Missouri for crimes against Southerners and he'd gone over to the enemy—the very same enemy who had cost his family so dearly. In peaceful times Billy might have felt compassion, now he felt only apathy.

Once the grave was filled, Quantrill and Bloody Bill approached the gravesite with Zack, the negro barber-turned-cook, following behind them. The men moved near Jack Mann. Jack, exhausted from his work, leaned heavily on his shovel, his body glistening with sweat. Quantrill said in a low, menacing tone, "You did a nice job on the graves, Jack. Time for your reward." He turned toward Arch Clements. "Finish him, Arch."

The black man stepped back from the shovel as fear twisted his face. He backed up slowly, hands before him as if to deflect the shot. His eyes stared wide and white in horror.

Arch smiled wickedly, delighting in inflicting torture. "Look at it this way, Jack, you shouldn't have turned on your masters. Goin' over to the Yankees like ya done." He shook his head as he talked. "Well, you know that just can't be tolerated." Two shots were fired, one right on the heels of the other, as Jack Mann clutched at his chest and sagged to his knees.

He looked down at the fresh blood on his fingers as though he couldn't believe it was real. He eyed Arch, shock written across his face. Arch said lightly, "At least you can't complain about the quality of the workmanship or how deep it is. You dug your grave, now lie in it." A third shot blasted from the smoking revolver and tore through the dying man's body. Slowly Jack Mann toppled headfirst into his grave.

Arch Clements looked gleefully at Bloody Bill and Quantrill. "One less traitor in the world." He began to reload his Colt.

Quantrill turned toward Zack. "Hurry up and fill it in, Zack. We want to make a few miles before sunset."

Zack looked over at Quantrill with eyes as big as saucers. "What if he ain't dead?"

"Then he'll be dead when you finish. I'm not askin' you again, Zack. You either fill the grave or you'll join him. Do I make myself clear?"

"Oh, yes, suh, I'll get on it right away." The small-framed man moved quickly to the shovel and hastily hurled spadefuls of dirt into the hole. The raiders began to drift away, preparing for the continuation of the march. Billy lingered near the grave, still captivated by Arch Clements' cold-blooded murder of Jack Mann. He heard the black barber whispering under his breath, "Dear Lord, please forgive me for what I'm doin'. Jack, it ain't my fault so don't you come back an' haunt me, friend. Lawd, I hope you understand. Least ways I know you'd be doin' the same to me if things had gone the other way.

Later, Quantrill's raiders rode south leaving two fresh graves in the lee shadows of the abandoned cabin.

35

Bushwhacker Feud

Billy Cahill opened his eyes slowly and glanced about the primitive log cabin. He'd slept his fill and now lay in his bedroll on the crude bunk recalling the last few weeks.

After Bledsoe's burial, the guerillas continued south until just a few miles above the Canadian River. There they met General Cooper's Confederate command. Quantrill's men spent a few days in camp with Cooper's men before moving on. Quantrill led his band fifteen miles northwest of Sherman, Texas. There, along the banks of Mineral Creek, Quantrill directed his men to construct log cabins for the winter encampment.

Once the cabins were built the raiders found themselves fighting boredom instead of enemies. This slack time provided the opportunity for the men to reflect on the campaigns of 1863 and wonder about their future. The seed of discontent began to grow.

The sound of rough voices coming from outside the cabin took Billy from his thoughts. He threw back his blankets and rushed outside, squinting against the harsh sunlight as he emerged from the gloom of the log cabin. Near Mineral Creek, Bloody Bill Anderson, George Todd, and Captain Quantrill were engaged in a heated debate. Out of curiosity, Billy approached them, anxious to discover the cause of the argument.

Billy heard George Todd shout boisterously, "I'm not afraid of any man."

Quantrill glared at George Todd. "What about me?"

George's cheeks flushed scarlet at Quantrill's question. "Oh . . . well, you're the only man I was ever afraid of."

Quantrill smiled in satisfaction while Bloody Bill Anderson looked contemptuous. "I've had enough of Todd's bragging. I'm goin' to town."

Quantrill's smile faded as he glared at Bloody Bill. "I want you and your men to stay here. You've spent enough time in Sherman causing trouble."

Bloody Bill faced Quantrill, his eyes burning with anger. "I'll do what I damn well please. I'd rather spend my time in Sherman in bed with Bush Smith than sit here and die of boredom."

"As long as I'm in command you'll do what I tell you or get out." Quantrill paused a moment, letting his words sink in. "Can't you find something better to do than spend all day in bed with some cheap whore?"

"You're a hell of a one to talk, Capt'n. After the Lawrence raid you couldn't get enough of Kate King. Hell, I had to run things most of the time because you were too busy to worry about it."

"That was different. Kate is no whore. She's a farmer's daughter and loyal to the cause."

"The only difference between the two of them is Bush Smith is honest enough to ask for cash for her favors, while Kate King looks for handouts, gifts, and special treatment for her old man."

"I've had enough of your insolence, Anderson. I forbid you from seeing Bush Smith or any of those other whores in Sherman."

"You can forbid all the hell you want. I'll do as I please. I command my men and I sure as hell don't need you." The silence between them was deadly as both men let their hands linger near their guns. Finally, Bloody Bill broke the silence. "Maybe I ought to marry Bush since you're so against it."

"I don't care what you do, Bill, just do it away from here. Ride out and don't come back." Quantrill turned toward the gathering crowd of raiders. He shouted loudly so others in the camp could hear. "Bloody Bill is leaving. Any of you want to trail with him it's fine with me, just don't come back. I don't want any man in my command who won't follow orders." Quantrill turned, walked to his horse, and slid into the saddle. "When I return, those going with Bloody Bill better be gone." Quantrill let his horse walk boldly out of camp.

Billy Cahill felt uneasy as he watched Bloody Bill's men prepare to depart. He noticed Bill Gregg studying the camp as the men made their choices. Quantrill's charismatic leadership had bound the loose confederation of several guerilla bands and leaders together. Now with inactivity the thin line of loyalty was disintegrating.

Even within his own band Quantrill's leadership was being questioned. George Todd's more violent nature found favor among the younger gang members including Riley Crawford. Billy Cahill followed Bill Gregg's lead and supported Quantrill.

Since their arrival in Texas, several Southerners were found robbed and murdered. First a man named Froman was killed for three hundred dollars. Next, Colonel Alexander, who lived about two miles south of Sherman, was found dead; Jim Crow Chiles, John Ross, Fletch Taylor, and Andy Walker admitted murdering him. Another victim, Major Butts, lived north of Sherman. All were Confederate soldiers murdered by Quantrill's dissidents.

The murders reflected badly on Quantrill and his command and profoundly upset many of his original followers. Quantrill wanted the men arrested and court-martialed for their offenses, but Bloody Bill Anderson and George Todd sought to protect those who were guilty. This rift served to deepen the chasm between the various guerilla members.

Other problems plagued the command. Quantrill lost faith in the Confederacy's chances for victory in the wake of the fall of Vicksburg and the defeat of Lee's army at Gettysburg. In addition, he was losing faith in the Confederate commanders in the region. Recent reversals in the Trans-Mississippi region only intensified his feelings. His men naturally wanted to follow a leader who still believed in the ultimate victory of the cause. George Todd began to exert his desire for leadership to fill the void. Many of those in Quantrill's band who favored a more bloody course and robbery for personal gain began to ally themselves with him. Still others felt disheartened by the dark direction the guerillas were taking.

Half an hour later, Bloody Bill led nearly fifty men toward Sherman. Meanwhile, Todd and his followers drifted off to get drunk in celebration. Those who remained in camp gathered near a campfire. Forty lean, hard veterans stood disgruntled and disillusioned by what they had witnessed since their arrival in Texas. Among them were Cole Younger, John Jarette, Billy Cahill, and Bill Gregg.

Cole Younger, his eyes pinched with concern, peered at Gregg. "What do you make of this, Bill?"

Bill Gregg toed the ground. "I don't like what I'm seeing. Todd and Anderson's boys have gone plum crazy and Quantrill is allowing Todd too much control. It doesn't matter which side a man is on anymore as long as he has something worth stealing. How low have we sunk if we allow our men to kill our own kind for the sake of plunder?" Silence met his gaze. "It's gettin' where a man's life ain't worth much more than a sheep-killin' dog and there's no honor in it, boys, none at all."

Cole Younger sat near the fire. When he spoke the others turned to listen. "I don't know what's wrong with Quantrill. He's lost touch with the men and he's losing control. I think Todd intimidates him."

Bill Gregg nodded in agreement. "The time is coming when there'll be a showdown. George isn't content to be second in command and he sees a weakness in Capt'n Billy. Mark my words, boys, he'll make his move someday and try to force out Quantrill. When he does, we'll have to choose sides."

Billy Cahill listened intently. He decided to speak his mind. "I don't know about the rest of you, but I'm starting to feel dirty. When we started out we fought to stop the Jayhawkers and the Red Legs. Now, we're turning on our own kind and we have men murdering and stealing against our civilians. I never intended to end up like a Jayhawker. Even if we don't do the killing, or robbing, we can't let our men get away with it, it just isn't right." Billy hesitated as he gathered his thoughts. "I felt proud when I rode with Shelby's men last winter. I haven't felt that way for a long time."

Bill Gregg said, "Maybe it's time we quit fightin' from the bush and join the regular army."

John Jarette squatted down on his haunches as he poked the fire with a stick. "Just how do you plan to go about it? You signed on with Quantrill and gave your word to fight with him. You can't just run off, it'd be desertion."

"I don't know. Maybe we can get Quantrill to sign a transfer, or let us muster out. Then we'd be free to enlist in regular service."

"You're fools if you think George Todd or his followers will stand by and watch you ride out peaceful-like," said Cole Younger. "They'll mark you for a turncoat and a traitor."

"I'm not afraid to face them, Cole. I've got to stand for what I believe in and I can't agree with the direction this outfit is taking. I have to live with myself when this war is over."

"I'll go with you, Bill," said Billy Cahill. In many ways Bill Gregg had become a father figure for Billy. In Bill Gregg, he found the tough-as-nails fighting man of principle he wanted to become. Bill Gregg had taken him under his wing and Billy knew he'd follow him wherever he led.

The meeting continued for a while as each man dealt with his feelings and tried to decide what he must do. When Quantrill returned to camp the group separated and returned to their camp routines. Later that night, George Todd and his followers returned, drunk and disorderly, a confusing end to a dismal day along Mineral Creek.

Bloody Bill Anderson's group took control of Sherman, the nearest town to the encampment. They allowed Quantrill's men to come and go freely as long as they rode alone or in small groups. Back at Mineral Creek, Quantrill followed suit and allowed his men more freedom. While staying overnight in Sherman on one of their forays, Billy Cahill and Bill Gregg determined it was time to ask Quantrill for permission to leave the command. The next morning they saddled up and rode for the Mineral Creek encampment.

Billy rode along the trail at an easy gallop just a few

feet behind Bill Gregg. He tugged his coat collar up around his neck to ward off the chill of the autumn day. Overhead, dark clouds chased by an angry wind scudded across the sky. The gunmetal gray skies matched the gloom he felt inside. Quantrill and his men had taken him in when he had no place to go and now he must say good-bye. He felt the emotional tug-of-war inside him as he prepared to turn his back on the past and look forward to the future. At least in the regular army he would serve that much closer to Elizabeth Kimbrough. His thoughts of her gave him comfort. Riding under the black flag meant win or die, for surrender meant death in a war where prisoners were executed. How different it would be to fight in a more civilized war.

As they rounded a bend in the road, Bill Gregg stopped his horse. Riding toward them were their good friends and fellow Bushwhackers David Poole and John Jarette.

Bill Gregg yelled at them first. "Whoa, boys, where ya headin'?"

David Poole rode up close, a broad smile stretching across his face and a half-burnt cigar hanging in the corner of his mouth. "We're headin' into town to blow off a little steam. There's a pretty young redhead up at Bush Smith's bordello I've had my eye on. I've heard that gal could suck brass off a doorknob." He took another puff on his cigar, blowing the smoke out through his nose. "I reckon I aim to see just how good she really is." He gave a sly wink at Billy.

Bill Gregg eyed John Jarette. "John, are you headin' up to the sportin' house, too?"

"It can wait. First thing I want is a hot bath and a shave. Then I want to fill up on a good home-cooked meal and see if I can't find me a hot piece of pie somewhere. Then, if I still got the energy and the money, I'll see if I can handle the ladies." He pushed his hat back with his thumb as he smiled broadly. "Where you boys headin'?"

"Back to Mineral Creek camp; I want to talk to Quantrill. I've given it plenty of thought and I think it's time to leave the outfit. Is Quantrill in camp?"

Dave Poole looked surprised as he took another draw on his cigar, turning the tip to a cherry red. "He's there and so is George Todd and his buddies. You ain't the most popular sort with Fletch Taylor and Jim Little. If they find out you're cuttin' tail and leavin' the gang they'll be gunning for you."

"I'm not worried about 'em. Billy and I can handle ourselves in trouble."

"Just the same, I'd really watch my backside if I were you. I'd ride right on back to Sherman and forget leavin'."

John Jarette nodded his head in agreement. "He's right, boys, I wouldn't risk it. If you're dead set on going I'd do what Cole Younger did. Just ride out without saying a word and head for the headquarters at Shreveport and ask for reassignment. It could save your lives."

"I've never run from trouble in my life, boys, and I don't intend to start now. Capt'n Billy is a fair man and I owe it to him to do this right."

"How about you, Cahill? Are you as stubborn as this old mule?"

Billy didn't hesitate. "I'll stand by Gregg. We've fought side by side and lived in the bush with Quantrill's raiders. I owe it to Capt'n Billy to do the right thing instead of slippin' away like a thief in the night."

John Jarette shook his head in exasperation. "I've tried to talk sense to you boys, but I reckon I could've done as well talkin' to a fence post. George Todd is as dangerous as a loose cannon on a ship's deck. If he thinks you're crossin' him, hell itself won't save you." He offered his hand to Bill Gregg; then he shook hands with Billy. "Good luck, youngin'. You're a real wildcat in a fight and I'm gonna miss ya." He tipped his hat as he spurred his horse toward town.

Dave Poole took the soggy stub of his cigar out and flipped it into the dust of the road. "Keep your powder dry and your pistols close to hand. Best of luck, boys." He touched his fingers to his hat in a salute as he spurred after John Jarette.

36

Farewell To Quantrill

As Billy rode into the Mineral Creek camp he felt the glare of watchful eyes. Some sixth sense told him someone was watching him and when he glanced around he looked into the cold, blue eyes of George Todd. Unable to maintain eye contact, Billy looked away.

He followed Bill Gregg until they reached the log shack that served as Captain Quantrill's headquarters. They tied the reins of their horses off to an improvised hitching rail in front of the cabin. After a couple of brisk raps on the door, Quantrill emerged.

"Capt'n, Billy and I would like to have a word with you, if we may."

"Please, step right in, boys, and make yourself at home." He turned his back on the door and moved near the improvised fireplace where hanging from a steel hook sat a hot coffeepot. He used a piece of leather to grip the handle and poured himself a cup of coffee. "Would you boys care for a cup? I brewed it fresh this morning."

"We'd be obliged, Capt'n."

Quantrill removed two tin cups hanging from nails on the wall and poured generous amounts of the dark, steaming liquid. The aroma filled Billy's nostrils and the warmth of the coffee in the cup felt good against his hands. The ride had been colder than he had expected and his fingers were still cold.

Quantrill eased himself down on the edge of a rough-cut homemade table. "Sometimes, I think the best deal I ever made was trading the ambulance we took from Blunt for four bags of coffee beans. God, I'd hate to try and make it through another winter without coffee." He looked up from sipping his strong, black coffee and studied the boys. "I'm glad you're here, Bill. I was going to send for you, but now I can tell you in person." He hesitated a moment as if carefully weighing his words. "I want you boys to go away. You have some enemies in camp."

Bill Gregg had been trying to find a way to start his conversation. This quick speech by Captain Quantrill caught him off guard. Bill Gregg glanced quickly at Billy Cahill and turned to face Quantrill. "Who are these enemies?"

"Jim Little and Fletch Taylor are lookin' to settle a score with you ever since you called them thieves. John Barker is also carrying a grudge."

"Let them carry them. On the Plattsburg, Missouri, raid they should have split the money equally with the men. The two of them kept the six thousand they took and wouldn't divide with the rest of us. George Todd sided with them and I was surprised you didn't make them split the money. I said they were thieves and as far as I'm concerned nothing's changed."

"I know how you felt, but George didn't want them to divide and I didn't want to cross him. His men are good fighters and I didn't want them to ride out on us over a little money. Looking back, maybe I should have."

Bill Gregg set his coffee down after swallowing a large gulp of the hot liquid. "They're thieves and they stole from us all after Plattsburg."

"Yes, they are."

"I've been a good soldier and an officer. I've been an honest man and yet you want me to leave and the thieves to stay?"

"All three of them are Todd's men and loyal to him. If I go against them I'll have to deal with Todd."

Billy had listened carefully to the conversation as he nursed his cup of coffee. Twice he tried to sip it, but the coffee burned his lips. Try as he might, he'd never succeeded in learning to drink hot coffee successfully. Billy couldn't understand why Bill Gregg was arguing to stay when they had come here in the first place to ask permission to leave. Why couldn't he count himself lucky and just go?

The men sat in silence for a while, lost in thought. Finally, after a few minutes, Bill Gregg said, "I want a leave of absence for myself and Billy. Will you grant it, Capt'n?"

"Yes, of course, and I'd suggest you leave immediately."

"I intend to ride down to Shreveport and ask for assignment to another outfit. I hope they'll let us ride with Shelby's command."

"I hate to see you go, Bill, but if you stay, there will only be trouble. You and Billy have been a credit to the command. I'll write out a leave of absence for you and Billy for ninety days. I'll also give you my permission for reassignment." Quantrill sat at the crude table and shuffled through some loose papers. Finally he drew out two unused pages and laid them before him. He pulled a pen and a brass inkwell from the corner and began writing. When he finished he gave the signed pages to the men before him. Bill Gregg saluted Quantrill and then shook his hand.

Quantrill gave him a grim smile. "Best of luck, Bill."

"Same to you, sir." Gregg let go and moved toward the door.

Billy Cahill moved forward and repeated the process. "Capt'n, I wanted to thank you for taking me in when I came to you."

"I must admit, Billy, when your mother first brought you to me I thought you might be too young. You had fire in your eyes and hate in your heart and you turned out to be a man I could depend on in a fight. Best of luck to you, Billy."

Billy swallowed hard as the words of praise sunk in. He turned quickly away, afraid he might break down and cry. As he reached the door he took one last look at William Clarke Quantrill. He couldn't find it in himself to say more and after a silent moment, he quietly closed the door behind him.

The two men untied their horses from the rail and led them toward their log cabin. Once inside they began to pack. Gregg finished first and slipped out the door while Billy continued to gather his things.

Billy heard the door creak open on its dry leather hinges and felt a gust of cold air blow across his back, sending a shiver down his spine. He glanced over his shoulder at the backlit silhouette standing in the doorway. The door slammed shut loudly and swung back slightly ajar from the impact. The silhouetted figure stepped forward into the dimly lit cabin.

A familiar voice said icily, "Word going around camp is you're leaving. Is it true, Billy?"

Billy stopped folding his extra blanket. He studied Riley Crawford for a moment before he answered, "Yeah, it's true, Riley. Gregg and I plan to join up with Shelby."

"I never thought I'd see the day you'd turn your back on your friends and run off."

"Things have changed, Riley. Sometimes I don't think this outfit is fighting for the cause anymore. Everyone seems more interested in the loot they can steal than driving the Yankees out of Missouri."

"So when did you become holier-than-thou? I know about the money you took out of Lawrence. I didn't see you giving it to any widows and orphans."

"I never said I was better than anyone else here, but things just aren't the same anymore. All the bands are beginning to fight among themselves in a bid for power. Bloody Bill has stormed off and you can't tell me you haven't noticed George Todd trying to push Capt'n Billy out."

"So, what's wrong with that? Quantrill is weak and going soft. You've heard him. He doesn't believe the South can win the war anymore. He's only interested in survival."

"Listen to yourself, Riley. Capt'n Billy drew all the various bands together and led us on every successful raid we've had. Loss of enthusiasm is no reason to desert him. Where would we be without him?"

"I admit once he was good, but those days are over. We need new blood, a younger and stronger man."

"Someone like George Todd?"

"Yeah, like Todd."

"He's power-hungry, he's bloodthirsty, and he sides with the wrong people. He isn't gonna stop until someone blows him away." Billy threw his hands up in exasperation. "Sooner or later he's going down and he'll take everyone with him. I don't want to be one of them."

"You've gone soft, haven't ya, Billy?"

"I'm not afraid, Riley, but I'm not gonna throw my life away. George has surrounded himself with guys that kill for the fun of it. They take what they want and they don't care who gets killed. It's not about right or wrong anymore and it isn't about revenge. It's about killing and robbing for the sheer enjoyment of it."

"So . . . what's the matter with that? Nobody ever gave me nothin'. Whatever I got I went out and took."

"Not from your own people, Riley. It's wrong. I can't do it anymore. I'm going back to Shelby's brigade 'cause I want to feel good about myself again." He slipped his blanket into his canvas bag and pulled the string tight. "I'm leaving, Riley, good luck."

Riley stepped forward and shoved Billy hard in the chest. He flew backward, pawing the air for balance, until he tripped over the bed and slammed into the wall. Riley towered above him, his finger waving in his face. "I'm tired of your bull crap. This ain't about George and the boys, it's about that Kimbrough bitch back at Batesville. You're lookin' for an excuse to turn your back on us so you can go back and moon over her."

Billy kicked his foot hard, landing it in Riley's belly. The air rushed out of Riley in one quick gush as Billy pushed himself off the bed. He landed an uppercut square on Riley's chin, staggering him off balance. Billy pursued him, ramming his shoulder into Riley's chest. Riley landed flat on the floor and in a flash Billy straddled him. In a blink of an eye, Billy pulled his Bowie knife and pressed the tip to Riley's throat, tightly gripping a handful of the boy's hair. "You leave Elizabeth out of this, you son of a bitch. I ought to kill you." A single ruby-red drop of blood welled at the knife point.

"Do it!" shouted Riley. "If you got the guts, go ahead and do it." Riley's eyes turned wild and a strange, cruel smile crossed his face. "You ain't any different than the rest of us."

Riley's words hit Billy like ice water in the face. Suddenly, he realized how close to the edge he'd come, how close he was to slitting Riley's throat. Billy willed himself to relax. Before he could withdraw the knife point from Riley's throat, he felt cold, hard metal pressing against his temple and he felt the vibration through his skull as the hammer clicked into position. Billy swallowed hard.

Riley whispered softly, "Can you do it, Billy? Can you slit my throat? Do you have what it takes? Me, I know I got what it takes. I can blow your brains all over the walls with just a twitch on the trigger."

"This is stupid, Riley. What are we doing? Aren't we friends? Are we gonna kill each other?"

The craziness seeped out of Riley's eyes. His smile faded. He pulled the revolver barrel slowly away from Billy's head and eased down the hammer. Billy removed his knife from Riley's throat and stood up. He offered his hand and pulled Riley to his feet.

Riley was the first to break the silence. "You want to leave, then go, damn you! I won't stand in your way. You're the closest I've ever come to having a friend, but you walk outa here and it's over. Next time you see me expect trouble."

"It doesn't have to be this way, Riley. You could go with us."

Riley's cold stare was his answer. Billy reached down and grabbed his duffle bag. He slung the bag on his shoulder and went to meet Bill Gregg, who was waiting with the horses.

"Did you get things settled with Riley?" Gregg asked.

Billy swung into his saddle and slipped the duffle bag around his saddle horn. "We talked." Billy neck-reined his horse and headed out of camp at a walk while Bill Gregg spurred to catch up.

After they had ridden three miles the leaden skies darkened and a driving rain began to fall. Thunder rolled and echoed off the land while jagged white-hot bolts of lightning streaked across the sky. The cold water sheeted off Billy's hat and trickled beneath his rain slicker, chilling him to the bone. At the sound of each roll of heavy thunder Bess skittered and skipped under him. Shivers racked his body as he gripped his knees tightly to his horse.

Bill Gregg periodically checked over his shoulder, watching their back trail even after dusk made seeing difficult. After covering nearly five miles, he spotted four riders at the crest of a ridge, backlit by the heavens' jagged lightning bolts. The big man leading the trailing pack was George Todd.

As the light dimmed overhead and the thunder rolled away, the figures faded into the mists of the sheeting rain. Bill Gregg urged his horse off the trail and Billy followed. In the cleansing rinse of the cold downpour and the cover of the gathering night, the two riders managed to lose their pursuers.

Billy was glad for Bill Gregg's uncanny sense of direction as he followed him cross-country. A few hours later the two riders approached a dilapidated barn. Only the flash of sheet lightning bouncing off the unpainted walls of the barn kept them from riding past it in the darkness. After bedding the horses down for the night, Billy chewed for a while on a couple of strips of beef jerky he found in his pocket. He made a bed in a corner of an empty stall and slipped into a restless sleep.

The next morning they rode into Sherman. The two men considered bypassing the town to avoid trouble, but Bill Gregg pointed out their lack of supplies. They would have to risk it. They dropped their horses off at the livery closest to the edge of town, paid extra for grain and feed for their horses, and asked the stable hand to keep them ready to ride.

Billy felt an uneasiness walking through Sherman. He kept his eyes peeled as they headed to the mercantile and the general store. They bought their supplies, carried them to the livery, and put them away without interference. Billy began to relax a little. So far they hadn't seen anyone who posed a threat. Traffic along the streets seemed normal, so when Bill Gregg suggested they eat a decent meal before they hit the trail, Billy agreed. At least they would start with a full stomach.

Billy strolled out onto the wooden sidewalk leisurely. A belch worked its way up unexpectedly, and he felt better although slightly surprised. He looked around to see if anyone standing near him noticed.

Bill Gregg smiled wryly. "Yeah, I heard it. I wish you weren't so darn proud when you burp. If you'd slowed down on polishing off your steak and two helpings of beans you wouldn't be so full."

"It was good, Bill, and a sight better than your cookin'." Billy shot him a mischievous grin. "You think the belch was bad, wait until the beans do their magic."

"Thanks for the warning, youngin'. I'll be sure to stay upwind from you for the rest of the day." Billy chuckled and Bill laughed as they walked along. Under his breath Bill Gregg muttered, "Never did understand why youngin's were so darn proud of belchin' and passin' gas."

They turned a corner and headed toward the livery. Immediately, Billy's belly tightened as he spotted George Todd, Fletch Taylor, John Barker, and Jim Little walking toward them on the opposite side of the street.

Todd and his Bushwhackers stopped walking when they spotted Cahill and Gregg. They circled together, talking and looking nervous. Billy and Bill walked on slowly, alert for any hostile move.

As the distance between them closed, George Todd shouted, "There goes the sons of bitches, now kill 'em." The three men with Todd froze, hesitant to draw their guns on their former companions.

Fletch Taylor shook his head no and said, "I won't kill Bill or Billy. They're Southern men and good soldiers. If you want 'em killed your gonna have to do it yourself, George."

George shot an angry glare at Fletch Taylor. "They're runnin' out on us. We need to set an example for others. We can't just let 'em run off."

Jim Little turned toward Gregg and Cahill and said loudly enough for them to hear, "Why the hell can't we? Plenty of others have taken off and no one is hunting for them. Them boys have saved my bacon a time or two and I reckon they got a right to leave if they want."

George Todd, surprised by the lack of support from his comrades, looked frustrated, but didn't make a move. Billy Cahill and Bill Gregg finally reached the livery. Billy glanced back through a crack between the door and the hinge to see if they were being pursued. He let out a long and slow breath when he noticed the four Bushwhackers walking away from them.

"That was close, my friend, too damn close," said Bill Gregg. "Let's get out of here before they change their minds." Moments later the two Missourians headed their horses toward Shreveport.

Epilogue

November and December 1863 ushered in inclement weather and a temporary end to military campaigning. The cold cloak of winter wrapped itself tightly around the opposing forces as both sides settled into camp to wait for the spring. The battle would now turn from the enemy to a struggle against the elements. Although the frigid conditions had brought a temporary halt to the fighting, the war would rage on, spreading its black cloud of death and destruction for another year and a half. Both sides had grown weary of the conflict and prayed for an early end to the fighting, yet neither side was willing to concede defeat.

The war was bringing about sweeping changes, but nothing could be decided or finished while it continued. The Kimbroughs and those around them were swept up in the events of the war as though caught on a giant swell, building at last into a gigantic wave which threatened to smash them all against a rocky shore.

The struggle was as impossible to resist as the combined forces of nature with the power to destroy all in their path. For those who lived through it, nothing would remain the same. Only time would reveal their future as they rushed toward the final cataclysm.

About the Author

When you talk to Randal L. Greenwood, his lifelong love for American history comes shining through. Since he was in the fifth grade he has been fascinated with the American Civil War and western history. "My mother's family were Missouri Confederates and all my ancestors on my father's side were Union Veterans. For some reason the Rebel in me has always ruled my heart."

Randy has lived most of his life in Hugoton, Kansas, in the southwest corner of the state. He received his B.S. in History from Kansas State University in 1972.

"I've been a full-time professional photographer since 1978. Photography offers a visual creativity to my life; writing gives me other outlets to express myself. I feel photography helps me visualize."

His interests include reading and writing novels and collecting books on the Civil War, western history, and the WWII European theater air war. "My favorite hobby is watching and following Winston Cup Racing. I collect diecast. These guys are my heroes and I follow them like other fans follow baseball or football teams." He also watches boxing, horse racing, movies, and enjoys playing slot machines.

Randy is married to Rebecca Richmeier Greenwood and is the father of three children, Evan, Amber, and Ciara.

THE BEST OF TOR/FORGE
HISTORICALS

☐ 50747-9 *PEOPLE OF THE LAKES* $6.99
        Kathleen O'Neal & W. Michael Gear $7.99 Canada

☐ 53536-7 *FIRE ALONG THE SKY* $5.99
        Robert Moss $6.99 Canada

☐ 52377-6 *THE WOMAN WHO FELL FROM THE SKY* $5.99
        Barbara Riefe $6.99 Canada

☐ 52293-1 *DEATH COMES AS EPIPHANY* $4.99
        Sharan Newman $5.99 Canada

☐ 53013-6 *NOT OF WAR ONLY* $5.99
        Norman Zollinger $6.99 Canada

WESTERN ADVENTURE
FROM TOR/FORGE